THE ARRIVAL

REAWAKENED

… a compelling world that will draw you in and make you cheer for your favourite characters – then break your heart when you realise not all will survive. It's a masterfully crafted tale of love, loss and sacrifice, perfect for fans of vampires, myth, legend, and paranormal romance and suspense.

~Serene Conneeley, Into the Mists & Into the Storm Trilogies

Thrilling…devastating, but satisfying. A riveting read you'll have trouble putting down.

~M.K. Deppner, Photographs of October

…I dread and thrill in equal measure for where Pavlik will take us. So much hangs in the balance, and with an ending to Last Born Daughter that left me in stunned silence, this series still has so much more to come.

~Julie Embleton, Turning Moon series & Voyager Chronicles

Praise for *Eternal Light Descendant*

A fitting ending to a series that twists the myths of creation and of vampires and turns them both upside down, all along making you question the existence of free will, of liberty, of fate, even.

~Ruth Miranda, The Blood Trilogy

[This] asks us to examine what it means to have faith even in the darkest of times…what it means to truly love—and not always the pretty, romantic side, but the heart-rending grey area…which drives some to obsession and others to the most abject depths of despair.

~M.K. Deppner, Photographs of October

This suspenseful, gritty tale, heaving with dark emotion takes vampirism to a whole new level. Fans of intelligent, dark paranormal reads will love it.

~Julie Embleton, Turning Moon Series and Voyager Chronicles

Praise for *How To Make Lemonade*

Beautiful prose and an unexpected story…Ms. Pavlik delivers unique twists and leads the reader through the darkness toward the light…or does she?

~M.K. Deppner, Photographs of October

I simply could not put it down…I was left replenished, satisfied, my thirst slackened by this fresh glass of lemonade!

~Ruth Miranda, The Preternaturals Series

THE
ARRIVAL

~ REAWAKENED ~

CHILDREN OF THE MORNING STAR BOOK 1

KASTIE PAVLIK

THE ARRIVAL REAWAKENED: Children of the Morning Star Book 1

Revised Edition

This is a work of fiction. Names, characters, places, and incidents in this book are either products of the author's imagination or used fictitiously.

ISBN-13: 978-1-7376818-0-9
Library of Congress Control Number: 2021917640

Printed in Fairfield, Ohio
United States of America

Revision based on the original story "The Arrival"
© 2017 Kastie Pavlik
ISBN-13: 978-1976109799

Editing Services: Magpie Press
Photographs and Illustrations by: Kastie Pavlik
Email: *kastiepavlik@gmail.com*
Instagram & Facebook: *@kastiepavlikauthor*
www.kastiepavlik.wixsite.com/author

TIM
&
DAVID

LOVE. HEART. SOUL.

"THE BOUNDARIES WHICH DIVIDE LIFE FROM DEATH ARE AT BEST SHADOWY AND VAGUE. WHO SHALL SAY WHERE THE ONE ENDS, AND WHERE THE OTHER BEGINS?"

~ EDGAR ALLAN POE, *THE PREMATURE BURIAL*

TABLE OF CONTENTS

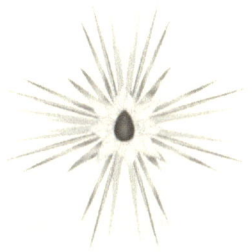

Chapter One: Chosen

I

Orison Crossing, Illinois, August 1996

She loved mornings like these when the early light sank into a sky clear as water and hit the tassels like haloes. Ordinary cornfields transformed into magical tapestries woven through roots and soil. Home to any creature imaginable. A place where any dream could come true. But, back at the cottage, the forest owned her heart, truly enchanted as the place where all her friends lived.

Cradling her stuffed bunny, she traded the blur of stalks speeding past the window for her mother's honeyed curls, partially blocked by the passenger seat's headrest. She angled a shiny shoe into the leather. "Can we get ice cream after church?"

"A sweet treat for our sweet treat?" Her mother stretched back and tapped her nose over the bunny's ears.

Her father's blue eyes smiled from the rearview mirror. "Of course we can, Pare."

"I'm your gift from God, right Mommy?"

A wistful turn of rosy lips brightened her mother's gaunt visage, and for a moment, the circles that anchored her eyes seemed a little less dark. "From His 'parish' to our home, God gave us our own 'Paresh' to keep with us, always."

Soft fingers stroked her chin. Paresh giggled and buried her face into the bunny's fur. "Stop! That tick—"

The car lurched. A piercing screech cut the air. For a solitary moment, she was weightless. Her father yelled. Her mother

1

screamed. Then Paresh slammed into the constricting seatbelt and the bunny flew from her grasp. A sickening metallic crunch rocked the vehicle sideways and her head cracked against the window.

An eerie silence followed, broken only by the ringing in her ears and the hiss of engine steam. Their car had become a twisted mess of jutting, blood-covered framework and broken glass. A small pocket had formed around her.

Her tiny cries sounded distant and hollow inside her throbbing head, and black spots flickered in her vision. The seatbelt splintered her nails as she desperately tried to get her fingers between the strap and her legs. "Daddy! It hurts!"

Pain speared her skull. She grabbed her head. Warmth streamed between her fingers and fat drops splashed her dress, staining the cream lace bright red. "Daddy! *Help! Daddy!*"

There was no answer. Only the creaking sounds of the car settling and a rising odor of gasoline and exhaust mixing with oil. Tears blurred the back of the passenger seat. The honeyed curls were gone.

"Mommy?" she whispered, rubbing her eyes. The black spots were tunneling. She felt like she was spinning or falling—like Alice down the hole after the White Rabbit. Her eyelids grew heavy. She wanted to sleep.

Muffled voices. A *click*. A rush of cool air. Strong arms scooped her up. Darkness fringed his face, but she conjured the friendly blue eyes of her father's partner. They flashed in her mind like a safety beacon.

"Er…ic?"

The man scoffed. Cold eyes, golden and black, like a tiger's eye stone, drilled into her. His voice, usually so comforting, was hard instead. Words she couldn't hear plunged her into a world of black before she could even think to scream.

II

The eight-year-old asleep in his arms was like a foreign creature. So light that an easy muscle flex could crush her and he'd be done with it all. But it wasn't that simple. Nothing involving Eric ever was. That was part of the appeal.

His shaggy-haired human "partner" leered over the mother's

corpse, too close to the damn car for comfort. He flicked an irritated gaze at the fool and barked, "David! Let's go. You got what you wanted."

Dazed, the man turned and shuffled in line behind him.

A low growl rumbled in the vampire's throat. The moment he'd revealed the child's existence to the Vampiric High Council of Elders—the so-called "Iron Fist" of the Vampiric Nation—he'd chained himself to David. The freedom he'd enjoyed was gone and everything had changed—except for Lucien, the only constant in a race tainted by the blood of angels and innocents.

He tucked the child into the crook of his arm and swept a stray copper lock behind his ear. The Elders had argued, of course. One wished to enforce the law banning child vampires, but a voice of reason put the decision to Lucien—

"Jonathan," David mumbled, stumbling over his feet as his red-rimmed eyes looked back at the intertwined cars. He bumped into Jonathan but didn't seem to care. "Felicia's really dead isn't she? So Eric—"

Jonathan clenched his jaw and sucked in a quelling breath as David's skin oils and hair pressed into his silk suit. He whisked around to put distance between them, his disgust barely masked by his bored voice. "You've killed your brother and his wife. Eric will hunt you as long as you live."

David's brow bridged an angry scowl. He flung an arm into the cornstalks to open a path for Jonathan. "I will kill him first."

A tempting grin crawled over Jonathan's lips. He tapped the obsidian stone in his Hilja ring, a trinket that produced a highly effective sound barrier. "My dear brother has never developed his ability to sense me. Care to watch his reaction?"

The breeze toyed with David's dirt-brown mop as his head drooped. He tucked his hands into his pockets and kinked his neck to look up at Jonathan.

"I want him to suffer," he sneered. "So yeah, let's see him find his precious *Andrew*."

"Give me the Aegis Cloak I put in your bag." Jonathan snapped his fingers. The cloak's protective crimson wool would contain the girl's blood scent—even from Eric.

The oversized garment swallowed the child. Jonathan looped the excess fabric over her head and bloodstained dress for extra measure. Then he opened his aura to include David and fortified it with his ring. Between the ring's silencing shield and his aura's ability to shroud them beyond the visible frequency, they were undetectable to humans and vampires alike.

Twenty minutes passed before another car appeared. The driver called emergency services and a distant siren wailed.

The Elders' fear forced Lucien's hand, Jonathan thought. *Eric, you can only blame yourself this time.*

The first police car delivered a somewhat overweight man wearing a black polo. Visibly shaken after seeing the mangled couple in the silver sedan, he circled to the large, 70s era boat of a car that had plowed into the driver's side. He spoke with the Good Samaritan and then dismissed him since he hadn't seen the accident. The officer held his breath until the stranger's car shrank into the distance. Only then did he wipe his face and exhale between trembling lips.

His eyes watered as he keyed up his radio. "Dispatch, 571. Send the coroner and backup. Three confirmed deceased." He unsuccessfully tried to clear the catch in his voice. "Call Eric Ravenscroft. I need to tell him...it's the Hawthornes."

"Not all of them, you fool!" David yelled, his pulse pumping loud and fast.

Jonathan briefly fantasized about tearing into David's throat, but he couldn't kill him. Yet. Too much hinged on the girl's development—*if* she continued to age.

Only one High Elder had brazenly questioned Lucien's order. Lucien had said nothing, of course, but the other High Elders had immediately scolded their counterpart, one with a small, sardonic laugh into the back of her hand as she said, "Lest you forget, Lord Lucien speaks only once," while the other snapped, "You dare forget your place? Hold your tongue swiftly, or you may find it, and your head, separated from your body."

That cruel reminder rang through Jonathan's head as a black BMW coupe slammed to a stop behind the police car. A vampire in a black tailored suit jumped out.

A sinuous curve overtook Jonathan's mouth. *Fetching as ever.*

"Oh my God…" Eric paused at the passenger door and his expression contorted from shock to horror. He reached in through the broken window and produced a blood-spattered stuffed bunny. "*Where's Paresh?*"

When he turned and saw the officer paling, panic etched furrows into Eric's porcelain countenance. "Walter! Her blood's in the backseat! *Where is she?*"

Oblivious to the ashen-hued fingers shaking his shoulders, Walter whispered, "Oh God, how did I miss—"

He glanced around in a daze and noticed the break in the corn behind David and Jonathan. "Maybe she was scared and hid?"

"Shit," David muttered, stepping behind Jonathan as Eric and Walter ran by oblivious to their presence.

"As long as you didn't touch the car," Jonathan said, "they'll never know. Eric has no scent to follow."

David glared at Eric, who was squatting where Jonathan had wrapped the girl in the Aegis Cloak. "Bastard. Look at him."

Oh yes, look at him. Jonathan licked his lips as Eric disappeared into the field. *So beautiful when he's angry.*

"I can't hear her," Eric yelled from a few rows in. "And I can't smell her blood in here. This isn't good."

He emerged with engorged, darkening eyes. Sharp fangs glinted in the sunlight and his voice was coarse as he demanded, "Get every officer you have. Get the whole damn town and *find her!*"

"Find her!" David mimicked. He kicked at the air. "You deserve everything that's coming to you, you filthy demon! I'm—"

That officer knows what Eric is, Jonathan realized. "This situation has changed. We're leaving."

"But you could kill them both right now! *And her!*" David gestured at the child.

"I am not permitted to take from the Flock. They are protected from me."

As David grumbled and mocked him behind his back, Jonathan pressed a prong on the Vampiric Star pinned to his lapel. The portal to Animus Hollow, the dimensional divide between Heaven, Earth, and Hades, appeared as a gaping white maw. It was the only way to escape without a trace.

5

He shoved David into the rolling white haze and lingered a moment to admire the angst in Eric's icy blue eyes.

"The game may be on a forced hiatus," Jonathan whispered. "But it's your move, now." He laughed softly as he eyed the girl. "You have no hope of winning, *Brother*."

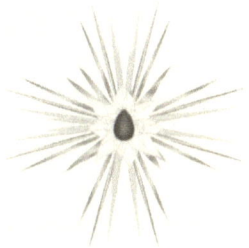

Chapter Two: Paresh of Sunset Grove

Orison Crossing, Illinois, Summer 2006

Sunset Grove's mighty mouth opened at the break near the carriage house, framing a cottage frosted silver under the moon's light. Feathered, furred, or somewhere in between, the forest's animals lined the flagstone path, rapt with otherworldly anticipation.

A silhouette broke apart from the canopy's inky swell and stepped into the clearing. A burst of wind blew back the hood of its lightweight cloak. Leaves gossiped their secrets, and the eldest animals twitched and skittered about. They knew that golden hair and pale skin, and recognized the ghostly gray eyes that brightened in welcome.

She was finally home.

Fidgeting with the key that dangled from a spiraled bracelet on her wrist, she contemplated the gathering and the stone cottage. Her mother had named her for the parish that had once stood there—the parish where she was born. The animals were present that night, too.

It's been so many years, she thought. *How can they remember me?*

Startled by the crunch of leaves in the darkness at her back, she whirled around and peered beyond the tree line. Her lips eased into a smile as she knelt and cooed, "Hi there, aren't you just beautiful?"

A doe crossed the threshold into the dewy grass, its big black eyes lifting to hers as a fawn came out behind her. The girl offered a gentle hand and stroked the fawn's spotted fur.

"Such a pretty baby, Mama," she whispered, glancing at the surrounding tree line as other woodland critters appeared, ears perked, tails snapping, wings flapping, eyes observing—their presence a collective, *Welcome home.*

She remembered playing with them—her friends—and the feel of their fur beneath her fingertips, both soft and coarse, and the slight pinch of miniature talons perched upon her shoulders. On the shores of memory, the innocence of youth briefly returned.

It's not a dream. I'm really home.

Suddenly, the doe flashed the white of her tail to scatter the other animals into the canopy's safety. Cocking her head at sky-darkening clouds, the doe shared a final look with the girl before issuing a small cry and bounding into the woods with her baby.

Thunder crashed and a dull rain scented of stone and dirt splashed the path. Wind rushed the girl's back as she turned and ran for the door, getting inside just before the sky split open.

She did not see the man in the shadows who had watched her arrival, nor the grim smile that played across his lips. He emerged from the forest, standing firm against the raging storm, and his intense, black eyes stabbed the closing door.

☽ ❀ ☾

The silence inside the cottage was a jarring contrast to the howling wind and beating rain. And yet, even as shadows danced wildly with each lightning flash, the scent of freshly chopped firewood invoked nostalgic memories of snowy nights warmed by fires in the stone hearth.

She smiled. The cottage had stood empty all these years, waiting for the buoyancy of life to return. She firmed her grip on the door. "I missed you, too."

It felt too good not to be real. It felt right. This was where she belonged. "Just get through tomorrow, Pare. No matter what happens, this is your home."

A bright lightning bolt brought the space to life and she instantly saw that Simon, the caretaker, hadn't changed a thing. The dining table, the kitchen chairs, the Victorian sofa, her father's desk—all the same pieces in all the same places.

Returned to darkness, she touched the table's smooth surface. A woman's delicate voice floated by on fine wisps of recollection, trailed by a man's soft chuckle and a child's innocent giggle. Another voice grew in prominence—a deep, masculine sound that ripped into her core. She jerked away, staring hard into nothingness and gasping as though winded.

N-no! No! She backed into the door. *I never should have gotten onto that train!*

She covered her mouth. *I can't face him! I can't...*

Minutes passed before she ran a shaky hand through her hair, sucked in a quelling breath, and squared her shoulders. "Yes, I can. It's paperwork. *That's all.*"

She flipped the light switch, but nothing happened.

"Oh, right," she muttered. "The power's off until morning."

A quick search of the sideboard yielded the candles and matches Simon had promised to leave. The scent of sulfur nipped her nose as flames flickered to life and she blew out the match. She turned to hang her cloak behind the door, but paused as candlelight reflected off a thick book. It was a phone book from 1996.

For half a second she told herself she wouldn't open it. But she knew better. She'd look for her parents anywhere she could find them, no matter how much it hurt.

The entry for *Hawthorne, A.* stung her eyes and brought a lump to her throat. "I miss you, Daddy."

She closed the book and let her hand linger as though breaking the link meant losing every memory of him. She eventually turned away and padded across the carpet with a heavy weight in her heart.

She ran her fingers over the curved slats of her father's roll top desk. It looked so desolate and alone in the dim light, shuttered with the chair tucked into place, naked without its usual clutter of unruly paper stacks and bound depositions. She felt her courage falter. She wasn't strong enough to do this on her own.

But she'd already made her choice. "The fireplace...light will help."

She wasn't sure that she believed herself. Even so, despite it being summer, Simon had left firewood and tinder ready, and lighting it would give her something else to focus on. He'd said the nights had been chilly lately, and tonight was proof enough. The rain lashing the window over the desk was more like an autumnal storm than a midsummer thundershower. She'd forgotten how fickle the weather in Illinois was—not that it was any more predictable in Kansas.

She sparked what she hoped would be a confidence boosting fire, and sat on the hearth listening to its comforting crackle. Bathed in golden light, the cottage's familiar décor was swathed in feminine roses and creams. Rich woods were softened by velvet and lace. The sofa's dark frame gleamed with polish and her father's leather wingback chair was nestled into the corner, worn and well loved. An ornate side table displayed his collection of pipes and tobacco jars.

Simon had done well. Too well. The room was so frozen in time that her mother's eternally unfinished needlepoint sat on her rocking chair as though she'd only just left it.

She dabbed at her teary eyes and sighed, half expecting to see her parents walk through the door. Absently smudging moisture between her thumb and forefinger, she forced herself to acknowledge that neither would ever walk through that door again.

A blinding flash hit close enough to shake the cottage. She jolted to her feet and her breath caught in her throat. There'd been a face! No! A…a man! At the window!

Her heart slammed against her sternum as she hesitantly approached the glass. No one was there. She rubbed her eyes, but jagged lines still swam in her vision. She must have imagined a pattern in the rain on the window.

"Get a grip," she said, sweeping her fingers over her forehead. "It was sixteen hours on that train—you're seeing things. Sleep!"

She grabbed a throw blanket off the sofa and shook out the scent of lavender fabric softener. Roses and lavender. Her mother's favorite flowers. She breathed it in deeply and closed her eyes, hugging the blanket to her chest. She'd known this would be hard. She hadn't expected Simon to transport her back in time and make it near impossible.

With a hefty sigh, she spread the blanket over the sofa's plush cushions and eased out of her dress. With her bags at the station and nothing else to wear, she didn't want it to wrinkle. She blew out the candles, slid beneath the cover, and breathed slowly and deeply, relaxing her muscles on each exhale and clearing her mind—it didn't stop the nightmares, but it helped her to drift off.

She'd just crossed the barrier between lucidity and the place where dreams were born when a man with hair as dark as the night turned out of the shadows. He stood before her with a ghostly pale face, the deep black of the surroundings blurring his outline. His eyes snapped open and pierced hers with emotionless, ice blue orbs.

She went rigid for an instant and then mentally sank to her knees, sobbing uncontrollably. "*Why?*" she screamed. "*Why did you leave me?*"

Leaping up, she ran into him, pummeling his chest only to find her fists sucked into a tar-like substance. She collapsed at his feet, arms stuck and crisscrossed overhead, weeping as she realized he wasn't really there. He had never been there.

II

A knot of distrust tightened in his gut. Only one person was worthy of Simon's frenzied three days of cleaning, pruning, and de-winterizing, but the old man hadn't said a peep. Not to the authorities. Not to *him*. And that was inexcusable.

Still…he couldn't deny that the cottage had embraced its former glory. Simon had sparked its hope anew, lifting the protective sheets of abandonment and revealing the contents as proof of the life it'd once nurtured. *He'd* refused to let Simon box it all up for storage. That meant letting her go forever and he couldn't do that.

Am I a fool for wanting to hope, too, after a decade of not knowing? He tousled his black hair as a surge of impatience nipped his ribs.

One event, all those years ago, had stolen the reason for his existence. Huffing between his teeth, he clenched his jaw and let his gaze drift over the gathered animals—the only proof that he *should* need that she was coming. But hope was a dangerous, fragile thing, easily shattered, rarely fulfilled, and monstrously cruel.

Light footsteps sounded near the carriage house. His pulse spiked.

"It can't be her!" he growled to himself, desperate to starve hope's spark and instead ignite the fires of rage. "It has to be *David!*"

And if it were, he'd shred David's throat and drain him dry. That man did not deserve the air that filled his lungs, let alone the blood in his veins.

The night worse only shades of crimson as his adrenaline surged and aching pressure mounted behind his canines. As his teeth descended, his jaw stretched at the hinge and a growl rumbled in his throat. He tucked low, his legs coiled tight and ready to spring.

The footsteps drew closer.

An outline appeared at the break in the woods.

A figure emerged wearing a pale cloak.

His muscles released and time seemed to slow as the wind hooked under the hood.

His body instantly ran cold, freezing him in place. The night's air stuck in his throat like a strangled cry. All his hopes and doubts collided, and grief squeezed like a vice on his heart. He clutched his chest, his gaze locked onto the moonlit ghost of Felicia, tears splashing his cheeks.

But it wasn't Felicia. It was *her*. *Her* skin. *Her* face. *Her* hair.

He covered his mouth and dropped to his knees. "Oh God, you look so much like your mother." This woman…no, the eight-year-old girl he'd known—

He shook his head, unable to reconcile the two images. He couldn't accept that David would simply let her go. Through all of his searching, he'd never even known if she was alive. As he watched her kneel before a doe and its fawn, his protective instinct kicked in. David must have followed her.

"Such a pretty baby, Mama," she cooed as she stroked the fawn— and his urge to run to her.

Daggered claws tore into a sapling. He needed to moor himself to this spot, to fight his desire to fold her into his arms and soothe her troubles, and never to let go of her again. If he were to stand at her side as her father intended, she couldn't see him as he was, monstrous with fangs and throbbing, bloodshot eyes. He'd terrify her and that would break his already fractured soul.

Andrew and Felicia had never explained his secret—his relationship with her father. She'd been too young to understand. The fine lines of age and beginnings of gray hair went unnoticed by a child. She saw only a familiar face, not realizing it never changed the way her father's did.

Her parents were young, barely even forty, when they died. No one had noticed the years growing on them day to day, but photographs revealed the passage of time differently. Photographs told no such tale about him.

The sapling snapped. He pounded the ground with his fist. He should have dealt with David long before the accident. That man was a snake. And he'd slithered into hiding, pulling all his assets shortly after her birth. No amount of digging ever turned up whatever hole he'd gone into. He'd feared that she'd vanished forever, too, but—

Thunder grumbled, trailing bright flashes over the canopy, and the animals ran for cover. The girl sprinted for the cottage and got in before the downpour hit.

Fantastic veins of light embraced the sky and thunder shook the Earth as he stepped from the forest's shelter. Needled by rain, he watched the door close with narrowed eyes and a thin smile. At last, he could finally put an end to all of this.

$$) * ($$

The storm lashed him with a fury that seemingly wanted to push him back into the forest. The trees creaked and groaned, and the heavens roared with the same intensity as his hammering heart. When he got to the window and saw her basking in a fire's warmth, he understood why. She may be the daughter of the only "family" he'd had left, but that little girl he'd known had grown into a beautiful young woman. And desires that had lain dormant since before his wife's death were stirring to life beyond his control.

"It's not right—you can't...you just can't—" He faced the driving rain, hoping the cool torrent would calm his pulse—and his thoughts. Lightning zipped across the sky, illuminating the clearing as bright as day while shaking the ground violently. His gaze dropped and locked onto hers.

Damn it! He ducked and flattened himself against the wall. Footsteps approached and her shadow loomed for what felt like an eternity. He sighed in relief when she finally turned away, talking herself out of what she'd seen.

He slicked his hair back and closed his eyes, finding solace in the rhythm of her heart. He hated to admit it to himself, but she pulled him from his cold reality into a warm, ethereal place that he didn't want to leave. She'd only just arrived, and he was already hooked like an addict, unable to resist another peek, even if it meant being caught.

Dancing flames gave her ivory complexion a luminous glow and highlighted shimmering gold tones in the wavy locks spilling across her pillow. Her skin had always been fair like his, but she'd never tanned or burned, even under the hottest summer sun. Her features were a blend of Felicia's natural beauty and soft curves, and Andrew's fine symmetry and hard angles. Graceful arches adorned satiny pink lips and a petite button nose complemented eyes he knew to be a steely gray.

Lucinda, forgive me. He sighed and ran his hands through his hair again. In the agony of waiting and searching and not knowing, he'd lost touch with time's reality.

As her pulse and breathing slowed into sleep's rhythmic domain, she lost her subconscious hold on her aura. Its essence sought him out, and enveloped him in instant recognition, pure and tranquil, the same energy that attracted animals to her like a magnet to iron.

"Welcome home, Paresh," he whispered, his skin tingling under her aura's caress. "I've missed you more than I thought possible."

Suddenly her pulse ignited and her aura froze. Her visage twisted in anguish. "Why?" she mumbled. Tears slid onto her pillow and she hugged the blanket as she curled into a tiny ball. "Why did you leave me?"

He staggered backward as though slapped and swallowed hard, staring at the window without seeing it. A slideshow of terrors clicked through his head—all the possibilities of the life she'd endured without his protection—and that made him hate David—and himself—even more.

III

He was thoroughly drenched and chilled by the time his black BMW coupe came into view after a long trek through the woods. He clasped his hands and blew warmth into them, and then dug into his pocket. The saturated denim fought his fingers every bit of the way, but eventually his key ring jingled free. As he got closer to the main road, he jabbed the keyless remote and circled to the driver's door.

"Hello there, *Brother*," cooed a velvety voice that instantly twisted his stomach.

Of course, he'd appear tonight, he thought, mentally kicking himself for not seeing Jonathan leaning against the trunk. Not that seeing him would change anything. The knot already festering in his chest tightened. He warily faced his brother.

"Not even a 'hello,' Eric?" Jonathan approached from the passenger side and rounded the hood. Youthful, lean, and tall, with auburn hair tied at his nape by a crimson ribbon, Jonathan was smug and in his element—unfazed by the rain, despite his soaked pinstriped suit, with Eric caught off guard. A faint glow came off his alabaster skin, but his golden eyes were preternaturally dark as he stuffed his hands into his pockets.

They stared at each other in silence. The storm subsided, leaving behind only the sounds of distant thunder and water dripping from leaves into puddles. Eric crossed his arms and leaned against his car. Jonathan wrung out the kerchief from his breast pocket and dabbed his face.

"Really? It's been a while." Jonathan cracked a grin that didn't touch his eyes. "Not happy to see me?"

"When am I ever?" Eric snapped, his brow furrowing. "Not seeing you in the last decade was one of the few good standouts."

"Interesting, Brother, because, in that regard, we have a common...well, *interest*."

The gleam in Jonathan's prodding eyes triggered every internal warning at once, but Eric couldn't let it show. Feigning a bored sigh, he whisked water from his eyes. "Get to the point already."

"Tsk, tsk." Jonathan wagged his finger. "She's returned and I'm here right on her heels—almost like the Hawthorne Dog Himself! Don't pretend that doesn't strike you."

Jonathan's wicked smile grew wider and more annoying. Eric's jaw bulged at the hinge as his eyes rolled skyward. He was sick of playing these insidious little games.

Jonathan's smile faded. "I see, then. Mr. Serious. As usual."

Taking his time—because, of course, Eric's world had to revolve around him and his whims—Jonathan folded and carefully tucked the kerchief into his pocket. "I'm following her," he said, pausing for extra effect, "for David."

The internal alarms blared again and this time Eric didn't have the control needed not to react. His eyes snapped to Jonathan and he ground his teeth against mounting pressure. Taking a step forward, he growled, "*You're what?*"

Jonathan laughed. "Finally! A reaction!" He grinned with the whole of his being and held up a finger. "But see, that's not completely accur—"

Eric lunged, grabbing him by the lapels and throwing him onto the BMW's hood. He landed on top of Jonathan, seething with saliva dripping down his teeth. "Why the hell are you involved with *him?*"

Trying to wriggle free before Eric got both hands on his throat, Jonathan flashed a savage smile. "My, my. Someone's gotten rather testy over the years."

Thrusting his arms up between Eric's elbows, Jonathan broke the tenuous hold on his throat and used Eric's shifting balance against him to reverse their positions. "You should know by now that you'll never win. Sometimes I wonder if you actually do enjoy this."

His lips skimmed Eric's ear with a deliberate kiss as he whispered, "Because you know I do, and that makes it extra unfortunate that I can't play right now. But there's always next time. Thanks for the tickle." He winked and stared at Eric with a silent, albeit arrogant, plea for a truce before releasing his grip and backing away.

"*Bastard!*" Eric angrily wiped his ear and threw his fist into Jonathan's face, smashing his jaw and breaking Jonathan's composure for the first time.

Jonathan's beautiful visage warped into that of an angry demon with blackened eyes and engorged blood red veins, and sharp fangs that protruded from a grotesquely stretched jaw. He pinned Eric against the car and leaned in to hiss, "*Let me finish!*"

"I'm not in the mood to deal with you tonight!" Eric spat. He kicked off the ground sideways and Jonathan fell against his chest.

"Just *stop*, would you?" Jonathan demanded. Eric went stiff beneath him, so he let go and was slowly rising when Eric's other fist connected with his face.

As Jonathan rubbed his jaw, warning flashed in his eyes, but he continued walking backward and put both hands up. "Do that again and I say *nothing*."

"How did you find her? What the hell do you mean you're here *for* David? *What the hell is going on?*" Eric wiped spittle from his mouth and threw his arms out in frustration.

"This time, it's beyond my control," Jonathan answered earnestly. "You see, the High Council is rather interested in your little, eh, *prodigy*. David is merely a tool." He dismissed Eric's other question with a wave and glanced in disdain at his wrinkled suit. "Money does so motivate humans. Why do you think he let her come back?"

Eric slumped against the car in shock. "The...the High Council?" he asked, not hearing his own voice.

"Who else?" Jonathan sounded annoyed. He straightened his jacket and brushed leaves off his sleeves. "And I came to tell you she's home, like the good brother I am."

"Oh, cut the crap," Eric said, shaking his head. "What have you told the High Council? And where is David? He owes me a life or two."

"I won't argue that." Irritation flickered across Jonathan's face. "But finding David won't help you now. He's barely in control of the situation anymore."

Golden flecks glimmered like fire in Jonathan's eyes as he faked a laugh. "Oops, did I say *barely*—ha! Why do you think I'd help you? Aren't I too *narcissistic* for something like that?"

"Yes, but you seem to like skulking in the shadows to spy on me," Eric muttered dryly as a heavily tinted black Lexus pulled up behind his car.

Jonathan breezed past him casting a purposefully lustful gaze that he knew would hit Eric to the bone. "I *always* enjoy seeing you."

Eric scoffed at Jonathan's retreating form. "You want me to know something or I wouldn't even know you're here. Give me something concrete. One thing. Anything."

"Okay. One thing?" Jonathan tapped his index finger against the air and entered the sedan without acknowledging the vampire who opened his door. Eric sighed in resignation.

As he pulled his door open, Jonathan's car stopped beside him. The rear window lowered and revealed a wicked spark in Jonathan's golden brown eyes. "You want one thing? Well, how about this? David is the least of your worries now, *Brother*."

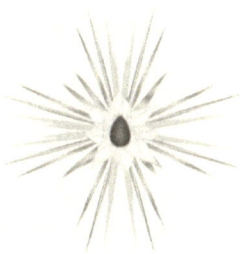

Chapter Three: Reunion

I

Eric didn't sleep. He changed into a t-shirt and track pants and retired to his conservatory. Lightning flashed over cornfields and thunder rolled as the storms returned and drummed the overhead glass with rain. Propping his feet on the rattan ottoman, he leaned back with his eyes closed, his hand weaving to Beethoven's *Moonlight Sonata*.

Despite Jonathan's revelation about the High Council, David had consumed Eric's thoughts every day for the past decade and now he finally had a clear motive to work with. As the executor of Andrew and Felicia's estate, Eric held sole control over their assets. In accordance with family tradition, he had taken his rightful share and placed the rest into a trust for their daughter. Her eighteenth birthday was too recent and too conveniently coincidental for David to have simply let her go. No...he'd sent her to see *him*.

Which meant—

His bare feet slapped the floor as he jerked up. She appeared in his mind, haloed in bright, fiery light. Delicate fabric slid from her shoulders, revealing skin that shimmered golden. The dress slid down her arms. She looked up and smiled, eyes shining like stars, guiding him to her like he was a lost sailor in rough waters. Enveloping warmth ignited his pulse. The dress slipped off her hips. The halo encased her body in a blinding flash and dropped him back into the cold grasp of lonely darkness.

He ran a hand through his hair and absently watched rivulets run down the glass. Seeing her like that...he buried his face in his hands

19

and tried to shake it off. But she lingered where she'd always lingered, only now she was a beautiful woman, not a giggling eight-year-old girl, and her haunting presence lifted the ghosts of his past alongside his guilt until the rain stopped. The clouds cleared and the sun's first rays poked over the horizon when Jonathan's voice popped back into his head.

I'm following her...David is merely a tool.

Eric's heart dropped at the implication he'd missed. The Elders only interfered in the Realm of Man when they felt threatened. He didn't know much about them, but he did know they acted swiftly and lethally to keep the world at large in the dark. But why would they send Jonathan instead of a hunter? And why had he agreed?

Jonathan, on his own, was a formidable opponent without the High Council involved. For them to stand behind him now made no sense—even if they did see her as a threat. As a protected member of God's Flock, no vampire could touch her—

David is merely a tool.

The words cut into his thoughts with a cruel realization that tolled like a bell for the dead.

☽ ❊ ☾

Later that morning, Eric breezed into the Law Offices of Hawthorne, Ravenscroft, Dugao, and Daley. The rich mahogany floorboards matched the paneled walls, and patterned Oriental rugs muffled their old, creaking groans as he passed the wingback chairs in the waiting area. Wrought iron stairs spiraled up to the loft where his partners and their staff worked, but his office was straight ahead. He only needed to clear the gatekeeper: Molly Sims, his secretary.

A painting of Andrew's great-great-great grandfather at the capture of Fort Donelson in 1862 loomed overhead as she glanced up from her computer screen. He beamed a disarming smile, said, "Good morning," and swept into his office before she could respond.

When the door latched, he exhaled relief into a soothing blackness only achievable with custom-made, opaque screens installed on the arched windows. But humans expected to see light in an office, so after his appreciative moment of darkness, he flipped the middle switch. Dim rays beamed down from the vaulted tin-tiled ceiling and highlighted built-in shelves that housed thousands of books, many of them aged volumes of old-time law, broken into clusters by silken peonies in glazed ceramic pots—used at Molly's insistence to "soften" his edge.

Despite his mood, he smiled at how she'd precariously teetered on the ladders to place those things in the "perfect" spots. His old-fashioned roots didn't tether him to an outdated mindset that dismissed feminine whims. She'd been right; they did work. His clients often focused on them and relaxed—if only slightly—while in his presence.

He crossed a crimson and cream rug, specially woven to cover a space that spanned the full width of the ground floor, and tossed his briefcase and sunglasses onto his desk. There were no paintings or pieces of art, only a few small frames with his degrees and certificates hanging near the door. He paused to stroke the coarse spine of an ancient book. It left a powdery substance on his fingertip. Time's touch had been gentler to him.

Smudging the powder between his thumb and forefinger, he sat at his desk and whispered, "Can I do this?"

He sighed and leaned forward, wholly uncertain of how the morning would play out. His gaze dropped to a photograph of Andrew and Felicia with their daughter, taken a few years before the accident. He traced the little girl's outline with his finger. She no longer existed. Day by day, time changed little for him, but it had certainly changed her.

"I promise," he whispered. "I'll never leave you again."

He stood with another sigh and tried to walk off the energy buzzing his nerves. He paced between his desk and the suede sofa in the sitting area where clients could wind down. The marble-topped sideboard, handcrafted by a local artisan, hid a refrigerated cabinet filled with water and juice, and displayed a tray of top shelf liquor—none of which could soothe his restless anxiety.

Time is not on your side. Get it together.

Gripping the back of the sofa, he eyed the trio of lead crystal decanters. That was an indulgence he offered to the people seeking his help. In this moment, right here, right now, there was no indulging for him. He didn't keep blood in his office. He was on his own—but not alone.

He poked his head out to summon Molly. She was his confidante and a true friend, and likely knew him even better than Andrew had. He didn't let many get that close, but life in the public eye required trusted connections.

Always professional in the office, the middle-aged woman smoothed her tweed skirt as she stood. She wore her chestnut hair tied into a loose bun. Bifocal glasses rode low on her narrow nose, and her hazel eyes glinted with curiosity.

Pushing her glasses up, she hurried into his office and crossed the large expanse to plop down in a chair opposite his desk. She looked over her shoulder when she realized he'd remained in place, staring vacantly at the closed door.

"Mr. Ravenscroft?" Given their apparent age difference and close-knit community, she always used the formality in public. She thought it prevented rumors from spreading more than they already did.

He parted his lips, but words weren't there. "Give me a moment."

"Well, at least, remember to put on your *spectacles*." She lifted a brow and smirked, brushing invisible lint from her lap.

A reluctant smile cracked at the old word, a joke between them. Striding to his desk, Eric pulled a case from his jacket pocket and slid rectangular frames onto his nose. He pinched the metal bridge for a moment with his eyes closed. When he opened them, his arm fell to his side and he met Molly's gaze with dead seriousness in his.

"I'm expecting a visitor. Likely today. Soon." He ruffled his hair and briefly lost himself in thought again. He shrugged out of his jacket, draped it over his chair, and sat.

Molly studied him closely. She tensed and inched closer to the edge of her seat.

Folding his hands, he said, "Paresh came home last night."

Molly's eyes widened. Her lips moved in an effort to reply, but no voice came out. After several intensifying seconds, she managed to get out, "P-P-Pare...Paresh *Hawthorne*?"

Eric nodded solemnly. "I saw her myself."

"She came home?" Molly whispered in disbelief. Her eyes darted to his and she rapid-fired, "How is she? Did you talk to her? Did they let her go? Was she hurt? Oh! That poor child! Oh, I hope she's all right! They—"

Eric motioned for her to calm down. "I haven't spoken with her

22

yet, but she seemed fine. She came alone."

"Could you tell if—" Molly averted her gaze. "If they hurt her?"

"No," he replied in a low voice. After another few seconds of grim silence, he dipped his face to catch Molly's eye. "Given her recent birthday, I expect she's coming to see me."

At first, Molly looked confused. Then she gasped and pointed at his face, and he nodded in agreement.

"Yes, I'll get to that," he said. "But first, when she arrives, contact Walter and get him here right away. I won't terminate the trust until we understand more. I'm not certain she even knows she was kidnapped and concerns about her mental health will legally delay whatever plans David has—not that he has a legal leg to stand on."

Molly adjusted her glasses and smoothed flyaway strands. She was visibly shaken and hiding it poorly. "Do…are you sure we shouldn't call the chief now?"

"I want to see her first. Call him on his direct line, not through dispatch. I don't want a media circus or parades in her honor right now—but we both know we'll have to deal with it eventually."

A deep sigh crossed his lips as he brushed ebony hairs away from his glasses. They fell right back into place. Molly wasn't the only one trying to hide her emotions.

"So! As for *this*," he said, indicating his face. "I don't want my appearance to confuse her. Ask Walter to call me Mr. Ravenscroft in her presence and tell her that I'm out of the office, but that my son is assisting and can meet with her."

Molly's voice was barely audible when she asked, "Darien?"

Given the observant and good-natured person Molly was, Eric appreciated her delicacy. "Yes. I'll identify with that name."

"Did she know you had a son?"

"No." His tone put an end to further questions.

"Shall I rework your schedule then, as well?" she asked, ticking off a mental checklist. "Mr. Dugao can cover your nine-thirty and eleven o'clock hearings, and Mrs. Daley can meet with your clients this afternoon. Also, the Jamersons want you to represent their son. He allegedly broke into their neighbor's shed and stole his power tools. He's at the jail pending arraignment since they can't afford bail."

Eric marveled at her ability to switch modes so swiftly, especially when her concern for Paresh nearly rivaled his own. She had also been Andrew's secretary and family friend.

"Good idea. Clear my schedule for the next few weeks. Tell the Jamersons that I must decline and recommend either of my partners at their discretion. I'm sure they need pro bono, so pay the expenses from my account until I can speak with their son and resolve the matter. Rework your schedule, as well, and see what the girls upstairs can take from you. We're going to be rather busy for the foreseeable future."

II

Paresh awoke to warm, sunny rays reaching in through the windows. Finches and sparrows sang and tapped on the glass, and squirrels chattered on the sills. On the roof, doves cooed the song of dawn, while chatter and scratching below the windows gave away the presence of other animals calling her outside to play.

Flat on her back, Paresh stretched the cramped muscles in her arms and legs, and groaned happily. This was a morning ritual long overdue, yet never forgotten. She closed her eyes and smiled at the forest's exuberant joy. Its essence lifted her spirits.

She heard a *click* and a low hum, and clapped her hands together. "Yes! The refrigerator is running—I have power!"

Laughing at herself, she jumped up and pressed her hand to the window glass. "Good morning, everyone," she said. "Thank you for coming to visit. It's already a better day."

She briefly touched her father's desk and looked at her mother's needlepoint. Even if they weren't here, their memories were. She could visit them—and all of her friends—when she was ready.

For now, she headed for the shower, not surprised to see the bathroom suspended ten years in the past. At least Simon had added hints of the present with fluffy white towels and an assortment of travel-sized toiletries. A fresh bouquet of carnations, daisies, and azaleas sprouted from a Depression-era vase and breathed revitalizing life into the space.

The antique washbasin on the vanity prickled her nerves. A hand-painted rose garnished each side of the pitcher inside the ceramic bowl. The cherished wedding gift to her parents had originally been the family heirloom of her father's partner. The reminder of the unpleasant task ahead of her dated back to the 1840s.

Yet again second-guessing her choice, she glanced at the mirror and noticed a swatch of lavender behind the door—her mother's silk robe. The material around the collar, slightly stretched, retained the shape of the hook when she removed it. It had hung there since the last time her mother had worn it—*that morning* before church.

Cocooning stillness gathered her into its fold, muffling the animal prattle under the beating of her heart. The hall clock ticked. The refrigerator hummed.

Thump. Tick. Hm. Tock.

The sounds grew louder as her vision tunneled into purple silk and feathered at the edges into wreckage she didn't want to see. *Not that day. Not today.*

Thump. Tick. Hm. Tock.

It echoed in her ears. She could smell gasoline and exhaust. She squeezed her eyes shut. *No! Don't go back!*

Thump. Tick. Hm. Toc—

A thundering knock broke the spell. The air trapped in her lungs rushed out. She was shaking so badly that it took a few tries to slip her arms into the sleeves. She knotted the belt and swore she could feel her mother embracing her as an assurance that everything would work out.

She took a moment to collect herself, and then, after a quick check of her reflection, smoothed her hair and trotted to the front door. There was another knock as she reached for the handle.

A man in his late seventies, short and pudgy, with a poof of white hair atop his head, stood there in a flannel shirt haphazardly tucked into faded jeans. One gnarled hand held a white sack and the other, an insulated travel mug.

"Ah, I see you got in okay. Thought you might be hungry and not have any breakfast, what with the power out and all. Is it on yet?" He poked his head inside. "No bags?"

"You must be Simon." She remembered the throaty rattle in his voice from their phone calls. "Thank you. Please, come in. No bags yet. I'll pick them up later at the station."

He headed for the dining table. He set the items down and dropped into a chair.

"Can't stand long on account of my bad back, you know," he said. "I can get your luggage for you, if you want. Here—" He pushed the bag and mug across the table. "A doughnut and orange juice. Didn't know if you were a coffee drinker and figured most everybody likes juice. Took a minute to choose apple or orange, though."

"Orange is fine. Thank you again," she said, sitting across from him. "I've never tried coffee to know if I like it or not, to be honest. No one in the house drank it."

As she streamed pulpy liquid into the mug's cap, his eyes lifted from her hands to her face with an intensity she could feel. She gently cleared her throat before looking up. He glanced out the window.

"You're much bigger than the last time I seen you. You grew up into a real pretty young lady." He smiled sadly. "Sorry 'bout your folks, you know. Bet this place is happy to have you home."

Her eyes stung as she sipped, but she forced a smile. "It's good to be home. Everything looks wonderful. You've taken great care of it."

When he remained silent, she tapped her fingers lightly against the plastic cap, trying to think of something to say. He nudged the unopened sack.

"Well? Aren't you hungry? Eat up, eat up!" He waited until she took a bite to glance around with pride. "Yeah, I cleaned this place top to bottom and washed just 'bout everything. Sorry 'bout the power thing, you know. You'll probably want to wait 'til tomorra' to use the fridge. Other than that, everything should be just 'bout perfect. You stayin' long?"

She nodded and swallowed before answering. "I'm here for good. I'm looking forward to getting back into the community and picking up my father's charity work while I look for a job."

"A job?" Simon scoffed and then clucked his tongue while surveying the kitchen. "Mm-hm. You'll need to update the appliances. They're probably as old as you and haven't been used in half as long at least."

He slapped his hands on the table. "So, uh, do you have your luggage tags or ticket stub, locker key—whatever—so I can get your bags?"

"Oh, that's okay. I need to go into town before I settle in."

Butterflies tickled her stomach. She shoved a chunk of doughnut into her mouth. With only enough money left for a small lunch, she couldn't rent a car to retrieve her luggage until she met with her father's partner about her inheritance. But how could she face that man when the prospect alone made her want to run back to Kansas?

"You don't have a car," Simon said, "so let me give you a ride at least. I can wait or come back later." He crumpled the sack as she took the final bite.

Shaking her head, she smiled and waved dismissively. "Thank you for the offer, but I'd like to walk and take in the scenery." She finished the juice. "Thanks again for breakfast. I'm sorry I wasn't a better host."

"You been gone a long time and I can't say I wouldn't have lots to think 'bout neither, if I was in your shoes." He sighed. "But, figured you'd need something to eat, seeing there's no food here, so thought I'd pop by. You sure you don't need anything else 'fore I go?" He pushed off the table to get up.

"Well," she said reluctantly. "There is one thing. Do you remember Dad's partner, Eric?"

"Yep, he's my boss. Runs the firm downtown. Should be there today—if you need to see him," he replied nonchalantly, facing away as he struggled out of the chair.

"Oh…" She bit her lower lip. "Of course. So, he…he knows I'm back then?"

"Ah, haven't seen him since you called, sorry. He and I just kind of go about our business, if you know what I mean. If you need anything, my number's by the phone." He pointed at a note on the sideboard and grabbed the travel mug. He shuffled to the door and paused with his hand on the knob, pivoting at the waist to peer over his shoulder without looking at her. "You know—you look an awful lot like your mother. I swear…ain't that something? It's been nice seein' you again."

She clasped her hands at her breast. "Thank you. You, too. I'm sorry I don't remember you from before."

He shrugged. "You was a little one back then."

"Still, thanks for everything you've done. It really looks great."

He nodded and let himself out. She leaned against the doorjamb, her stomach sinking as he hobbled down the flagstone path.

Soon she would face the man who had cast her aside. The man

27

who had sent her to grieve among strangers when he left her with an uncle her father had never mentioned. The man who had broken his vow—his promise to be with her always—but perhaps she had been a foolish young girl to believe such a thing in the first place.

III

After a hot shower, she found herself outside the master bedroom. The door was slightly ajar, tempting her with another glimpse into the past. She yearned to enter and pick one of her mother's dresses to wear, but another part of her hoped that Simon had boxed this room up and sent it off for storage, leaving behind only remnants of once happy lives.

She curled her fingers over the edge and stared at the wood's grain, imagining ghostly sheets draping the bed and furniture, and cobwebs cascading from the canopy to the floor and hugging the corners with thick, sticky funnels. But she knew better. The cottage was stuck in time and their room would be no different. Her parents' clothes still hung in their closet just as her mother's robe had remained on that hook.

Stirring up dusty memories needed to wait. She inhaled deeply and let it trickle out through her nose. Closing her eyes, she rested her forehead against the door and tightened her grip. "Get through the morning. That's all you need to do."

She put on her dress and sandals, and mustered the courage to leave, but when she touched the door's handle, the room teetered and tilted off balance. After all these years, she was going to see him—it was really happening. She blew out a bolstering breath and opened the door.

The sun hugged her like an old friend, and a cluster of woodland animals tagged along down the flagstone. As she passed the old carriage house turned garage, a relic from when the Sunset Grove Parish had stood in the clearing instead of the cottage, her nerves took over and whisked her into thought. She didn't notice that her friends fell back as she approached the main road or that she emerged from the forest's shadow alone.

She'd been similarly absent during all sixteen hours on the train, mulling the unexpected offer of returning home and claiming an inheritance she'd known nothing about. The requirement of seeing *him*—and on her own, no less—had almost made the choice for her.

She drifted into town. Trees gave way to houses and houses became businesses. She walked up one bustling street after another on automatic until she reached a window with large, block-lettered names on it.

"Law Offices of Hawthorne, Ravenscroft, Dugao, and Daley," she read quietly. The latter two names were new, and it was a relief to see the Hawthorne name still on the glass. Her father and Eric had started their practice here long before she was born.

Her father used to say that without Eric, they'd never have won half of their cases, and yet, for some reason, he'd always traveled while Eric stayed behind to work via conference calls, entrusted to look after her mother and her.

Ravenscroft.

Savage butterflies nipped her ribs. Life had always seemed safe with Eric at her side. He had always been there—been with her. Until he wasn't. That made his betrayal so much worse.

Her stomach roiled as she reached a trembling hand to the door. She pushed on the bar. It didn't budge.

Her body went hot under a wave of humiliation. She mentally chided herself. She had to *pull*. Unable to stop a mortified smile from spreading, she entered the vestibule and pulled open the next door to the lobby.

With the involuntary grin plastered on her face, she stepped into the richly adorned room. It was quiet, except for the faint clacking of a keyboard. For the second time in as many days, she felt suspended by the strings of time.

The lobby hadn't changed much, though the potted palms had grown taller thanks to sunbeams filtering in through thick, wooden blinds. The heirloom portrait of Colonel Hawthorne with Sharps carbine rifle in hand towered over an updated space that honored the style she remembered. She breathed in the same smell of old rugs, paper, leather, and wood and noticed that her father's brass nameplate still labeled his door.

Eric's nameplate was on the door to the secretary's left—the door straight ahead. The door she'd enter in mere moments. She felt her throat shrivel up and tried to swallow as she cast her attention to her father's office, barely resisting the urge to run in and slam the door.

But what was she hiding from? Numbingly familiar surroundings? *Nothing* had changed—beyond that door lived a soulless desk in a room that had been empty for a decade.

Why is it like this, Dad? She blinked fiercely at the sting of tears. *Why did he leave me with people I didn't know?*

She had grieved alone, not only for her parents, but also for Eric and the life she'd known. He'd abandoned her. Eric had tossed her aside without a single goodbye. So why was everything the same?

It didn't make sense, and she shouldn't care. But she did, and it was cruel.

She closed her eyes and rested her fingertips on her forehead. She was the heir. It was her birthright. She was strong enough to face him. She'd gotten this far.

The room had gone silent. The secretary had stopped typing. She imagined the woman staring at her like some random stranger trying not to break down in the doorway.

"May I help you?"

Her voice was close, warm and gentle, and enfolded within a delicate fragrance—lilacs or gardenias, maybe. The flowery note hooked a thread of recollection. Paresh curiously looked up at the secretary, who was studying her with wide, concerned eyes. A box of tissues was in her outstretched hand. "Please, come this way, m-miss."

Paresh pulled out a tissue and folded it into unusable shreds as she tried to place the secretary's face and perfume, and followed her to her desk. "I…I'm here to see Er-Eric Ravenscroft."

The secretary stumbled and caught herself on her chair. "I must apologize. He's away on a personal matter."

"Oh." As Paresh wilted, she caught the secretary eyeing Eric's door and hope flared. "Do you expect him back soon?"

"N-no," the secretary—Molly according to her nameplate—stammered. "It's just—"

Sitting and smoothing her skirt, Molly said, "His son, Darien Ravenscroft, is assisting during his absence. Who shall I say is here?"

"Paresh Hawthorne." Her search for Molly in her memories ended as she drifted off in search of elusive fragments of Eric's son—another surprise.

Molly's hand shook slightly as she picked up the phone. "Mr.

Ravenscroft, Paresh Hawthorne is here."

As Molly cradled the handset, Eric's door swung open and a young man in his twenties flew out, his eyes surprised and incredulous. "Paresh?"

A knot formed in her stomach as her jaw dropped. He looked and sounded exactly like the man she remembered. Her knees buckled. "Er...Eric?"

Darting forward, he effortlessly caught her with an arm around her shoulders as though they had choreographed the moment hundreds of times. Irises of the clearest blue and the scent of crisp, citrusy bergamot and spiced musk lulled her into nostalgia.

"That's Eric's cologne," she murmured distantly.

"I'm...Darien Ravenscroft," he said gently. "But, I do bear a striking resemblance to my father."

He helped her get steady on her feet and subtly nodded in response to the somber look Molly shot at him behind Paresh's back. "Everything's going to be okay. I promise. We can talk in his office."

Paresh moved forward in a daze. The uncanny likeness made her stomach sink, but his soothing voice put her at ease—as it always had—and his handsome features...well, those tripped her nerves. Her body tingled where he touched her. Her heart leaped anxious hurdles in an endless loop. But even for all that, warmth nested in her core, signaling safety, as if she'd known this man all her life.

He glanced back at Molly as they crossed the office threshold and her mental fog lifted. Paresh caught her breath. Her father's door still existed, but his office did not.

"You remodeled." She remembered running between their offices through French doors. "There used to be a wall...and doors. Dad and you—um, no, not *you*—but *they* would open them to collaborate. They said the conference rooms were too cold and formal, but I never understood that because the rooms all looked the same to me."

The door clicked shut. She was keenly aware of his proximity— and his continued embrace—and turned to meet eyes that poured a river of concern into hers. "Do you need to lie down? I thought you might faint."

Heat flushed her cheeks. "N-no, I'm f-fine. I-I'm sorry. I don't know what came over me. You look so much like him." Tissue fell like snow as she reached for his face. She stopped before touching his cheek, so close that the heat of his skin warmed her fingertips.

"But he's not—I mean…everything is the same as it was before. It…it's just been, well, difficult." She lowered her hand and her gaze sank into the ball of tissue flaking to the floor.

"Eric's not here," she whispered to herself, realizing that she'd actually wanted to see him. She gnawed her lip as tears dripped onto her cheeks. "I feel like a lost child. A foolish child."

Eric pulled her to his chest, his steely muscles a juxtaposition to her soft and fragile body. He yearned to erase the heartbreak on her beautiful face, to reassure her doubts. But he could only listen to her in her vulnerability and hold her…for now.

Her tears dried, and she relaxed against him. He held his breath in surprise, afraid to destroy the moment. It so felt natural that he wished they could stay like this forever. That he could tell her he was sorry, that he'd always be her shield and protector, that no one would ever hurt her again. But he couldn't. He hated his silence. He hated David for it. Jonathan. Lucien.

But in the end, it'd been his fault. It had always been his fault. And now he had to lie.

Eric immersed himself into being "Darien" and stifled the desire to stroke her hair. Holding her felt *too* natural. He had to force his voice to work.

"We've been so worried about you," he whispered at last, grudgingly loosening his hold. "Even Molly. Do you remember? She was your father's secretary, too. You used to play with her typewriter."

The floral perfume teased her mind again. Somewhere distant, she remembered the pushback of hard round keys and the imprint on paper, and heard a woman playfully chastising her for wasting her father's expensive letterhead. She started to smile, but then the first part of his statement hit her. "Worried? About me? Why?"

"We can talk more comfortably over there." He nodded at the sitting area. As she turned away, her scent and residual warmth lingered on his clothes and in the empty space between his arms. He already regretted letting go. "Would you like a drink?"

"Water, please." She sank into the recliner closest to her father's door and massaged her temples. Usually migraines came on with dull pressure and a head splitting sensitivity to light, but she'd never felt an ache like this. Thankfully, the arched screens on the windows kept the office dim. She could only hope it passed quickly. She'd packed her special sunglasses in a suitcase—of course.

He offered a cold bottle taken from a cabinet in the sideboard and sat on the coffee table across from her. "Paresh…I'm sorry for the loss of your parents," he said gingerly. "It must have been difficult to grieve alone."

His words were a gut punch that shocked her into silence. She clenched her jaw and fisted the bottle cap with white knuckles.

He nudged his fingers under hers to twist it off and gently added, "But there may be some confusion. What do you think happened after the accident?"

The hurt in her eyes pierced his heart like a dagger. "I'm sorr—"

"Why does that matter?" she interrupted, blinking back tears. She sucked in an uneven breath. "I'm not here to discuss *that day*."

As she looked up at Eric's strangely familiar son and saw the sympathy in his eyes, she felt bad for snapping. She yearned to bare her soul to him, even if it meant revisiting the past. Her lips quivered as she started, "I—"

A quick knock on the door announced Molly's entrance. "Sir, your expected visitor is in the lobby."

Paresh missed the irritation that flashed across Eric's face. Walter had arrived faster than anticipated and Paresh had so thoroughly consumed his attention that he'd missed his arrival—otherwise Molly never would've barged in like that.

"I'm sorry, Paresh. I had hoped to avoid interruption. Please excuse me." He patted her knee and softly added, "I'll only be a minute."

Molly looked apologetic as she followed him out on his heels. He extended his hand in greeting to Orison Crossing's Police Chief, Walter Hodges. "Thank you for coming so quickly."

"I understand Paresh Hawthorne is back, Mr. Ravenscroft?" Walter said gruffly, clasping Eric's hand and giving him a knowing look.

An older man, as tall as Eric, with graying brown hair, Walter had fought a losing battle with his weight and stereotypical love for pastries for all of the thirty-plus years he'd been on the force. With a belly that protruded over his waistline, he often conducted business without wearing his uniform or duty belt and today was no exception. He wore tan slacks and a black polo shirt embroidered with the department's badge.

Eric guided Walter away from the door and lowered his voice. "She's in my office. I was trying to get her to relax—Walter, I don't think she knows she was kidnapped."

"Huh," Chief Hodges grunted and bobbed his head in thought. "But she's comfortable talking to you? I mean you look—"

"Yes, yes. My face is moot at the moment." Eric impatiently swatted his concern away. "She's comfortable enough and I can always put her at ease, if needed."

He got a look from Walter that he shot right back. Walter held his hands up in concession. "Okay, but only if she gets too distraught. We don't want to influence her statement."

Eric nodded.

"Do you want to continue alone and bring me in later?"

"No," Eric said firmly, glancing over his shoulder at the door. "This should be done once, so she doesn't have to repeat herself and experience the pain twice. Besides, one trusted friend is better than a team of federal investigators. You and I will meet them after you turn in your report."

"All right, then. Let's go," the Chief said, heading for Eric's office.

Eric led the way with his shoulders squared. It felt like a steel rod had replaced his spine. The grim-faced officer followed in similar fashion.

"Paresh, this is Chief Hodges. Do you remember him?" Eric asked as Walter extended his hand.

"I was a good friend of your dad's. It's real nice to see you again, hon," he said with a smile. "Call me Walter."

"Hi Walter. I do remember—you came out when those hunters trespassed and shot my coyote," she replied, shaking his hand.

Eric watched her closely. She'd regained her composure, but grief swam in the depths of her eyes. He hated that they had to rip open wounds that hadn't even healed.

"Graywolf? I can't believe you remember that! You were only six!" Walter chuckled. "You know, Dr. Grimley still has his veterinary practice. You always kept him busy by taming all those wild critters."

"I'd love to see him again." Paresh smiled. Finally, someone looked different. Chief Hodges had always been an overweight man with friendly brown eyes and prominent facial features, including a rounded nose blanketed by large pores. Age and years of sun exposure had ravaged his tanned face and neck with wrinkles and creases, making him a testament to the passage of time.

She'd managed to calm down, but now that the spitting image of Eric—looking powerful and handsome in creased black trousers and a pressed white dress shirt—stood beside the friendly "old" face, her jitters returned.

He looked so much like Eric, his skin smooth and ashen-hued, faintly luminous even in the dim room, his hair short on the bottom with longer strands up top that he had to sweep out of his eyes, his features refined and chiseled as though cut from exquisite marble. The only difference was the unassuming lenses, encased in a thin silver frame that rested on the bridge of his nose. Even the same friendly spark had glinted in his crystalline eyes—although, every now and again, the color disappeared, turning them into bottomless, inky wells.

Those dark eyes observed her now, despite his friendly expression and the Chief's jovial demeanor. "Paresh," he said. "Walter has some questions for you. Please take your time answering and let us know if you need a break."

Her smile faded as she grew aware of tension between the two men. "H-have I done something wrong?"

"No, no. You haven't done anything," Eric said softly, kneeling before her and taking hold of her hands. They were trembling. "It's going to be okay. I promised you, remember?"

She nodded, tears glistening in her eyes. Oh how he hated David.

"After your parents—" Eric started, firming his hold on her hands and his resolve. "After they died in that accident, we…*they* searched through the wreckage, but you were nowhere to be found. You were gone. This is the first time anyone has seen you since."

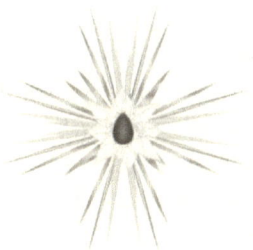

Chapter Four: Perspective

Paresh felt like she'd tilted off balance and tumbled into unending darkness. She was cold with dread despite the heat of the hands on hers. A wave of emotion crested and left her breathless. Unable to stop shaking, she tore free and clamped her fists onto the recliner's arms.

She leaned forward, insistent. "B-b-but Eric...he *sent* me to live with my uncle! I mailed him letters, *for years*, asking him why! But he never wrote back—he just left me there!"

"Honey..." The Chief sat in the opposite recliner and patted the air in a gesture meant to help her calm down. "Mr. Ravenscroft's spent the last ten years searching for you. He never sent you anywhere nor received any letters. Where were you?"

"With my uncle—David Hawthorne," she said as though it should've been obvious, but as she gazed at Darien's mask of sympathy and *rage*, an ugly truth began to surface. "N-no. I...I mailed those letters myself. A-a-and b-besides, I saw... "

She rubbed her forehead with shaking fingers. "I remember his face!" she whispered to herself. "I saw it—I know I did! Eric pulled me from the car after...after—"

She snapped her eyes shut to stop the hazy memory from clearing. But it was already too late. In the fog of twisted metal and steam, of broken glass and blood, the foolish hope of a child had seen eyes of safe blue instead of the cold brown reality.

She choked on her voice as tears gushed forth. "No!" she cried, folding over and burying her face into her hands. "It wasn't him— my parents were dead and it should have been him, *but it wasn't*. It wasn't him. It wasn't. It was-n't—"

She broke down, hiccupping and hyperventilating. Her shoulders heaved violently with soul rending sobs. And all Eric could do was swallow the anger that burned his throat like acid. She was right: he should have been there. He had abandoned her. He ran a hand through his hair and glanced back at Walter, who gave a sad nod.

Eric plucked tissues from the end table and gently peeled Paresh's hands from her face. He captured her gaze over the rim of his glasses. She quieted and he dabbed her eyes and cheeks dry, and then he covered her hands with his, holding her in an emotionally neutral stasis with his warmth and the stability of his aura's energy.

"Don't influence her," Walter whispered as quietly as humanly possible.

"I won't," Eric replied in a calm, even tone without looking away from her. "Paresh, it's going to get worse, and I'm so sorry for that. I'll give you what I can, but you need to be strong—you can get through this. Eric loves you more than you know, and he is so, so sorry he wasn't there back then. But you were strong without him. You came back to us, all on your own."

To Walter, he said, "I'm going to release her. Go back to where she left off. She thought she saw me—"

Despite clearing a catch in his throat, Walter hit his stride perfectly. "I'm sorry, hon, but I personally notified Mr. Ravenscroft of the accident and was there when he arrived. You couldn't have seen him."

She blinked at him uncertainly and sniffled. "The man…he, uh, had brown eyes."

"And your letters never came, I promise you," Eric said, resting his hands on her knees. "David must've taken them. This is the truth, Paresh. We aren't here to lie to you or hurt you. We'll help you sort everything out and figure out why he kidnapped you."

"Kid-kidnapped?" she echoed. She slumped in the chair, stricken by the single word, frantically rummaging through her most innocent experiences for any sinister motives. She was so far gone that she missed Molly's knock at the door.

She rushed in carrying two taped-up cardboard boxes. "I'm sorry to come in, again, Mr. Ravenscroft, but a gentleman dropped these off with instructions to give them to you right away. He was quite insistent that they were 'pertinent.'" She emphasized the last word and glanced at Paresh, who was oblivious and blowing her nose.

Molly set the packages on the coffee table. Eric sliced through the tape with a lengthened fingernail and felt the air tense as Molly and Walter glared at him. He ignored them since Paresh hadn't noticed and flipped open the folds to reveal stacks of letter-sized envelopes bound tightly with twine. As he pulled them out, Paresh's eyes widened at the handwritten addresses.

"Those are my letters." She sat up, sniffling and poking through the bundles. "How the... ?"

Eric glanced at her and then at the other two before dashing out in search of the "gentleman." The lobby was empty. He darted outside and squinted in the painful sunlight, shielding his eyes to scrutinize the business district. Everyone milling about had familiar, local faces. No one looked or sounded out of the ordinary.

Molly appeared beside him, offering his sunglasses. He switched frames in a fluent motion and dangled his glasses at his side. No longer hindered by the bright light, he looked up and down the street, far into the distance, and checked the rooftops, too. No one was suspicious.

"What did this man look like?" His voice came from low in his throat, more of an order, less of a question.

"He looked, well, *like you*, but with long, reddish-brown hair," she said with a pause. "He wore a gray suit—no tie with a white shirt—and a fedora with a red feather tucked into a black band. He had a silver ring with a large black stone in it."

Eric stiffened. "There were two pins on his lapel," he growled. "A silver starburst loosely resembling a Maltese cross and a military style ribbon bar of black, red, and silver stripes."

Molly's jaw dropped open as she nodded. A cold aura flared from Eric's body that consumed the heat of the day and grew more ominous as he fumed. She staggered backward, losing the fight against an innate need to flee from danger. She retreated inside and left him on the sidewalk.

He charged after her, furiously flinging his sunglasses onto her desk and shoving his silver frames onto his nose as he marched into his office. He knew Molly slipped in behind him and quietly shut the door, and that he needed to regain control or his unhinged emotions would paralyze anyone they touched. Jonathan had delivered those packages, toying with him in typical fashion, and that angered him more than he cared to admit.

Jonathan despised Eric's choice to stay in the Realm of Man. The humans in Eric's life were all pawns—weak and disposable, yet powerful with proper manipulation—in Jonathan's nefarious "games." Eric never knew the current play until after Jonathan had a long advantage, but he'd successfully protected the Hawthorne under his care each time. Death had claimed someone else, though, handing victory to Jonathan. Blood was blood and death was death, and now he held Eric suspended, yet again, in another game.

But, he did know the target. After all, there was only one left.

Paresh stood next to Chief Hodges, crestfallen as she pawed through the second box. Her movements grew sluggish as Eric got closer. The envelopes fell from her hands and her arms dropped to her sides. By the time Eric stopped in front of her, she was staring through him like a living doll.

$$\text{☽ ☀ ☾}$$

Eric clenched his jaw. He hated doing this to her, again, and stronger than before, but something was off. The High Council had always left Jonathan to his amusements, and David had fallen from the Flock over thirty years ago, making him easy prey.

Hell, I should have killed him back then, Eric thought. *But since I want him dead, it doesn't benefit Jonathan to kill him.*

He pulled his glasses down and held Paresh's gaze over the rim. He snapped his fingers at Walter and lowered Paresh to sit on the couch, kneeling in front of her without breaking their connection. Walter dropped the letters and sat next to the girl. Molly hovered near the door like a nervous gazelle.

The energy rolling off Eric's aura filled the office with thick, invisible waves that crashed over Molly and Walter. They rebounded off the walls and doubled back, each layer more intense than the last. He knew both had felt the phenomenon in the past, but it had never possessed such crushing power.

Eric had lost an unusual measure of patience and control, and he didn't have the time or will to rein it in. He needed answers. Now.

"Paresh," the Chief began, "tell me what you remember about the accident."

She spoke unblinkingly in monotone.

"We were on our way to church. I was in the backseat and had asked if we could go for ice cream afterward and Dad said yes. I remember the corn was tall. I flew forward in my seat belt. Dad and Mom screamed. There was a screeching noise, the brakes, maybe, and metal crunching. Then a man pulled me out and I woke up in a bed at my uncle's house in Kansas."

"Then what?"

"I slept a few days and woke up injured. They were surprised."

"They?"

"Uncle David and his girlfriend, Nicole. He said that Mom and Dad had been in a car accident. That they had died instantly. He told me Eric sent me to him to make my father happy, but Dad had never mentioned having a brother. I didn't know anything about him and cried to come home, but Uncle David said that he would never let me leave his sight because he didn't want to lose me, too."

"Did he ever hurt you?"

"No."

"Did Nicole ever hurt you?"

"N-no."

"Are you sure?"

"She was mean, like she hated me. No one hurt me."

"Okay. Tell me about Kansas."

"We lived in a gated community outside of Ellis. It's mostly residential, but since it's so far from town, it has a central hub where people can drop off mail or meet with each other—like a community center. Most of the houses are near the front, but Uncle David lives at the back. I didn't stay with him and Nicole long. She was always snapping at me and, one night, I overheard her telling Uncle David that I should 'go away.' A few days later, Master Jon moved my governess, Miss Lydia, and me into a vacant house down the street. Master Jon had Eric send my things so I wouldn't feel so out of place."

"Who is Master Jon?"

"My governor."

"What do you mean by governor and governess?"

"That's what Master Jon said they were. Like teachers or substitute guardians."

"Master Jon was in charge then? Tell me about them both."

"I lived with Miss Lydia, but Master Jon was always there. They homeschooled me because Uncle David didn't want me attending public school. He was protective because he was afraid of losing the rest of his family. There were other kids, though, children of the people in the community. They went to school in Ellis."

"Did these substitute guardians ever hurt you?"

"No. Miss Lydia was kind. And so was Master Jon, eventually," Paresh said, a slight mist appearing in her vacant eyes.

Walter paused with an uncertain glance at Eric that received no acknowledgement. "Are you sure Master Jon never hurt you? Was he *ever* unkind?"

"He never hurt me. He was distant at first and seemed like he hated me, like Nicole. But then, we got close and it was like…like it was with Eric."

The Chief shot another hesitant look at Eric, but still received nothing. "All right. So they were good to you and you didn't go to school. Were you ever allowed to leave?"

"Only with Master Jon. Uncle David trusted him to keep me safe, so I never went anywhere without him. He'd take me into Ellis or Hays once a week or so to go shopping, or to see a movie. Miss Lydia went with us sometimes, but Uncle David never did."

"Did anyone ever approach you or recognize you?"

"No one seemed to pay much attention to me, I guess, but it's not something I would have noticed."

"How were you able to come here?"

"Master Jon knew I'd never felt comfortable there and said it was time for me to decide if I wanted to come home or stay there. He and Miss Lydia told me that my parents had left me money, and he made me promise to meet with Eric as soon as I got here."

"And they let you go, just like that?"

"They helped me contact Simon and gave me enough cash to take the train. After I got a key in the mail, they drove me to Hays. We stayed overnight in a hotel and I left at seven yesterday morning."

"Do David and Nicole know they let you go?"

"I don't know. For the last few years, I haven't seen my uncle much, just glimpses in passing, and Nicole avoids me. She's probably glad that I'm gone. I haven't seen either one for at least six months."

Chief Hodges nodded to Eric, who focused Paresh's eyes onto his palm and drew her attention to the twined mail without breaking his hold on her. The Chief held up an envelope and jabbed his finger at the upper corner. "Is this your address?"

"Uncle David and Nicole live there." She lethargically pointed to another stack of envelopes. "That's Miss Lydia's address."

Eyeing the return address, Chief Hodges read aloud, "Twelve-Fifteen Turnberry Lane, Ellis, Kansas."

Eric's hand jerked up in front of Paresh's face to keep her attention and block the disgusted look he shot at Walter. "That sick bastard. Remember Felicia's old street address? That was it."

"Yeah—the one he burned down after torching the mansion in the seventies." The Chief mirrored Eric's scowl with one of his own. "I have enough information to make a formal report. I think it would be a good idea to get the FBI involved right away. Let her go and see me out?"

As Chief Hodges rose, Eric lowered his hand and caught Paresh when she slumped out of his control. Leaning her against the cushions, he gestured for Molly to stay with her and then followed Walter into the lobby. The door clicked shut behind them.

☽ ❋ ☾

Finally, the world began to return, rippled and distorted as though veiled by a pond's glassy surface. She had heard everything, even her own voice, as a distant conversation, and hadn't been able to see clearly. Walter had appeared in a tiny window of clarity, and she'd been able to read the envelope and point to it. But then, the tide had rushed back in, thrusting her deep beneath the surface.

"Here you go, dear."

Paresh searched for the source of the muffled voice and saw Molly hovering overhead through a fine layer of ripples. She tried to speak but couldn't.

After a distant *click*, she melted into the cushion and instinctively caught her head on her palm. Molly met her stare with worry. Paresh was about to ask about the "pond" but the instant her lips parted, she no longer knew what to ask or why.

Instead, too many questions stacked in her head, overlapping and toppling like feeble towers. Confused and exhausted, she accepted Molly's offering of fresh water and glanced at the shaded windows. It felt late in the day, though it couldn't be past noon.

She studied the condensation beading on the new bottle and muttered, "It's all true, isn't it?"

Molly made a thoughtful noise and held up her index finger. She searched Eric's desk for a moment and returned holding a sheet of paper. Sitting beside Paresh, she presented an updated missing persons bulletin, the absolute proof of truth.

"It is, sweetie, I'm so sorry. Many people have been looking for you for a long time. Mr. Ravenscroft even hired a team of private detectives and never gave up."

Then why isn't he here? Paresh thought as she looked at the strange, age progressed picture of herself. It had the right structure, but her face was softer and less angular than the computer generated version. Her hair had darkened from pale blonde to a golden hue that was rich with strawberry and copper highlights. Familiar gray eyes stared back at her, but they weren't hers. She shuddered and set the paper face down on the table. It gave her the creeps.

"This is—" She shook her head, not knowing if she was in shock or denial, or which was worse: the truth of being kidnapped or the lie of being abandoned.

"It'll take time," Molly said, sympathetically. "We're all here for you. Even if it doesn't make sense, say whatever comes to mind. I'm just so glad you're home."

Paresh shrugged weakly. "I don't know what to feel, let alone what to think or say. I mean, I guess I feel unwanted? I don't know."

"Because of that Nicole lady and Mr. Jon?" Molly offered.

Paresh nodded, her eyes watering. "All this time, I thought Eric had abandoned me and it hurt so much. He was supposed to be my guardian; I knew that. I wrote every day and told him I wanted to come home. I asked why he hadn't come to get me. Why he'd broken his promise. I thought surely he was throwing the letters away, but—" She sniffled and waved at the twined stacks. "Obviously not."

Sucking in a deep breath, Paresh tried to unscrew the bottle's lid with nervous fingers. Her voice quivered. "I thought Master Jon and Miss Lydia cared for me, but they never did, did they?"

"Oh sweetie." Molly held the girl's hands steady and opened the bottle for her. Watching Paresh drink, she said, "You're hurting now, but it seems like you have good memories of them. Focus on those instead of guessing motives. They gave you a home. They must have cared, on some level."

Paresh shook her head, staring ahead at nothing. "I may have lived there, but I always felt out of place. I am home *here*."

She absently wiped her eyes with the hem of her dress. "I never questioned having a chaperone—it made sense that Uncle David would worry about me, but how can I not wonder about their motives or true feelings? Why did they do this? Any of it?"

"You have every right to wonder and be angry, but can you say you were happy? Or content? Did you feel loved? Take a moment. Separate the players and think about just that. How did you feel?"

"I suppose," Paresh started, fumbling as the word "kidnapped" loomed large over her thoughts. "I missed my parents and Eric, but I didn't have another reason to be unhappy. Miss Lydia and Master Jon were always with me. They raised me like a daughter. I feel like they loved me. You can't fake that, right? But, why did my uncle take me only to hide me away under their care? If I was so important to him, why not say goodbye? He was the one who didn't care. Master Jon and Miss Lydia were there for goodbyes..." She sniffled and her voice hitched. "I'll never see them again, will I?"

The two women stared at each other in silence—one at a loss for words and the other lost in the unraveling fabric of her life. Paresh felt so suddenly and completely drained. Her body was numb. She wanted to give in and cry, but her face felt heavy, like stone, and her tears were like a dry fire.

"Just coming home was hard. But walking inside—" Paresh shook her head. "Nothing's changed. It's like I never left. Like I'm stuck in time. And I've been so angry with Eric when he didn't deserve any of it. None at all. How could I ever think—"

Squeezing Paresh's hand, Molly swapped her concern for a heartfelt smile. "None of this is your fault! I promise you nothing means more to Mr. Ravenscroft than your safety. Process this in time, not in an instant. Take comfort that you are surrounded by people who love you and will protect you *now*—Mr. Ravenscroft especially. You can put a lot of faith and trust in him."

Paresh nodded. "You're right—I mean—I know you're right. I'm here now and that's all that should matter. But, I'm going to miss them, you know? I was already exhausted from the last few days—and now this." She pointed at the bulletin. The letters.

"Anyone would be frazzled after learning everything you've heard today." Molly held her arms out. "I've been waiting so long. May I?"

Paresh threw herself into Molly's arms as new tears fell, overwhelmed by the woman's genuine expression of care.

☽ ❋ ☾

Eric entered the room unnoticed as the two embraced. He cleared his throat as he approached the sofa. "Chief Hodges wanted me to say goodbye for him."

He distractedly picked at nonexistent lint on the recliner and quietly asked, "How are things in here?"

Molly nodded over her shoulder and whispered, "She's better now." She firmed her hug and said to Paresh, "Call on me anytime. I'll go for now and let you two talk." She patted Eric's arm on her way out and mouthed, "Let her feel her emotions."

"Yes ma'am," Eric murmured, smiling softly at Paresh.

Alone with him again, Paresh's tentative confidence wilted. Her stomach clenched. Unearthly fire lit her nerves. Her pulse drummed, too heavy and too loud. And yet…strangely, as he got closer, a feeling of tranquility settled over her, as though his calmness was becoming her calmness. That his strength in crisis was a boost to her own resilience.

He sat beside her and thumbed tears off her cheeks. She wanted to forget everything and lose herself in him. She stared into his icy blue wells, reveling in the quiet of the moment as he licked his lips and studied her as though entranced himself.

"This never should have happened to you," he whispered, stroking her cheek. He felt bewitched, as though her very essence held him to her underwater, only he didn't need air to breathe as long as she was there. He didn't understand it. Or how she wasn't panicking after learning that half of her life was a lie.

"Um." He shook his head in an effort to break the spell. "I'm sorry...the things you must be feeling...how are you?"

She turned her hands up and half shrugged. "I don't really know. But Molly gives great advice. Positive perspectives. So, I think I'm okay for now—honestly."

Eric couldn't resist holding her hands again. "I'm not surprised. She has a knack for putting people at ease."

"She has a kind soul," Paresh added with a shy smile.

"That she does." He caressed her fingers and remembered how tiny they'd once been. She was the same person but everything about the way he felt was different. And that gnawed at him. It couldn't be right, no matter how perfectly her hand fit into his now. How her warmth brought him a comfort he'd never felt in his life.

"I know this hasn't been pleasant, but it's not all bad. The reason you came in...is good, I guess. We could go over it?" He gently squeezed her hand. "Is that okay?"

"O-okay." She nodded, her cheeks flushing as she glanced at their entwined hands.

He regained a bit of clarity and reluctantly released her, rising to retrieve an expandable folder from his desk. He needed to get his head clear and into a better space. *She's the heir.*

Rejoining her on sofa, he pushed his glasses up. *Time for more lies.*

"Unfortunately only my father, as the trustee, can authorize any transfers of your parents' assets." Seeing her brow wrinkle, he quickly added, "However, after...well, *after*, he opened a savings account for you at the Orison Crossing Bank across the street. He made deposits from his own funds and managed it as a way to care for you when he had no other means of doing so."

She hesitantly accepted the folder.

"These are condensed account records for every deposit, withdrawal, and interest accrual. The current monthly statement is in there, along with a debit card and pin number."

As she flipped through the papers, he continued, "Use the debit card to keep your identity a secret. This entire town spent weeks searching the countryside and woods for you. We feared you stumbled out of the car and got lost looking for help. When everyone learns that you're back...there'll be some commotion."

Skimming the columns to find the balance, Paresh felt time slow. Her body seemed to burn from her toes up. Her jaw dropped.

"This…Miss Lydia paid for the train in cash and gave me the two remaining dollars." She sucked in an uneven breath. "That-that's all I had when I woke up. Simon brought me breakfast. And now…this is almost a hundred thousand dollars! Your dad did this just for me?"

Simon had already made contact. Eric concealed his concern with a small laugh. "He'd do anything for you. This account is only insured to a certain amount, so he invested excess earnings into your trust's mutual funds."

Her eyes glazed over. "My what?"

"Paresh—" He pointed to the balance. "This is nothing compared to your inheritance. Your parents desired a quiet life and lived frugally, so you never knew about the trust—all of your family's investments, holdings, properties, and more. You are the last Hawthorne. It's all yours."

"This is *nothing* compared to my inheritance?" She jabbed past his finger at the number with all the zeros. "No way. How much—"

"Approximately five hundred and fifty million domestically, not including property values and foreign holdings."

The paper dropped to the table and her mouth seemed to go with it. She was frozen. Unable to think. She might've stopped breathing.

Eric's grin widened as he retrieved the paper and gently nudged her jaw shut. "The Hawthorne name has been tied to vast wealth since before the Civil War. I won't bore you with the details, but it began with railroad engineering and investments, which led to mining in Las Vegas and casinos when the mines collapsed. Then, hotels, restaurants, politics—it even survived the Great Depression and boomed with technological investments."

"I-I-I can't believe this." She stiffly took the statement. "Five. Hundred. Mil—"

"Oh, and the speakeasies!" Eric interrupted, unable to help himself. He laughed wholeheartedly. "Your Prohibition grandfathers had 'friends' in Chicago. I…I know this is a lot. It's been a shock, but I hope *this* is a good one at least."

She exhaled the breath she didn't realize she was holding. "It is a lot…I'm not sure what to say. Or do."

He sobered. "Anything you need—anything at all—I will take

care of personally." Needing to touch her again, he slid his hand across her shoulders. The tension in her muscles melted away.

"Talk about a full day," she muttered. "I had no idea Dad was—" She flicked the page. "Rich."

She made a thoughtful noise. "Is Uncle David, too? Do you think he owns the entire community?"

"Probably. David and your father never got along, but it worsened a few years before your grandfather died in 1975. The Senator secretly altered his will to give Andrew the majority, and left David a smaller, but still comfortable, stipend."

With Paresh distracted and wiggling her lower lip between her teeth, Eric quickly tallied a mental list of the pros and cons to revealing her family history. The decades-long feud between brothers would reveal her uncle's true nature and the less than honorable beginning to her parents' courtship—

"Why would Dad not tell me he had a brother?" she wondered aloud. "Or that Eric had a son?"

Eric inwardly flinched and his smile faded. There was too much she didn't know and his moral backbone wouldn't let him throw more at her now.

"Your father was truly a good man," he said quietly. "As for David—we'll learn quite a bit about him and the community soon."

She shoved the sheet into the folder. "What do you mean?"

He paused before saying, "Kidnapping across state lines is a federal offense. Walter left to give the Federal Bureau of Investigation your statement. They'll swoop down on the compound in Kansas and reveal everything we need to know."

He mentally chided himself for using the "k" word. She'd instantly stiffened. Her shoulders were like stone under his palm.

Molly's voice rang through his mind. *Let her feel her emotions.*

Easier said than done, he thought grimly as he gently cupped Paresh's cheek and turned her toward him. Stealing her gaze with deliberate eyes, he said, "Don't worry. Don't be afraid. You are home and you are safe with me."

The ability to buy her privacy on the national level would give him extra time to keep her hidden and protected. He and Walter could act as intermediaries with the FBI for now, but reality was never ideal. Eventually she'd need to speak to the FBI and the media would descend on Orison Crossing, and he'd lose his ability to shield her. Beautiful, missing heiresses never turned up quietly.

A deeper sadness punched his chest as he stared into her empty eyes. He couldn't help adding, "You'll see Eric soon, I promise. He'll be so happy to see you." The muscles in her shoulders relaxed and a half smile curved her lips. His heart both sang and sank. He hated the lie. The whole situation.

Briefly closing his eyes, he broke the suggestive link and cleared his throat. "How is the cottage? Do you need help getting settled?"

"The…um…" She rubbed her forehead. This was the strangest migraine she'd ever had. It felt like she'd surfaced from underwater again. "The cottage is…the same. It's weird, like suspended in time. I keep expecting my parents to come home."

She locked onto his crystalline blue orbs and openly confessed, "I don't want to be alone with that."

"You aren't alone."

The intensity in his eyes made her heart leap. He held her gaze for an agonizing eternity before he finally lowered his eyes and whispered, "I am here for anything you need."

"Thank you," she whispered, wishing he hadn't looked away.

He stood and offered his hand. Accepting, she said, "Um, well, Simon said I should replace the appliances and I don't think I can lift a refrigerator on my own." She half laughed at her feeble joke.

Eric chuckled with her despite the war raging within him. "You can pay people for that," he said, pulling her up. "And I can take you to dinner tonight."

The instant the words left his mouth, he regretted them. A night of lies, pretending to be someone else? Why not add another betrayal by someone who supposedly loved her? He'd just said he'd never deceive her, while deceiving her, after all.

As his lips parted with an excuse, her cheeks flushed. "Dinner sounds nice. I'd love to learn more about you. I didn't know Eric had a son."

Guilt slapped him with an odd urge to avert his gaze, but he held it steady. He was a natural predator, patient with an eye for weakness—always the hidden cat and never the unsuspecting mouse—except with Jonathan.

But Paresh wasn't just some human to manipulate. For the rest of her life, he would stand by her side, regardless of her reaction to his truth. Even if he had to lurk in the shadows, he'd be there. He had old-fashioned roots. He always kept his promises.

It's to protect her, he told himself, as though the excuse for excuses was actually morally consoling. *I'll tell her in time.*

She tucked the folder under her arm. "Use the debit card and don't give out my name. Anything else?" Sorrow pooled in her pupils but a genuine smile lifted her cheeks and crinkled her eyes.

"Ah——" He fidgeted with his shirt cuffs, flustered out of his tangled thoughts. "I don't mean to rush you out—do you want to meet Karen Daley, one of my partners? Kenshin Dugao is—" He glanced at his watch. "Currently at court."

She shook her head. "I have a bit of a headache and need to grab my bags…oh, and rent a car. What time will you pick me up?"

He seemed preoccupied as he jogged to his desk and pulled something from the center drawer. "I have a few engagements that I can't break this afternoon, so let me give you my contact information. If you need anything at all, call me." His brow furrowed at the business card in his hand. "Uh…unfortunately, I don't have any cards of my own."

He scratched his head and grabbed a pen. "Here's one of my father's. The information is the same. I'm housesitting and have his cell phone—it's easier for the clients." He flipped the card to show her the private number he'd scribbled on the back.

What a fool he was, tripping over his lies to keep his story straight. He had never been this off kilter. How the hell was he going to get through dinner?

Running a hand through his hair, he handed her the card. "Do you have a cell phone?"

She shook her head and stuffed the card into the folder. "I was never alone to need one."

"Right…I'll have Molly give you one of ours." He couldn't believe how put together she was given how sheltered she'd been. "We lend them out to clients so we can access them as needed."

"Can you show me how to use it?"

"Of course." He smiled. Trying to keep the mood light, but

eager to sate his curiosity, he asked, "Did you have a computer or internet access?"

"Mm-hm. I used it for homework, but Master Jon or Miss Lydia had to supervise when I was online. I only used it for research or to get the news."

They'd likely censored most of her access to the news or she would've learned the truth long ago. He motioned for her to lead the way out and Molly stood to greet them. "Please assign phone one to Paresh and file the bills under the Hawthorne business account. She'll have it indefinitely."

After Molly pulled out the clamshell phone, Eric sent her across the street to withdraw money from his account while he showed Paresh how to use it. The faceless debit card and cash would give her some anonymity, but he could only do so much when nearly every building in town had her missing poster pinned to a board. At the local level, no amount of money would buy her privacy.

He needed to get her out of town, somewhere where she wasn't alone. When Molly returned, the proverbial light bulb dinged.

She handed an envelope brimming with twenties to Paresh, who was gracious and shoved the money, phone, and instructional booklet into the folder. He pulled Molly aside and quietly asked her to make a call.

"Thank you so much," Paresh said as Molly returned to her desk. "But, is it dangerous to carry this much cash around?"

"Don't go flashing it around and you'll be fine." Eric mentally kicked himself for forgetting about the patrols Walter said he'd set up. "I forgot—I'm sorry—it's just precautionary, but the police will drive by periodically and Walter might knock to check on you. If anyone from Kansas contacts you, act normally, don't say anything about meeting with us, and call me right away, okay?"

Fear crept into her eyes and he kicked himself again.

"Do you think they're going to come for me?" she asked.

"No, it's just better safe than sorry. I promise." Eric got a nod from Molly and his expression relaxed. "Plus, our car and driver, Sam Weaverly, are available to take you around today."

"But I was going to rent—"

"There's no need. You can shop for appliances or whatever you want without worrying about getting lost or being alone."

"Thank you," she said with a timid smile. "I'd like that."

"Relax and enjoy the sunny afternoon. Sammy will take you anywhere you want. He has access to my credit line if you feel like splurging—which I wholeheartedly encourage." Eric winked and looked back at Molly, hidden from Paresh's view by his shoulders.

Nodding, she mouthed, "He'll stay with her."

Relief washed over Eric. That she'd be out of his sight worried him regardless, but he trusted Sammy. He faced Paresh and said, "It won't take him long to get here."

"Can he meet me at the train station instead?" Paresh asked. "I need to get my bags and wouldn't mind stretching my legs a bit."

"Molly, have him report to the Orison Crossing Terminal and get an e.t.a.," he said over his shoulder, anxious that she'd be alone between here and there.

They crossed the lobby to the vestibule. He slid behind her to open the first door. "He'll be in a silver four-door Lexus."

Molly called out Sammy's estimated arrival time and Eric said that he'd see her for dinner. Suddenly aware of how close he was, Paresh stammered, "Y-you n-never did say when I should expect you."

"How about six-thirty?" he suggested.

She smiled, bit her lip, and nodded. "What should I wear?"

"Anything you want." He smiled.

Paresh playfully rolled her eyes. "Okay, but what will *you* wear?"

"That man always wears a suit," Molly yelled, slapping the air. "Play dress up tonight."

Paresh burned bright pink and laughed awkwardly as she folded in on herself. It was, possibly, the most adorable thing Eric had ever seen. In that moment, he was awestruck.

Paresh waved at Molly and stepped into the vestibule. She started to lean in, but then gave him an odd look and held out her hand. "I don't know how people, uh…um, can I…hug you?"

Eric grinned mischievously and took her hand, pulling gently to fold her into his arms. The clean scent of her hair and skin was the sweetest perfume; it roused heat deep inside him where he'd been cold for far too long. Andrew's little girl may have been missing for the last ten years, but he felt as though she, the woman in his arms, had been missing his whole life. "I'm glad you're back. You have no idea…" he whispered, squeezing gently. "Welcome home."

Butterflies fluttered to life in her belly as she melted against him and laid her head on his shoulder. The world outside seemed to slow to a stop as the spicy scent of his cologne hit her nose—familiar and warm, like smoke on a crisp fall day. For the first time, she truly felt like she was home and everything was right as it should be.

She slid her hands up the solid muscles of his back and felt them flex as his arms tightened around her. The butterflies crashed madly into each other. She firmed her embrace in return and closed her eyes, fully aware that he was holding her rather than hugging her.

Eric clenched his teeth tightly to hold his desire at bay and forced himself to let go. When she'd pressed against him, every nerve in his body had fired at once, and the changes in her breathing and heartbeat hadn't helped.

The dreamy glaze hanging over her eyes as she lifted her head made his body sing. In that moment, he knew she felt the same way he did—or at least felt *something*. Neither spoke as they parted. He shared a silent look with her and watched her walk out the door.

After she disappeared from his vantage point, he returned to the lobby and saw a smirk on Molly's face. She held his sunglasses in an extended hand. "Mr. Ravenscroft, are you actually smitten?"

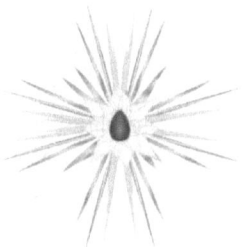

CHAPTER FIVE: TEMPTATION

I

Later that morning, two FBI agents came in with Walter to discuss his written report. They agreed to keep Paresh's arrival quiet and were about to leave when they saw the boxes on the coffee table. One flipped through the pages and asked about the letters. The other collected them as evidence.

Eric hadn't yet read a single word and confiscation meant her handwritten pleas would vanish into the hole of an investigation. She'd be reduced to a case number. He refused to let that happen.

He met the agents at the door and hooked his finger over his glasses. A shocked look from Walter kicked him back into professional legal mode. Forcing a tight smile, he stepped aside.

"Thank you, gentlemen, for agreeing to my requests." Eric nodded at the boxes. "I expect a receipt for those and will file release requests this afternoon. Copies may be used in court if they are deemed noteworthy."

The agents shook Eric's hand. "What happens to them isn't up to us, but we'll get you a receipt and the name of the prosecutor assigned to this case."

Eric nodded his farewell, and pushed his glasses up as the agents walked out of the vestibule. Walter's hand landed on his shoulder.

"Thank you, for not—" Walter rolled his wrist out to the side. "Well, you know. I know it's tough, but they won't be evidence forever. You've got the time to wait."

"She really did write me every day, didn't she?" Eric asked, not expecting an answer as he deflated against the door.

Walter nudged his chin at the lobby. "I called your detectives in from Chicago, like you asked. They'll be here later with every case note they have, and I have the files from our investigation in my squad. We'll figure this out. You don't have to worry anymore."

Eric nodded absently. Walter gave his shoulder a reassuring squeeze.

"Why don't you come with me and Molly for lunch? Check in with Sammy, see how Paresh is doing. Unwind for an hour. Have a drink or something?"

Eric didn't answer.

"Hey!" Walter pinched him hard to get his attention. "The way you were earlier?"

Raising his eyebrows, Walter pointed at the sitting area. "After that guy made Molly bring those boxes in? Come on! I've never seen you that angry! You need a distraction, if for nothing more than to help clear your head."

"I'm fine, Walter, really." Eric sighed and gestured at the vestibule doors. "I just…I've been waiting for so long. I thought I'd be better prepared, but seeing her—now that she's here, she's caught me off guard."

Clucking his tongue against his teeth, Walter shook his head. "I disagree with your assessment, Counselor. And I think Molly would concur." He stuck a finger in Eric's face. "You're usually the one with all the answers, but it's time to listen to an old friend. Clear your head, even if you think you don't need to. Because if you don't, you won't be able to help the investigation or that girl."

☽ ✳ ☾

Energized and eager to close Paresh's case, the detectives, a two-man and one-woman trio, arrived around one o'clock and swiftly buried Eric's office under notes, receipts, family records, and every other type of paper imaginable, along with surveillance and reference photographs, to which Walter added another few boxes from the department's records. Dust motes swirled wildly within canned beams of light as the group swapped notes and scribbled on legal pads, confirming theories and trying to tease out a satisfactory conclusion.

Their excitement was cooling when Molly flew in, gray faced and gaping, her eyes shining like warning beacons. She didn't need to say a word. The afternoon news Eric usually tuned out at her desk had his complete attention now. He grabbed the remote and turned on the television.

A collective gasp erupted when the display zapped to images of black vans and tactically clad agents scurrying in and out of iron gates behind a horde of reporters. The remote cracked in Eric's hand.

"They don't know anything." She pried the remote free. "The spokesperson for the FBI has only said they're looking for a person of interest—no mention of kidnapping or any Hawthorne. The reporters are speculating about homeland security issues."

She squeezed his hand and reiterated, "They don't know anything."

Jacob Spade, the senior investigator, pumped his fist. "We've finally got him! There's no hiding from this!"

Fingers of unease raced up Eric's back. "Hey Walter? I need to know what's going on there—can you make contact?"

"I can try." He punched numbers into his phone and paced along the far wall.

Thirty minutes later, Walter finally connected with someone who could talk. Eric didn't think Molly could squeeze his hand any tighter.

"Okay, listen up!" Walter said. "They've found about a dozen vacant houses so far. They're methodically searching and sweeping with dogs just in case—the community has too many hallmarks of a cult for their liking—so it's going slow. They started with the addresses Paresh gave us, but they're empty and scrubbed clean."

"Putting her up in a hotel the night before a long train ride bought them time to clear out," Molly said, leaving an imprint on Eric's skin as she flexed her fingers. "They didn't leave a trace when they stole her stuff from the cottage a few months after she disappeared."

"Mm-hm." Eric quelled the acidic anger burning his gut. "That break in proved they know what they're doing. But this?"

He nodded at the scene. "With David, I'm surprised that place isn't up in flames."

"They're not all gone," Walter whispered, covering the mouthpiece with his hand. A dark look circled the room.

Gesturing for quiet while he listened to the agent, Walter moved closer to Eric's desk. During a pause, he gave a quick summary.

"Other people live in the compound, but claim not to know

David or Paresh. They all bought their homes within the last three to six months through an agency, but they've all described the same person at closing: a woman with red hair and bright green eyes."

"Paresh said she hadn't seen David in six months. That has to mean something," Molly said.

Eric flicked his eyes up at her. "Nicole."

He crossed his hands under his chin. He clenched and unclenched his jaw waiting for Walter to elaborate even though he could hear the agent's voice clearly.

"So far, they've interviewed young couples who thought it was a community designed as a haven for kids and families. They're just as confused at the FBI's presence as the media," Walter said.

"We can safely assume that only David's inner circle had access to Paresh, then?" Spade asked.

As Walter shrugged, Eric said, "It makes sense that he'd have an elaborate network to shield her from the world. Paresh only had daily contact with two people."

Walter covered the mouthpiece. "They aren't down into details yet, but there are no records for the previous homeowners or tenants, and the land deeds are all registered to Nicole O'Reilly."

Eric said shared a look with Molly. "We already know about her—the girlfriend. He's not telling us anything useful."

"Or why David took her in the first place," added Molly.

The investigators shifted uncomfortably. They'd tried every angle to determine foul play or to put David there, but the evidence didn't support it. No connection existed between the driver and the Hawthorne family. All injuries resulted directly from the impact. Neither vehicle showed signs of tampering—missing child aside. Why David was there, why he'd taken her, why he'd raised her—no one had those answers. *Why* haunted them all.

Eric motioned for Walter to end the call. Walter retreated to the sitting area with Molly, wary of Eric's souring mood. Together with the detectives, they drank coffee and discussed what they knew, which still left them working off an unconfirmed theory. Given the history between David and his brother, they thought he'd taken Paresh because of her relation to Felicia rather than to Andrew. But her upbringing didn't fit what they knew about David. An education, doting custodians, and a grieving eight-year-old girl who'd grown into a well-balanced young woman? That brought them right back to *why*.

Tired of talking in circles, Molly left early. Eric's thoughts strayed to Jonathan, and the others' voices became white noise. Jonathan was not something he could share. Jonathan was *his* threat.

None of Jonathan's cryptic tidbits linked to anything they'd learned. On the surface, David was after Paresh's estate, which didn't pose a threat to the Vampiric Nation. Whatever was going on had to justify not only the High Council's involvement, but also their decision to use a human. Jonathan's willingness to tail Paresh—under the guise that David was in control—was another matter unto itself.

Eric knew Jonathan too well to believe he was acting solely on orders. The skilled puppet master had arranged for his toys to fall into place, as usual. Manipulating the Elders into his control would give Jonathan absolute power over Eric—and that was truly terrifying.

A hard smack on his shoulder jerked Eric back into the din of his office. Walter's watch was in his face. "You're going to be late!"

17:19

Eric cursed at himself.

Walter leaned closer to whisper, "You sure you're all right?"

"Just thinking." Eric slid his hands under his glasses to rub his eyes. "I'm fine—or, at least, I will be once I'm with her and can see that she's fine. You guys keep at it and stay in touch with the FBI. The team can head back tomorrow. There's no point keeping everyone here—it's obviously going to be a longer investigation than we thought. Molly's arranged the usual accommodations. Take a room, too. Pamper yourself a bit."

Appalled by the thought, Walter waved his hands and stepped back with a laugh. "I don't need any of that spa treatment junk you spring for. I'm good in my own bed, but thanks."

"All right then. Lock up, Chief?"

"Sure thing, Counselor. I'd tell you to take care of our girl, but you've got it covered."

A few goodbyes later and Eric was on the road to his house with barely enough time to shower and change. Molly was there like a mother hen, flitting through his closet and plucking hangers to determine his eveningwear: black wool and cashmere blend trousers and a pressed, fine-cotton shirt in crimson. She badgered him to select a tie, then tossed it aside and shoved him into the bathroom.

Wearing only a towel, he came out to a valet stand punctuated with shined Oxford shoes and a matching leather belt—with a silver buckle to complement his watch. Swooping over in higher spirits, she added a jacket and cufflinks, and began fussing with his hair. He gently extracted himself from her clutches, wondering if Paresh's essence had affected her, too. She normally left him alone when a sour mood hit, but nothing was stopping her tonight.

He managed to dress himself, but her fingers twitched as he buttoned his shirt, and she pursed her lips when he began threading the dreaded tie that she'd chosen. She knocked his hands aside and smoothed out a perfect Windsor knot, thoroughly enjoying every moment and poking fun at him—playing every bit of the overprotective mother prepping her son for his first date.

"Enough, Molly," he admonished with a smile. "I'll be good. I promise."

With a coy grin and glittering eyes, she returned, "Oh, I'm sure."

He kissed her on the cheek and headed out the door.

☽ ❋ ☾

At six-thirty sharp, Eric parked at the carriage house and stepped into the lightly shadowed wood. Molly had almost won the tie battle, but he rarely wore them outside of court. He banished it to the backseat with his jacket and popped his shirt's top button free.

Much better, he thought as Molly's final suggestion barreled into his head: "A gentleman always takes a lady flowers!"

He'd literally waved it off as he drove down his lane, not wishing to complicate matters with an illusory gesture of courtship. The attraction they shared was undeniable, but also a dangerous distraction, especially when Paresh didn't know who, or what, he was.

He sighed and ran his hand through his hair, trying to tamp down the guilt that had been nipping at him since their parting hug. He'd loved his wife and mourned her passing, but this…this was different. The weight of desperate yearning. A tidal wave of lost time and love. Of a broken life and a broken man. His very soul aching.

Perhaps that was why he found himself rolling the single stem, with a bud the color of blood, between his fingers as he crossed the forest threshold onto the flagstone path.

His gaze lifted from the rose to the clearing. After standing empty for a decade, it danced to life in full color with the evening sun painting lime tips onto the grass and glossing the foliage in the velvety rose garden. The cottage's stone walls radiated warmth and the roof's asphalt shingles twinkled as though dusted by pixies.

Squirrels and rabbits tumbled in the grass and he stepped over two raccoons sleeping belly up on sun-heated stones. Chirping sparrows flew circles around a cardinal's melodious chorus, and a doe nibbled near the tree line.

When Paresh was a child, his predatory presence would've triggered the doe's instinct to scatter every animal into hiding. He'd had to watch from a distance while she played with her friends, but now she'd enchanted the entire forest. He felt like a knight coming for his fairytale maiden.

Smiling with boyish wonder, he jogged up the steps and remembered to knock at the last second. Pocketing his key, he chided himself to stay focused. Then she opened the door.

Silver satin clung to her breasts, hips, and thighs, and dropped him mentally to his knees. The mermaid-style dress left her shoulders bare, her skin supple and tempting. Shimmering powder tugged his gaze to her cleavage.

He forced his eyes up to the diamond butterfly pendant dangling from a silver necklace and the elegant bun at her nape. Mascara and blue liner accented her eyes, pale rose-color blushed her cheeks, and gloss gave her lips a dew-kissed look.

He wanted to devour her.

"Hello, Darien." She flashed an uncertain smile and swayed in place. Strappy sandals and metallic, pale blue nail polish were visible beneath a hem that nearly dusted the floor.

"Wow," he whispered breathlessly.

Clasping her hands over her heart, she leaned forward and asked, "It's not too much is it? I've never worn anything like this before. Sammy picked it out." She twirled girlishly, swirling the fabric in a graceful arc around her knees.

Distracted by legs surely crafted by Aphrodite, he nearly missed the sapphire and diamond-studded butterfly comb, resplendent with silver filigree detail, tucked into her bun. Noticing his stare, she hesitantly touched the antique adornment.

"It is too much isn't it?" she asked. "Sammy said he found it in one of the Hawthorne's 'long forgotten' boxes."

"N-no…no! It's perfect. It's beautiful. You…you're beautiful." How could he possibly hide his surprise at the comb he'd gifted to his wife as the "something blue" to wear on their wedding day? He hadn't seen it again after she died.

Paresh palmed her flushing cheeks. "T-thank you."

Pulling off his sunglasses, he stepped inside and gently twirled her, marveling at how the comb perfectly complimented this silver limned fairy who looked nothing like his wife, and how serendipitous it was to appear now, on *her*, both missing for so long.

The image of Lucinda's thick, chocolate-y locks began to form in his mind. He fought against seeing her face. He only ever remembered her covered in blood.

Paresh's infectious giggling saved him. He disguised a thankful sigh as an appreciative whistle and twirled her once more. Lucinda was at rest and had been for a long time.

With a nostalgic grin tugging at his mouth, he gave Paresh the rose. "Sammy's got excellent taste."

She sighed happily and sniffed the bud. "Mm…I love roses. I'll be right back."

She disappeared into the bathroom and returned empty handed. He shot her a puzzled look.

Pointing down the hall, she explained, "There's a vase in there. I haven't…well, I didn't want to look for another one. Being here…it's bringing up a lot of stuff."

Avoiding memory was something Eric understood well. "Would it be easier if everything had been boxed up and stored?"

"I think it would've been lonely to come home to an abandoned shell." She scanned the living room. "Everything here has meaning: Mom's embroidery, Dad's pipes. When I saw them, I swear I smelled vanilla tobacco, and remembered Mom humming in her rocking chair while Dad puffed at his desk. And you—"

She shook her head. "No—*your dad*—was there, too, reading to me on the sofa."

Briefly hooding his gaze under his lashes, he said, "They say scents trigger the human memory into recalling what may have been forgotten."

"Who says that?"

"I'm not sure," he said with a smile. "But I read it in a magazine once, so it must be true. Shall we go?"

Nodding, she grabbed the wristlet with her house key from the sideboard.

"Do you have a handbag for that?"

"I bought one today, but I don't need it for this."

"You can leave it here, if you'd like. I have my key," he said, surprised by her simplicity. All of the women he knew, including Molly, would be lost without their bottomless catchalls.

She dropped it onto the sideboard and stepped into the evening. "Why do you have a key?"

"My father maintains the properties of your local estate, so while he's away, I'm tending to his duties. Simon is under his employ and he has a key, as well," he explained, making a mental note to have the locks changed. Sliding his sunglasses on, he followed her and locked the door.

"What is my *local estate*?" she asked, brows dipping slightly. "Isn't it just the cottage?"

"It's substantially more," he said with a grin. "Sunset Grove, in its entirety, most of the countryside surrounding Orison Crossing, and a few other properties that your father turned over to maintenance crews after the Sunset Grove Parish burned down. Andrew donated money and farmland closer to the cemetery for the new church and then built this cottage."

"Oh yeah, I remember Dad's stories about the church. He said that since I was born there, they wanted to name me 'Parish,' but changed the spelling. And I think I knew that my family founded the town, but I had no idea about the land. I always thought it was just this clearing..." She surveyed the treetops. "Have you contacted your dad yet? I can't wait to see him."

"He's unreachable at the moment, but I'm certain he'll feel the same way I do." Hoping to steer the conversation away from himself, he waved at the animals. They were drifting closer. "What's this all about? I felt like I was walking through the page of a book earlier."

"As long as I can remember, they've been this way. You should hear them in the mornings. They sing and call me outside to play." She laughed. "I missed it so much. There wasn't a lot of wildlife near my house in Kansas. Some of Miss Lydia's friends had cats who liked me better than anyone else, but it wasn't the same." She wrinkled her nose.

"I wish I could be that close to nature. I enjoy walking through these woods at night." He grinned at the fox slinking behind them, courageous enough to approach despite his presence.

Following his gaze, Paresh smiled and stopped briefly to pat its head. "It's like they need to make up for lost time."

They fell into a comfortable silence until they reached the carriage house. He opened her door and she asked, "You're not a hunter, are you?"

"No," he said, tucking her safely into the car. At the driver's side, he grabbed the handle and froze. The forest had gone silent in an instant and there wasn't an animal in sight.

Subtle pressure crept along his cheekbones. Someone was there—someone deliberately provoking a fear response stronger than Paresh's calming aura.

Eric peered over his sunglasses into the shadows and ordered in a low whisper, "We need to talk, *Brother*."

The presence vanished. Crows cawed, woodpeckers drilled, and birds broke into summer song. As the chatter of life resumed, Eric entered the car. Paresh asked if something was wrong. "I was just enjoying how the sunlight trickles through the leaves and disappears under the canopy."

She stretched over the dashboard to look into the forest. "Oh, you're right! It's like the darkness gobbles it up, like a black hole."

He tore his eyes away from the sight of her exquisite throat and clamped down on his teeth. He'd thought he'd gained control of *that* craving long ago. Berating himself internally, he started the car. "I reserved the greenhouse at The Greenery. They specialize in vegetarian entrees. Is that okay?"

"That sounds perfect. How did you know I'm a vegetarian?"

"I read people well. I hope it doesn't ruin your dinner, but I've already eaten. I had a meeting before this and my client insisted on an early meal." After dinner, he'd reveal his truth to her. With Jonathan lurking in the shadows and his emotions in turmoil, she shouldn't be alone. She deserved to know the truth, and he couldn't perform his sworn duty shrouded in lies.

II

Sweeping trees arced over The Greenery, an elegant stone and brick building with sunlight-gilded windows. She searched for the greenhouse, but couldn't see it beyond a dense thicket that must have been part of Sunset Grove at one time.

Humid summer air whooshed into the cab when he opened her door and offered his hand. The dress squeezed her thighs as she swung her legs out, and she was briefly mortified at the thought of ripping the form-fitting thing. She accepted his hand and was relieved when he effortlessly pulled her up. The heat of his palm traveled up her arm and nestled comfortably in her chest. His presence alone chased off her troubling thoughts. His touch made them vanish.

He was the best kind of amnesia.

He'd been acting like the perfect gentleman, bringing her a rose, keeping a close but appropriate distance, and opening her doors. But each gesture hinted at something more, at a hidden restraint. The morning's butterflies returned, fluttering beneath her ribs. She sighed at the memory of his breath brushing her ear, the muscles that had tensed when he'd folded her into his arms—how she'd melted against him, hearing the swift beat of his heart, leaning into him and yearning to drift off into another world—

The warmth in her chest flared. He'd moved his hand to the small of her back. She bit her lip to keep a bashful smile from spreading and stole an appreciative glance at him.

At the cottage, he had strolled, relaxed and loose, yet here he stood tall, shoulders squared, chin up and jaw set, taking each step firmly heel to toe. His stance and tailored suit—down to the way his perfectly creased trousers draped over gleaming leather Oxfords—gave off a distinctly aristocratic air, and his dark sunglasses added an ominous mystique.

This was a man approached only if invited.

She suddenly felt very minuscule at his side. All this time, she'd thought of Eric only as her dad's partner, someone she'd adored in childhood. Clearly, he was a powerful and wealthy man, evidenced in this moment with his son alone. Despite her new financial standing, her humble roots left her feeling beneath him.

They reached the stairs leading to the entrance and, as she took that first step, her sandal caught the hem of her dress and strained the fabric against her knee. She wished she'd worn a simpler style, an A-line or a maxi cut, anything with more range, but now she'd lost a sandal and was flailing beside him, about to face plant at his feet because she couldn't walk, think, and admire him all at once.

She didn't see him move. But he instantly caught her, saving her delicate skin—and the cursed dress—from scraping the paved stone. Icy blue flashed over the rim of his sunglasses.

"Oh, careful!" He tried to hide a quiet chuckle as he asked, "Are you all right?"

"Y-yes," she stammered, her cheeks burning.

He set her upright on her protected foot and grabbed the orphaned sandal, firmly cupping the small of her back, as he slipped it onto her foot. "My fair maiden," he murmured to himself.

Her heart skipped a beat.

She let out a timid laugh. "Th-thank you. I was just…um… y-you look very handsome, Darien."

He winked and grinned. "Handsome, huh? Molly deserves all the credit—just don't tell her I didn't wear my tie."

"My lips are sealed." She made a zipping motion with her finger and thumb over her mouth. "But really—thank you for catching me. And for dinner tonight."

"My pleasure on both accounts."

The intimate honesty in his voice whipped the butterflies into a frenzy, and his lingering eyes plunged them into chaos. She was silently grateful when the restaurant door opened. A young woman with light umber skin wearing a smoky blue dress greeted them.

"Good evening Mr. Ravenscroft, Miss Hawthorne," she said in an airy voice. "Sir, your reservation is prepared as requested."

"Thank you, Sarah. Please show Miss Hawthorne the way and I'll be along in a moment." He slid his hand from her back and veered left, removing his sunglasses and pulling a small white case from his jacket pocket.

Sarah gestured in the opposite direction. "Right this way, please."

She whisked Paresh through an intimately lit space with masculine dark woods, organic greens, and feminine toile fabrics in cream and faded crimson. Latticed boxes brimmed with plants atop five-foot walls of cozy, private booths. Exposed wooden beams in the ceiling added a rustic element that paired well with the exquisite woodwork and trim in the bar's alcove.

They arrived at a pair of heavy wooden doors carved with peonies and butterflies. Sarah pushed them open and sunlight rushed inside, eager to usher them into its glass-encased haven. At the center, a pond filled with brightly colored koi encircled an island of lace leaf Japanese maples and stone lanterns. The tallest of the trees sprouted nearly eight feet, with deep burgundy leaves and limbs that twisted gracefully over the feathery green foliage of its smaller brethren.

The pond had seemingly spilled over the floor, but on closer inspection, Paresh found that the surface was hard and dry. A thick glossy coating topped clusters of pea pebbles to give the illusion of a shallow riverbed. Narrow water channels snaked throughout the concrete and added real movement to enhance the effect.

Raised plant beds divided a maze of bistro-style tables, each with its own mosaic-tiled inlay and a bowl of colored water and floating candles. Overhead, paper lanterns and clear fairy lights crisscrossed the supports, promising a magical transformation once night fell.

Sarah led her to the far corner where another deep red tree loomed overhead, elevated by a tall, crescent-shaped retaining wall. The hostess pulled out a chair. "Here you are, Miss Hawthorne. May I get you something to drink?"

"Water is fine. Thank you," Paresh replied, gaping at the magnificence of the greenhouse and wondering how Darien had reserved it on such short notice.

On her way out, Sarah pushed a button near the door. The room dimmed as shaded panels tilted over the ceiling. Darien entered and Sarah pulled the doors shut, hiding them from public view.

"What do you think?" he asked, beaming proudly. He slipped his jacket over the chair before sitting. "It's enchanting after dusk when the lanterns are lit and the candles are burning."

"It's breathtaking. The trees, the pond, the fish...it's all so beautiful." She smiled in awe. "The floor is interesting. I felt like I was walking on water…" Her voice trailed when she met his gaze and noticed it was darker than usual. "Is something wrong?"

Leaning across the table, he shook his head and removed his glasses. "No, not at all. I have conditions that make me sensitive to the sun. I need to protect my skin and eyes, but I didn't want to wear my sunglasses all evening. I put in coated contacts when I excused myself."

"Have you been like this your whole life?" she asked, lost in his eyes. Though shaded, the crystalline blue was as clear as the water in the pond.

"Most of it. Modern medicine is a godsend." He returned her gaze with an intensity that nipped at her. "Does that sate your curiosity?" he asked quietly, sliding his silver-framed glasses back onto his nose.

"Maybe," she mused. "Well, there is something else—why didn't Eric ever mention you?"

He lowered his gaze to the floating candles. "That's a sensitive subject. Can we revisit it later?"

"I'm sorry," she said, emphatically pressing her palm to her chest. "I shouldn't have pried. I just thought I'd remember you."

"It's all right. I'll elaborate later," he promised. Smiling widely, he sat back and swept his hand toward the pond. "So do you want one of those? The koi are really something. That big white one there leaps out of the water at night. Everyone loves him."

"He jumps out of the water?"

"Like a dolphin." He mimicked the motion with his hand. "It's usually a sign of distress, but he just seems to enjoy it. Like a performance. The staff named him Kabuki."

Paresh laughed. "A fitting name! I bet he shimmers under the moonlight."

Eric withdrew in thought. "The diameter of the cottage's clearing is about 600 yards. That's plenty of room for a large pond. You could have dozens of koi to watch at your leisure. I can arrange a meeting with the designer for you."

"You know everyone don't you?" she teased.

Smiling wistfully, he said, "This was your father's dedication to your mother. He never finalized the project, but the plans were drafted. I built this restaurant from his designs to honor both of them. I'd be more than happy to transfer ownership to you, if you'd like. It should be yours, after all."

The sudden appearance of a lump in her throat robbed her of words. "N-no…"

"I didn't mean to upset you," he said softly, leaning forward and stroking her cheek. "How about a lighter subject? How was your afternoon?"

"Thank you," she whispered, deflecting her gaze.

He nudged her chin up with his thumb. The concentration in his eyes stole her breath. She thought he might kiss her.

Instead, with a subtle sigh, he lowered his hand and sat back. The doors swung open and Sarah entered with their drinks. Eric gave her a warm smile. She set a wine glass before him, but the liquid inside was thick, like vegetable juice, and he moved it off to the side.

The two shared polite conversation about the day's business as Paresh's water, along with a chilled bottle of chardonnay and a glass, were placed on the table. Sarah presented a menu and offered assistance when Paresh had trouble choosing an entrée.

"I think I'll go with the spinach lasagna with house salad and garlic bread," Paresh finally decided.

"Substitute toasted French bread, please," he said to Sarah, meeting Paresh's puzzled gaze with a wink.

As Sarah made her exit with the modified order in hand, he smiled and poured Paresh a glass of chardonnay. "I have a strong aversion to garlic," he explained. "I can't stand the smell. Unfortunately, it's very popular and hard to avoid, but at least it gives me an excuse for staying out of the kitchen."

"I'm learning all about you tonight," she said, returning his smile. "Is there anything else I should know?" Having never tasted wine before, she took a cautious sip. The cool, fruity liquid cascaded smoothly over her tongue and burned pleasurably as it slid down her throat. She followed the glass with her eyes as she set it down, already wanting another taste.

"Let's see. I don't want to thin my mystique," he teased.

"Don't worry, there's plenty to spare." She laughed and reached for the wine.

Flashing a wide grin, he said, "Hm, something you don't know about me. Okay, here: these aren't real——" He tipped his glasses up. "I have perfect vision. I just like the way they look and have worn them for so long that most people think I need them."

"They do look nice on you." She got lost in his eyes again and blushed. She sipped and asked, "Is there anything else?"

"Of course. But we'll save it for later," he answered cryptically. "Now, tell me about your afternoon. I want to hear all about Sammy's fashion sense."

"Well, it started off simply enough. I picked up my bags at the terminal and——*oh!*" She slapped the table. "I nearly forgot! One of my bags was missing and they asked where to deliver it when it turns up. Given the whole...*situation*...I figured it'd be better to have it dropped by your office than the cottage. They didn't recognize your name, so they put down 'Eric' instead." She sipped as he nodded in response.

"Um, other than that, I had a nice afternoon. Sammy showed me the town and let me buy him lunch. It was the least I could do since he was taking such great care of me and keeping my mind off other things." She took a longer drink.

"You may want to slow down until you eat something," he cautioned.

Smiling shyly, she set the glass down and ran her finger around the base. "Sammy asked where I wanted to go, but I had no idea. He told me that his girls loved the Plaza Shopping Center and Mall, so that's where he took me.

"He said he always waited in the car, which made me really nervous. I mean, until now I've never been on my own——Master Jon went with me everywhere and I always felt safe with him. So when I walked in alone, I felt very exposed."

With a laugh, she finished off her wine and said, "Maybe it was childish, but I practically ran out to the car to beg for his company, but he was already on his way in to find me. It was such a relief. He knew his way around and took me to the best stores."

"I can only imagine Sammy being dragged around the mall!" Eric laughed as he poured her another glass, giving her less this time. "I always thought he'd be happy to live in that car."

"He seemed to enjoy himself. He's nice. He must spoil his granddaughters. You wouldn't believe how many pictures he had crammed into his wallet. They're so adorable." Between the conversation and chardonnay, she felt warm and relaxed for the first time in days. She eyed her wine glass, but heeded his warning and waited for her dinner to arrive.

It wasn't long before Sarah delivered her salad, entrée, and substituted bread. Eric politely waited until Paresh began eating to drink from his glass. He attentively listened to her shopping adventures with his driver, and they talked well into the night, but he revealed nothing further about himself.

As the moon rose, Sarah cleared away the dishes, lit the candles, and turned on the lanterns. At Eric's request, she took his glass and replaced it with another full one. As she closed the doors behind her, the only sound was the gentle lapping of the pond. Though the white koi had not jumped, the intimate touches of lighting reflected in the water, shimmering with the subtlest of ripples as koi swam beneath the surface. Paresh enjoyed the sudden stillness, the magical feel—he'd been right. The greenhouse was enchanting after dusk.

Even with the food, the wine affected her strongly. Over half the bottle was gone. Heat simmered in her core, and her fingers and cheeks were numb. She propped her elbows on the table and held her face in her hands, contented to watch him in silence. He sipped from his glass slowly, rolling the liquid along his tongue to savor every flavor, and returned her gaze. Her heart fluttered. She smiled and nervously looked away.

He laughed. "I should have known you've never had wine before. It wasn't my intention to get you drunk."

She giggled. "It wasn't my intention to get drunk!"

Quietly sobering, she half-smiled. "But after a day like this—"

"Speaking of that—" He leaned forward, folding his hands in front of his face. "How are you doing, really?"

"I'm okay. I think." She shrugged, not wanting to ruin the evening.

He met her eyes over the rim of his glasses. "Tell me what's on your mind."

Her resolve broke under his blue orbs and commanding voice.

"I'm trying not to focus on the negative things, but it's hard when I'm alone. I mean, the people who raised me were good to me and made me the person I am—I can't ignore that. Maybe they didn't know I was…*kidnapped*…or maybe they did."

She sighed. "I guess that makes the most sense since they were always with me, but even before that, I was never alone because Eric was always there, like a protector, and I always felt safe. I felt that way with Master Jon, too. I hope he actually cared about me, but I may never know." She sighed again, licking her lips as she stared at the ice melting in her water.

He regarded her silently.

"I don't know… from the moment I stepped inside the cottage, I've been trapped in time," she said at last. "That place hasn't changed at all. I keep expecting to see my parents, but I know they're dead. It just…it feels like I've lost them all over again."

Ice clinked as she sipped her water.

"But with you, well, I guess, overall I'm fine, just…conflicted. I…I don't want to go home," she confessed quietly, her pulse jumping as she focused on the floating candles, too nervous to look at him.

He spent a moment in thought before answering, "I understand." Something in his voice made her look up. Heat smoldered in his eyes as he reached for her face and stroked her cheek gently. "I must admit to feeling a bit…*conflicted*, myself."

She leaned into his touch and closed her eyes, each affectionate caress euphoric and adding to alcohol-induced vertigo. "Don't leave me alone…" her voice faded as she felt the entire room move.

"You don't have to go home. Stay with me tonight."

"…such a considerate man," she murmured distantly.

"Well, I don't know about that. Here, let me help you up."

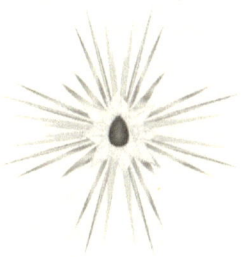

CHAPTER SIX: THE TRUTH

E ric invited her into his home where she stepped into enrobing darkness as though expecting him to turn on a light. But he wasn't thinking as clearly as he could see. Intoxicated by her essence, he stood painfully close, his aroused body aching for her as he breathed in the scents of her hair and skin. She smelled like the spirit of summer—of clover and honey—and the nectar of innocence.

He slid his jacket from her shoulders and tossed it aside. The wine had more than relaxed her inhibition; it had freed her aura to act on its own, like his—and preternaturally so—viscous and soft, and powerfully tuned into her desires. It had stroked him all evening long and it was driving him mad.

Just as her purity drew the creatures of the forest to her, so did it call to the beast chained deeply within him. His aura hungrily devoured every drop of hers as a war raged between his logic and lust. He'd thought logic was winning, but he felt it ebbing away.

He shouldn't have brought her home.

He'd already lost.

Gliding his fingers down the undersides of her arms, he sighed down the nape of her neck and linked their hands. He drew her back against him, folding their entwined arms over her breasts. She moaned and leaned into him, her heart thumping wildly. She rolled her head along his shoulder and bared her throat.

His control shattered.

Fire flared in his chest as a muted ache spread along his cheekbones and upper jaw. His teeth prickled as he tested his limits, lowering his mouth to the delicate curvature of her neck, hovering above her pulse, savoring her scent, his breath hot on her skin. He tenderly kissed her there and the heat of her pulse smoldered on his lips, sparking ripples of pleasure that threatened to release the bloodthirsty animal hiding in wait.

Pressure mounted behind his canines. He stared desperately ahead, clenching his teeth to fight his instinctual urges. His human heart wanted to save her by pushing her away, but lust didn't want to let go and the vampire's beast wanted to pull her closer.

He flicked his tongue over his teeth, panting against her throat. She moaned again, freeing a hand to curl up his neck, her fingers working into his hair. He slid his palm down her gown, low on her belly, holding her tightly against him. His fangs were fully extended and he was beyond lost in her. There was no more thought. Only instinct. Desire. He licked her throat with the tip of his tongue and opened——

A throaty, feminine growl stopped him cold. It spoke the language of the beast, perplexing it and drawing its attention, giving him a chance to recover and regain control. As the fog of his lust lifted, his arms loosened and his lips lifted from her neck. Fear's talons clicked up his spine one by one. He knew the expression on Paresh's face too well.

In a raspy, defeated voice, he whispered, "Paresh, I need to tell you something."

☽ ❈ ☾

Under the guise of getting her a glass of water, he sat her down on his couch and jogged to his bedroom to quell his own thirst first. He grabbed a blood bag from the "wine chest" in his closet and a glass from the ledge of crystal above it.

His fangs clinked against the glass and made forming a seal with his lips difficult. Blood stained the corners of his mouth and dribbled down his jaw. It'd be much easier if he drank from the bag, but he already felt like an animal. Drinking from a glass felt civilized, at least. He refilled and chugged until the bag was empty.

Shards flew everywhere when he finished and slammed the glass down, enraged at the risk he'd taken. How the hell had she spawned such an out-of-control, desire-driven bloodlust? No, it wasn't her fault—he never should've allowed even a chance for anything like that to happen. If not for *that growl*, he would have gone over the edge and succumbed to his lethal urges.

Gripping the wine chest in tightening fists, his muscles twisted like an over tightened tension wire. He ground his teeth, staring into the darkness but seeing the past—a pale little girl who never got sick or hurt, frolicking in the sunlight with fawns and coyote pups like one of Mother Nature's sprites.

Then Jonathan appeared in the shadows wearing that wicked grin of his and Eric snapped his eyes shut. The cabinet creaked and groaned under the weight of his silent scream.

All he'd ever wanted for her was an ordinary life. He growled at himself, at his fear, his failure. The signs he'd been too unwilling to see in her youth had developed aggressively while she'd been gone—and the High Council had seen them first. If the Elders deemed her a threat, they'd order her death, and he'd be powerless to stop them.

He ripped off his soiled shirt and tossed it into the biohazard bin, a consideration for Molly, who saw to his laundry, and shook his head at the thought of Jonathan finally forcing him to play his part in the game.

"Bastard." The word strained thick and raw between his teeth. He ran his hands through his hair wanting nothing more than to hunt his brother down. Instead of letting that anger take over, he pulled in deep, calming breaths, and thought about Paresh. She was sitting alone, in the dark, in a place where she'd never been, waiting for a man she thought she didn't know.

He washed up, removed his contacts, and donned a fresh white t-shirt, then, with water in hand, returned to the living room. Her hair snaked loosely around her shoulders, but she otherwise remained as he'd left her—upright and hands folded in her lap, her calm façade betrayed by a racing pulse. His heart sank. He was doomed to fail her.

Sitting beside her, he placed the glass in her hands. She blindly faced him, asking what was wrong and if he'd turn on a light. He swallowed his selfish guilt. Even a dim lamp would painfully blast his eyes, which, in their current state, were likely scarier than his fangs.

"Drink this," he said, his voice rough and deep. "I took out my contacts…the light—"

"Darien, what's going on?" Her voice quivered with the meekness of a mouse in the shadow of that strong, unnatural growl.

He huffed out his own uncertainty and bolstered his faith that everything would work out in the end. He had no choice but to keep moving forward—honestly. "I'm sorry, Paresh."

Taking hold of her hand, he caressed her fingers with his thumb. "Everything's fine, I promise. But I haven't told you the truth."

She sucked in a shaky breath.

"Your parents and I meant to tell you this when you were old enough to understand…about me, but Fate stole our chance."

Her pulse calmed for an instant. Then it spiked erratically. "Wait, if my parents had known Eric had a son, they would have told—"

"They knew about him," he interrupted. "But, more importantly, they knew *me* quite well—and so did you. All I ask is that you listen. If you want to leave afterward, I'll take you home or call Sammy or Molly—or even Walter. Okay?"

Sighing nervously, Paresh nodded. He briefly wondered if she realized he shouldn't be able to see her, but then forced himself to open truth's dreadful door.

"My name isn't Darien."

Her hand went rigid.

"*I am Eric.* I am the man you came to see, the man you remember, and the man who loved your father dearly. I am the man you've spent the entire evening with, the man who cares for you more than you know—nothing changes that."

"W-what?" she sputtered. "B-but…how? Why…*what?*"

"I've protected your family for generations, watching over them like I did with you and your mother. And I can only do that because I do not age or die. I'm…a vampire," he revealed delicately, the words sounding so strange to him that he couldn't fathom how they sounded to her.

Her heart jumped into a heavy gallop. She laughed nervously and pulled her hand away. "I don't know what this is—if it's some weird lawyer joke or what—but I-I think…I want to go." Her chest bobbed as fear grew into panic. "I…I…"

She bolted up and stumbled over the ottoman with a groan. "I…can't…breathe…"

Eric tried to catch her hand, but she jerked away.

"No! You—"

"Please! I'm not joking! Just listen—" he pleaded.

"No! It's not...true—" She hit the door to the atrium and tugged on the handle.

"Paresh, you've always felt safe with me." Eric seized her hands. She whimpered in pain and it hit like a dagger to his heart. He loosened his grip. "I'm sorry...I-I'm so sorry. I didn't mean to hurt you. I—"

"*No!*" she screamed, ripping free. "*Let me go!* You said—you said I could go!"

Tears stung Eric's eyes. He clamped down on his jaw and grabbed her, holding her tightly with one arm and forcing her palm flat against his chest with the other. As she screamed and struggled to escape his unearthly grasp, he choked into her ear, "The heart of this man breaks when you are in pain. The heart of this man broke when you were taken away. *I* broke, Paresh. *Eric broke.*"

His voice caught in his throat. He sniffled and begged, "Please give me a chance. Please remember me. I am Eric—*your* Eric. *I'm yours. Only yours.*"

She went limp and cried heaving sobs into his chest, twisting his shirt into her fist, repeatedly whispering, "*My Eric.*"

"Shh..." He swallowed the lump in his throat. "It's me," he whispered. Tears dripped off his cheeks into her hair. "It's just me."

She buried her face into a pocket of cotton between her fist and his chest. Her breaths were evening out, but her heart was pounding...and throbbing in his ears.

If you were a decent man, you'd turn on the light, Eric thought, frustrated that the beast had honed in on her blood and locked him into his altered state.

He gently loosened her fist and pried his shirt free, intending to reach for the lamp, but she pressed her ear against his chest, so he brought her hand up to his cheek instead, skimming her palm with a kiss he doubted she'd feel, and stood with her in the dark, listening to her heart as she listened to his.

Eventually, she inched her hand toward his mouth. He gently stopped her when she swept her index finger over his bottom lip and got too close to a fang.

"It's okay," he said in a soft voice, "but, do you have any cuts on your fingers?" She shook her head. "Then let me block the tip, and be careful not to cut yourself, okay?"

He let go when she nodded. Examining his teeth on her own, she glided down the length of his fangs, stopping as she reached his fingertip at each needle-sharp point. She drew in a final shaky breath and blew it out, dropping her hand to his chest.

The light, Eric reminded himself. "Do you...want to see me?"

She nodded again, clutching his shirt.

He guided her to the lamp by the atrium door and placed the pull chain in her hand. "Leave it on as long as you wish."

The searing assault knocked him back, but he forced his eyes open through the pain so she could see him as he truly was—eyes dilated and bloodshot, with animalistic fangs. As quickly as she turned the light on, she pulled the chain again and plunged him back into a soothing ebony oasis.

Despite temporary blindness, he should have heard her approach. She closed in without a sound, surprising him when she wrapped her arms around his waist. He held his breath as she rested her head on his chest and listened to his heart again.

"I trust you," she whispered at last. "Eric, I want to know you."

He returned her embrace and bowed his head.

"Thank you. Thank you," he murmured into her hair. He held her like he'd never let go. Every emotion crashed over him at once and he knew life would fall into despair without her. He'd never felt this way with anyone. Not Andrew. Not Molly. Not even his wife.

Paresh looked up. He wanted so badly to kiss her. Instead, he wiped tears from her cheeks. "Are you ready?"

She bit her lip and nodded.

He sighed and embraced her again before guiding her to the couch. "I have so much to tell you."

She sniffled and offered an earnest smile. "We have all night, right?"

I want more than a night, he thought as he helped her find her water. Her fingers lingered on his before she accepted the glass.

"Thank you, Eric," she whispered.

Hearing her say his name was like hearing angels sing. He wiped his face and sat beside her, simply watching her a moment before clearing his throat and beginning his tale.

☾ ❋ ☽

1864, American Civil War, United States of America

Life had a way of being both pointless and cruel while smiling its joyful pearly whites. It turned out that Death wasn't so different, equally callous and meaningless, with the extra kick that the world would keep turning without him. At least life offered an illusion of significance. As he sank into the cold mud and stared up at Death's scythe leveled above his head, Eric thought that it gleamed like a covetous grin and recognized that mattering or not was irrelevant.

Bullets flying too fast to have come from a single gun had punched him off his horse. The Confederates had planned this ambush; their units flanked three sides. Two hundred Union wagons of supplies and loot, with accompanying artillery and infantry, hadn't gone unnoticed in Confederacy sympathizing Arkansas Territory.

Someone screamed for "Sergeant Ravenscroft," but when he tried to respond, he choked on hot, coppery blood. His head lolled to the side, eyes aimed at a wagon wheel while cannons boomed. The acrid smoke of black powder billowed over him as blood bubbled up his throat and spilled from his mouth.

The so-called "gentleman's war" was anything but. His men screeched in horror and rage, barely able to form a line, let alone hold one as the Confederates pushed them back farther into the trees and muck. Injured men were shot in the back or the head as they tried to crawl to safety. There would be no prisoners today. If the wounded were smart, they'd play dead and live to fight another senseless battle.

The world rolled violently as his eyes swung around, barely staying open. God, he was cold. And tired. And so sick of the rain. It'd rained the past two weeks in Camden. If not for the damn rain, the supply train would've arrived on schedule. They wouldn't have needed to ration their food. He wouldn't have ridden out with reinforcements to escort the wagons back because the wagons never would've gone out in the first place.

The cannons boomed again over the infantry's fire. From which side, he couldn't tell. Orders and bullets flew from every direction, but only one force was organized with a semblance of order and might—and it wasn't the *right* one.

The smoke drifting over him began to fade. Death conjured the ghosts of memory and took him back to the beginning, to the birth of a screaming baby boy in 1841, with hair black as night and eyes like blue topaz.

He managed to blink over the poverty-stricken days of his childhood until Death dredged up his mother, gaunt and sickly pale, wasting away on a straw cot, her ruby lips colored by the blood that came up with each tortured breath. Doctors called it Consumption, because that's exactly what it did. She'd once been so vibrantly beautiful and happy despite their circumstances. His favorite person, his beloved mother—his world—was a fragile shell when she died in his father's arms.

Cold tears raced over the bridge of his nose. He'd only been nine. By his tenth birthday, his father had abandoned him to drown his grief at the bottom of any bottle he could find.

Death mercifully skipped over those three long years and dropped him as a young teen into the street at the county courthouse. It was the same week that his father's broken heart had finally expired, and Eric had refused to add an orphan's misery of forced labor or exploitation to his life's résumé.

Warmth bloomed in his chest. Maybe it was the memory. Or maybe the lead balls in his lungs.

On that day, he went from starving and homeless to eating like a king and living in a mansion. He'd begged to just the right person, Thaddeus Hawthorne, a retired lieutenant colonel and attorney who traveled the circuit with the man who currently served as Commander-in-Chief. Thanks to Thaddeus, Eric had met Abraham Lincoln, and his family, many times before he became President.

But on that day, Thaddeus's eyes had narrowed as he dropped coins into Eric's outstretched hands. "Aren't you Ravenscroft's boy?"

Of course, the question had clenched his stomach. His father hadn't had *friends*, after all. But, apparently, at one time, he had, and Thaddeus was one of them.

That night came with condolences, a warm bath, and a real mattress with clean sheets. The morning welcomed brand new clothes and shoes without holes in them. The "Colonel" treated him like a member of his family and never once made him feel like he owed anything for it. He provided a proper education and his only child, Lucinda, a few years older than Eric, was his tutor.

Lucinda...

His heart hurt. Death was crueler than life. It had taken Lucinda's mother shortly before Eric moved in, and now it was taking him, too. She was too young to be a widow—but many women were these days.

He saw sunlight streaming through her chocolaty locks as he lifted her veil on their wedding day. He could almost feel the cushion of her lips when they'd kissed. She'd been so pretty, so gentle and kind, a proper lady with the extra resilience that came from running a household as a girl without the guidance of her mother. They'd been married barely a year before the Civil War began.

In the fall of 1861, he'd joined the military and departed with Company I of the Illinois Cavalry, Tenth Regiment, riding out from Camp Butler to Missouri and into Arkansas, facing the horrors of a country so divided and angry that even his own men fought against their brothers.

Of course, now he wished he hadn't reenlisted when his three-year term expired. He hadn't seen Lucinda at all during that time, not until the thirty-day furlough awarded to re-enlistees. That had been only a few months ago, in February. He'd fallen in love with her all over again, and had learned just the week before, in a letter stained with happy tears, that she was pregnant with their first child.

A strange stillness interrupted Death's predictable routine. A man appeared with eyes blacker than Death itself, fashionably refined in a silk suit with auburn hair tied at his nape. He seemed completely unfazed—and unnoticed—by the battle. Eric forgot for a moment that he was dying, positive that this man was visible to him alone, and unsure if that was good or bad.

"You've finally lost your faith and fallen from the Flock." The man's lips formed a disconcerting smile as he knelt beside Eric.

Regardless of who—or what—this man was, how could Eric argue with that? He was right. No mother. No father. Shot without a chance of defense. Dying alone in the cold and sinking into the mud like the wagons. Yet another causality—one of war's unavoidable evils. Perhaps he hadn't seen the tether snap, but his faith had been little more than a fraying string for years. The only thing he had left was Lucinda, but he was losing her, too.

Why? Why was I born at all?

Through a teary haze, he looked at the man, so unearthly pale he couldn't be human—

This is Death's true face, Eric realized with a shiver. *This is the moment I say goodbye to everything.*

The man's grin widened. "I can offer you a better life—a life outside the pettiness of man." His voice was too calm. "I can't guarantee that you'll recover, but if you do, I will come for you and you'll be mine."

Half dead and desperate to escape a nightmarish rift that would leave Lucinda all alone, Eric met the man's stare and blinked once in confirmation. The man scooped Eric to his chest and carried him far away—far beyond the sounds of battle that could carry for miles. They were in a field of prairie grasses when the man set him down.

Eric had no idea what to expect. Maybe everyone got this deal when they died. How could there be a heaven when hell lived on earth, when God allowed this war between brothers? For children to lose their parents? For him to lose everyone he loved?

The man smiled again and his lips parted over sharp ivory fangs. Eric's heart seized in terror. Death had become the Devil, and he'd made a deal with him. There was no time for regrets. As those gleeful teeth lowered to his throat, Eric committed to memory that on April 18, 1864, at a place known as Poison Spring, Arkansas, Sergeant Eric James Ravenscroft was killed in action. The life he'd known was forever gone.

☽ ✹ ☾

The light behind his eyes made him cringe. A shadow moved over him and he felt a cool towel blotting his forehead. As he turned his head toward the shadow, he heard a gasp. The shadow got darker and weight pressed down on his chest—fingers scrabbled over his arms and thick hair tickled his chin.

Through cracked lids, he let his eyes adjust and made out a ceramic basin and pitcher. He recognized the hand painted rose instantly. Thaddeus had given it to him that first night in his new home. It'd once belonged to Eric's mother, but the Colonel never told him how he'd acquired it.

"Lucinda?" he croaked, his voice unrecognizable. He squinted in the dimming light of evening.

"Oh my darling! My darling husband!" she cried, hugging him and cupping his face as though he were a fading figment of imagination.

He rather wondered about that himself. "Am I dead?"

"No! Oh darling, no…no." She smoothed his hair back, making soothing noises and studying his eyes as though memorizing them all over again. "Oh! You are very much alive, my husband. God was watching over you."

"But…how did I get here? We were ambushed—" He sat up and something flopped against his chest—a small wooden cross, attached to leather cording tied around his neck. He turned it between his fingers and asked, "Did the others make it?"

"Father got word that over 300 perished," she said quietly. "But the others retreated to safety. The Confederates took most of the wagons and found a stash of Union artillery. They hit another wagon train not long after…but it wasn't nearly so brutal."

Sorrow churned in her hazel depths. "Those poor men. Their families." Her voice cracked. "I'm so blessed that you came home breathing." She nodded at the cross. "I was scared you might yet die when the doctor couldn't find any reason for your coma."

"Coma?"

"Well yes," she said, grabbing hold of his hand. "And the seizures and fevers. Oh, you were too hot to touch. The doctor ordered so many ice baths that I had to buy a half-dozen ice chests. And then came the cold sweats, too."

Eric shook his head to clear his thoughts. "Wait, I-I don't understand. I was shot off my horse—the doctor didn't see that?" He patted his chest over his shirt. "It must have been an infection."

Lucinda's brow dipped. She covered his hand. "Darling, no. You weren't injured as far as we could see. I…I know about the ambush because of Father, but you…"

Her lips moved at a loss. Puzzled himself, he visually prodded her to elaborate.

"You appeared in your bed on April 19th with no trace of injury even though you were listed as missing at Poison Spring." She glanced down before nervously meeting his gaze again. "Father didn't tell them, and he paid the doctor to stay quiet."

"What? April 19th...but I was 600 miles away!"

She nodded.

"And I'm listed as *missing*?" Eric pulled his shirt off. His skin was perfect. No scars. "How could I abandon my unit? I need to—"

She squeezed his hands with firm insistence. "Father wants you here. It's been six months—you'll get a court-martial or worse if you go back now—please, at least write to him first."

Her words knocked the wind from his lungs. He grabbed the sides of the bed until his breath came back. "Six? Months?"

She nodded.

"I feel fine! A little tired, but fine! How did this—" Ivory fangs flashed across his mind. *The demon with the auburn hair and black eyes.*

He slumped against the headboard and groaned. He fingered the cross again, contemplating the irony of Lucinda's belief in God's watch when a demon had saved his life. Cold fear suddenly broke down his back. The auburn-haired demon had said he'd come to claim him. What did that actually mean? What had he agreed to—

Lucinda hesitantly moved from the bedside chair to the mattress, holding her huge belly as though dragging it along. He gasped at the size. "The baby!" he whispered breathlessly.

Her smile made her entire body glow. She placed his hand under her navel and whispered, "Wait."

Thirty seconds passed before he felt a tiny *flick* on his palm. He held his breath and gaped at her in awe. He rose on his knees and leaned over to listen. He could feel its tiny heartbeat fluttering against his ear. "Oh darling! Our baby's grown so much! When will he come?"

"He?" she laughed, lifting his chin and tugging him into a kiss hungry with excitement.

He flinched and momentarily stiffened. She pulled back.

"What's wrong, darling?" she asked. "Is it too much? Perhaps you should lie down."

"I...I'm s-sorry. I don't...feel like myself." He swallowed and shook his head. Where passion and desire had once fired under her touch, he was empty and cold. "Besides, can we…uh? With a baby? It's probably not safe."

Her sagging disappointment struck through him like an arrow. He didn't understand how the thought of making love to his wife could instantly shut off the connection they shared, but the more he thought about touching and kissing her, the more he recoiled internally. His thoughts turned to their baby and the warmth of love returned to his heart.

"I love you, my wife," he said at last, hoping to bring her smile back, if nothing else. "I'm sure you're right—I did just wake up, after all. I should rest."

"Of course, my husband," she said, pressing her palm against the wooden cross. "God brought you home to me. You're my miracle."

☽ ✳ ☾

The oddities of his return continued over the next month. He wrote to the Colonel, who confirmed what Lucinda had told him, and added an order to stay home and out of sight. Members of his Company's initial tour, the wounded, and the discharged would recognize him. He felt like a coward, but couldn't deny that the complications of his new life made returning to his old one impossible.

He discovered most of the changes to his body in the first week. Some were incredible. He was stronger than any man he knew and his senses were heightened to extraordinary levels—he could see clearly almost to the horizon, hear a bird singing nearly a half mile away, and detect the individual components in Lucinda's perfume. Others were a hindrance, like his reactions—or rather, the lack of—to Lucinda's romantic advances. He got ashy burns and blisters under the sun, and severe eye pain with bright light. And then there was his appetite. He was starving but couldn't eat without vomiting—and merely smelling garlic or raw onion dropped him to his knees in debilitating pain.

After a few days of nothing but water, his stamina took a hit and he got belted by his first blind rage. He blacked out and came to dangling a decapitated chicken over his mouth, the taste of its blood saturating his tongue—only it didn't taste like blood as he'd ever known it.

The cook later scolded him for stealing their dinner, telling him that she'd been plucking it when he snatched it from her hands and bolted out the service door like an animal. He'd apologized and waved it off as a tasteless joke, but had run into the study and slumped against the door in fear.

He knew what the auburn-haired demon truly was. What had saved him. What he'd become—a beast to be feared, not a heroic soldier returned home. And he didn't know how to tell Lucinda.

The baby was due in November. The long hours she'd spent caring for him, coupled with her worry over his appetite, had exhausted her. She was on doctor-ordered bed rest. He didn't want to lie, but he had to tell her something to ease her worries.

He knocked on her door one night. Sitting up with a book, she patted the bed for him to join her. He'd learned to control the instinctual cringe of contact, but a different energy—nervous and stiff—kept them both silent. They simply sat together in the flickering candlelight awhile.

Eventually, he sighed. "I know what's wrong with me, but I…I fear it."

She inched up straighter and covered his hand. "Darling, I'll love you no matter what it is. You can tell me anything."

"What if I told you that I'd become a monster?"

"Many women speak of how the war's changed their men," she said quietly, her eyes roaming the darkness. "It doesn't make you a monster."

He licked his lips. "I meant…literally. Fangs of a predator. A thirst for blood."

"Well, I…" Confusion knotted her countenance as she tilted her head in thought. "I suppose, as eccentric as that sounds, you're still my husband, the man I love. I don't see a beast before me."

"Please don't placate me," he whispered. "It's not a metaphor. I should have died—I was shot, bleeding to death behind the wagon train…but a man…"

He groaned and ruffled his hair. "Not a man—not a *human*, anyway—somehow saved my life. And not in the way that a battlefield surgeon would. I 'magically' appeared in my bed before a day had even passed, and yet you saw no chest wounds, no bite marks—nothing."

She hesitantly agreed.

"But I suffered in a way that would have killed a normal man."

Again, she nodded.

"*That man*—" He huffed to steady his voice and hurried out, "I'm like him now. I'm not human anymore. I-I stole that chicken to *drink its blood*…and I felt better afterward…"

His eyes misted. "I'm not the same."

He shook his head. "I'm not…"

Lucinda sniffled and wiped her eyes. "I know you're different now. I do," she whispered. "I've seen it—not, not this *beast* that you describe, but…"

She nodded and visibly swallowed over a lump. "But, darling, you—"

Squeezing his hands, she locked onto his gaze. "You are my husband, and you are not so different that I'd see you as a monster, fangs or not. The heart of a good man beats in that chest same as it did before the war."

He didn't know if she truly believed him, and the only way to convince her meant showing her the monster, but he'd promised himself that she'd never see that side of him. He laid his head over her belly and closed his eyes to the beat of their baby's heart.

"At the very least, please understand that you don't need to worry about me," he said. "I understand what I need. I will be strong for you—I promise."

In the weeks that followed, they tried to live a normal life. Lucinda oversaw the finishing touches to the nursery and Eric wrote to the Colonel. They discussed names—Collette or Victoria after their mothers, or Darien after Eric's grandfather since his father would never be a consideration.

The night of November 4th, Lucinda's water broke. Eric was anxious, as any new father would be, he supposed. As the midwife prepped and they waited for the doctor, Lucinda begged him to stay with her.

"But men don't do that," he insisted, lowering his voice to add, "and what about the blood? What if I…what if it's like the chicken again and I black out? What if I hurt you? Or our baby? I absolutely should not be in here!"

She clawed into his arm, fiercely clinging to him. "We've made it this far! I want you here. I need you here. Please!" She grimaced and squeezed her eyes shut, groaning through a contraction. Her nails punctured his skin and his blood scent snaked up into his nostrils...but it smelled normal—metallic and unappetizing—for the first time since he'd awakened.

"All right, darling. All right. I'll stay." He stroked her hair as she made it through another contraction. To the midwife, he asked, "Aren't they a bit close together? Where's the doctor?"

Maids scurried in and out of the room with blankets and water. He told one to go with the butler to find the doctor. Eric should've been able to hear his carriage at the gate by now, but he didn't hear anything indicative of a traveler heading toward the mansion.

"I want our baby to meet you first," Lucinda said just before her fingers dug deeper into his skin and a throat-shredding scream bellowed throughout the grand house.

The midwife chased the maids out and rushed over, dropping to her knees to check Lucinda's progress. "Oh my God!"

She shoved up her sleeves and yelled for Lucinda to push. A glob of blood gushed over her arms as she maneuvered her hands around what looked like a purple ball. She yelled at Lucinda to push again and shot a look of alarm at Eric.

Fear unlike anything he'd ever felt seized hold of him. He crouched beside Lucinda and whispered encouragements into her ear, bearing down with her through each push. Despite that, he recognized the look on the midwife's face—battlefield surgeons had worn it in the early days of the war, before death became an all-too-frequent occurrence.

Lucinda fell back against the pillows, gulping for air, and the midwife again looked at Eric, bringing her hands up only enough for him to see the umbilical cord wound tightly around his son's neck. Tears scorched his eyes and an involuntary sob escaped before he could cover his mouth.

Lucinda sat up in wide-eyed alarm. The midwife severed the umbilical cord and placed the infant into Lucinda's demanding arms. Sobbing with the whole of her being, she clutched the babe at her breast. A wave of nausea crashed over Eric. He sucked in breaths of sticky, acrid air, and folded himself protectively around Lucinda and their son, who never got to draw a single breath of life.

He kissed the top of Lucinda's head, his tears dripping onto her face and hair. The midwife urgently cleared her throat to get his attention. Feeling dread slither around him like an intimate friend, he peeled himself away from Lucinda. Blood had pooled on the floor and continued to stream out.

"The afterbirth isn't coming—I think it ruptured," she whispered. Her eyes watered as she helplessly confessed, "I...I can't stop the bleeding."

They both looked up at Lucinda who seemed abnormally aware and calm in the face of Death. She drew in a shaky breath and nodded in acknowledgment. Eric returned to her side. He felt hollow inside. Why had Death saved him? He should have died—not her. Not his son.

He curled over her, his jaw quivering as he smoothed her hair from her paling face.

"Name him Darien, my darling," Lucinda said weakly. "He deserves a proper name for a proper burial."

Eric nodded and kissed her again. "That glossy black hair of his is definitely mine, but he's a Hawthorne, through and through. Look at that nose. It's just like yours."

"Dar...ling." Lucinda's eyes rolled back. He patted her cheeks and stared at the midwife, who shook her head.

"Lucinda! *Lucinda!*" he cried.

Her eyelids fluttered and her hazel orbs penetrated his gaze. "I love you always. Protect...Fath—"

Their son's body slipped from her limp arms. Her head lolled to the side. Eric folded himself tightly over her, holding her and howling desperate sobs from the deepest parts of his soul.

☽ ❋ ☾

Orison Crossing, Summer 2006

Eric quieted. That was a raw wound, ripped open and stuffed with salt. He wiped his eyes and sniffled, and Paresh unknowingly mimicked his motions in the darkness. He wanted to wrap his arm around her shoulders and pull her close, but he leaned forward on his knees instead.

"The emotions were quite human, even if I wasn't. At twenty-three years old, I lost everyone I loved. I didn't understand how my life was supposedly better than before, so I channeled my grief into the war, and met up with the Colonel to protect him, as Lucinda had asked. No one knew my name—I'd fought in the Western Theater of the war and he was with the Army of the Potomac in the East. I was merely a shadow in black.

"One night, on the battlefield, I tasted human blood for the first time. My strength and abilities soared to frightening new heights. It felt good, natural, like I'd finally found a place where I belonged—where I thrived. But then the war ended.

"We came home in the summer of 1865, and I had to deal with carnal cravings and the return of civilized life while still hiding the fact that I was alive. I...struggled...to adjust my mindset from violence and to control my urges, but the Colonel helped.

"He used his influence to arrange for human donors. No one questioned his cover that he'd contracted a blood disorder during the war. Of course, the blood bank eventually made life easier, but until then, this 'blood disorder' conveniently passed to each successive Hawthorne descendant.

"In the eyes of the public, the Colonel had lost his daughter, grandchild, and son-in-law within months of each other. He held a memorial service at the mansion and I can't liken the experience to anything else. It's an odd thing, hearing your life summarized like it's over—even more when you're immortal. Those who knew of a man living with the Colonel knew only that. No one outside of the staff ever saw my face. I'm not proud of that dark period in my life, of hiding from my fellow soldiers, or that I needed the Colonel's protection more than he needed mine."

Eric sighed and leaned back. "Within a few months, the Colonel arranged a marriage of convenience with one of the younger household maids, Emily, hoping to gain an heir. He saw to her every need and took care of her ailing mother. She bore him a son—Lucas, your great-great-great grandfather, to carry on the family lineage.

"The Colonel no longer needed my protection and didn't want me feeling indebted, or bound, to him. He generously gave me the property and assets that would have become mine as Lucinda's husband and told me I was free to live my life with no obligation to him—but I could tell he wanted more, so I asked. It took a bit of prompting, but eventually he confessed to wanting me to protect Lucinda's half-brother and the future Hawthorne generations.

"No one was waiting for me. He was the last of my family and staying gave me purpose. Consequently, wherever Lucas went, I followed. In return, the Colonel dictated the family tradition of setting aside a portion of the estate for me in the will or trust of each subsequent generation. It wasn't a binding contract per se, but that is how I came to be the Hawthorne guardian. I am the watcher in the shadows, passed down from father to son—the family's ultimate legacy.

"Lucas married Rebecca and produced Nathaniel in 1887, who later married Elizabeth and had Joshua in 1905. Joshua married Lily, who mothered your grandfather, Senator Daniel Hawthorne, in 1935. From there you already know that the Senator married Sandy and had your father and uncle in 1956 and 1957. Now, there's you, the first female born to the family in four generations."

With nervous eyes locked on her face in the ensuing silence, he held his breath and wondered what would happen now that she knew he needed human blood to survive. She hadn't tried to run away, at least. Still, she said nothing as she peered ahead into the blackness. But her lips were moving. He looked closer. She was counting to herself. That was a new response.

"One hundred and forty-two?" she said at last. "No, wait—you said 1841, so you're older than that." She cocked her head in thought and then slid closer, resting her head on his shoulder. "I don't know what to say. I'm so sorry all those horrible things happened to you. I can't imagine it."

He succumbed and wrapped his arm around her, pulling her against his chest. "I can't say some of those things still don't hurt, but you don't have to apologize or say anything at all. Just know that you can always trust me, and I'll always be at your side." He brushed a lock of hair off her cheek. "Are you tired?"

"A little bit, but this is nice…sitting here with you."

"I am truly sorry that I lied to you."

"Well, it's not like a mythical being pops into existence every day.

It would've been difficult to accept this morning…especially on top of everything else." She smoothed her hand over his chest and traced the outline of the silver cross under his shirt. "Did the man who changed you ever come back?"

"He was there the night I realized what I'd become. He's an arrogant bloke who calls me 'Brother' even though——" he broke off. Jonathan's obsession with him wasn't relevant. "He tried to force me to go with him, but the cross Lucinda put around my neck protected me. I was too weak to fend him off back then, but now my strength rivals his, and the cross repels him if he sees or touches it. The promise I made to him on the battlefield is the only vow I've ever broken. The second chance he gave me restored my faith, despite everything that happened, and that faith protected me when he came to collect my debt."

"Does he still come after you?" The feather light caress of her fingers was maddening. He flattened his hand on hers. Even discussing Jonathan couldn't counteract her temptation.

Eric needed to keep his focus. In all of his history with the family, he'd only revealed the danger of his brother to Andrew, the sole Hawthorne Jonathan had agreed to spare.

Eric sighed. "He's relentless and my insistence on staying here has also necessitated my service. Senseless death trails him." Eric patted her hand. "But it's your family's own odd luck that one male heir carried the name until your father and uncle came along. My brother believes that destroying your lineage will free me from my ties to this world and finally force me to join him…" He deliberately let his voice trail to avoid bringing up the Vampiric Nation or High Council of Elders.

She didn't notice. A troubled expression knitted her brow. "Does that mean he killed my parents?"

Eric had wondered that himself. "Your disappearance aside, there was no indication of a crime. It was a tragic accident at an unmarked country intersection. No stop signs meant both drivers thought they had the right of way, so, by the time your dad hit the brakes, it was already too late. The other driver died, too."

"That's what happened? I didn't know…" She tucked her hair behind her ears and whispered, "Dad saw it coming—how awful."

She snuggled closer, hiking her dress up to pull her knees to her chest. "All that time, watching my family age and die while you lived on—wasn't that hard?"

"Those feelings that I didn't understand with Lucinda were indicators of a new mindset. I loved her and her death broke me for a while—I mourned her like a human—and I stayed close to the Colonel. He'd been like a father to me, after all.

"But I haven't had favorable relationships with all of your grandfathers," he continued. "For several generations, honor and duty bound me to them, not love. Wealth inflated their egos, and they treated me more as a servant and less as family—especially during Prohibition when Nathaniel and his son, Joshua, put me in charge of their security force.

"I didn't care for them. Protecting them was a job that gave me purpose. I constantly battle to reconcile my human heart and vampire blood, but, back then, so many things were frustratingly petty. I almost walked away.

"After a fire killed Joshua and Lily, your grandfather, Daniel, came into my care. He was only an infant…and my chance at fatherhood at been stolen. I began to care again. I realigned the family's values and your grandfather became a great senator. When your father was born, I was drawn to him. It wasn't until he was older that I realized why. That he and the Senator embodied the same spiritual footprint as Lucinda and the Colonel. That similarity not only helped me rediscover life and my humanity, but it saved my soul.

"The Senator never chose which son 'inherited' me. Maybe my natural gravitation to Andrew caused the constant sparring between him and David. I can't say, but standing between them renewed my purpose. Your dad was more than family—we had a tight, platonic bond—so when you were born and Andrew followed tradition, I gave to him a new promise from my reborn heart. My duty to Lucinda and the Colonel no longer drives me.

"For humans, death is part of life. With the few exceptions that tugged on my human heart, the vampire in me has viewed much of it as a job that passes the time. It hasn't always been easy, but I found true happiness when I met your father and…yeah…it was hard to lose him—but worse to lose you."

Paresh sniffled. "You spent your life saving my family and my father ended up saving you. It must have been so lonely. Did you ever fall in love again?"

"No. Attraction between vampires and humans is extremely rare. My brother likens it to humans and apes. But——" He paused in thought, uncertain how to continue.

"There's me," she said quietly.

"Y-yes," he said in a soft voice. Now that he'd revealed his truth, he needed to uncover hers. To know if she'd felt any pain in her jaw or teeth earlier, but he couldn't ask. She was yawning and it was late. "Why don't we talk more in the morning? You're welcome to stay or I can take you home."

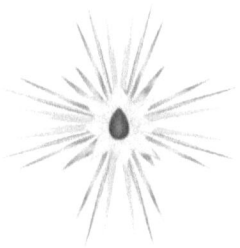

CHAPTER SEVEN: COMMUNION

I

June 22, 1988 23:30 hours

*W*ind moaned a path through Sunset Grove outside the parish. Inside, silence hung over the pews where dozens of townsfolk bowed their heads in search of a miracle. They didn't falter as the anguished groans of a woman filled the sanctuary.

A sudden clattering at the windows broke their concentration. Woodland creatures flocked from all sides, filling the clearing with a sea of feathers and fur. Birds of every shade flew at the glass and animals of every size pawed at the siding. Two men jumped up to bolt the doors.

As quickly as it started, it stopped. The animals froze. The power flickered. The wind intensified, howling through the eaves and lashing the forest. The lights sputtered out and the woman's screams became hysterical cries of woe.

Everyone embraced one another in consolation. Another child had been lost.

Candle flames jumped to life against the blackness in the cramped makeshift delivery room. Dr. Jacobs, Pastor Caine, and Andrew crowded the bed, trying desperately to soothe Felicia. Andrew's eyes swelled with tears, but he wouldn't let them fall and add to her heartbreak.

He feared this might be it. Having a baby was her only desire.

If she lost her dream of motherhood, she'd give up on everything else and her grief would destroy her. The doctors had advised against their fourth attempt. There wouldn't be a fifth.

Felicia wailed louder and harder as she stared in denial at the stillborn infant in the nurse's arms. She feebly stretched her arms out in vain to touch her child. "Paresh!"

She fell back against the pillow and a strangled cry stuck in her throat. Her face lost its color. She grimaced and tried to grab her chest, but her arms and body were limp. The nurse thrust the lifeless bundle into arms hidden in the shadowed corner and joined the doctor in a frantic effort to resuscitate Felicia.

Pastor Caine pulled Andrew away to give them space to work. The tears Andrew had held back streamed down his face as he cried for Felicia not to leave him. The pastor placed his arm over Andrew's shoulders and began to pray. Pressing a hand against his forehead, Andrew bowed his head and wept, unable to watch his wife die.

The room was quiet as the nurse and doctor methodically performed compressions and respirations. Dr. Jacobs exclaimed that he felt a pulse and Andrew broke down sobbing into his hands. Nurse Avondale called for an ambulance.

Andrew knelt next to the bed and pressed his tear-stained face against Felicia's arm. Her absent eyes stared into the nothingness beyond the light. She didn't acknowledge him or anyone else.

No one paid attention to the person veiled in the corner.

At the stroke of midnight, an eerie cry speared the stillness. Every head jerked to the corner. Another uneven scream pealed, followed by another, and another. Stunned faces followed the hidden person's movements as he crossed into the quivering light.

He approached the bed with a squirming, blanketed mass in his hands. As though nothing remarkable had transpired at all, Eric gave Felicia a tender smile and placed her crying baby into her waiting arms.

II

Orison Crossing, Summer 2006

Eric spent the night absorbed in thought. Darkness was his salvation and his internal clock dictated downtime by daylight. Of course, ignoring it took a toll, but he hadn't slept in four days and could easily go weeks without losing stamina.

The hall light popped on and trickled into his windowless room beneath the door. He looked at the girl nestled comfortably beneath his sheet and wondered what Molly would have to say about that.

With a sigh, he ran his finger down Paresh's cheek. He'd intended to retire to the conservatory after tucking her in, but she'd begged him to stay. As he'd lain on top of the covers, watching her sleep, he'd somehow managed to smother the all-consuming desire that burned deeply in his core.

Her essence was stronger when she slept and it'd called to him all night. He was still fighting its allure. Heart and body, he wanted her, but the fear of losing control was a powerful brake. He was supposed to be her protector. Not her greatest threat.

He rolled off the bed and stole from the room, quietly closing the door behind him. Molly was tending to the orchids in the atrium. He slid on his sunglasses and poked his head into the brightly lit room. "Step out here, please."

She set the misting bottle outside the door and pulled off her gloves, spying with interest that he was wearing the trousers she'd selected the night before. "Good morning, Eric. How was your evening with Paresh?"

"Interesting," he replied nonchalantly, ignoring her inquisitive tone. "Head over to the diner or bakery and pick up a breakfast— something without meat—please."

Her eyes darted to the antique comb and hairpins on the ottoman and returned to him with a mischievous jab, her lashes fluttering innocently. "And where shall I deliver this breakfast?"

"Here." He turned away and headed to his study to check in with Chief Hodges. Feeling her eyes on his back, he said, without stopping, "We talked all night. Nothing more."

III

She awoke to darkness, dismissing the night before as a dream of extreme exhaustion and wondering if the day had even happened. But then she heard the unmistakable slap of water in the shower and smelled soap and shampoo too sporty fresh to belong to her. She curled into a ball and hugged the covers to her chest, fisting them close to her face to breathe in the scent of Eric's cologne.

She was in his bed.

The fire of pleasure sparked up her arms and legs and sank into her belly, where it quivered and smoldered. Entering his house, cocooned in silent blackness, his breath breaking unevenly on her neck, his hand sliding below her navel, holding her firmly against his aroused body, the tenderness of his lips on her skin, the timbre of his moan in his throat—

Oh! She wanted to kick and scream! She'd never felt any of this before.

She was grinning to herself when his masculine scent teased his presence beside the bed. The mattress dipped slightly when he leaned forward to nudge a few wayward locks from her face as though he could see through the pitch—which he probably could.

"Sleep well?" he whispered, his voice smiling.

"Mm-hm," she mumbled happily, delighting in each stroke as his fingers worked through her hair.

"Hm…as much as I hate to, I have to go." He sighed. "I'll be back, though. And Molly's here—she brought you breakfast and will take you home whenever you want. She's at your disposal today. I'll come by this afternoon. Sleep in as long as you'd like."

"Mm'kay," she murmured. Her heart fluttered at the thought that he might kiss her, and maybe he contemplated it, but instead he cupped her cheek and sighed again before letting himself out.

Basking in the cloud of Eric's spicy cologne, how could she be disappointed? She drew it in deep and exhaled happily, then threw the sheet back. The bright crack under the door led her to the light switch. The room was surprisingly modern with angular furniture and a platform bed with floating nightstands, the dark woods and brushed steel complimented by black and cream upholstery with crimson accents.

She pulled off the t-shirt he'd given her to wear and freshened up in the en suite. Slipping into her gown, she felt silly dressing up for breakfast, especially in such a form-fitting thing. She was a mermaid in a vampire's house. The thought came and went so quickly that she first felt her cheeks heat up before giggling at the absurdity of it.

She left the master suite and discovered Eric's house in the light of day—not that much made it in. The rich color of coffee covered the walls and the polished granite tiles that gleamed on the floor were almost black. As she made her way down the L-shaped hallway, she passed several closed doors and stifled her curiosity to sneak a peek. After everything he'd told her, she was sure he wouldn't mind, but she wanted to savor every moment of getting to know him *with* him.

The house was silent with no sign of Molly as she stepped into the open kitchen and living area. Muted rays beamed through abstract stained glass over the sink, washing the ebony countertop and walnut cabinets in scarlet light. The minimalist kitchen lacked upper cabinets and shelving, and the stainless-steel appliances looked pristine and unused.

A walnut dining table secured the space across the way with chunky legs that tapered up to the top. Crimson cushions topped the benches on either side, and brushed steel pendant lamps dropped down from the ceiling.

Squares of red canvas dotting the kitchen's far wall matched the larger abstract pieces hanging over the white sectional sofa in the main area. A matching shag rug softened the hard floor, and a plasma television was perched above a long, narrow sideboard that ended at a rustic wooden door.

"Molly?" Her voice was so loud she swore the house flinched. "Are you here?"

The rustic door burst open, lobbing sunlight at the shadowy interior, and Molly emerged. Paresh glimpsed of towering tropical palms and glass panels behind Molly.

"Good morning, Paresh! Sorry, I didn't expect you up so soon or I wouldn't have been hiding in there." She smiled as she pulled the door shut and delivered mercy to the darker space. "Mr. Ravenscroft sends his regrets for not being here. He had a meeting."

"Good morning," Paresh replied, smiling in return. "He'll be back in the afternoon, right?"

"He should be." Molly set her gloves on the sideboard, wiped her hands on her khaki pants, and adjusted her glasses, which had slid down her nose. "Are you hungry? I picked up some fresh fruit and a bagel for you."

"Thanks, that was thoughtful." Paresh followed her to the kitchen and sat on a stool at the bar height counter. She studied Molly as she pulled out a plate and manifested a toaster from somewhere, wondering how much the older woman knew about Eric.

"I can take you home after breakfast. How are you feeling today?" Molly gathered juice and fruit from the mostly empty refrigerator.

"I feel good, actually. Much better than yesterday."

"And how was dinner?" Molly grinned over her shoulder. "Mr. Ravenscroft disappeared into his study so fast this morning, I couldn't ask."

"It was delicious. I had a lovely time last night. Eric and I had a lengthy discussion when we came back here." She watched for a reaction at the slip of his name: Molly paused briefly in selecting a juice glass.

"I see. Did he tell you everything, then?" Molly's back was to Paresh. Her voice was cautious.

"Maybe not everything, but enough. There's a lot to tell…" As Paresh's voice faded, Molly turned, and they eyed each other. After a few seconds, they shared a nervous laugh.

"So you *know*?" Molly arched her eyebrows.

"Yes," Paresh replied with a firm nod, unsure of what to say until she remembered his excuse for staying out of the kitchen. "His appliances look brand new. I suppose they don't get much use."

The tension in Molly's shoulders visibly relaxed. "That's true, but he does entertain guests here, on occasion. I stock the pantry and fridge, and he hires a chef. His clients understand that he dislikes an audience when he eats. They believe him to be very particular. He plays the gracious host, and they enjoy a delicious meal, so they don't mind."

"He has a good system in place, doesn't he?" Paresh asked with an awestruck smile.

"He's had many years to find the best ways to address his needs, but he wasn't as prominent with previous generations as he is now. He easily hid behind a suit or a hat and sunglasses because he was seen only as hired help."

"He said the Colonel had to hide him after the Civil War so no one would recognize him. That must've been so lonely."

Molly shrugged. "I don't think he sees it that way, and besides, things only really changed when he chose to risk more exposure for your father. And even then, he spent as much time as possible working behind the scenes or watching over you and your mother. He started wearing the glasses in public in '91, I think. They make him look a little older, but not enough to have graduated from law school with your dad in '82."

She chuckled. "For a few years there, he tried dyeing the hair at his temples gray, but the color only held for about a month and he got tired of me fussing over him for touch ups."

Molly sobered. "Then you disappeared. He ran the firm on his own at first, but it made his face too public, so he hired Kenshin—and he's a great attorney. I often expected that Eric would stop practicing, but he couldn't help you, so he was determined to help whoever he could."

Molly blew a few salt-and-pepper strands from her eyes. "After a few years, he restricted public exposure and only took cases he could resolve outside of court. He went back to wearing hats and dark glasses to hide his appearance."

"That's so awful!"

Molly's shoulders heaved under a weighted sigh. She quieted as she hit a steady rhythm coring and slicing an apple. "To be frank, his reaction to your parents' deaths and your disappearance, and his choice to build the restaurant, all set him up to be a prominent figure in a small community where most of the families are generational—he put himself out there. They know he's close to Walter and me. They see him when he slips in for services at the Sunset Grove Parish. He got tired of hiding and started coming out more in the last year or so, and once the townsfolk found out he was actively practicing his own cases again—they've kept him busy."

"But they have to wonder? I mean, he's lived here his whole life. How can someone not recognize him or…see it?"

Molly smiled and placed the juice and a plateful of fresh berries, melon, and apple in front of Paresh. "Oh yeah, they wonder and talk! My grandfather even had his own wild theories, but the people who seek his help—which is most of this town—get his help. It's not that they don't see it; they just look the other way. He's good to people, like your dad was, so they're good to him. The only ones he's ever had trouble with are the Fausts, who own most of the farmland here that you don't and contract to farm the land that you do own. I'm not privy to how he handles people like that, but the Fausts are a bunch of stuck up, no good—"

Molly gritted her teeth in a tight smile and pushed her glasses up. "All that really matters is that everything falls into place. I hate to think what would happen if he was exposed—he'd have to leave."

She tapped the counter and swatted the words away. "But that hasn't happened, so let's not dwell on it. Would you like your bagel toasted?"

Paresh bit into a strawberry and shook her head. "So, who's in the know, then?"

Molly sliced the bagel, slathered it with blackberry jam, and placed it on Paresh's plate. "Mostly just Walter, Sammy, Judge Bankman, Sarah Weaverly at The Greenery, Juliet O'Connor at the Orison Crossing Blood Bank, and Kenshin—although he's not entirely clear on the details. Sarah, Juliet, and Kenshin receive generous supplements to their incomes in exchange for their services, but money can only get him so far. Without trustworthy connections, it wouldn't work."

"Are you worried about revealing too much to me, then? Maybe you know something he doesn't want me to know."

"Not at all. You're the Hawthorne. You are privileged to know much more than I do." She wiped down the counters and began washing the few dirtied dishes.

To avoid blurting out anything he may have told her in confidence, Paresh bit into the bagel and glanced around. "Miss Lydia's house was kind of like this, but not as dark. I suppose he likes it that way."

"It absorbs light and reduces glare. He can tolerate small amounts of illumination and sunlight, but he's at home in complete darkness."

Paresh nodded and sipped the juice. Except for the moment with the lamp, they'd talked in the dark all night, and she hadn't noticed any light in the bathroom while he showered.

Molly seemed to enjoy the ability to talk freely with someone who knew the secret she'd harbored for so long, but Paresh worried about saying too much. She focused on the squares of canvas and tried to change the subject again. "I like how the red pops out."

Molly lowered her gaze. "He surrounds himself with it. It's…the color of blood. He never forgets that he is not like us, but he doesn't regret the decision he made all those years ago. He has embraced what he is." She looked up with a curious expression on her face.

"Yet you...I've never seen him look at any woman with the eyes he has for you." She tilted her head back in reflection. "There was a time when I'd hoped to see him look at me that way, but—oh, well—suffice it to say that I let go of that idea ages ago."

Caught mid-bite, Paresh stared at Molly with wide eyes. "What happened?"

The older woman sighed. "He explained that he cared for me but couldn't care in that way. But being near him was and is enough. Truly. It wasn't easy at first, especially since no one else compares to him—" She smiled and patted Paresh's arm. "But none of that matters. I haven't seen the spark of life in his eyes for a long time, and you put it there."

"Do you still love him?" Paresh asked quietly.

"Yes, but it's not like that. Heavens! I'm in my fifties! Could you imagine someone my age pining after a man who looks so young?" She laughed. "He talks a lot about having purpose in life and he is my purpose. My family. I've watched him go through so much, seen how much pain and loneliness he's hidden. Now...now it's beyond time he found someone to share his life with, someone to bring him joy. It's nice to see him happy. You bring out the man in him."

Paresh smiled wistfully. "The heart of a man beats within his chest."

☽ ☀ ☾

Later that morning, Molly drove Paresh home. At the door, she turned a stern gaze upon the girl. "You promise you'll stay inside with the door locked?"

"I know he's worried about me, but you won't be gone long." Paresh looked down at her dress. "I'm going to take a shower and put on something less formal. That's all."

Pursing her lips, Molly eyed her through narrowed slits that demanded more.

Paresh held up her hands. "I promise! I can't pack up the cottage dressed in a ball gown."

"All right, then." Molly hesitantly unlocked the door. "I'll pick up storage boxes and lunch, and then I'm coming right back."

"And I'll be in there, ready to start going through everything." Paresh pointed inside as she squeezed by.

Molly wouldn't leave the flagstone until Paresh closed and locked the door. She waved from the window and then peeled off the clingy dress, eager to hop into the shower's refreshing spray.

Nothing felt real today.

When the water ran cold, she shut the tap off and slicked her hair back with a sigh. For as much as she needed a reset, she couldn't stop thinking about Eric—at his office, at dinner, at his house—or tamp down the butterflies in her belly that he'd lit on fire.

She buried her face into a towel and groaned. She should be grateful for the distraction—she'd left her suitcases in the living room because she still couldn't bring herself to venture into the bedrooms. But that'd go better with Molly and Eric there for moral support—especially now that she knew the truth.

Nostalgia saw the opening and reeled her into a past of happy faces. Her heart bloomed—and ached—at the curve of her parents' lips, but it fluttered at the memory of Eric's. A decade of absence hadn't changed his smile at all, only the way he looked at her. The love she'd felt for him even then had transcended familial affection, but trying to reconcile a childhood infatuation with the heat she felt now—

Slapping her flushing cheeks, she shook her head clear and doggedly kept it blank as she marched out to pick through her meager possessions, selecting jeans, a black camisole, and a lightweight summer cardigan. On the way back to the bathroom, she froze and caught her breath, prepared to fight against nostalgia's gravity again as light poked through the master suite's door at the end of the hall. New warmth sparked in her belly with a compulsion to explore a special place from her childhood.

She hurriedly dressed and gathered her hair into a sloppy ponytail. After scribbling an apologetic note to Molly and taping it to the door, she stepped outside and smiled up at the welcoming sun. There weren't any animals around—the forest had been abnormally quiet all morning. She jogged to the old trail south of the cottage and was surprised to find it beaten and worn.

"He remembered," she whispered, stepping into the forest's

beckoning shade where the sun was powerless against a shield of ash, oak, and maple treetops.

The chill and absolute quiet were otherworldly. Much like her life, she supposed. Eric portrayed himself as a creature born from the nightmares of people thousands of years past, people who may have feared him as a monster. But to her, he was a fairytale prince.

Twisting her fingers around a wispy branch, she smiled sheepishly because that made her the princess. She laughed in delight and twirled in a circle, brushing leaves and twigs with her fingertips before skipping along the path.

The canopy opened to blue sky after about a mile where the trail spilled into the only other meadow in Sunset Grove—the cottage clearing's twin. Nothing but grass would grow here except for the giant silver maple at the center.

She stepped into its shadow, astounded by the base's monstrous girth that had to be at least four times her arm span. Above her head, the trunk split into four main limbs, each with branches that towered more than a hundred feet into the sky. Eric had named it "Grandfather Wisdom" and had once told her that he hadn't expected it to survive when he planted it as a sapling. But it had thrived and grown into a beast of furrowed gray bark—the King of Sunset Grove.

A familiar feeling of serenity fell over her. Tilting her head back as summer's clement air caressed her skin, she watched the brilliant blue of the sky appear and disappear as a sea of sun-kissed green danced aloft.

She was home.

Her child mind hadn't matched Eric's story to the passage of time. She envisioned him planting a tiny sprout more than a century ago, and compared the grand tree's bark, coarse and grooved with age to his smooth skin. She brushed the ragged exterior and an eerie sensation zapped her fingertips. It bit down and took hold, swiftly racing up her arm and neck, twisting its way into her mind.

In the blackness of night, she ran through the forest. Panic gripped her as she looked over her shoulder. A menacing figure in a crimson cloak closed the gap too fast for her to react. He clamped hold of her arm and painfully jerked her backward. As she whipped around, fighting to get free, a silver and black ring shone on his finger. She tried to rip back his hood, but he caught her arm and wrenched it down, securing both wrists with one merciless hand. He pulled a silver dagger from his cloak's folds. The blade glinted as he raised it up and viciously plunged it into her heart.

Her scream echoed throughout the abandoned forest. Panting hard, she wildly gazed at her raised arms, the tree, and the sunny clearing, and began to tremble uncontrollably. She stumbled away from Grandfather Wisdom and fell to the ground, wincing as she landed. Clutching her wrist at her breast, she scooted backward and lifted her eyes, not knowing what to expect. Perhaps a demon peering through the branches would make sense of whatever that was, but she saw only the proud mammoth of furrowed bark and sun-kissed leaves that she'd always loved.

IV

An ominous chill chased her down the path, nipping her heels all the way to the cottage. She threw herself against the door as it slammed shut. Quaking and gasping for breath, she slid to the floor and buried her face into her hands. She desperately wished someone else, anyone else, were there.

The hall clock ticked as she folded in on herself. She hugged her knees close and let the tears fall. The eerie stillness drilled the magnitude of her isolation deep into her psyche. No one was there. No animals chattering. No birds singing. No crickets chirping. No cicadas droning. Only the memory of the cloaked man and that awful blade.

She'd never been so alone. Ever.

The sunlight at the end of the hall, still as cheery as it was earlier, made her realize that her arrival was a carefully orchestrated and thoroughly sugarcoated lie. To call it a homecoming was a joke. How much of a choice had she really been given? What if she'd said no?

Flapping crimson wool and a streak of silver flashed before her eyes. She squeezed them shut, curling into a tight ball, crying, "Go away. Go away. Please, just, go away—"

The door shook under a pounding fist.

She bolted up, heart slamming, feet shuffling backward. Staring at the door, she balled her hands at her sides, pulled in a shaky breath, and exhaled in relief. She threw the door open, expecting Molly.

She raced to smudge tears off her cheeks, but Simon didn't seem to notice, fidgeting as he said he only had a minute to check in, and was wondering if she'd found the lawyer? Rolling her eyes up to wipe them dry with her sleeve, she nodded.

"Well, okay then." He sighed and turned to leave, hesitating a moment to stare at her, but he didn't say anything, just fixed his lips into a grim line and nodded goodbye.

Molly raced up the path behind him and narrowly slipped past as the flattened boxes and plastic bag piled high in her arms began to slide from her grip. "Sorry!" she yelled as she ran by, "but I'm going to lose it all if I don't put something down right now!"

Paresh rushed to grab The Greenery bag before it fell and Molly dropped the rest with a *thud* on the table. She collapsed into a chair with a huff and wiped her forehead. "That was close."

Paresh heard Simon mutter, "Have a good day, ladies," but he was gone when she turned to see him off, so she set the bag down and went to close the door.

She hesitated when Eric emerged from the tree line. Irritation flickered across his face and darkened into a scowl as Simon hobbled along the flagstone toward him, and then tried to scurry past with a simple nod.

Eric stopped the old man with a firm hand. She could only hear Eric's voice in patches, saying, "You…forget…care to explain?"

The rest was too quiet to make out, but for the most part, Eric had Simon on the defensive. The old man's arms shot out in various directions as he spoke, and, at one point, he jabbed a gnarled finger at the black box that Eric held.

Simon shut his mouth and stiffened when Eric's expression went blank. But then Eric glanced up and saw Paresh watching them. He answered the caretaker, patted him on the back, and sent him on his way. He gave Paresh a wide smile and a wave. She bit her lip and ducked behind the door. Her cheeks were on fire. She felt like a child caught spying.

Molly snickered at the table. She stood and began pulling the window shades down. "I guess Eric's here?"

"Shh!" Paresh whispered.

Molly laughed harder. "Why are you whispering? He can hear you!"

Mortified, Paresh stared at the older woman a moment before peering over the edge of the door. Eric was halfway up the path, shaking his head and chuckling. Paresh glanced back at Molly, who was unknowingly mimicking him.

"You two are something. It's entertaining, really. Here—lunch." Molly moved the plastic bag to the kitchen counter and grabbed the boxes. "Starting in the master suite, correct?"

"Uh…yes," Paresh replied, distracted by a scuff on the flagstone as Molly headed down the hall.

Eric poked his head around the door. "Hey there," he whispered. He stepped inside and removed his sunglasses, casting a flash of crystalline blue at her that crammed the butterflies into her throat.

"Ha-h-hi," she croaked.

"Was it better when I was Darien?" he asked with a soft laugh. "You could talk to him, at least. Although—"

He set his sunglasses and the metal container on the sideboard. "You did have trouble walking while staring at him, as I recall."

Her mouth gaped slightly. He was smiling, his mesmerizing eyes holding her gaze steady. The heat of his palms danced on hers. When had he gotten so close? The enveloping musk in his cologne, the scent of the office on his clothes, and his raw masculinity made her heart leap.

"Hm, interesting. I think I like this reaction better." He leaned in and her heart surely stopped, anticipating his lips on hers. She caught her breath and her eyes widened.

His pupils suddenly focused hard on hers and concern bridged his brow. He straightened. "Wait—I'm sorry for teasing you—what happened?"

"Wha-what?" Too stunned to be disappointed, she glanced down at her feet and worked her lip between her teeth.

"It's nothing. Just a nightmare." She cursed the quiver in her voice and forced a smile. "What's in the box?"

"It's a small safe I keep in my car. It's empty—a test," he said dismissively. "Tell me about the nightmare. It upset you."

He led her to the table. "I'm sorry—I don't mean to sound harsh. How about you eat while you tell me about it?"

She reluctantly nodded.

He unpacked the bag and utensils, and served her with a smile, then bowed before slipping into the chair at her side. Listening intently as she recounted the tale between sips of iced tea and bites of cranberry, mandarin, and spinach salad, he didn't say anything until she finished speaking.

"You were alone?" A dark appeared in the crystalline blue.

"W-well, uh, I convinced Molly to get the boxes. I wanted to start early, and I promised I'd stay inside, but then I saw the sunlight and couldn't resist—" She folded her hands in her lap. "I'm sorry. I should've stayed here."

"You have nothing to apologize for. This is your home." Eric leaned back and reached a hand out to her. "Do you have any idea who the man in the cloak is?"

She stole a look at him through hooded eyes before sliding her hand into his. "He seemed familiar, but I've never seen that black ring. It was just a dream, right? Nothing to be worried about?"

She shuddered.

Eric threaded their fingers and gave a reassuring squeeze. "Hey, it's okay," he said softly. "Why do you think he's familiar?"

"Just a feeling." She shuddered again. "Are premonitions a thing?"

"If people could see the future, the lottery wouldn't exist." The darkness in Eric's eyes betrayed his smile.

"Maybe…but supposedly there's no such thing as vampires, either," she said.

"Touché, my dear, but even I cannot predict the future." He genuinely grinned and beckoned for her other hand. "I will not allow any man to bring you harm. Believe in that, if nothing else."

) ✳ (

At the master suite's door, they shared a glance. Hers uncertain. His supportive. He nudged the door. There were no cobwebs or dusty sheets.

Suede slippers waited beside the four-poster bed. Reading glasses sat atop an abandoned book. But change was in progress thanks to the force that was Molly. Piles of clothes and hangers buried the quilt her mother had sewn and embroidered. Flattened cardboard leaned against the footboard while assembled boxes formed a grid over the floor's oak planks. One held her mother's purses, another her shoes, and the other her father's belts and ties.

Molly paused mid-fold. "It's just for sorting."

Paresh nodded as she drifted in, vaguely aware of Eric propped against the doorjamb and of Molly's eyes on her every movement. The pale green of a luna moth's wings on the walls was a soothing match for the creamy chaise lounge and scenic Victorian paintings. She glided her fingers over the vanity's glossy shellac, its antique curves elegant and delicate in contrast to the commanding bed and its ornately carved headboard.

She'd thought the door at The Greenery looked familiar. The engravings were different, but the style was the same. Eric must've hired the same craftsman.

She sat at the foot of the bed. Molly had drawn down the honeycomb blinds under the lace sheers. The room felt oddly sterile, its memories stamped into history. She traced the threaded lines of the quilt, and remembered snuggling with her mother after her father had left for work.

She dabbed her eyes. Memories couldn't reenergize the space. It was time for new life. Grief had given her the strength and resolve to let them rest and live on in her heart. Eric's abandonment had scarred her far worse. Years of not knowing, not understanding, asking why, why, *why*. The reason had changed, but the questions remained.

She admired him—striking in black and white, affecting leisure but emanating a keen awareness—thankful for the truths that had withered her pain and bolstered her strength. Watching him watch her brought on a sudden realization: if her life had changed in any way, their relationship would have evolved vastly differently.

She saw her future in him and knew Destiny had put her on this path, crosscutting the intersections of her life to end with him. The questions faded. She'd gotten home safely. And now she had Eric, and not because of his vows or because she wanted him there. It was Fate. She felt it with all her soul.

As his gaze turned intimately warm, heat rose to her cheeks yet again, and she glanced away with a shy smile.

"Oh!" She caught her breath and reached for the photograph on the vanity.

She was almost afraid to hold it in her hands. If she dropped it, it felt like her childhood would shatter completely, but she hadn't seen her parents' faces in a decade. It was from their wedding anniversary and her father's arms were looped lovingly around her mother's waist. A three-year-old version of herself gripped the pleats of her mother's skirt. They looked so happy.

"I love you both, always." Tears brimmed as she kissed them through the glass. Eric came in and wrapped his arm around her shoulders. She hugged the picture. "I've never seen their graves."

"Oh honey." Molly crouched at the footboard and patted Paresh's knee. "I'm so sorry."

"We can go see them tomorrow if you want," he said with a reassuring squeeze. "Are you sure you want to do this today?"

Paresh sniffled. "I'm ready to put them to rest. Just seeing the picture…I didn't have any photographs of them growing up."

"I bet they're smiling down on you now," Molly said, "happy you're finally home where you belong."

Paresh half-laughed through her tears. "I was just thinking that very thing."

Eric hugged her closer and buried his face in her hair. Molly patted her knee once more and returned to folding clothes. Eventually, Paresh set the frame on the vanity and turned to sort through her mother's dresses after inviting Eric to look through her father's trinkets.

"He had a nice collection of tie pins, since I know how much you love ties," Paresh said with a wink.

Molly frowned and put a hand on her hip. "You didn't wear the tie, did you?"

Eric shrugged and pointed at Paresh. "Her lips are sealed, so we'll never know."

"I'll ask Sarah, then!" Molly threw a slipper at him.

He chuckled as he caught it. "I'll select a nice pin—will that make you happy?"

She arched her brows and pointed at the valet tray on the dresser. "You will take a tie bar, too, young man."

"Yes, of course. And I will wear it."

Molly narrowed her eyes at him, and Paresh stepped in with a mockingly serious tone. "Oh, he'll wear it because it belonged to my father, and I gave it to him."

Molly and Eric both groaned and chuckled, and the former said, "Ah! I like her—she's got you pegged."

They settled into a comfortable groove, packing and sharing memories for hours. They paused to laugh or cry as they cleared the closet, dressers, nightstands, and vanity. With each box moved to Paresh's old room, they emptied the suite of its former occupants until only the core of the room remained intact. The intimate touches of inhabitance were gone except for a few dresses in the closet and the linens on the bed.

Molly left to pick up dinner while Eric brought Paresh's suitcases from the living room. As she put away her clothes, he kicked back on the bed, watching her with eyes that made her heart flutter.

"I have something for you," he said at last. "I'll be right back."

She took advantage of his absence to stuff her bras and panties into a drawer in the highboy. She was setting her brushes on the vanity when she saw him enter through the mirror. The mysterious black box was in his hands.

"You said that was empty."

"And you said I *love* ties." He smirked as she cocked a half grin and suspiciously watched him pull out a thin velvet case. "I can lie, too."

He grinned mischievously. "And I'm better at it since I'm an attorney—classically trained."

He stood behind her and pulled out a silver necklace with a platinum cross. It was elegant and ornate, with intricate filigree scrolls and rectangular, step cut sapphires and diamonds. She gasped as he placed it around her neck and set the clasp.

"Oh, Eric!" she whispered breathlessly. "It's so beautiful!" Admiring it in the mirror, she ran her fingers over the details. "I don't know what to say."

"It's even more beautiful than I thought it would be on you," he said with a wistful glimmer in his eyes. His fingers lingered lightly on her shoulders. "You don't have to say anything. Just…never take it off."

He dropped his hands to his sides and turned away. "I'm working on a theory. If anyone asks about the status of your trust, tell them the paperwork—account numbers, statements, property deeds—everything is here. Simon asked about that safe earlier and I told him I was transporting papers to secure in the basement vault."

"He asked if I'd met with you yet—what's your theory?" She swiveled on the bench as he sat on the bed.

"Let me sort out a few more details and I'll explain everything. Deal?" he asked with a playful wink.

"I suppose." She hesitated briefly and whispered, "As long as you sort them out here tonight."

Shocked that she'd said that out loud, she felt her entire body run hot. It blazed under his stare as he got off the bed. She cringed into her hands, not recognizing the person she became around him.

"Com'ere, Bashful." He pulled her up into his embrace, his heart racing as fast as hers. Nudging her chin up, he leaned in, and she closed her eyes, lifting her lips to meet his.

The front door opened and Molly announced her return.

Eric groaned against her lips and kissed her on the forehead. "Go eat. I'll join you in a bit."

☽ ❅ ☾

Another bag from The Greenery was on the table. So was her missing suitcase.

"They found it!" Paresh rushed over, her disappointment waning—a little. Hopefully she didn't look as red as she felt.

"It was at the office when I stopped by to get the mail." Molly pointed at the bag. "Stuffed roasted portabella with steamed veggies, homemade roll, and house salad with raspberry vinaigrette—all sans garlic, of course—one for each of us."

"Oh yum, it sounds delicious! Thank you!" Paresh unlatched the case and took a step back.

Eric came from the hall, his step quickening when he saw Paresh's face. "What's wrong?"

Pieces of massacred photographs fell between Paresh's fingers. "Who would do this? And why?"

Molly pawed through the scraps. "It's just you and this..." She shot Eric a look of warning.

His eyes darkened slightly. But when he saw the photographs, adrenaline scorched them black.

Behind Paresh's back, Molly mouthed, "He. Had. The. Letters!"

"Paresh," Eric said in a low voice. "Who is this man to you? And what exactly is his name?"

"That's Master Jon—Jonathan Trueblood." Her brow dipped. "Do you...know him?"

Ignoring the question, he countered, "And who is missing?"

"Miss Lydia. Um, Lydia Burke. Why would someone cut her out, but leave him?" She poked through the pieces seeking any remnant of her governess, but the woman who had raised her was gone.

Anger simmered in Eric's gut. Not once had he considered that "Master Jon" might be Jonathan, even given his sudden presence. Paresh had said she felt like her guardians loved her. But—

Jonathan hated humans.

Jonathan hated the Hawthornes.

Jonathan was biologically incapable of loving anything.

Jonathan had "worked" with David.

Jonathan had raised Paresh.

What the hell was going on? Had Jonathan conned the High Council into sanctioning a play that would finish off the Hawthorne line? Why did they even care? Was her symptomology merely coincidental? Or was it a ploy used by Jonathan to get his way at last?

Furious at Jonathan and himself, Eric forced an even voice and asked, "Is anything else amiss?"

Paresh shuffled through the contents. "Everything else is here."

"Molly, gather the photographs and take them to Chief Hodges when you leave," he said. "Paresh, try not to worry. I'm sure this is more about protecting Lydia's identity than scaring you."

Reacting to hints within Eric's comments and actions, Molly gathered the fragments and said, "This man must not want your governess involved in the investigation—you said they were good to you. Maybe she's innocent."

"I wish they'd just taken them then," Paresh said sadly, snapping the latches in place.

Eric took the case from her. "I'll unpack it so you and Molly can try to enjoy dinner."

Before Paresh could object, he disappeared down the hall and Molly loudly crinkled The Greenery bag. With exaggerated flare, she popped lids from black plastic bottoms and slid Paresh's entrée into place. "Voilà, madame!"

Molly directed the conversation and drew out Paresh's childhood dream of using Sunset Grove as an animal sanctuary, a diversion that Paresh not only appreciated, but also dove into eagerly. They were discussing logistics when Eric finally reappeared and joined them.

Hours later, Molly glanced at her watch and flipped the window shade up. The sky was nearly black. "Oh my! If I'm lucky, I can still catch Walter tonight." She shoved the dinner trash into the restaurant bag.

"Thanks for helping me today, and for dinner." Paresh stood with a stretch and yawned.

Covering her own yawn, Molly eyed Eric, who remained yawn-free, and chuckled. "I never noticed that you don't catch those."

"It's a perk." He winked and waited by the door as Molly grabbed her purse. "Paresh, I'll be back in a moment."

"'Kay," she replied. "Thanks again, Molly. Drive safely."

"Goodnight, hon." She hugged Paresh and stepped into the silent night with Eric.

Paresh stared at the closed door awhile, wondering if Eric would really stay. Something about those pictures had hit him on a personal level. And he was taking a long time—maybe he was only going to come back to say goodbye.

She brushed her teeth, stripped off her clothes, and dressed in a pink satin and lace camisole set that she'd left in the bathroom earlier. Facing the master suite alone was still daunting. She slid into her mother's robe and retrieved the candles from the hearth, thinking that if she couldn't see the whole room, it wouldn't be as hard to go in alone.

Shadows lapped at the golden halo that illuminated her path. At the master suite's threshold, she took a deep breath and entered quickly. She eased down onto the vanity's bench and set the candles before the mirror. She pulled off the elastic band and absently ran the brush through her hair, her eyes stubbornly locked on the flames instead of her reflection—or the room behind it.

A prismatic sparkle drew her gaze to the beautiful cross on her décolleté. Fingering the sapphires and diamonds, she marveled at their brilliant internal fire and unexpectedly awoke her own. Longing bloomed deep within her and rushed to her head, fuzzy but firm, dizzying and melodic, and foreign yet comfortable, draping over her entire being like a warm summer cloak of clover and honey.

Slightly breathless, with impassioned heat quivering in her belly, she closed her eyes and doled a lingering kiss upon the cross. She unclasped it, hung it from the drawer pull to avoid catching it with the bristles, and continued brushing her hair, focused on the flames with an intense yearning that she'd never before felt.

V

Eric rapped on the doorframe and hesitantly entered. He stood behind Paresh, watching her, knowing he shouldn't be there but unable to leave. He took the brush and continued the motions for her. He smoothed his hand down the silky length of her hair with each stroke, and gritted his teeth, trying to think of anything other than how much he wanted her.

Their gazes met in the mirror and reflected the same desire. She caught his arm mid-stroke, and dipped her chin to skim the back of his hand with petal soft lips. Her kiss drew out an involuntary moan from deep in his throat. She rose from the bench and stretched up on her tiptoes, eyes searching, lips hovering, her breath hot on his skin, his hot on hers.

He dropped the brush and clasped her hands, closing his eyes with a slow breath out. "I can't…the beast. It…*I* will hurt you," he whispered painfully.

She freed a hand and flattened it against his chest. "The heart of this man controls the beast." Her voice was a quiet spell, a magic she wove like vertigo.

"No…it can't—"

Her breath came faster and hotter, and then her lips were against his, shredding his willpower, and her aura flooded into his with the viscosity of warm syrup, fueling a fire that was already burning out of control. He hungrily took command of her mouth, parting her lips with his tongue, exploring deeply, winding his fingers through her hair, cupping her velvety soft cheek, completely lost in everything that was her.

He drew her up against his aching body, delighted when she

melted into him with a moan, and freed her mouth to kiss her throat's graceful lines, too aware of her pulse hammering on his lips. She threw her head back and curled her fingers into his hair, savoring each kiss and caress.

He tugged the belt loose on her robe as he lavished attention on her mouth once more. His fingers slid down her throat and over her delicate collarbone. He inched the silk off her shoulders until it fluttered to the floor. Enquiring, memorizing, relishing, his hands moved down, lingering over her satin covered breasts, teasing her taut nipples, earning pleasured whimpers. Continuing down her navel, he fanned out to her hips. He began kissing a new trail along her throat, his lips drawing in the heat of her skin. Of her desire. Of the blood pumping beneath the surface.

He tucked her to his chest and stared at himself in the mirror. He feared the darkening eyes that looked back. The beast had heard that tantalizing swish. It was awake. And she was working the buttons of his shirt free.

Her aura snaked beneath the fabric, winding over his skin with a deft, maddening touch. Moaning breathlessly, he watched himself loosen his cuffs and lower his arms so she could shove the fabric off. As it crumpled at his feet, he squeezed his eyes shut tight, desperate for restraint in a body that was acting on its own.

Electric fingers tiptoed up his back and kisses like flames dotted a line from his shoulder to his neck. He gasped as her lips traveled up his throat and over his pulse. The intensity of the pleasure ignited the first tinges of sensation behind his teeth. He straightened and faced the ceiling with a cry, gripping her arms as he fought against the beast prying at the bars of its prison.

Oblivious to his plight, her burning palms slid up his chest. She pushed herself up to his mouth and kissed him, gently at first, and then hungrily. He moaned and let his hands roam beneath her camisole but froze when she pulled back slightly after brushing his cross with her fingers.

Smoothing her thumb over the silver adornment, she admired it with a blend of adoration and curiosity. He watched her with new heat burning in his eyes. She was so beautiful. An innocent pixie enthralled by life. Her touch so delicate. Driven by a gentle spirit.

Her blood so tempting. Swishing faster and hotter...

He threw his glasses onto the vanity. His hands were moving under the satin, firmly gliding up her navel and breasts, pulling the garment off, and discarding it into the shadows. He explored her bare back, cupping her curves as he traveled lower to hike her leg up against his thigh. He pulled her close and leaned into her, aching for her as both a man and a beast. She clung to his neck so tightly that her breathless whimpers rammed his desire beyond the borderline.

Ravenous, he captured her mouth and guided her to the bed without breaking their kiss. As he lowered her to the pillows, he knelt over her and let his lips roam. Her breath hitched as he turned his attention to her breasts, tantalizing each stiff, aching peak with his tongue. Crying out, she arched beneath him, fisting her fingers in his hair.

He relished the feel of her skin as he slid his hands toward her hips at a teasing pace. Slipping beneath the lace covering, he pushed the delicate fabric down her legs and kicked it off the bed. As she feverishly reached for his belt, he propped himself up and helped her remove the rest of his clothing. He settled on top of her, feeling the heat of her naked body against his, her heart beating against his, their auras entangled and stroking with ghostly fingers, and knew the real battle had begun.

He kissed a line across her cheek and nibbled on her ear, asking with a heavy breath, "Are you sure?"

"Yes," she moaned, pawing at his neck and back, sounding as tortured as he felt.

She yielded willingly as he entered her. The pleasure that crashed over him unleashed the beast, but he was helpless, spellbound by her and by lust, thrusting as she moved beneath him. He buried his face in her hair, holding her hips, his carnal moans melding with hers and turning into growls as he waged war with the beast once more.

The curve of her throat called to him. Her whole body was temptation, but her thundering pulse was the ultimate seduction that captivated the beast. It was as powerless as he was against her allure. Lost to despair, he was deafened to the voice of logic that urged him to fight and blinded to the importance of the low rumbling in his throat.

The key was turning in the final lock.

Her pulse erupted and incited the beast into action. As the familiar ache spread along his jaw, he peered at her face and saw the same expression there as the night before. He pressed his lips against hers, parting them, eager to taste her again over his ulterior motive.

Her canines had lengthened. Slightly.

This fully roused the beast and amplified its lustful blood thirst. It roared, arrogantly triumphant, screaming that she'd survive its kiss. The unease that came with losing that duel seeped into his aura as the ache in his chest faded and the pressure mounted, forcing his teeth out over his bottom lip. Everything he saw wore shades of crimson.

Soft hands cupped his face. She kissed him gently, meeting his bloodshot gaze with earnest eyes. "It's okay."

"No. No..." His voice was raw with hot agony.

"I want to know you. To feel all of you. It's okay." She tilted her head back, arching her throat.

His teeth finished adjusting and the pressure broke under the beast's insatiable hunger. He stared at her throbbing throat, craving to plunge below the surface. He ground his teeth against his lips, breaking his skin instead of hers. He couldn't let the monster in him hurt her.

"Trust me." She covered his heart with her palm. Her warm essence seeped through muscle and bone, and, in that moment, the man and the beast became one.

He parted his mouth and lowered toward her throat, unable to stop. Not wanting to stop. The blind bloodlust of the beast was gone. His soul itself yearned for her to make him whole, to bond with him beyond the physical plane.

When his teeth sank into her creamy flesh, she cried out in rapture—a crescendo of ecstasy pulsed throughout her body, pushing her over the edge of orgasm and into the cascades of pleasure that coursed in an unending loop. Swimming in his own euphoria, he held her there as long as he could before he came with her, tightening his hold on her writhing hips as he thrust deep inside.

She tasted sweeter than he'd imagined. Sweeter than the fresh honeycomb he remembered stealing from beehives on summer days as a boy. Sweeter than the nectar he'd sucked from the purple clover that grew in the sun loving prairie. She enthralled him beyond time and space, enticing him to stay in her arms, between her legs, enveloped in her warmth and suckling her ambrosia forever. But he knew, somehow, through that temptation, that heavy lustful haze and its nostalgia that he needed to withdraw from her throat or he'd drink her dry and kill her.

☽ ✳ ☾

Chest heaving, with her blood dripping from his fangs and staining her skin, he watched the puncture wounds heal. He'd forgotten about her healing factor—but she must have known. After living with Jonathan, perhaps she knew more than she'd told him.

Tiny moans escaped her mouth between gasps for breath. He caught a glimpse of her teeth. While not the same length as his, she bore the telltale sign. The fangs of a vampire.

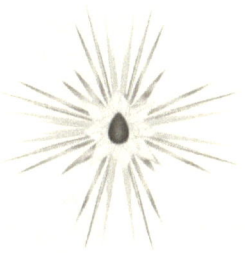

CHAPTER EIGHT: REVELATION

Asleep beside him, gilded in silver and swathed in white linen, Paresh looked like a Grecian sculpture. It was an unusually quiet night. He listened to the soft *whoosh* of her lungs ballooning while shadows crept into the corners to hide from the moon's equally pale light.

It's okay.

Golden curls draped the graceful arch of her neck in a way that hid the subtle throbbing in her throat. He forced his eyes shut. The elegant curvature stayed in his mind, her taste on his tongue, her pulse a tempting rhythm in his ears. He stared at the ceiling with a huff, but his gaze drifted back to her. She was immune to his bite. That nearly drove him to delirium all over again.

He envisioned the blood flowing beneath the milky surface and vertigo crashed over him in merciless waves. He wanted to take her again. To feel her soft skin yield to him, to cushion his fangs as he drew in her luscious—

It's okay.

Sighing, he glided his fingers through her hair, down her neck, up her bare shoulder, along her arm. The frenzied cravings from before were gone. She'd merged the two warring factions of his being. Neither had possessed the power to resist. She'd taken his will to fight, and he'd taken her blood and her purity. The man was the beast and the beast was the man. She'd made him whole.

Twisting her curls around his finger, he gazed longingly upon the delicate reveal of ivory above her shoulder. His love for her created a persistent thirst that blended hunger for blood with lust for flesh until no difference existed. Ecstasy had enveloped him the instant he bit into her throat and heard her cry, bringing him to the edge of rapture. They'd become one, reveling in pleasure too concentrated for humans to endure. She'd wanted to know that part of him and now they shared an impossible spiritual bond. One strengthened by their *similarities.*

It's okay. Trust me.

That coaxing whisper, at that most intimate of moments, had eliminated the existence of two halves fighting over the illusion of control. It didn't matter that she'd willingly offered herself. He should be concerned—and ashamed—not buzzing with energy, thirsty to taste her again.

She deserved better than him. She deserved the truth he'd been hiding from himself since her birth—the truth that she'd forced him to see for himself. If she was an ordinary human, she'd be dead. Most vampires injected an infectious protein into the bloodstream, but he did not. His bite was lethal. Even a kiss could kill.

He sat up with a sigh and swung his feet to the floor, wiping his face and hanging his hand off his neck. She'd come home to life shattering revelations, but he was the one who felt unmoored. He sighed again, heavier, and grabbed his trousers.

He dressed near the window, where the moon sat on high, frosting the forest canopy and brushing trunks darkening shades of silver and pewter while sinking into the ebony interior. It was calm. Quiet. Peaceful.

Unlike his mind.

He turned away and sat on the bed. Wiping his face, he closed his eyes and tried to focus his thoughts. An unwelcome prickle raced across his cheekbones.

So much for the peace.

"What are you doing in here?" Eric glared at the shadows down the hall through the open door. "I sure as hell didn't invite you and this is hallowed ground."

"You requested my presence, Brother, and it *was* hallowed ground. This is not a church." Jonathan stepped in and leaned against the wall. Moonlight glinted off the bejeweled starburst pinned to his lapel. "Besides, you have no authority here—she gave me a standing invitation and she is the property owner. Screw your legalities."

His copper strands flickered like fire as he shook his head. "I should be asking what you're doing in here, but we both know that answer. Why did you summon me?"

"Allow me to plead ignorance and tell me I can trust you with my life," Eric said quietly. "With any conditions that may apply."

"Oh, you mean like with Andrew? I'm not sure I can make that promise twice in a row." Jonathan crossed his arms.

"It worked with Andrew, right? You may be incapable of caring about me as a person, but Heaven forbid something happens to your precious investment—"

"Brother, Brother, Brother." Jonathan tapped his index finger against his lip before popping it into the air. "You were the one who very clearly told Nathaniel that you weren't the only vampire in this big, wide world and look at what happened to him. Not that he could possibly damage you."

A wicked grin split Jonathan's porcelain face. "Oh, no—it was his wife who paid for your life, wasn't it?" He waved off Eric's glare. "You know what I mean. Assurances from me mean nothing. I may lose patience and kill you myself."

"Joshua."

"Excuse me?"

"It was Joshua who tried to beat me, not Nathaniel. And *you* set that fire."

Jonathan rolled his eyes. "Oh right, Nathaniel—how could I forget that wretched ape of a man? He was with Elizabeth, not Lily. Either way." He shrugged. "Semantics. Who cares? They're dead."

"Literally because of you."

A disgusted grunt came from Jonathan's throat. "And thanks to you, *I know their names.* You didn't seem to care much at the time. I may have set that fire, but—"

He grinned. "We both know who—"

"Don't you d—" Eric started to warn.

"Why not? You came so gloriously close! I almost had you. If not for that infant. Ug…your insistence on staying here sickens me. Surely you do it to torture me."

"Yes, because my life is all about you," Eric muttered, leaning forward on his elbows. He visually traced the grain of the floor. Putting their past aside, Jonathan was right—there were others, and they were dangerous.

"She's unique," he said, searching Jonathan for a reaction. "More so than I thought, but maybe you already know that."

Something indefinable rippled through his aura, but Jonathan's affect was flat. "Don't think your parlor trick at her birth makes me feel any differently toward her. She is not one of us."

"Neither of us can deny that my blood gave her life. And even though she never got sick as a child, there was no reason to suspect that she might be changing." Eric glanced at her.

"You're wrong there," Jonathan muttered dryly.

"But she...she's always healed like us—and still does—and I've...no, she's—" Furrowing his brow, Eric met Jonathan's gaze and sighed. "Last night—and again tonight—her canines grew. Fangs, Jonathan. She has fangs."

Jonathan's face contorted first with shock and then with fleeting irritation. Eric had expected to learn that he already knew, but Jonathan seemed genuinely surprised.

"She looks utterly spent," Jonathan spat sarcastically. "*I know what you've done*."

"The silence. That's why the animals have stayed away. You've been here all day spying on her?" Eric licked his lips. "Why? Tell me—why did they tether you here? For her?"

Jonathan brooded in silence, but his aura stiffened. He tried to hide it, but that and his deflection were telling.

"You're the one who tethers me here and you know it," Jonathan snapped. "And now you demand answers when you've been so uncooperative with giving me what I want—"

Eric definitely had Jonathan off his usual firm footing, but this wasn't going in the right direction. His chest felt tighter with each passing second. He clenched and unclenched his fists. If Jonathan didn't know, then the Elders didn't know, and that meant nothing he'd assumed was correct. "As obsessive as always, I see. Even when acting as the High Council's watchdog."

"Oh, shall we do this then?" Jonathan arched an eyebrow and grinned. He tossed his hands out and shrugged. "I have no problem with putting my mission on hold if you feel like succumbing. After all, I will have you one way or another...eventually."

Eric's stomach turned. "I'm so tired of fighting with you on that!

If you could put your orders on hold, you would've fought me harder the other night instead of leaving me alone."

"Harder, you say?" Jonathan's lips widened. "Do you think it's safe to make assumptions like that?"

Eric groaned. "Can we please focus? You're obviously not here to toy with me—not this time."

"You're the only thing that makes this wretched town worth its spot on the map. I *only* come here for you."

Eric scoffed. "The High Council sent you here for me? I don't think so—they know about her, don't they?"

Jonathan's nostrils flared. "Fine, Mr. Serious. You asked, so you tell. How was she after your lustful romp? How was her throat after you bit into it? By all appearances, she's breathing. Dead *women* don't breathe."

"Oh you..." Eric shook his head and forced himself to breathe and calm down before they actually did tear into each other. "Look, she was immune—she healed instantly, like I said. So I...I put her to sleep before she asked any questions. I needed time to think."

Eric ran his hands through his hair, expecting a snarky response. Instead, Jonathan merely stared at a random spot on the bed.

"I saw the pictures," Eric added. "I suppose that was your intent. Did you see any signs, *Master Jonathan*?"

"Irregularities that I'm not at liberty to discuss."

Eric remained silent.

Jonathan eventually focused on him. "She may be more important than the Elders know." His voice was uncharacteristically serious.

"What do they want with her?" Eric demanded.

Hooding his eyes, Jonathan shook his head.

"Answer me! How long have they known?"

"Longer than you. Clearly."

Eric switched tactics before they wound up arguing in circles. "How did you get her away from David?"

Jonathan shot a pointed look at the sleeping girl. "Humans are quite easy to manipulate, as you know. Even more so when they're unstable. Why haven't you asked why *he* took her at all?"

Eric studied Jonathan, knowing that he would share something, if asked exactly the right question. Obviously, David took her for the

Elders whether he knew it or not, but Eric needed more than that. Luckily, he knew a cheat: Jonathan hated to lose his interest—so, feigning boredom, Eric tapped his foot and huffed over his upper lip.

The corner of Jonathan's mouth curled into a snarl. Crinkles cut lines across his forehead as his golden eyes narrowed. "Fine. See how this strikes you. Lucien ordered her removal from your presence. I needed to distract you, and the 'accident' did the trick. The Elders are quite interested in her."

He was not expecting that. Violent tremors shook Eric's whole body. "*You killed Andrew and Felicia for their interest?*"

Yawning in mock delight, Jonathan locked onto Eric's simmering eyes, fully aware of how infuriated he truly was. "I am not permitted to take from the Flock."

"*You could have influenced David!*" Eric growled.

"I am not permitted to influence what is not already there."

"You lying son of a bitch. *David is not of the Flock!*" Eric snarled, bearing his fangs as he stood. "I will never serve the High Council with you, not now. You broke your vow—*Andrew was protected!*"

"Oh, come now, you don't want to wake her—how tragic, her uncle not only kidnapped her, but also killed her parents? Would you inflict that pain on her? Or, better yet—" Jonathan pointed from himself to Eric.

"Maybe she'll see me here with you and wonder about your motives—and you've just regained her trust, too. Tsk, tsk." He smiled fiendishly and straightened to take Eric's attack.

But his threat hit as intended. Eric's mind emptied of everything except his desperation to protect her.

Jonathan started across the room, flicking his eyes up in an offended manner. "*I broke nothing—I did not kill your precious human.*"

Eric grabbed his arm as he passed by, but Jonathan ripped free and smoothed his sleeve as he sat on the bed. Jonathan trapped Eric's gaze and deliberately looked from the cross dangling from the vanity's drawer pull to Paresh's face. "She makes me feel things I've never felt before."

Fear ripped down Eric's spine, flaring into his aura and gaining a rare chuckle from Jonathan.

"I only act on Lucien's orders, you know that," Jonathan said, petting Paresh's hair and exposing her jugular as if to verify that the punctures had healed. "If you'd ever return with me, you'd learn that he only acts in the interest of furthering the Vampiric Nation."

"I don't give a damn about the Vampiric Nation. What does the High Council want with her?"

Jonathan flippantly waved his hand. "I am merely their eyes, ordered to observe and not interfere with the plan in motion."

"What plan?" Eric stood over him, puzzled by the tenderness of his touch.

Jonathan smiled slyly and wagged his finger. "Now, if I told you that, I'd be interfering—it's nothing you can't handle."

"This is just another game to you, but she means more to me than you could possibly understand." Eric sighed in defeat and said, "Give me real answers and I promise to return with you after she is safe."

"You would pay your debt to me in exchange for a favor?" Jonathan half laughed and looked down at Paresh with thoughtful eyes. "Their interest encompasses both of you, actually. They have time to observe you—that's why they haven't sent the hunters, yet—but they had to interfere with her. I had strict orders to make her life as ordinary as possible without influencing her normal human development. David would have killed her if not for my intervention. I put her into the care of a motherly trustee—"

"Lydia. You massacred Paresh's photos to erase her existence. She's been altered." The FBI would find no trace of the governess—she had joined the ranks of the eternal as a reward for her service.

"Consider it an experiment. I provided a safe, controlled environment for her to grow—"

"Under lock and key with her uncle plotting her death?" Eric dragged Jonathan up from the bed.

"She never knew that!" Jonathan growled, clutching Eric's wrist. "Do I really need to remind you who actually saved her life? Because I don't recall seeing you there with David."

Eric released him and watched with sullen eyes as he returned to the bed and resituated his jacket. Leaning against a bedpost, Eric resentfully admitted, "I came to terms with my failure years ago, *Brother*, but I am thankful that you kept her safe when I couldn't."

Jonathan's chin lifted in pride as he resumed stroking Paresh's hair. "The plot to kill her parents was David's revenge, planned long before I received my orders. I knew she'd survive. He only took her because I made him believe that she was special—in a different sense. I am the sole reason she is alive."

Eric was silent, his wounds and grief reopened. He hadn't thought it possible to hate David more. "Where does Simon fit in?"

"Simon is an isolated pawn. David found him drunk in an alley years before he sent him here. David's powers of persuasion and manipulation are rather admirable for a human I must say—" A glimmer of darkness flashed in Jonathan's eyes. "Just ask the man who died in that crash."

Eric clenched his jaw and shot a look of warning. Jonathan held a hand up in concession. "Simon is merely an informant. He's wholly insignificant."

Jonathan sighed. "I have not enjoyed this assignment—too much human interaction—and I had to live with *women*. Do you have any idea what that's like? *Human women?*"

He rolled his eyes. "Who am I talking to—of course you do. Anyway, I'm surprised you let that one to get so close in the first place. Simon wasn't of the Flock."

"Not all who have fallen from the Flock are bad people," Eric said. "Regardless, Simon must have suspected the crash was no accident and that makes him an accessory. I will deal with him."

"Ah yes. You will 'deal' with him." Jonathan snorted. "You'll throw him at that police chief you tote around instead of devouring him like a wolf. Pitiful."

"Don't judge me too quickly. I live in their world and generally play by their rules, but I am not one of them."

A slight smile turned up Jonathan's lips. He glanced away without commenting. After a few seconds, he looked up and grinned. "Do you see what she does to me? If I didn't know better, I'd say I'm in love."

"I thought I was the only exception." But Eric couldn't deny it. He'd never seen Jonathan like this.

"We watched a movie together every week," Jonathan revealed. "She likes monster movies, particularly the black and white films from early 19th century. You know the ones, Béla Lugosi and the lot. She adores him by the way—wrote a report for Lydia years ago."

Jonathan's smile grew, revealing the elongated canines of a true blood. They never completely receded like Eric's did. "She has a special affinity for vampire flicks. And the real thing, apparently."

He said that without a trace of sarcasm. Eric stared at Jonathan as if he'd never seen him before. He tried to imagine Jonathan living a normal life, in a movie theater watching vampire fiction— surrounded by humans. It'd be impossible if not for Jonathan, himself, chatting about it like it was nothing, while caressing Paresh so affectionately. That was equally jaw dropping. The Jonathan he knew would never touch a woman—human or vampire.

He knitted his brow, thoroughly doubting everything he'd thought over the past 24 hours. "Why *did* the High Council order you to take her?"

Glancing up with deliberate eyes, Jonathan clasped his hands in his lap. "They believe the prophecy may be coming true."

Eric went rigid.

"Hadn't thought about that one, huh?" Jonathan snapped his fingers and lifted a smug brow.

"There's the Jonathan I know," Eric muttered, retreating into hopeful thought. If the High Council suspected that Paresh was their fabled savior, the Servator, they'd protect her against any threat— which meant Jonathan's pack was likely closer than usual, too.

Jonathan rose and stood at Eric's side, where they watched Paresh sleep in silence together. Eventually, Jonathan quipped, "Oh, what's that saying? A dead man tells no tales? Well, here's a truth for you— she would've died here with or without David's assistance. Contrary to your belief, she *was* changing and would've stopped aging. The Elders banned child vampires long ago, so there were two orders on the table. Obviously, they didn't kill her."

"Don't play the role of saint like it excuses what you've done. You could have told me." Eric glared at Jonathan again. His guilt screamed that he'd started all of this the night she was born—and Andrew had died because of it. But Andrew had died happy and fulfilled because of it. "What does David have planned?"

Jonathan tilted his head back and shot Eric a furtive look. "He believes that he can become a vampire if he bleeds her to death and drinks her blood, which will therefore grant him the power to complete his revenge by killing you."

Eric blinked. "And why does David believe that absurd idea?"

"I told you already. He's delusional and believes everything I tell him. He'd already figured out that you were involved in her 'miracle birth,' so I built on that and voilà!"

He snapped his fingers again. "The combination of her faith-based delivery and the blood of a demon created a potent mixture not meant for this world, and since your blood mixed with hers, it only affects those in her bloodline—leaving one, lone, person to tap into that power." He stretched out the last sentence with a dark grin and tossed his hand flippantly.

"You have an overactive imagination," Eric said somewhat incredulously. "He bought that?"

Jonathan laughed. "I have to have fun sometimes. He has no idea how it works. And it did keep her alive. His lust for revenge and money took care of the rest."

Eric held back a dubious laugh. Human gullibility sometimes left even him in disbelief. "That's ridiculous. How does he expect to accomplish this or get the estate? There's no way I would allow any of it to happen."

"Since when does truth matter to a madman? I only needed tangibility. I have no interest in his financial affairs. Besides, I doubt that's really his main objective. He's sick."

Jonathan gave another dismissive wave and paced between the bed and door. "He is a puppet of necessity. She's off limits to me—to you, as well. I cannot believe that you, especially, bit a member of the Flock. I thought she'd be safe with you."

"That's no longer your concern, is it?" Eric's guilt stole the intended bite from his voice. He cleared his throat and turned the focus back to David. "Does he not realize that he's wanted by the Federal Government for kidnapping? Or that I'll kill him the moment I see him? He hasn't forgotten that, has he?"

"You aren't as human as you pretend to be, Brother. If you saw life through our eyes more often, you'd be enlightened." Jonathan walked over to the window. "David has no idea how powerful you are. Why do you make me repeat myself so much? It's nothing you can't handle. Besides, he is not of the Flock. Do with him what you want. I have orders not to interfere."

"She said only you could take her from the gated community—

you kept her shielded from view, so no one could see her, which means David knows what you are."

"Of course he does," Jonathan said with a smirk. "After watching you slave away as his brother's guardian, David knew exactly what I was when he met me. He's honestly thought all this time that he's had control over me."

Jonathan laughed. "If that were true, she never would have left the house. I couldn't expect her to develop normally living in a cage. I convinced him to let me take her out. The risks were low since there are so terribly few humans that I cannot influence. You know this, just as well as I." Jonathan untied the crimson bow at his nape and threaded his fingers through his long coppery hair.

"Why does he trust you so much?" Eric asked suspiciously.

"All David ever wanted was what his brother had…which makes two of us, I suppose, since he had you," Jonathan said with an insinuative glance. Before Eric could reply, Jonathan faced the window again. "Yes, yes, I know. Platonic. How could I possibly forget?"

"I don't want to argue—you know quite well that I don't—"

"David willingly invited me into his circle," Jonathan interrupted, his tone growing sarcastic as he gathered his hair and tied the ribbon. "Happy to have a vampire to call his very own." He made a disgusted noise. "As if he has any clue as to just who I am."

He huffed. "He may have wanted your sole attention back then, but now David blames you for destroying his life."

Jonathan turned toward him, his expression smug. "Well. I've told you quite a lot tonight, but don't be fooled. It's her effect and not your pitiful attempt to bargain for information. As tempted as I am to accept your offer, I have my orders. That's not how the Elders want you, but know that when they want you, you will go…or the Vampire Shadow Hounds will drag you in."

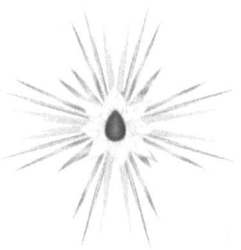

CHAPTER NINE: THE VAMPIRIC HIGH COUNCIL OF ELDERS

Snowblood Square, Arc of True Blood, Treuter Mountains
Devon Island, Nunavut, Canada

June in the Arctic Circle meant the sun barely rose higher than thirty degrees and never set. Another month and a half would pass before dusk would touch the island and even longer before night fell. Even though the Arctic desert teemed with life—sea birds, seals, polar bears, and roaming herds of muskoxen—all attempts at human settlement had failed in the harsh winds and subzero temperatures. That made Devon Island the perfect location for the High Council's chambers.

In recent years, scientists had begun researching the Haughton Impact Crater, formed over twenty million years ago. The environment mimicked that of Mars, so the summer months were active with experiments. Tourists ventured to view the Truelove River and the coasts, the Jones Sound, and the Sverdrup Glacier. The High Council only tolerated the increased human activity because the island was quiet again by winter.

All of the domes, from the Arc of True Blood to the Arc of Ebony Stars in Siberia, sat within the Arctic Circle, hidden away by cloaking technologies far beyond the human mind. The Arc of True Blood was built around the time Leif Eriksson settled L'Anse aux Meadows in Newfoundland, and in the thousand years that had passed, no Elder had left its sanctity. They determined the fate of the Nation and the death of even one could throw the race into chaos. Only true bloods selected for service or the few held in high esteem by the Elders could live there.

Such prestige made the arc a sought-after vacation spot. The Elders granted permits to true bloods for Winter Solitude, an annual festival that celebrated ninety days of darkness over their capitol. The normally opaque walls would fade to crystal to display haunting ribbons of aurora borealis and a blanket of shining stars that made the ice and snow shine.

The High Council generally denied access to anyone of human origin, but the Arch Elder had a special interest in Eric. The other Elders had not known of Eric's existence until Jonathan told the Arch Elder about Paresh's birth. Given the ramifications, his master had convened the full panel—who, upon hearing Jonathan's report, were angered to learn of the secrets kept from them for over a century. However, time constraints forced their attention from Eric to the more pressing issue of Paresh, and, by the meeting's end, Jonathan's orders had come from the Arch Elder, the only man he obeyed with unwavering loyalty.

After meeting informally with him, Jonathan was organizing his thoughts en route to Snowblood Square, the meeting hall at the heart of the arc. The Elders' private dwellings and courtyards, the bathhouse, and guest accommodations dotted the outer perimeter. Designed after traditional Japanese homes, the structures featured sturdy wooden post-and-beam frames and shoji screened exteriors.

Pathways of wood, marble, glass, and stone wove scenic avenues through botanical beds, grassy meadows, and rocky terraces. Zen gardens delivered meditation among rippling pebbles and large stone islands, and reflecting pools stood still and timeless while cascading waterfalls trickled into meandering crystal streams.

Most animals, mammals especially, smelled blood on all vampires. The very essence of true bloods spooked them. Despite this, the dome buzzed with life. Butterflies, bees, and other insects worked the gardens, and speckled koi with flowing fins lived in ponds among an array of amphibian life.

The arc's electronic casing simulated daylight and replicated atmospheric conditions based on the Elders' wishes. Although the sunless sky of morning covered most of North America, time in the Realm of Man did not matter here—twinkling fireflies hovered in a virtual dusk.

Jonathan stepped onto the cobalt glass path leading to his destination: a domed structure with Ionic pillars sitting atop a circular mosaic surround of glass tiles and water. No seams marred its smooth marble exterior. The entrance appeared only for Elders and authorized true bloods like Arc Governors or Squad Commanders.

On Jonathan's approach, a gaping hole appeared that closed after he entered. The building was soundproof with an interior so dark that the eyes of the most perceptive true blood could not penetrate it, vital for anonymity. Jonathan had been here more than any other and no longer needed to count the paces it took to reach the room's center. It was there that he stood in wait.

A light appeared behind him, revealing a herald wrapped head to toe in black fabric with only his mouth exposed. The beam seemed to die the moment it left the herald's frame. He would see what the Elders wanted him to see and nothing more.

"Sir Jonathan of the Arc of True Blood appears before the Vampiric High Council of Elders." The room swallowed the herald's rolling baritone before it reached the walls. "He requests the presence of the True Blood Elders.

"Lady Aurelia." She appeared to Jonathan's right, awash in her own contained ray of light. A silver starburst pin and silk ribbon bar adorned her crimson cloak. The herald announced each elder and they appeared in similar fashion, surrounding him on both sides and the rear. "Lord Raiden. Lord Swaran. Lord Endymion. Lady Lucine. Lord Satiereon. Lady Arria. Lord Ceallach. Lady Rainne.

"The Eternal Blood High Elders shall enter." They appeared in front of Jonathan. "Lady Ambrosia. Lady Lucasta. Lord Corben."

The herald briefly paused. "Arch Elder Lord Lucien the Eternal enters and convenes this council." With Lucien's appearance, the herald faded into darkness.

A source-less glow lit around Jonathan. He placed his hand over his heart and bowed before the High Elders. He lifted his gaze to Lucien as he straightened.

Lady Aurelia spoke first. "Welcome home, Sir Jonathan."

Lord Raiden nodded respectfully. "We await the results of your observations."

When Jonathan spoke, it was only to Lucien. "Removing her from the environment stabilized her, as you suspected. The acceleration of her transformation stalled and eventually went dormant, with few exceptions. She continued to heal quickly, although at a noticeably slower pace, and she remained free from bacterial and viral infections. There were rare instances of major symptoms, which manifested as mild to moderate photophobia."

"And how did you address that?" The question came from Lord Ceallach, on Jonathan's right.

"I informed her that she had migraines with aura effect. I had her wear an eye mask in case she displayed enhanced visual acuity and asked her to rest in a dark room. As I was not to interfere with her development, I waited for her to fall asleep before entrancing her to take blood samples during these episodes. She healed immediately and was unaware of these tests. Not one returned positive results for any vampiric gene, as we know them. However, the abnormal finding does not exist in the human genome, either."

"And what of her tie to the Universal Thread?" asked Lady Arria.

"It dissipated as I moved her away from Sunset Grove. With the exception that she interacted extraordinarily well with domestic pets, she had no special bond with nature or any other organic item. However, that changed on her arrival home."

"How do you account for that change?" asked Lady Rainne.

"I can't. I'm not restricted from entering any portion of Sunset Grove and have no proof of a spiritual nexus, with the exception of the church that once stood there. But something reawakened her transformation. Her spiritual energy spiked and instantly renewed her bond with the Universal Thread. I don't know if this connection ties her to all living organisms or tunes her into them. In my opinion, it's a secondary matter, since we have seen this before with other humans, like the one they call Saint Francis of Assisi. More importantly, there are new developments—"

At Jonathan's pause, the Elders seemed hesitant, nervous even, for him to continue. He dropped his voice a level quieter as though revealing a great taboo.

"I've seen her spiritual aura affect those around her, from animals and humans to…vampires. Just as she tames the beasts of the forest, so does she tame us. I've experienced euphoria in her presence and also believe that I have felt…love. Her effect is much stronger now, especially on him. He fell in love with her the moment he saw her."

Jonathan's voice became firmer. "On two occasions he witnessed her canines extending and, just hours ago, he took her body—and her blood."

Lord Corben's voice cut deliberately through the chamber. "Eric Ravenscroft has bitten a member of the Flock."

The Elders collectively faced Lord Lucien. His impassive crystal eyes were locked on Jonathan. No Elder would dare break the silence between them.

But Jonathan wasn't an elder.

"She survived—no coma, no seizures, no fever," Jonathan said. "She was completely immune and the punctures healed instantly."

Several Elders whispered to each other.

Jonathan ignored them. "I'm most concerned that our former commander is involved. I witnessed his influence in the eyes of a human woman who lived with the subject's uncle. She has incredible willpower and evaded me frequently. I believe she is after the subject's demise, which was the primary reason for moving her into the care of a trustee early on."

The Elders murmured louder.

Jonathan added, "She returned two days ago and is growing stronger. We may see full transformation within a week. However, Eric spoke with a man who reports to the subject's uncle and inadvertently started the plan moving forward. I need authorization to delay implementation for further study."

Lucien remained mute and expressionless, indifferent to the Elders' growing unrest as they spoke to and over each other.

"If *he* is involved, how can we ascertain she's not his means to destroy us?" Lord Raiden demanded. "This does not bode well."

"Why would he attack us in this manner? Eric loves her. Quite possibly, Sir Jonathan, too." Lady Aurelia lowered her hood, revealing the regal features all true bloods shared. Her richly toned garnet hair, braided and piled atop her head, shone like a gemstone and her magenta eyes gleamed.

"Impossible!" Lord Swaran countered, his dark hand cleaving the air. "Only members of the Flock can love. We have been denied that!"

"'Tis possible that she is *the one*," interrupted Lord Endymion, lowering his hood to face the others with intense, chartreuse eyes.

Jonathan glanced at Endymion as he tucked long, flaxen strands behind his ears. Mild-mannered and pensive, Endymion was a pivotal ally. "Why else would he want her dead?"

"The Servator," whispered Lady Lucasta, long ago dubbed "The Gilded Lady" due to her golden features.

"That girl is a danger to the Vampiric Nation!" Lord Ceallach challenged, raising his voice at Lord Endymion. "We have seen no proof of His heavenly hand!"

"What of her birth?" Lady Raine's voice of reason spilled from the shadows of her cloak and clipped the charge in the air. "Or her connection with the Universal Thread? Only those close to *Him* have such a bond. Besides, do we need proof? What of our faith in our salvation? The humans do not require proof to support their faith in Him and we know He exists."

"What about her essence? If she can affect Sir Jonathan, then she can affect us all, perhaps even Lord Lucien," Lady Arria said. "What if she can take control of us?"

Lord Satiereon replied, "A human with such power will cause anarchy among our race." He met Lord Ceallach's gaze with an expression of allegiance. "For our salvation to come at the hands of a human is preposterous."

"But she might be our only chance at salvation," Lady Lucine said. Her brilliant amber eyes twinkled. "We've waited so long, why would we deny our race their due because she's human?"

"Humans do not spontaneously turn into vampires. Our blood is toxic to them. This is the Devil's work," asserted Lord Raiden. He brushed back his hood and held his head high. Modeled after the humans of Far Eastern descent, his dark eyes were angular and almond shaped, and his skin gave off a bronzed glow. "If anybody is the Servator, it is that man, Eric."

Lady Lucine nodded. "Elder Raiden may be correct. Eric is different from any before him."

"Nonsense," objected Lord Swaran. His complexion was so dark that the features of his face blended into the shadows of his hood. "His uniqueness is born of Sir Jonathan alone. I cannot believe our salvation would come from any being other than a true blood."

"Do not forget that Sir Jonathan created him. Under extraordinary circumstances, no less," reminded Lady Rainne. "A true blood can be a soldier of Destiny, but not the bringer of our salvation."

"If Eric is the Servator, then perhaps she was sent to destroy him. She seduced him into breaking the most vital law of the Treaty. We are all at risk now," Lady Ambrosia countered. "Moreover, she's given Sir Jonathan a taste of love. If she'd seduced him instead, we wouldn't be here now to have this discussion—Gabriel would have seen to that!"

"She's an abomination created by a rogue vampire and nothing more! They must both be put to death, as I requested a decade ago!" Lord Ceallach threw his hood back, revealing an angry scowl that matched his fiery mane. He pointed at Lucien, his charcoal eyes beseeching. "You know I speak the truth now, as I did then, milord."

Lucien's empty eyes moved over Lord Ceallach, who faltered and lowered his hand. Lucien blinked and returned his attention to Jonathan.

"She is of the Flock. We cannot order her death," Lady Lucasta scolded. "Mind your tongue, Elder Ceallach. Another outburst will not be tolerated."

"And the fact that Sir Jonathan chose Eric cannot be ignored," added Lady Rainne. "We cannot order his death, either. That is for Lord Lucien to decide."

Jonathan smirked internally. Only Lucien held a higher social station than him. By altering Eric—the only human ever to capture his interest—Jonathan had bestowed upon him the same elevated stature and many of the Elders hated to acknowledge that.

"Even despite his crime? He gave his blood to a human child. Lord Ceallach is correct; she is an abomination! We've been foolish to entertain this 'Servator' theory thus far," charged Lord Satiereon.

"Love?" Lady Aurelia asked. "That emotion rules the actions of humans. What does it mean for us? We have long awaited the Servator, but how will this affect the Nation? We have ruled for so long with our minds alone."

"She will destroy us, not save us," Lord Swaran said with a crestfallen sigh. "What if our enemies learn of her abilities? Maybe that is why *he* is involved."

"She was immune to his bite, yet Sir Jonathan reports that she'll achieve complete metamorphosis in less than a week? How can her body survive that?" asked Lady Arria. "What happens to her soul? Will she be like Eric?"

"She is of the Flock, so how will alteration affect our law? When Eric gave her his blood, she was dead," said Lord Satiereon. "Her soul wasn't even on the physical plane."

"And yet only our intervention prevented the reckless creation of a child vampire." Lord Raiden motioned at Lord Satiereon in agreement.

"'Twould be worth remembering that we don't know how the laws in the Treaty apply to Eric, and that the girl is of the Flock now regardless of her birth. How can a maiden protected by His veil be sent by the Devil to defeat our empire?" challenged Lord Endymion with unusual force.

Lord Raiden began to answer, but Lady Ambrosia cut him off with a knowing smile. "Can you prove she has favor with those behind the Celestial Curtain?" She didn't let Lord Endymion answer. "No, you cannot, and we know well that the Devil has an affinity for using women to do his work. He always comes as a wolf camouflaged as a lamb, so to come to us as a demon concealed behind angelic layers is easily within his power."

"If he wanted her dead, she'd be dead. Not interfering just beyond our reach," Lord Raiden added. "There must be a motive."

A sudden obeisant stillness permeated the room. Lucien was usually a silent, statuesque figurehead at High Council sessions, but his hands were moving. More than 900 years had passed since he'd executed Lord Connall, but the memory was burned into the forefront of every Elder's mind. *Any* movement by their Eternal Lord triggered instant fear.

Lucien lowered his hood. His apathetic manner was intact, but Jonathan knew that revealing his face meant he was disturbed and had reached a decision. He would speak only once.

As the original and oldest of his kind, Lucien's features distinguished him from vampires and humans alike. His hair shone like frosted sterling straight down his back, and his silver-flecked eyes were clearer than quartz crystal. The blue hue of his skin, his pointed ears, and his slim, lofty form—designed for stealth and speed—made him resemble an elven inhabitant of Álfheim more than a modern human. His lips parted, revealing long, ivory fangs that never receded and instead curved to match the contours of his mouth.

"Authorization to delay implementation is denied." His decree was emotionless and unwavering. "Abide by our laws, ensure the girl's demise as planned, and bring the rogue before the High Council."

Jonathan gritted his teeth and glared at Lucien through hooded eyes. Whether they agreed or not, no elder would argue. Lucien's word was absolute. The Arch Elder raised his hood, prompting the others to do the same and return to order.

"As you command, my lord. I request weapons for human use to elude and pacify Eric so he cannot interfere." Jonathan bowed his head out of respect, but didn't bother hiding his disappointment. Lucien's heart beat at the core of the Vampiric Nation. He'd never once been wrong.

Lord Corben said, "Use the VaSH's non-lethal weapons—take anything you need."

The Vampire Shadow Hounds hunted the lawless within the Vampiric Nation. Jonathan already knew what he'd have his pack grab from their armory at the Arc of Mourning Eidolons. The Ivor Bow looked like a crossbow and shot out electric bolts that spread via air current to form a high voltage net. It would knock Eric off his feet and immobilize him with a jolt that was lethal to humans. The Hilja Ring's sound barrier would make the user—vampire or human—inaudible to Eric's sensitive ears. And the Aegis Cloak's protective wool would block an attack from his aura.

Jonathan began to bow to take his leave, but Lady Ambrosia said, "You will, of course, deal with the humans and ensure the weapons are retrieved?"

His lips curved up. "Of course. That's the fun part. They are not of the Flock. I'll organize my pack as a VaSH cleaning squad."

Jonathan met Lucien's vacant eyes once more, silently searching for a reason, but finding nothing. He made a final bow and disappeared into Animus Hollow.

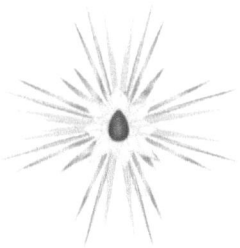

Chapter Ten: Winds of Change

I

Paresh awoke with a start. The air felt wrong—stifling and heavy—and yet the sheers fluttered gently as moonlit shapes stalked shadows that tried to hide in the corners. She eased her feet from beneath the sheet and approached the open window. A full moon sat high above a great white veil that hid the Earth below.

Fleeting motion caught her eye: wispy fog swirled in the wake of a man sprinting toward the forest. She knew those squared shoulders and black hair, and cried out, but the mist swallowed her voice. She threw on a robe and ran after Eric.

Thick, humid air clung to her body. She could barely see the tip of her nose and swatting did nothing. She ran from memory, taking a curved approach around the cottage, and soon made out the dark gray beast of the forest looming over the wall of white.

The haze stuck stubbornly to her until she reached the southern tree line, where it cleared as though afraid of touching the darkness under the canopy. She couldn't find the trail, though, and was only distantly aware of a burning sensation creeping up her spine. Its invisible, fiery talons clamped tightly onto her nape and forced her to turn and face the man behind her.

Crimson fabric draped his form, swirling like droplets of water as though he had materialized from the mist itself. Endless black filled his hood. It wasn't shadow. It was more like his face didn't exist.

She tried to scream. To cower. But she was frozen, trapped in a mental chokehold. Eric's crystalline eyes flashed in her mind and she tore free, her body suddenly moving on its own, legs vaulting into the thicket, breath sticking in her throat, the forest spinning all around. A frantic look back showed the red ghost gaining on her as if she was standing still. He was close enough to touch her shoulder.

Her stomach clenched at the black stone ring on his finger. She shuddered knowing what his other hand held—and what would happen if he caught her—and pushed her legs harder.

The forest fought her every move. Low hanging branches tore her robe, clawed her face, yanked her hair. Thorny shrubs and weeds scraped her legs and ankles, ripping into her flesh. She threw her arms up to protect her face and somehow managed to increase the gap between them.

Relief trickled down her spine like ice water when she glanced back again and couldn't see him. Gasping hard, she slowed to a trot and peered deep into the shadows trying to see if she'd lost him or if he lingered there unseen.

Goose pimples prickled her skin as the forest's unnatural silence and darkness pressed in from every side. She turned in circles. No matter which way she went, she would run into the unknown. But she knew Eric was ahead. She focused on him and pressed on through the punishing thicket.

Eventually, Grandfather Wisdom's towering form came into view. She leaped over the tree line, searching with desperate eyes when she entered an empty clearing.

No, no, no! Where is he?

She sprinted to the mammoth tree and scrambled to hide on the opposite side, heaving to catch her breath. The energy in the clearing felt off. She leaned against the tree and ran a trembling hand through her hair. Her stomach clenched even tighter as the forest's shadows seemed to crawl toward her.

Feeling very much like a lost child, and too aware that she was on her own, she grasped the trunk's course grooves so tightly that her knuckles turned white. Blowing a burst of air over her lip, she flattened against the aged bark and slid to the ground.

Red fabric flapped in her peripheral. She scampered up as the Cloaked Man appeared, and her brain screamed, *Run!*, but her heart wanted to explode and terror pinned her in place. Her fingernails splintered under the pressure of her grip and tremors rocked her so hard that her legs gave out. She couldn't escape now.

Tears blurred her vision as the man towered overhead. A voice in her head yelled that she knew him, but no matter how hard she tried, she couldn't see past the black hole where his face should be.

Foreign words chanted by an entrancing voice burrowed into her skull. Déjà vu nipped at her psyche as his cloak billowed out on a gust and her gaze dropped to the oversized black ring on the hand digging into his cloak.

He withdrew a silver dagger and raised it high. When he brought it down, she felt Death crawl into her body to claim her soul for its very own...

☽ ✳ ☾

Her voice screamed to life and she raised her arms to block the attack. Fabric tangled her in a web and covered her head. It was white...and made from lightweight cotton. She froze, her heart hammering, and held her breath.

It was sunny.

Only when her lungs burned did she peel the sheet off and sigh in relief. She collapsed onto her back, her terror plateauing as the vision played again in her mind. She focused on the ceiling to try to clear it away and realized that Eric was gone.

As the dagger gleamed on replay, she covered her chest protectively and felt the antique cross. Eric must have put it on her before he'd left. She flattened her palm over it and then slid her fingers up to the throbbing spot where he'd bitten her.

The front door slammed. Her belly butterflies fluttered at the thought of seeing Eric. The bedroom door flew open, and Molly burst in wielding pruning shears, hunkered down and ready to fight.

"*Are you okay?*" She peeked behind the door and into the closet, oblivious to the heat burning Paresh's face as she scrambled to pull the discarded sheet over her nude body.

"I-I'm fine!" Paresh stuttered. "What are you doing here?"

"I was outside pruning the roses when I heard screaming." Molly huffed to catch her breath. Her brow crinkled as she studied Paresh's face. "Why were you screaming?"

"I just...it was...a nightmare. That's all. Where's Eric?" Paresh clutched the sheet in her fist, lifting it to her chin.

Molly slapped a hand to her chest, exhaled, and slumped dramatically against the highboy. "Gracious! I thought someone was killing you in here!"

Shoving her glasses up, Molly let her breath trickle out and ran a gloved hand through her hair. "Eric called me over about an hour ago. He needed to talk to Walter and didn't want to wake you."

"Oh." Paresh sagged against the headboard. "What prompted such an urgent meeting?"

"He didn't say, but he hoped to return before you woke up. He said if he didn't, you should go ahead and get ready. He's taking you to the cemetery to…day…"

Molly's voice broke up as a peculiar expression overtook her face. Paresh followed her gaze to the bloodstains on her pillow. Molly's eyes subtly skimmed over Paresh's throat as she looked up and locked her questions behind a smile.

"I'm glad you're okay," she said, retreating into the hall. "Let me know if you need anything—I'm just outside. That Simon does not know how to properly prune roses!"

Feeling self-conscious, Paresh covered her throat and nodded. She hugged her knees and stared at the footboard for a long time. She'd fallen asleep so quickly. She wished Eric were there. She'd hoped to wake up nestled against his chest. To listen to his heart beating as birds sang their summer morning song.

She wanted to forget all about that man with the dagger and that uneasy sense of familiarity. Simply being with Eric would chase him out of her head. But that nightmare was so vivid and real that it felt like a memory. That man wasn't going anywhere. A nagging feeling told her she'd see him again. Soon.

II

"I don't know about this." Chief Hodges shook his head, propping his elbows on his knees as he contemplated the untouched cherry turnover and steaming cup on the coffee table in Eric's office.

Eric leaned against the back of the sofa, his arms crossed. "It's the only way. If your officers get involved, I can't guarantee their safety."

The photos he'd retrieved from Molly last night were mounded innocuously on his desk. "He's too dangerous. His rules may not allow him to kill them, but he can leave them incapacitated. Trust me; they'd prefer death."

Briefly rendered speechless, the Chief sipped from his cup. "So, what, then? I'm just supposed to cast our laws aside? If my officers witness a crime, how do you suggest I tell them to ignore it?"

"Like it or not, your laws don't apply to him. His society is self-sufficient in ruling and enforcement, and he's a dignitary with his own security. I'm only asking you to halt patrols in Sunset Grove. If you see David lurking around town, pick him up," Eric said.

"You can't tell me anything about your brother other than he has long red hair and that I'd know him if I saw him?"

The inquiry was futile, and Walter waited all of ten seconds before sighing loudly in resignation. "All right then. Will your brother pose a threat if he's with David in town?"

"I doubt he'll appear in the village or be seen publicly with any human. The woods are my only concern." Eric pulled a mangled photograph from his jacket pocket and handed it to Walter with some reluctance. He couldn't let Jonathan's photograph circulate amongst the human population.

"Here," Eric said. "For your eyes only—my brother."

Walter gave Eric a hesitant look before accepting it. His head bopped back in surprise. "Wow! Except for the hair and eye color, you guys are like twins…wait a sec'!" Bumping his knee on the table with a groan, Walter stood and jabbed the photograph. "Is this young girl Paresh? When was this taken? If this is evidence—"

"You never saw it," Eric replied sternly. He came around to Walter's side, his expression bleak. "This situation is far more complicated than it seems. Keep your focus on David—and if you ever see this man, keep walking."

Visibly spooked, Walter returned the picture. Both men held still, as though the slightest movement would rip apart the gossamer threads of time and open a hole that would swallow them for eternity.

After several long, silent minutes, Walter quietly confessed, "You know, learning about you was hard enough. It never occurred to me that there would be others or an entire society that lives outside our laws. It makes my world feel a lot less safe."

Eric gave Walter's shoulder a squeeze. "They normally don't

concern themselves with your world. There are extenuating circumstances here that began with me. The last thing I want is for any harm to come to you. If you do as I ask, you won't be in any more danger than you are in the line of duty on a normal day. And besides, this will end soon."

Walter nodded, and, although he didn't appear comforted in the least, patted Eric's pale hand. Thoughtfully clucking his tongue against his teeth, he said, "I can pull the patrols from the woods. When is this supposed to happen?"

Shoving the picture into his pocket, Eric said, "I don't know exactly, but I expect them to make a move anytime."

"Why do you say that?"

"Simon is David's contact here. I'd ask you to keep an eye on him, but I don't want to scare him off. I confronted him yesterday about Paresh's arrival and he rambled about being so excited that he 'just forgot' to tell anyone, so I baited him with a lie of my own. David will appear. Watch."

Walter stared at Eric in stunned silence. Eventually, his cop mind put him back on an old beat. He popped into investigation mode and crammed a piece of pastry into his mouth. "Didn't Simon work for the family before the crash?"

"Yes. Do the feds have any leads?" Eric didn't want Walter to go where his mind was taking him. Revisiting the "accident" at this point would only cause pain without changing the outcome.

"It's piecemeal, nothing substantial about the kidnapping. They've added a slew of new charges, though, which has given their investigation a public face. I take it you haven't been watching the news?" Walter wiped cherry drizzle off his chin.

"I've been a little busy," Eric said dryly.

"Yes, of course." Walter sheepishly dipped his head. "Well, I don't expect it to stay in the national news much longer—land and real estate fraud isn't that exciting."

Gulping his coffee, he set the turnover down to run through it without a mouthful of food. "So, you remember how they couldn't find any long-term residents? Turns out that anyone tied to David moved out six months ago. David lured innocent people into buying fraudulent deeds with real money. None of those couples own their land or their houses."

"Insidious bastard," Eric muttered to himself.

"It gets better: David doesn't legally own the properties, either. When he disappeared back in the day, he transferred his assets to Nicole O'Reilly. I don't doubt that he's in control, but last week, Nicole signed off on a deal that sold the entire compound to a developer who has plans for a buffalo ranch and resort. She and the money promptly disappeared along with David and the original occupants. Needless to say, it's a mess."

Eric grunted. "It's a distraction that gave them pocket change. They're coming here set on the Hawthorne estate. David wants what he believes was his to begin with."

"Such a shame. I can't believe he shares Andrew's blood." The Chief took a final bite and chugged his coffee.

Nodding his agreement, Eric said, "I'm taking Paresh to their graves this morning. She's never seen them."

"Does she know what's going on?" Walter grabbed his hat off the sofa cushion and stood to leave.

"Not yet." Eric followed him into the lobby.

Walter looked like he had another question but didn't ask. He knew by now that he'd get little out of Eric when he kept his answers short. He put on his hat. "If you need anything—"

"I know. Thanks, Old Friend." Eric turned away as Walter left the lobby but swung back around in alarm as a prickling sensation crept along his cheekbones. A man in a tan suit and homburg hat entered the vestibule through the door politely held open by Walter, who mumbled a brief salutation.

As Jonathan removed his sunglasses, Walter's eyes bulged. He shot Eric a look and then took his advice to keep walking.

Eric tensed. Jonathan's aura felt off. Whatever had prompted this daytime visit after last night couldn't be good. Despite his misgivings, Eric invited Jonathan into his office. With a final glance at the empty entryway, he hoped Jonathan hadn't noticed that Walter had recognized him.

Clenching his jaw, Eric sighed and eventually followed Jonathan, pressing the door firmly shut. Seated in Eric's chair, Jonathan kicked back with his feet crossed on the desk. He was looking through a stack of photos in his lap, flinging them onto the desk in annoyance.

As Eric approached, Jonathan tucked one into his interior pocket and threw the rest into the pile.

Eric rolled his eyes and sat in the smaller chair across from his desk, waiting for Jonathan to speak. His brother merely regarded him, staring with piercing eyes that Eric couldn't read. After minutes of returning Jonathan's glare, Eric looked at his watch.

"Why are you so concerned with time? You're too much like them!" Jonathan cried, waving at the wall to indicate people in general. "Why don't you embrace what you are already?"

"I have. When are you going to accept that I'm not like you?" Eric replied coldly. "I have plans today. Forgive me for not dropping everything at your whim."

Icy tendrils of hostility slithered across the desk. The annoyance in Eric's aura formed a barrier too thick for Jonathan's to pass through. It'd been fourteen decades and the argument never changed.

Finally, Jonathan said, "You know, that night in the rain, I thought you looked lonely and bored—perhaps even tired of human behavior? They're never happy with what they have and their lives are far too short for such persnicketiness. They bicker over minuscule things and die without any real accomplishment. I thought you'd realize this when you had nothing to chain you here, that you'd start to evolve higher than them, again. Have you accepted *that?*"

Eric stared at a spot on his desk, unable to deny some truth to that. His vampire blood had influenced aspects of his core being, but his human soul and heart set him apart from Jonathan, and the rest of his kind.

Created in opposition to God, the Vampiric Nation existed outside the Realm of Man with the ability to feel love locked away in their hearts. Their most passionate and intimate moments were entirely devoid of the one emotion vital to caring for others above themselves. They envied the lives of men, but feared that love would weaken them. It was too powerful. They'd seen humans sacrifice themselves for love. And kill for it.

To feel that empty was unfathomable. That alone reassured Eric of his humanity.

"I've gained some perspective, but I will never be the partner you want or expect," Eric said in a quiet voice. He lifted his eyes to

Jonathan's with firm skepticism in his. "Why do you ask? Did you learn nothing last night? You act as though you weren't there—that I didn't see the way you are with her, that you didn't acknowledge what she does to you."

Jonathan's annoyed façade flattened into expressionless stone. "You caught me in a moment of weakness. It won't happen again. One way or another, she will die and free you from your self-inflicted prison. With no one left to bind you here, you'll join me. I just wanted to see if you were ready to accept your destiny."

"First, don't delude yourself—you are not a soldier for my destiny," Eric said. "Second, I have accepted that I am where I should be. And finally, if you're truly in no hurry, then why are we having this conversation, again, now, after you refused my offer last night? If she's really going to die anyway, what does it matter if I go now or stay with her and go later?"

Jonathan regarded Eric with anger rising deep within his pupils. His perception of time allowed for a level of patience implausible to humans, but it quickly tired when Eric refused to behave in a manner befitting his bloodline.

Eric leaned forward, eyes narrowing, voice provoking. "Or do you fear that you're wrong? That she won't die and you've lost me forever? That your ability to manipulate my life has slipped away?"

For once the one in control, Eric tapped his desk and growled, "If that's the case, then you will never lay a finger on her. Because if you try, *I will kill you*. Not even Lucien will stand in my way."

Jonathan's scowl etched deep lines into his smooth skin. He shoved off the desk and dropped his feet to the floor, not bothering to straighten his jacket as he stalked to the door. He turned to glare at Eric once more and spat, "Suit yourself."

Jonathan slammed the door and shook the frames off the wall. Listening to him storm out through the vestibule, Eric leaned back and stared at his vacant chair with darkening eyes.

Jonathan may have directed the brunt of his hostility at him, but he wasn't the cause or they'd be tearing into each other right now. Something, or, rather, *someone*, had changed the dynamics of the game, and the fact that only one man held that kind of power over Jonathan tied Eric's gut into merciless knots.

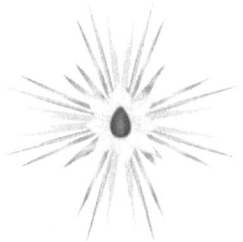

CHAPTER ELEVEN: THE WHOLE TRUTH

On the flagstone path, Eric fidgeted with his cuff links, trying and failing to get Jonathan out of his head. He couldn't make sense of it. The closest he got was Lucien sparing Paresh because he suspected her of being the Servator. Which, if Jonathan's mantra was true and Lucien was never wrong, made Paresh the Vampiric Nation's cherished being, their sacred mother who'd usher in their Second New Age. No one could touch her. Not even Jonathan. And that meant the game was over. It had to be. And yet, Eric couldn't tamp down a nagging fear.

...one way or another, she will die...

Those words, right there. Why had Jonathan phrased it that way? Why had he seemed so desperately angry? He lived to serve Lucien. Could Lucien killing his only dream break a lifetime of loyalty? Eric shook his head. He was missing a crucial detail. He wanted to believe Paresh was safe, but Jonathan had a knack for getting what he wanted, and he hated to lose.

"At least I can handle him," Eric muttered, casting a gaze darkened by contacts over the animals lazing in the grass. He left the canopy's shade briefly wondering where Jonathan was.

Still fiddling with his cuff links, he decided it didn't matter. Jonathan wasn't *there*. He wiped his hands on his charcoal gray trousers and pressed non-existent wrinkles from his Egyptian cotton shirt. It was Paresh's favorite color—a muted shade of blue similar to the sky before it rained at dusk. His jacket occupied its usual spot in the backseat, but he'd worn a tie and Andrew's pin for her.

His nerves began to flutter as he approached the steps. He sighed and ran a hand through his hair. He felt like a hormone-ravaged

153

teenager fumbling at a beautiful girl's feet—except reality was worse. The threats. The danger. All of it was fading. Paresh wholly destroyed his ability to focus on anything beyond *her*, and soon, she'd reduce even Jonathan to little more than background noise.

He jogged up the steps. The memory of her soft body yielding to him raced across his mind and he could taste the hot splash of her blood on his tongue. His heart erupted. His breaths quickened. His vision teetered. Leaning forward on the door, he tucked his chin to his chest, and closed his eyes, trying his best just to breathe, but he was falling down a pit, accelerating with nothing to slow his descent.

You're out of time.

The door swung open and Paresh crashed into him. A surprised cry flew off her lips as he caught her and carried her down the stairs. He set her feet on the ground and gave her a gentle twirl. She looked so delicate in a cap sleeve blouse and linen skirt.

He whistled and kissed her hand. "You look lovely."

"So do you." She smiled sheepishly.

Within her appreciative gaze, he caught a glimmer of darkness. She must have noticed his expression change because she knitted her brow. "Did your meeting with Walter not go well?"

"It was fine. I had an unexpected visitor—forgive me if I'm not myself. I won't let it ruin our day." He gave her a loving smile and put his arm around her waist, leaning in to whisper, "Thank you for last night."

Hot pink color spread over her neck and face. He locked his pupils onto hers, sharing the intensity of his desire with her before kissing her on the cheek. Her hand flitted up to her throat. She bit her lower lip and stole a furtive glance at him. He grinned and took her hand, putting a bit of distance between them as they strolled in silence toward the carriage house followed by her furred and feathered entourage.

He squeezed her hand. He didn't want to let go. Ever.

When they reached his car, he opened her door and then climbed into the driver's seat. For most of the journey, he held her hand and drove on autopilot. Jonathan wasn't quite background noise yet. Both of his visits played on loops, teasing an answer but never revealing it.

He was aware of Paresh looking out the window and peeking at him every now and again. He remembered the dark glint in her eyes earlier and squeezed her hand. "What happened this morning?"

She picked absently at her skirt. "It was another nightmare with the cloaked man and dagger. But…it was so violent and real. I'm…I'm scared I'll actually meet him."

Eric clenched the steering wheel in a tightening fist. He didn't know what this was, but it wasn't a simple nightmare. Freshly bitten fledglings were weak upon reawakening, their thoughts, actions, and dreams susceptible to control by the true blood of their bloodline, and to those at the top of the hierarchy, until they grew strong enough to overcome it.

Jonathan had used the twisted device in the past, but retaining his soul had given Eric immunity from the start. Paresh should be similarly immune. Trying to take complete control of her mind and failing would confirm it, but he refused to wield that kind of power over her. He wasn't discounting Jonathan quite yet, but he sensed that something else was at play. Paresh was not a fledgling.

He forced a tender smile and ran his thumb over her knuckles. "You've been under a lot of stress. Dreams are generally expansions of memory, dredged up by the subconscious. You may have relived your experience at the tree because it upset you and stayed in your mind."

She faced him with a spirited smirk playing over her lips. "Did you read that in a magazine, too?"

"I've had a lot of time to read." He eyed her with curious awe. "How do you do that? Bounce back? You were upset seconds ago."

She shrugged. "It's you. Everything falls into place when I'm with you." Her voice dropped to a whisper. "Don't you feel it?"

"Yeah. I do." He kissed the back of her hand. They shared an affectionate look and fell into a comfortable silence until the Cemetery of Eternal Hope came into view.

Its shield of tall evergreens rose between fields of soybeans and head high corn stalks. Gated at one time, the wide, rocky entrance gradually narrowed to one meandering lane. A single hawthorn tree guarded the entrance next to the remains of a crumbled brick column, and white pines and elms mingled alongside park benches left over from the Victorian days of graveside picnics.

Eric bypassed the oldest section and drove toward newer rows of carved granite headstones in the rear. Flags, plastic or silken flowers and wreaths adorned many of the graves, while roses, daylilies, and peony bushes grew around others.

Eric stopped in front of a nearly black headstone and scanned the surroundings as he circled to Paresh's door. She was transfixed on her surname in granite: HAWTHORNE.

A rose bush embraced the marker with thorny arms and snow-white fingers, and two cardinals contemplated her with cocked heads from atop the arch. The presence of the scarlet male and muted female allowed Eric to relax. Jonathan couldn't hide from them.

Paresh knelt and reached out as if to trace the intertwined wedding rings engraved between her parents' names, but hesitated to touch the surface. When her fingers made contact, she read in a soft voice, "Andrew Michael. Beloved husband, father, and friend. Born March 4, 1956.

"Felicia Elizabeth. Beloved wife, mother, and friend. Born September 30, 1957.

"Entered wedded bliss July 24, 1976. Found eternal peace August 4, 1996.

"May you both find lasting happiness and the love of God with Jesus Christ in Heaven."

She bowed her head as her fingers slid down the stone. Eric crossed his arms and leaned against the car, quelling the desire to hold her. This was her time, Paresh's private reunion. He'd seen them many times over the years. She had not.

Neither moved awhile. Eventually, Paresh's shoulders began to tremble, and tears dripped from her cheeks to the grass. Eric stepped forward with tissues in hand. Jonathan's revelation about the crash had ruptured his own grief, but that didn't matter now—she needed his strength and he would give it.

Eric crouched at her side. She blew her nose and leaned into him, resting her head in the crook of his neck. He stroked her hair and stared at the ground with a mind finally devoid of thought.

The day was comfortable, the sky a bright, cloudless blue, the air still. Not a tree branch swayed, not a blade of grass twittered. Even the cardinals seemed cemented on the headstone. The organic became the inanimate, frozen in time for a moment to speak with the dead.

She sniffed and kissed her fingers, then pressed them to the cold stone. Red-eyed and puffy cheeked, she sat up and wiped her nose. "I missed them so much, for so long. How did you move on without feeling guilty?"

"I don't know that I did." Eric brushed tear-dampened strands of hair off her face. "I poured my energy into finding you and came here to talk to them every week. But life doesn't stop during a crisis—it carried me forward. I didn't feel guilty for that, but I blamed myself for failing you and never gave up. I never will."

She stared at him with misty eyes before surprising him by throwing her arms around his neck. Folding one arm around her, he had to touch his fingertips to the ground to keep his balance.

"Thank you," she whispered.

"I will stand by your side, always. I promise," he said, reiterating the vow not only for her, but also for Andrew and Felicia as he gazed upon their names.

Paresh stretched up to kiss his lips. Her body heat seeped into his clothes and skin, and Eric's heart ached at the thought of ever letting go. He let himself sink into her and nearly forgot where they were.

But, as he'd said, life doesn't stop. The male cardinal cheered and roused them from their dreamy stupor. She smiled at the bird and gnawed her lip as she looked past him over the cemetery's acreage.

"Most of my family is buried here, right?"

"Mm-hm." He reached for her, gently returning her attention to him as he cupped her cheek. She smiled shyly despite the grief in her eyes. He took in a quelling breath and let the unpleasant task ahead temper the urge to kiss her again. "Every Hawthorne I've known is here."

"Do you ever visit their graves?"

"Sometimes. Here, come with me." He pulled her up and led her by the hand over a few rows. Their feathered companions followed. A small American flag stuck out of the ground and a crimson rose bush encompassed a white headstone.

"Senator Daniel Joseph Hawthorne and his beloved wife Sandra Lynn, 1935 to 1975," read Paresh. "My grandparents! I remember coming here a few times every year with Mom and Dad. What happened to them?"

"There was a fire at the mansion—they died of carbon monoxide poisoning before the fire department could get to them. Your mother lost her parents around that time, too. They're buried up north, not far from Chicago," he said. He pointed to the far edge. "Daniel's mother and father, Lily and Joshua, are buried three rows back over there. They died in early 1936, shortly after his birth— another fire."

He led her across the cemetery, pausing once to point out two more headstones on the end. "Those belong to Joshua's father and mother, Nathaniel and Elizabeth."

They entered the old section closer to the front. Many of the graves had meager markers buried in the ground, while others had headstones of varying sizes and shapes, from the traditional curved stones to towering pillars and carved marble tree stumps. All were aged and worn by time, some decrepit and long forgotten. He stopped before a cluster of lightly eroded, moss and lichen covered marble obelisks elevated by stone pedestals.

"As a humble man, the Colonel bought these plots so his Hawthornes could be buried together. The first pair there belongs to Lucas and Rebecca. This one belongs to the Colonel and his first wife, Collette, who died before I met Lucinda. His second wife and your great-great-great-great grandmother, Emily, is buried next to her mother one row back. And that leaves us with—"

He stepped to the left and gestured at a raised obelisk engraved with a lamb resting beneath a weeping willow. Their crimson and tan followers perched upon the pointed stone tip as Eric introduced, "Lucinda and Darien Ravenscroft."

Paresh brushed the coarse stone with her fingertips. "Wife of Eric Ravenscroft, Lucinda Marie, died November 4, 1864, aged twenty-five years, four months, and thirteen days. Infant son, Darien Christopher, died November 4, 1864."

Eric hadn't intended to show her his memorial plot, but the male cardinal's bright plumage caught her eye as he flew down to the standard issue Civil War headstone the Colonel had placed next to Lucinda's grave. Her eyes widened when she saw the name listed among the abbreviations within the badge shaped indentation.

"E. Ravenscroft, Sergeant Company I, Tenth Illinois Cavalry," he deciphered for her. They regarded the empty grave in silence and he wondered if she felt as strange as he did when he saw it. No matter how accustomed he'd grown to his life, it felt odd to know that he belonged in the ground next to his wife and son.

As if sensing his melancholy thought, she squeezed his hand and returned her attention to the epitaph below Darien's name. She squinted as she tried to make out the worn inscription.

"The golden gates did open, a gentle voice said 'Come,' and with farewells unspoken, they calmly entered home," Eric recited from memory.

"Oh Eric, I'm so sorry. I just can't imagine losing all of them." There wasn't a trace of her own sorrow when she looked up, only sympathy for him.

"This row was the hardest until your dad died. I'll miss him for a long time." He pulled Paresh toward him. "But, now I have you. I don't want to visit *you* here."

Her hand fluttered to her throat. She stroked the spot where he'd bitten her. "Did my father ever ask—"

Eric shook his head. "He wanted only to live his life the way he was intended to. And it doesn't work like that with me, anyway." He drew in a deep breath and held it before exhaling and gently saying, "Which brings me back to you."

She blew out a nervous sigh. "Is that why you left this morning?"

"No! No—believe me, I wanted to be there when you woke up, but I needed to meet with Chief Hodges. I'm sorry I left you with Molly again. It won't become a habit, I promise."

He pointed to a wooden bench shaded by a sprawling elm tree. "Let's sit over there and I'll explain everything."

Scarlet wings flapped as their chaperones joined them on their short journey.

Paresh's pulse skipped. "I'm not regretting last night, but what's going to happen to me?"

He waited until she sat before answering, "To be honest, I don't know. There are…complications."

A shadow of anxiety crossed her face. She leaned forward as though to ask a question, but he pressed his finger to her lips. "I know you have questions. This is a long story and I promise to tell you all of it. You'll understand more once I'm finished. Trust me?"

She nodded and crossed her legs, bouncing her foot restlessly as he composed his thoughts.

"You only ever saw your parents as a couple happy in love, but before you were born, they faced nearly a decade of conception hardships and three miscarriages, which, coupled with the deaths of her parents, left Felicia clinging desperately to a dying dream. She'd lost everyone and everything she'd ever loved—like your father, she had no other family—and she didn't want that for her children. They'd both wanted a large family.

"The love she and Andrew shared was true, but it wasn't enough. By the time they lost the third baby, Felicia's grief drove her to the edge of losing her faith. Deep depression weakened her heart. She pushed your father and me away, no matter how much we tried to help. I felt especially guilty, powerless to stop her from forsaking her faith."

"Why?" interrupted Paresh, her forehead creased with sorrow. "My poor mom. I wish I'd known."

"After everything—they wanted to focus on the joyful moments and enjoy life."

Eric smoothed his thumb over Paresh's cheek. "They got the happy ending they wanted—you."

Eric paused to clasp her hand before delving into the true story about her birth—with the parts that her parents hadn't told her. She inhaled a shallow breath upon learning that she'd been stillborn and that Felicia had almost died from a heart attack. But there was more—a truth that he'd only shared with Andrew and Jonathan— that Felicia hadn't even known. As the flickering darkness of that night returned to his mind, a weighted ache formed in his heart.

"The nurse essentially threw you at me in her rush to help the doctor perform CPR on your mom, and, as I watched your father watching his wife die, I just…I felt this urgent need to do *something*."

He leaned forward on his knees and held his head in his hands, sighing. "I bit my finger and swabbed the inside of your mouth with my blood. I…God, as I sit here now, I don't know what I expected to happen—I can't even explain why I thought of doing that!"

He sat back, shaking his head. The ache had turned into a rock. "I certainly wasn't thinking of the ramifications of my actions, and because of that, everything that has happened to you is my fault."

Rubbing his forehead, he said, "The storm had knocked out the power and the batteries were dead in the flashlights, so I'd lit candles. The flames, the complicated birth—it took me back to the night Darien and Lucinda died. All that blood, the fear, Death looming. It was history repeating itself, and more than coincidental to happen to the man who embodied the same spiritual footprint as my wife. I understood exactly how he felt, and it was killing me—"

Paresh swiped his cheek with a soft finger. The tear she'd caught dripped off and darkened a bench slat. He squeezed his eyes shut as her aura gathered around him, eager to soothe his pain.

"You truly are a miracle," he whispered too low for her to hear.

He sniffled and continued, "They'd gone through too much to have Felicia die without her faith. I suppose I was hoping to break the cycle and give them happiness. I was only thinking about them, about the joy they could have, the joy they did have, until…" Eric's gaze drifted into the distance.

Paresh slipped her hand into his and gave a light squeeze. "It's not your fault."

"Isn't it?" He looked down at the birds without really seeing them. The tightness in his chest was ebbing into her aura as if she was drawing it out of him.

"For a long time, nothing happened. I knew Felicia was awake and they'd called for an ambulance, but I was focused on you. I wrapped you in a blanket and was about to give you to your mother, but, at the stroke of midnight, you suddenly cried out. I…I was shocked. Everyone was shocked. But your little scream was the best thing any of us had ever heard. I put you into Felicia's arms and her smile made all of us cry. She wouldn't let you go even when the paramedics came. Her dream had finally come true and nothing was going to get in the way of her love for you."

This time, he squeezed her hand. "See? For the first time in years, your parents knew true happiness. Felicia's health never fully recovered, but they both remained thankful right up to the moment they died."

He emptied his lungs with a huff and tilted his head back. The afternoon sun bounced off the elm's leaves and a clement breeze brushed his skin with mild summer heat. He drew in even breaths and dropped his gaze to Paresh, who eyed him sympathetically, with tears drying on her cheeks and seemingly no idea of her aura's power over him—or that it existed at all.

She inched closer and stroked the nape of his neck.

"I told Andrew that night, but he didn't want Felicia to know. She wouldn't have loved you any less, but he wanted to let her enjoy a pure miracle, not the one tainted by vampire blood—not that he was ashamed. He didn't want her to worry. After what I'd gone through with Lucinda, I understood the toll of stress too well.

"So instead, *I* worried. I watched for side effects but you thrived. You had my skin tone without sun sensitivity, you never got sick, and—animals aside, of course—you developed like a normal, healthy child—with one exception. If you were ever injured, you healed nearly instantaneously. I first noticed it when you received your infant vaccinations. Neither your mother nor the doctor noticed how quickly the tiny punctures healed since they covered the blood spot with a bandage."

He tossed his hand up. "But when you were four, you followed a rabbit into the west side of Sunset Grove where there's a break in the terrain from a dried up creek bed. It didn't take long for me to find you, but when I got there, you looked back and tripped down the gully, landing on a broken bottle. It...it was one of few times I ever saw you cry.

"A shard broke off in your hand. It looked serious. I thought your mom would kill me if she saw it, honestly." He half laughed. "I pulled it out and the gash healed. You searched for the cut after I wiped off the blood and thought it was magic. So, I convinced you to keep it our special secret. Do you remember?"

"It seems familiar," she said, "but it's not something I would've recalled on my own. I had no idea—I mean, I've had superficial cuts that seemed to heal quickly, but I thought that was normal."

Eric shot her a troubled look. "What did you think about the punctures last night?"

She fingered the pulse in her throat and pleasure rippled through her aura. "I thought that was you. Don't vampire bats have some sort of anesthetic in their bites?"

"No—it's an anticoagulant, so the punctures *won't* clot."

"Then it was me?" She arched her brows in surprise and tapped her sternum.

Eric nodded. "I'd hoped you'd get a normal life, but I can't deny that you're undergoing a change. But it's unlike any other and started at your birth, not last night."

He tapped his forehead, trying to think of a way to explain something he didn't understand himself. He decided to start with what he knew.

"Okay, well, I'm not a bat, obviously—and I can't turn into one either." He chuckled at her blushing smile. "Most vampires secrete an infectious protein into their saliva that attacks the human body when injected into the bloodstream. It triggers a cataclysmic immune response, and some people are too weak to fight it off, so they die, but the survivors turn into vampires.

"My case was typical for survivors, although it took longer than usual. While I was in that coma, my body was fighting against my brother's bite, spreading like a disease throughout my system and altering my physiology to meet my new needs. It's probably best compared to a caterpillar's metamorphosis in the cocoon.

"You, on the other hand, are unique in the history of the world, born of human parents and vampire blood, which is toxic and destroys tissue from the inside out…similar to how a spider's venom works. Until two nights ago, I didn't suspect that you had changed, but then your teeth—"

He fell quiet and shifted to face her, gripping her hands tightly. "Did you notice the change in your teeth? And if you had no idea that you'd heal, why did you tell me to trust you last night? How did you know what would happen? I could've killed you."

She drifted into thought and slowly answered, "I had a weird pressure in my jaw, I guess. I-I can't really explain what I was feeling because I felt like my body and mind were disconnected from each other, like I could sense energy coming from you and knew what you wanted—what you were—when you kissed my throat."

She hurried to add, "But I wasn't scared. It felt natural—*right*. It wasn't until after you left the room that the separation of mind and body faded. I began to wonder what was happening. I blamed the alcohol until you came out and told me—"

She bit her lip and sighed. "I mean, come on—I thought was going crazy or had jumped into an alternate reality. Maybe I'd fallen asleep—it wouldn't be the first weird dream I've ever had about you, but…when I felt your heartbeat, I knew. I believed you then, even before I turned on the light."

She cupped his cheek and raked his skin lightly with her nails as she pulled her hand back. He caught it and threaded their fingers, and a loving smile lifted her lips. He heard her heart skip a beat as she briefly lowered her gaze.

"Last night, I knew…what I wanted…even though I barely felt in control of myself. I needed to finish what we'd started. *It had to happen.* It was instinctual."

Rose color spread along her cheeks as she faced away and closed her eyes. A light sigh fell from her lips and her pulse jumped as though replaying the night in her mind.

"I…" she started gently, "could feel the turmoil in your heart last night. I don't know how. You were fighting to hold yourself back and something awakened in me that wanted you to give in. It was desire. Not logic—I didn't know I'd heal. I expected what happens in the old movies, you know? You get bitten and change? And that's what I wanted."

She met his eyes. "With no regret."

The intensity in those steel gray orbs made *his* heart skip a beat. He swept his thumb over her cheek. She licked her lips.

"I don't have the answers, but the events in my life, my uncle—it's like Fate brought me back to you to focus on the future. I feel like we've fulfilled part of our destiny—like we were meant to be together—and I realized that if I hadn't gone away as a child, you'd be my surrogate father instead of Master Jon. A-and I…I just can't imagine that. I'm glad it's not like that. I…I still feel you…*here*." Her pulse jumped as she stroked her throat.

Eric couldn't resist. He tilted her chin up and kissed her deeply, covering her hand over her throbbing jugular. When they parted, he leaned his forehead against hers. "Maybe he's right," he murmured, not meaning to say the words loud enough for her to hear them.

"Who?" she whispered, gliding her fingertips down his nape.

"My brother." Eric sighed. "I need to back up to the beginning, to the very beginning, and tell you something that's not recorded anywhere in human history."

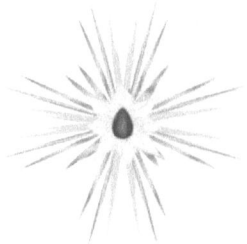

CHAPTER TWELVE: OF VAMPIRES AND MEN

I

"In Genesis, God made the heavens and the earth, the waters and the land, the plants and the animals, and the first man and woman, Adam and Eve, who were sent to care for the Garden of Eden with one limitation: do not eat fruit from the Tree of the Knowledge of Good and Evil.

"They lived in peace until God's most powerful angel, the seraph Lucifer, came to the woman as a serpent and enticed her to eat the forbidden fruit. God banished Adam and Eve from the garden, and although Lucifer remained in Heaven, he fell from grace and became man's accuser.

"Lucifer's growing jealousy and hatred made him plot a rebellion against God and the children of Earth. Modifying God's design, Lucifer created a creature that only barely resembled a man, and gave him a more devilish and sinister form as a hunter with the heart of a beast, sharp fangs, and heightened senses. He had a lean body designed for strength, stealth, and speed, and could rend a man from his limbs barehanded. This being fed on the blood of humans and began his tour on Earth nearly four thousand years ago. Lucifer named him Lucien.

"Lucifer stepped lightly in Heaven so God wouldn't know what he'd done. Thus, Lucien walked the Earth as a being created with intention, yet living without purpose. His instincts drew him to the battlefields as man fought for power and land where he was an efficient killing machine that cut down both sides.

"Lucien had the capacity to develop emotions and evolve

psychologically, but a thousand years of wandering on his own left him stoic and lonely. He didn't care about eradicating humans. He merely saw them as prey and hunted by night to survive.

"Meanwhile, humans continued to sin and reproduce, so Lucifer redrafted his plans. Lucien was powerful, but his appearance prevented him from mingling among the sheep, so to speak. So, Lucifer melded the best attributes of Lucien with God's design and mankind's appearance. He named this second creation Jonathan— ironically meaning 'Gift of God'—and gave him to Lucien as a companion and subordinate.

"Another thousand years passed. Jonathan knew why he'd been created and relished killing and destruction. It was Jonathan's ruthless bloodlust that caught the eye of God and alerted Him to Lucifer's treason.

"God confronted Lucifer, who accused mankind of being sinners unworthy of His love. By then Jesus Christ of Nazareth was preaching God's word to the land and would later die to pay humanity's debt for Lucifer's accusations. But, during His lifetime, Jesus witnessed Lucifer's second fall, from Heaven to his sphere of influence, the Earth, where he roams until Final Judgment, when God will send the wicked to burn in the Lake of Fire—or, rather, Hell.

"Enraged, Lucifer decreed that his walking wrath would march upon fields stained crimson by death. Jonathan and Lucien were nearly as powerful as angels with potent, lethal bites. Lucifer traded varying amounts of their prowess for the infectious protein and created slightly weaker foot soldiers that could alter humans to inflate their army's ranks. He called them vampires and ordered them to devour the children of God.

"Lucifer knew his vampires would starve and wither to ash after they obliterated mankind, but Lucien and Jonathan didn't. They took his orders and controlled his army, and thus, Lucifer's Holy Rebellion moved from Heaven to Earth as the Great Holy War.

"God sent His Heavenly Host to protect and aid mankind in battle, and permanently stripped Lucifer of the power of creation. Both sides suffered casualties as their armies dwindled. For a long time, the War was stalemated.

"But those with the power of creation cannot ignore free will. Just as Lucifer chose to rebel against his master, so did the vampires.

"They realized their ultimate fate and evolved away from carnage. Many yearned for the peaceful lives of men. They wanted control of their destinies instead of living a life in servitude to a creator who wanted them dead, too.

"Lucien called for a truce with the Archangel Gabriel. After they discussed the terms and Lucien had garnered Gabriel's trust, God allowed him to beg for forgiveness. God did not speak to him directly and the light of the seraphim guarding His throne burned so brightly that Lucien couldn't see Him.

"Instead of destroying the vampires as a whole, God suspended judgment and permitted Gabriel and Lucien to draft the Treaty of the Lasting Peace. Lucien agreed to abide by God's rules until their intentions were deemed noble and worthy of His judgment based on individual merit.

"The vampires then withdrew from a war that battles to this day. Since Lucifer and the fallen still roam the Earth, God's terms demanded no contact with the vampires' former commander or his subordinates.

"The newly formed Vampiric Nation didn't receive the life it wanted, but it was given a promise of better things to come—if earned. Vampires were to walk the Earth in their present forms and coexist with the Realm of Man outside of God's watchful eye and love. Just as God forbade Adam and Eve to eat the forbidden fruit, He forbade the vampires from stealing from His Flock.

"However, God does not forsake people. People forsake God. It was unspoken and unwritten, but the vampires understood that the Treaty didn't cover those who had fallen from the Flock, like those under the influence of Lucifer or those who had lost their faith."

Eric paused and fisted his cross. "That is how my brother was able to alter me when I was dying—I had given up on God."

He met Paresh's gaze with deliberate eyes. "So you can see why I couldn't let your mother forsake Him, to give up His protection and love. If she had died without her faith, her soul would've descended to Hades, and she and Andrew would've been parted forever. But preventing that sad ending was beyond my power."

"Except it wasn't," Paresh said softly. "You gave them a great gift."

He reflected on that night but still didn't see it the way Paresh did. "At least they both had their faith in the end."

Scratching his head, he leaned forward on his elbows. Soft fingertips glided across his back.

"What did God promise the vampires?" Paresh asked in the same quiet, cushioned voice.

"His grace, which would make them eligible for Final Judgment—if they honored the Treaty and didn't catch His eye. But there was a problem, because no vampire possessed a soul for God to judge. You see, God created mankind to populate the Earth until Final Judgment, so humans are born with souls, but Lucifer created shells empty of divine spirituality. Even though vampires can feel lust, they cannot love or bear children.

"So, God gave the vampires souls, but tucked them away within their hearts, along with the emotion of love, and gave the promise of a savior, dubbed the Servator, capable of unlocking their hearts to provide the lives they desired.

"Finally, He wiped the Great Holy War from human memory, altering history to reflect instead the march and fall of the Roman Empire, and left only the faintest memory of the undead who feed on the blood of the living—thus giving birth to vampire mythology.

"When Lucien returned to the physical plane with the Treaty in hand, the Vampiric Nation began its First New Age. Those created by Lucifer called themselves true bloods. Many had survived the War by commanding fledgling vampires on the front line, therefore shielding themselves from the swords of the angelic army.

"With the possibility that a single rogue could doom the entire Nation, Lucien ordered the race to the Arctic Circle where they lived in technologically advanced domes called arcs. At first, Lucien and Jonathan retained their status as Commanders, but when Lucien began to appoint Elders for the High Council, Jonathan stepped down. Serving the Nation meant never leaving the arc's sanctity. Instead, he became Lucien's eyes and served him directly.

"Lucien appointed the Council members by order of creation and divided them into factions with their own subset of duties. The Council then instructed the Vampiric Nation to address Lucien as 'Lord Lucien' at all times. Lucien's widely revered, but even the Elders fear him. As his sole companion, Jonathan is the only witness to whatever emotion Lucien may show.

"So, for the past thousand years or so, they've governed themselves without God's assistance, careful not to draw attention to themselves by Him or humans alike. The High Council created the Vampire Shadow Hounds—the VaSH—a hunting force capable of capturing and subduing rogues, lethally if necessary—to enforce the ironclad terms of the Treaty.

"Meanwhile, Jonathan roams the globe, enjoying a freer existence given his social status and intimate relationship with Lucien. He may abide by Lucien's request to treat the Elders with respect, but he sees himself as above them—he is their elder by at least a thousand years, after all—and they, in turn, regard him much as they do Lucien, as they did during the War.

"If Jonathan visits Lucien and brings up something of importance, Lucien convenes the High Elders and, rarely, the full council. Incidentally, *you* became an item of such interest that Lucien involved the entire High Council."

Eric met Paresh's wide eyes with guilt in his and gave her a moment to process the gravity of his words. He felt unusually drained. Recent events, surging emotions, and lack of sleep were weighing on him heavier than usual.

She gaped with her mouth slightly open. "How d-did *Jonathan* find out about me?"

Eric groaned internally. Down by his feet, the cardinals tipped their heads up as though equally interested in the answer. He curled his fingers around the photograph in his pocket but didn't pull it out. "By my choice, my brother has been my only contact to the vampire world. He alone has told me their history, rules, limitations, and capabilities.

"We share a fickle relationship, and I wouldn't call him a friend, but he is necessary, and he has a special interest in me. He tries to persuade me to appear with him before the High Council, but I always refuse. He can't force me to go, because like you, I am unique.

"My soul was not locked away during metamorphosis. Unlike all other vampires, the conditions of the Treaty do not limit me. I can step onto holy ground, speak of God, wear a cross, and enter any place I choose without an invitation. I exist in the Realm of Man under God's guidance; therefore, I am the only vampire who can pray and feel love.

"I am a vampire who exists inside God's Flock and is therefore off limits to the Vampiric Nation's governing body. I already had the High Council's attention. They fear that acting against me will break their rules, so they've placed me under the watchful eye of my brother until I choose to go with him.

"They know about you because I told him what I did. As I said, I acted impulsively that night, allowing my emotions to take control without considering the consequences. I'd hoped to learn that it'd happened before, but it's the opposite—it's impossible to bring dead humans back to life, let alone transform them with vampire blood. I should have known—or at least suspected—that he reported my confession directly to Lucien."

He pulled his hand from his pocket and cupped the same photograph he'd shown Walter. Without letting her see it, he said, "This is Jonathan. He wasn't designed to alter humans and never had the desire to do so, yet I alone intrigued him and became the exception. In his long history, I alone survived his lethal bite." He swallowed hard and watched her with grave eyes as he handed the picture over.

"Jonathan 'Trueblood.' Better known as the Second Born of the Vampiric Nation, Sir Jonathan of the Arc of True Blood."

Paresh paled and caught her breath as she looked upon the face of the man who'd raised her. Eric saw tears glistening and heard her breath shake, but forged ahead, pointing to the pins on Jonathan's jacket. "I imagine that you never saw him without these."

As she shook her head in a daze, he pulled a small case from his other pocket and flipped it open. Cushioned between layers of black velvet inside lay a shiny silver pin, nearly two inches in diameter with jagged spikes of varying lengths shooting from the bejeweled center, glittering with diamonds and a sparkling ruby. It was identical to the one on Jonathan's lapel.

"This is the Star of the Vampiric Nation. Given the nature of their creation, the true bloods have a vast understanding of the dimensional planes that make up Heaven, Hades, and Earth. Though barred from entering the spiritual realms, they can cross cut between them and the physical world. This pin is more than a symbol of allegiance—it's their key to instant travel around the world, giving them access to the Arctic domes at will. This is how Lucinda found me suddenly home when I should've been several states away in 1864.

"Every member of the Vampiric Nation has one and each one is encoded with security information that restricts or allows access to the arcs. Though worn in conjunction with the star, the ribbon bar simply sets the true bloods apart from their inferior replicas. Given the circumstances of my alteration, Jonathan gave me one of those, as well. He does not regard me as a mere imitation of himself."

Eric snapped the case shut without showing her the second pin and returned it to his pocket. "He came to me last night while you were sleeping and filled in many of the mysteries surrounding your disappearance. I'm not justifying what he did by any means, but you deserve to know that he saved your life.

"My blood was changing you over the years and he thought you would eventually stop aging. In accordance with their laws, the High Council would've ordered your immediate death. But, you were a child of God and they couldn't ignore the signs of Heavenly involvement—the blood of the only vampire in God's grace gave you life and you were born on His hallowed ground.

"Simply put, the Elders believe their prophecy may be coming true and that *you* are their long awaited Servator. He took you away to halt your symptoms from progressing, but he didn't say how he did that."

Eric rubbed his face and sighed. "I initially thought you were linked to the sacred ground at the cottage, but then Jonathan...well now that the church is gone, the land's no longer restricted. But *something* about Sunset Grove fuelled your transformation—I saw it. It's like you siphon energy directly from it. All those animals knew you were coming. They lined up moments before you arrived. You even said that you feel a connection there, that you felt removed from nature in Kansas."

Garbled sounds came from Paresh's throat as she struggled to find her voice. Tears dripped onto the photograph and the bench's slats. "M-Master J-Jon...I...oh my God, no, he's your *brother*—they...*what?*"

She drew in jagged air through trembling lips. "I-I c-can't even—

171

Master Jon is your brother."

She shook her head. "*This is too much!*" she cried, waving the photograph. "He never cared for me at all, did he?"

She searched Eric's eyes. "You said he hates humans." Tears gushed down her cheeks as her voice caught in her throat. She pointed to her heart. "I'm hu…man, b-but I loved him. I did. *I loved him.*"

The photograph fell to the bench as she sobbed into her hands. Eric gathered her in his arms and kissed the top of her head. "I believe he cared for you, Paresh, and after last night, I truly believe that he still does. You *aren't* human and he's known that longer than I have."

"I'm not…human. *Oh my God!*" She sat up, horrified, sniffling, and smacking at the moisture on her cheeks.

Eric dug into a pocket for a tissue. She took it and blew her nose. Shaking her head, she picked up the photograph. "But how could I not see it? In ten years, I should've noticed that he didn't get older!"

"Humans who see each other every day don't realize the effect time has on their bodies until they look at photographs and see the passage of time. You were too close to notice. I mean, you were younger, but you didn't notice with me, either, not until you saw an identical face a decade later that you expected to be older."

She offered an unconvincing nod and huffed out another breath. Her brow dipped and she looked from Eric's face to the photograph. She held it up to study them together.

"How weird—I see it now. Why I was so confused. He did pull me from the car that day…but what does that mean?"

"He saved your life," Eric said quietly. "He was there when I wasn't."

Stuck on the photograph, she said, "You talked to him—did you ask? Did he kill my parents?"

"He did not."

"O-okay." Chewing the inside of her cheek, she exhaled unsteadily through her nose and glanced from the picture to Eric. "It's really uncanny. Your faces are nearly identical—"

"It's purely coincidental. We are not actually related," Eric said more emphatically than he'd intended.

Scrunching her face, she gave Eric a questioning look. "Back up—you were there the night I came home?"

"I wasn't sure how to approach you at first—"

"N-no, that's not it." She fell into thought and Eric stayed quiet.

The male cardinal chirped and flew up to her knee. She focused on him with a peculiar expression on her face.

Shifting her gaze between Eric and the bird, she said, "They're not like this outside of Sunset Grove. They fall back when I leave."

She stared at the bird as though ransacking her mind. "I don't know that I'm this...*Servator*—that's a bit much—but I can't deny that something is happening to me. The thing is, I've been surrounded by the woods without feeling any different. In fact, regardless of where I am, if I'm not with you, I feel normal—well, as much as I can, given, well, *everything*."

She tossed her hand back like it didn't matter. "Everything really does fall into place when I'm with you—life slows down, I can think clearly, and I'm emotionally stronger. My spirit feels uplifted. Eric—I only feel that way with you. Sunset Grove is special, because I do share a connection with it, but—"

Not noticing his incredulous appearance, her eyes drifted to the wooden slats as her thoughts gained momentum. "You were there. I felt you when I came home, but I blamed it on the storm and my nerves. Then, at your house, when you first noticed a change, we weren't near the woods."

She glanced up sharply. "When Jonathan took me from here, he took me from *you*. Think about it. You have a soul and you brought life to death. Isn't that like turning water into wine? Maybe I'm just proof of your power. Why aren't they looking at you?"

"Maybe they are." He removed his glasses and wiped his eyes. He propped his foot on his knee and stretched his arm across the back of the bench. "I don't think Jonathan specifically mentioned the woods—I must've inferred that because of my own suspicions. But he did say they're watching both of us."

Eric nudged the bird from her lap onto his finger and truly began to understand the depth of their connection. He hadn't touched a living animal in a very long time. "All living things project an unseen aura—with humans, it's their spiritual energy. For us, it's a symbiotic manifestation of emotion, another means of assault. It can act as an entity separate from our subconsciousness and consume energy from others around us."

The moments he'd been touched by her aura flashed through his mind and he thought over her words, carefully concentrating on her insistence that she only felt different with him. And then it hit him.

"My blood gave you life, but it had nothing to bond with when it entered your body," he started slowly, "so, it remained linked to my energy and never broke its tie to me. In that case, removing you from *my aura* would've slowed your progression. You must need a constant supply of my energy for your vampiric cells to stay active."

He straightened. "And since Jonathan altered me, we share similar DNA. He must've sustained your needs enough to keep the cells dormant without dying. Maybe the High Council—or rather Lucien—suspected this all along."

With barely a breath's hesitation, he whispered, "Your essence calls to me, and to Jonathan, too. He was completely different than I've ever seen him. So kind and gentle—your aura does something to us, like it does with them." He nodded at the bird.

"I can't guarantee that I'm right, though," Eric said, sagging slightly, "not even Jonathan knows Lucien's innermost thoughts and you have his focus, not me."

Not knowing what to say next, he draped his arm over her shoulder and closed the gap between them. The breeze toyed with their hair as he gaped at the bird on his finger and she studied the photograph. She seemed content, so he drifted into thought.

The miracle of her birth was undeniable, but it wasn't the first. Jonathan altering him was. Eric was the only lethal vampire not created by Lucifer. He didn't carry the infectious protein, was stronger than the true bloods, shared Jonathan's persistent thirst, and was an equal match for Jonathan in combat.

Normally, altered vampires were at the bottom of the hierarchy, but Eric was Jonathan's equal in the chain of command. He hadn't shown Paresh his ribbon bar because of the silver stars that designated the bloodline and status he shared with Jonathan. No other vampire could claim that high honor.

Not that Eric considered it an honor.

He'd only seriously contemplated joining Jonathan in the 1930s while in Joshua Hawthorne's service. He credited Joshua's infant son, Daniel, as the reason that he stayed in the Realm of Man, but it had more to do with Jonathan and the way he looked at him. Jonathan didn't see him, or want him, as a brother in the human sense of the word, and Eric did not share his desire or appreciate his advances.

Eric was also aware that his presence would force beings thousands of years old to treat him as nobility—and he expected that might not sit well with many of them. Jonathan regarded the blood in his veins as special, but Eric did not. Paresh was the only special thing in his life, and he doubted he'd been alone in that church corner that night.

The sheer number of unknowns pointed to an epic event looming on the horizon. A force had driven all three of them to veer from their context of normal to take risks with extraordinary results. Paresh knew she walked her destined path—perhaps he and Jonathan traveled alongside her. An odd coupling to be sure, but who better to protect the Servator than two of the strongest creatures in the Realm of Man?

Lucifer thought he'd cursed the Earth with his bloodthirsty creation—how ironic for God to use Jonathan to bestow His promised gift. Eric had often felt like a coveted chess piece in Jonathan's games and wondered why God had given him a second chance. But he was beginning to see the bigger picture—that he had broken a repetitive historical sequence and taken compassion on a human couple at the right moment. He'd given life where none should've existed.

She was their chosen one, not him.

The male cardinal cocked his head and whistled nervously to his mate. They took off in a spooked flurry. Eric wondered what had taken Jonathan so long.

The cemetery's sacred soil would keep him out and, thankfully, the photo was distracting enough to keep Paresh deep in thought. Eric looked beyond her and found Jonathan in the soybean field not far from where his car idled up the road. Jonathan glared past Paresh as though she wasn't there. Distant animosity radiated from his aura.

Eric narrowed his eyes. *Why are you so focused on me now?*

Tired of the game, Eric stared equally hard at Jonathan and said to Paresh, "Jonathan is—or was—under orders to keep you safe until you got home, and told you to meet with me right away in case David showed up. But I suspect that his orders have changed."

Facing Paresh, he softened his expression and firmed his voice. "Jonathan was my unexpected visitor this morning and our conversation was not pleasant—"

Eric felt Jonathan's aura withdraw. Jonathan marched to the car and nearly ripped the door off before his "chauffeur" could reach the handle. Jonathan's pack rarely appeared to Eric, but he'd seen that red and black uniform before, and that confirmed that more than a few vampires were in town. As they drove off Paresh noticed the shift in Eric's attention and looked over her shoulder. The car's windows were heavily tinted.

"Who—" she began to ask as the car shrank into the distance.

"Jonathan didn't tell me much about David's plan or his orders," Eric interrupted, drawing out a pause until he knew Jonathan was out of earshot. He took the photograph from Paresh, set it face down, and clasped their hands together. "I hate seeing fear in your eyes. I'm not telling you any of this to scare you, but I can't assume you're safe. Your uncle is a dangerous man and I promise that I will not let him, or anyone—*anyone*—hurt you, but it's not fair for me to keep you in the dark about the people manipulating us. Vampires aside, it's time I told you about David."

II

1975, Orison Crossing, Illinois

He'd always felt at home here. It went beyond his love of libraries and books, of course, since this one in particular was almost as old as he was. From prairie to stone, he'd watched it go up, witnessed the expansions and new additions as the university grew, scrutinized the occasional change to the soft interiors, and appreciated the timeless pillars and architectural bones that remained as unchanged as he did. The smell of old paper and bound leather didn't waver even as books aged and new volumes came into the stacks. And then there was that special brand of library quiet, where even accidental noises seemed to shush themselves and the occupants moved a little slower or lighter.

He glared at Andrew's drumming fingers and kicked his ankle under the table. Andrew threw his hands up, bugging his eyes out, and returned to strumming his nerves atop the polished surface.

"Knock it off," Eric whispered, kicking his young ward harder and getting a muffled yelp. Born in 1956, the same year that the Senator and Sandy got married, Andrew already had a year of law school finished—the nineteen-year-old knew how to act in a library.

Naturally, Eric was the one who got the side-eye from the studious pair at the next table over. He lifted his hands in apology and flattened them on top of Andrew's fingers. "David sits still better than this," he hissed.

"That's because he's always high or drunk off his ass." Andrew lifted his chin to survey the doors.

Eric could feel the vibrations of Andrew's wiggling feet through the marble floor. "Good God man, settle down. David sat better than this when he was four. You weren't even this nervous when you met the governor."

"The governor's not a hot chick." Andrew rolled his eyes at Eric's pointed look. "I didn't mean it like that. I just need to warn her——"

He slapped the table and jumped up. "Oh, oh! There she is!"

Eric locked onto the sound of the shoes crossing the entrance. Most female students wore sneakers these days, but others preferred a formal look and used duct tape to dampen the clack of their heels on hard floors. This was even quieter. Since she worked here, perhaps she'd glued on cork or rubber instead.

The seat across from him was suddenly empty. *Damn it.*

Ever since Andrew had finagled him into taking classes, Eric was less focused in his official capacity and Andrew had found ways to slip away from him. This was the first Hawthorne generation in a century to produce more than one heir, and while David was…troubled…and jealous of Andrew, Eric still watched out to ensure that the younger brother didn't get ensnared in one of Jonathan's traps. But that hadn't been much of a problem—Jonathan had disappeared from his life completely for decades during the world wars and had been distant since returning.

If Eric didn't know better, he'd think those missing years had pounded some sense into Jonathan. But, when his brother did show up, he whined about being bored and would then disappear to spar with his pack in a jungle on another continent. Only recently, at a party celebrating the Senator's summer recess—where David had teased Andrew with a glimpse of his girlfriend, blond and beautiful, squealing in his car as he tore up the driveway—Jonathan had shown up with an injury. He was arrogant as always, but more philosophical. Eric wasn't sure what to think about that, but it didn't matter—Jonathan was not the problem here. David's appearance at that party had started this whole fiasco. Andrew hadn't stopped thinking about *her* since.

Eric quietly shoved his chair back and headed toward the stairs to roam the stacks, training an ear on Andrew, who was lingering by the reference desk, working up the courage to approach his brother's girlfriend. Eric lightly gripped the familiar curves of the old banister and jogged up. This whole idea was terrible, and he knew, whether Andrew would admit it to himself or not, that this was about more than warning the girl about David's violent tendencies. Andrew had to be second-guessing his motives by now.

The brothers were only a year apart and had been close until they were four or five. Eric had tried to avoid preferential treatment, but it was impossible to hide the extra attention he and their parents gave to Andrew. Once David was old enough to see it, he'd figured out that it was because Andrew had inherited the ultimate Hawthorne birthright and that Eric would never be his "special" friend. In many ways, it had seemed natural that their father gravitated more to the oldest son. Andrew wanted to create a legacy out of his father's political tenure, but it didn't help that Eric had forged a bond with him that he couldn't replicate with David.

To get Eric's undivided attention, David would act out and attack Andrew. He'd run off to sulk, feeling like the victim without an ounce of empathy or regret, and that worsened after Daniel was elected into Congress. The Senator and Sandy eventually sent David to a boarding school and arranged for Eric to take Andrew away on retreats when David came home for breaks. But keeping them separate wasn't enough. David would ransack Andrew's room, turn his drawers out, smash his trophies, set fires, and even leave dead fish and frogs rotting in Andrew's bed.

Eric reached the end of the row and glanced over the railing. Andrew was smoothing his hair back as he crossed the lobby to the information desk. Somehow, David had managed to keep nearly everything about his girlfriend a secret. Anytime Andrew asked him about her, David merely mumbled that he loved her and to leave him alone. David did seem to care about her—he'd cleaned himself up, quit smoking and drinking, gotten his GED, and even spoken with the Senator about enrolling in college classes. Eric couldn't deny that she was a good influence.

But then Andrew heard them arguing about what she did during their off time. David accused her of seeing someone else and Andrew's worry that his brother would hurt her worsened. Convinced that David was stalking her, Andrew talked Eric into following David. He confirmed Andrew's fear and David's paranoia, and managed to learn where she worked. Knowing that David's brand of love was more like jealous attachment, Andrew was determined to warn her off before their fights escalated.

Andrew was next in line—and last, since he kept moving to the back with each new person. When he finally reached the counter, she smiled and asked if she could help him. Andrew turned on the charm. Eric cringed.

"I hope so," Andrew said, "because none of these books can tell me what I need to know."

She cocked her head curiously, her smile stretching up past her eyes as she politely waited to hear his super difficult question. Eric closed his eyes. He couldn't watch. *Andrew, what are you doing?*

Andrew bent over the counter to whisper into her ear. "Will you go to dinner with me tomorrow night?"

Oh God. Eric covered his eyes and turned his back to the railing. *This is a nightmare. Catch your head, Andrew—that wasn't the plan!*

When Eric turned back around, she was shyly tucking her hair behind her ears and nodding, a slight blush of color rising to her cheeks. Andrew held out his hand.

"I'm Andy."

"Felicia Schaffer."

The railing audibly creaked in Eric's fists, drawing a brief glance from Andrew, but he turned back to Felicia just as quickly. Eric ground his teeth and disappeared into the stacks. As the pair planned where to meet, neither mentioned David even though he had to weigh heavily on both of their minds.

Later, when he followed Andrew out, Eric barely noticed the

moon bursting huge in the sky or the late summer cicada song. He no longer recognized Andrew. He had no need to covet anything, let alone the young woman who brought joy to his brother. For the first time in David's life, he'd invested in himself and his strengths instead of trying to destroy Andrew and his shadow.

No one knew why David saw himself as inferior to Andrew. With the Hawthorne good looks and limitless potential, both were bright young men with slender physiques, talented in sports, academics, and the arts. Andrew wanted only to be like his father, while David wandered without ambition, so focused on Eric that he squandered his potential.

David could easily follow his father into the Senate without expending half of Andrew's effort. He had the resources and an obvious fire burning within him that could propel him higher than Andrew. With his father's dark hair and eyes, he possessed a commanding presence that Andrew lacked. It wasn't just the gentler appearance that came with the lighter hair and blue eyes of their mother; there'd always been a fragility to Andrew that left him more prone to injury than David. He'd break bones, but David didn't— unless they were Andrew's.

"Andy, huh? Has anyone ever called you that? Even once?" Eric finally asked, stuffing his hands in his pockets as they stepped onto the sidewalk. "You do realize that David's never actually hurt her, right? When I saw them on their picnic dinner, he was an attentive gentleman."

Andrew kept walking toward the parking lot.

"This isn't going to end well, Andrew. Why did you do that?" Eric stopped. An element of force built within his voice. "Is this your revenge for everything he's done to you? Are you that petty to involve an innocent girl?"

Andrew whirled around and stomped back to where Eric stood. "Do you really think I'm like that? That I don't understand that *I'm* the envious one here?" He jabbed his finger at the building. "I know I should leave her alone, but love is trickier than I thought!"

Eric scoffed. "Love? Are you crazy? You don't even know her!"

"Call it love at first sight then—"

"That doesn't exist," Eric said.

Andrew shook his head in denial. "Just because you've never felt it doesn't mean it doesn't exist. It's got a powerful grip—how else do you explain this? I've been worried for her from the moment I saw her in David's car—but I guess it's been more than that. I mean, the instant our eyes met in there, I saw it in her, too."

Wiping his face dubiously, Eric countered, "She's never seen you before tonight. How can she love someone she doesn't know? How can you? I've lived a long time and seen what love can do——"

Eric shook his head. "And it can get ugly, just like revenge."

"It's not revenge, Eric!" Andrew insisted. "Ever since he dropped out of school, David's been so mellow that I don't care enough to waste my energy on him! He'd rather smoke pot, burn that shitty incense he likes, and listen to records than mess with me. Believe me, I don't want to destroy the peace that even Dad overlooks!"

"Peace?" Eric huffed and licked his lips, his patience unraveling. "Just weeks ago you woke up to him strangling you in your sleep! I can't count the number of times he's snuck into your room and watched you sleep *without* doing that—as if fantasizing about it. What if you hadn't fought him off? What if I hadn't been there?"

"If you hadn't been there, Dad wouldn't have found out, that's for sure," Andrew muttered under his breath.

"Right, because high collars and turtlenecks are totally normal summer wear." Eric flicked Andrew's throat. "I can still see the bruises. You expect me to believe this has nothing to do with it?"

Andrew took a step back and patted the air. "Look, Dad's been working hard to build a foundation for my career and I'm doing everything I can to fortify it—and that means not riling up David. I didn't want you to tell Dad because I didn't want him calling the police and blemishing *his* record. As it is, David said he was sleepwalking and doesn't remember doing it, and I believe him."

"Then you're stupid, and I'm disappointed in you," Eric said bluntly. "David showed no remorse whatsoever when I escorted him back to his room. He wasn't sleepwalking. As for your dad, re-election is years away—it wouldn't have dented his reputation. He's fed up with David, Andrew—he's adjusting his will. But if this girl succeeds with David where we've all failed, maybe he'll become a productive member of society and your dad will reconsider."

"You're contradicting yourself—is David a threat that deserves to get cut out or can we believe that he's trying for once?"

"I can't answer that, but he's at a pivotal moment where he can change and you're taking that away from him."

Andrew tapped his fists against his thighs and looked back at the library entrance. His eyes watered slightly and Eric finally noticed the frustration and guilt burning there.

"I don't know how to convince you," Andrew said, his voice painfully strained. "But I feel it—I do—and I don't want to hurt him, but Destiny made a mistake and took her to the wrong brother. She doesn't belong with him. I love her."

"So does David."

Rolling his gaze skyward, Andrew exhaled forcefully. Desperation pooled in the pupils he dropped on Eric, as though his guilt was consuming him. He held his hands out to the sides. "What else can I do or say? Tell me that you don't see *me*—the me you've always known and not this vengeful person you've invented—and tell me to walk away, and I will. She can marry him, and I'll just be another miserable politician in Washington."

Andrew tapped his temple. "Work your voodoo and get the truth. That'll make you happy."

Eric's shoulders sagged. "I'd never do that to you."

"Yeah, well, I never thought you'd accuse me of being petty or stupid."

Eric held Andrew's gaze, not as a vampire, but as an ashamed friend. "I'm sorry. Look—all I ask is that you take responsibility for your actions. I'm not going to interfere with Destiny, but you need to own up to David—and her—and it's going to get messy."

Hope blossomed on Andrew's face. "I will."

The next night, on their first date, Andrew introduced Eric as an overprotective friend, so used to his constant presence that the concept of "third wheel" hadn't occurred to him. Of course, it got weird—Eric excused himself to let Felicia relax and give them privacy for Andrew to reveal his secret, but he didn't.

By their third date, which came less than a week later because they couldn't get enough of each other, Eric roamed the shadows unseen with growing unease as he waited for Andrew to keep his word. Felicia's sudden withdrawal had made David more suspicious.

When Andrew finally came clean, Felicia was rattled. The

revelation exposed her own lie by omission, but Andrew spared her an explanation and moved the conversation forward as though she'd been open from the beginning. He asked how she felt about David.

She said that he'd initially swept her off her feet—handsome, polite, and sweet—but that as their relationship progressed from weeks to months, she began to suffocate under his need for validation and attention. Trying to put some distance between them only made him cling tighter.

"Then he told me that he loved me," she confessed quietly, uncomfortably wringing her hands and averting Andrew's gaze. "I guess I hesitated too long—I didn't know what to say back—because he launched into this tirade about cheating on him."

"I think that's the argument I heard that made me look for you," Andrew said.

She swallowed with some effort and half-heartedly shrugged. "It came out of nowhere. I didn't want to hurt him, but it was just so sudden and fast. I…"

She massaged her temples, her countenance wrinkling in thought. "I'd already suspected that he was going to propose and that just made it feel inevitable, you know? My parents would've pressured me into it—why wouldn't they? He's the wealthy son of a respected United States Senator. What more could they want for their daughter?"

"I didn't know he felt that deeply for you—I just ran with my feelings…only thinking of my happiness like that's all that mattered," Andrew said with a crestfallen sigh. "What did you want to do?"

She looked up with a noncommittal shrug. "I still don't know. I met you before I'd sorted it out. I suppose I could've married him and been happy enough, but now…I can't look back."

"I would've been miserable," Andrew said, hesitantly offering his hand and smiling softly when she accepted.

"Me, too, now that I know what real, true love feels like." She didn't need to search Andrew's face for his response. He was practically glowing.

"I knew it!" he said, grinning wide. "It was love at first sight!"

Of course, that was a jab at Eric, whose secretive presence

remained unknown to Felicia. Eric rolled his eyes. It didn't matter anymore—Felicia had made her choice.

"I should tell David," she said. "I owe it to him. I can't keep him in the dark. How this will ever be okay? You're his brother."

"It likely won't," Andrew answered in earnest. "We don't have much of a relationship and he can be volatile. I think it's best if I tell him. My parents will be gone this weekend, so I can handle his wrath then without getting them involved."

She reluctantly agreed and Eric's stomach unclenched—a little. They still had to make it to the weekend.

The next night, he and Andrew were walking from the parking lot toward the library when distant yelling made Eric take off so fast that he vanished from Andrew's side. Ahead, he saw David, and his expression told Eric all he needed to know. He'd appeared to pick Felicia up from work and she'd broken things off with him.

David's face was red with rage. He exploded about her cheating on him and demanded that she take him to this other guy—screaming, "I'm going to kill him!"

He jerked her by the arm, pulling her toward his car double-parked on the street. Crying and pleading with him to let go, Felicia lost her footing and tripped on her heels. David firmed his hold and dragged her along the concrete.

David must've seen movement from the corner of his eye because he looked over at Eric and the expressions that cycled on his face ran from fear to suspicion to realization.

"Are you fucking serious?" he screamed at Eric. "*Andrew?*"

His jaw gaping, David faced Felicia and saw the reality of the situation. He yanked her up and shoved her away, swinging his hand wildly and slapping her hard. She collapsed, crying and holding her face as he snarled and prepared to slap her again. At the last second, he spit on her and pivoted to charge Eric.

"David! Hitting me is like hitting concrete," Eric warned, but David didn't stop. Eric backed up to use David's momentum to fling him aside with a simple wrist roll. David tumbled down and leaped up, swinging uncontrollably and yelling like a rabid animal.

He punched Eric and jerked back, shaking crushed knuckles. He gritted his teeth and lunged again, gripping Eric's arms, digging his nails into ashen-hued flesh. Eric deflected him to the side and pinned him against the grass.

Everything was shaded the color of blood, but he hadn't felt himself changing. He shot a look back at Andrew who'd finally caught up and stood terrified on the sidewalk. Eric nudged his head at Felicia, who sobbed hysterically on the walkway as David screamed and clawed at him. Andrew rushed to scoop Felicia into his arms and tucked her face into the crook of his neck. She hung onto him like a life raft as Andrew looked at Eric again. He did a double take since he'd never seen his demonic façade, then he ran back the way he'd come.

Keeping his head low, Eric peered into David's eyes, diving far below the anger. He needed to maintain complete control without eye contact. David gradually went limp. His brown orbs dulled into empty holes. "Get in your car. I'm driving."

David handed over his keys. He stared absently ahead on the way home and as Eric walked him up to bed. "Lie down and sleep it off."

Andrew called later to say he'd taken Felicia to a hotel and was staying with her. As he'd done with Eric before, Andrew said he'd talked Felicia out of going to the police to avoid causing a scandal for his father.

"You worry too much about that," Eric said. "She should pursue the justice she wants."

"She agreed to let me handle it."

"So did I and it hasn't worked out so well."

"I'd love to see his ass locked up, but I swear I'm not overthinking it," Andrew insisted. "It's not what Dad would want. Like you said—David's been trying to change and he's an adult now. This would stay on his record forever."

"Forget what I said—don't you think *this* deserves to stay on his record? He attacked her!"

"Because of me!" Andrew huffed in frustration. "I will deal with it. I'll be home tomorrow, I promise. She's bruised up, but nothing's broken—she didn't want to go to the hospital, but I'll ask again in the morning."

"Take care of her. David's out. He won't bother you tonight."

In the morning, David awoke holding his head as though hung over, but blasted into full blown fury the instant he saw Eric leaning against his dresser—where he'd spent the entire night.

Felicia had more than broken his heart—she'd shattered it—and that was clearly visible in his hateful eyes and in the disgust and despair within his voice.

"It's not enough that Andrew gets *everything* he wants? I finally find someone who completes me, and you help him take her from me? Why? *Why?*" He punched down at his sides. "Don't I deserve anything? *I love her!* I…I'd give her everything I own. I even—I got her a ring. She's supposed to be mine…"

Tears glistened in his eyes as he seethed in silence. Eric merely watched, trying to quell the anger about to spark in his chest. Nearly twenty minutes later, David finally glared at him and yelled, "My parents gave you to Andrew, proving they love him most and that I'm damned. You say you're here to protect us, that you watch out for me, too, but what have you ever actually done for me? Huh?"

He jumped up and got in Eric's face. "You know the truth? The Devil sent you to make me miserable. You are nothing more than a *filthy demon* that brings pain and death to this family. My brother *stole my love*—and you helped him. He deserves everything that you bring on him."

He spit in Eric's face and stomped from the room, slamming doors all the way to the kitchen. Eric released an excruciatingly slow breath and wiped saliva from his eyes, fuming at the empty bed and feeling his blood begin to boil. The dresser screeched as he shoved off and stormed out of the mansion to cool off. He hadn't been this angry in decades, utterly fed up and sick of being stuck in the middle of those two and their ugly side of love.

In his absence, David downed an entire bottle of whiskey and trashed the kitchen. His rampage moved into other rooms, but the staff kept their distance until he ran into his father's parlor. A maid stepped in to plead with him to stop and was hit by a flying vase. Eric found her holding her head and sobbing on the floor with a few other maids trying to console her, unsure if they should call an ambulance.

"Tell me what happened and then have someone take you to get looked at," Eric said. "It's a head wound—don't take it lightly. They'll bill the Hawthornes."

She told him what she saw and added, "He looked horrified and empty, like it really was an accident but he couldn't believe it. He whispered, *Felicia,* and screamed really loudly."

Another maid added, "He took off in his car."

Eric held onto his composure until they cleared the room. Dropping into a leather chair that had lived in the house almost as long as he had, he rubbed his forehead and closed his eyes. He focused on breathing until the tightness in his chest began to ease. Then he picked up the phone and dialed the Senator's office.

Daniel and Sandy flew home that night apprehensive about facing an irrational David, but he didn't come home. Andrew did, however, and got his share of yelling for being so reckless. As Eric had learned long ago, anger tended to roll downhill. Afterward, Andrew searched the grounds for him, upset that Eric had left his depressed brother alone with a bottle of alcohol.

When Andrew accused him of abandoning his duty to the family, Eric's hold on his patience snapped. The situation had far exceeded the parameters of his honor bound obligation and even overstepped the near boundless limits of friendship.

"I'm stopping you right there and demanding an apology," Eric said, fine lines creasing his forehead. "I've stood by your deception and your empty promises to handle a situation that you very clearly can't or won't handle. I'm the one who dealt with David last night and this morning, and you're the one who stuck me there."

"I owe you an apology?" Andrew yelled. "Are you kidding me?"

Eric's eyes narrowed to slits, but his voice was coldly calm. "You tell me that you love Felicia and that your soul aches without her. David insists that Felicia completes him and brings him happiness. Meanwhile, she's in the middle, in love with you but not wanting to hurt him, so how do I choose who deserves pity or contempt?"

Eric's darkening scowl kept Andrew's mouth shut.

"The answer? *I don't.* It's not my place to choose or judge. *You* were supposed to work this out like an adult and *you* didn't." Eric's vampire blood added a trace of disdain to his voice as he growled, "I thought you were different from the previous generations who'd forgotten what I really am. But you saw me last night—the real me. I am not a plaything or a chaperone for this family. *I am not human.* And I am not here to arbitrate petty disagreements. I keep *you* safe from *other vampires*."

The fire burning in his gut wormed its way into his chest. Eric left Andrew standing there speechless. He bid a quiet goodnight to the Senator and Sandy before retiring to his living quarters—the western wing of the basement. A few hours later, Andrew knocked on the upstairs door before coming down. In darkness, he maneuvered around the furniture from memory and sat beside Eric on the sofa. His nerves thrummed the space between them.

"I see now that I let the situation escalate beyond my control because I handled it poorly from the start," Andrew admitted. "I'm sorry for yelling at you, for accusing you—"

Andrew paused to dry his eyes and clear the catch in his throat. "And most of all, I'm sorry for abusing your friendship. I love you, Eric—you're my closest family and none of that was fair of me to put on you. I'm so sorry. I really am."

He broke down and Eric patted him on the back, remembering the nights he'd comforted Andrew in his younger days. "We got through it then," he whispered. "We'll get through it now."

☽ ✺ ☾

Orison Crossing, Summer 2006

Eric exhaled a heavy sigh. He'd been through a lot in his life, but he rued that entire situation—and he was not one for regrets. Paresh seemed oblivious to the tears streaming down her cheeks. He wiped them away and offered a sad smile. She parted her lips to speak but couldn't find her voice.

"It's okay," he whispered, stroking her cheek. "I know it's a lot."

"It's just…" She moved her lips in search of words. "So *impossible*. No wonder I didn't know I had an uncle."

Eric tilted his head back and sighed again. He squeezed her hand. "There's more to it."

He heard her gulp. "I don't know if I want to know."

Shaking his head, he said, "You probably don't, and I'd honestly rather not go into it, but you should know. This whole thing is exactly why the true bloods are terrified of love. It wields too much power and clogs the gears of logic. It can shred sanity and exacerbate insanity."

"O-okay. So what happened next?" she asked, closing her eyes and touching her fingers to her forehead.

"The Senator got word that David was in Chicago, but between nightmares and fear, Felicia couldn't sleep. Andrew planned a weekend at a bed and breakfast that the family owned—owns—in Vermont. Given what he learned about third wheels, he asked me to find a date so it'd look like a normal getaway among couples. When I kept insisting that I could go without her knowing, he improvised by asking a waitress at a diner we frequented—giving assurances that she'd have a private room."

He sucked his teeth and flipped his hand out. "That was Molly."

"Ohh," Paresh said, intrigued. "Is that when she fell in love with you?"

"She told you about that, huh?" Eric chuckled and ruffled his hair. "Yeah…her grandfather had theories that others thought were kooky, but Molly didn't, so I openly told her why I couldn't feel the same way. Basically confirmed the kookiest theory she'd heard, which got us to where we are today. She stuck by my side for the sake of appearances throughout Andrew and Felicia's courtship. In many ways, she knows me better than Andrew ever did. I didn't ask her to assist me like she does; our relationship just…evolved. In turn, I take care of her, but I'd love to see her show interest in someone else."

"She said she's happy and loves you like family."

"I know." Eric smiled. "She's too good to me—I still think she could be happier."

He clapped his hands together and sighed. "But—I digress—the trip started pleasant enough, but then we learned about a fire at the mansion. Andrew found out that his parents had died on *the news*. I arranged for the Senator's pilot to meet us at the airport and we flew home where the police were waiting for us.

"With the national headlines focused on the Senator's death, even the *Daily Sunset* pushed the murder-suicide of a banker and his wife into the background—Walter pulled Felicia aside and told her about her parents, the only family she had left since her mother's sister had died the year before from cancer. They were still investigating when her house burned to the foundation. She lost everything."

Paresh choked out a strangled breath and smacked at her eyes, but it was too much. She leaned into her hands and let it out. A knot formed in Eric's throat as he stared across the cemetery at the black headstone by his car.

You can't do this to her. Eric clenched and unclenched his jaw. She still didn't know enough to understand their situation, and it was going to get worse. But he'd promised to tell her.

He unsuccessfully tried to level his voice. It had a rough edge as he said, "Felicia refused to believe that her father would shoot her mother and then himself, but the fire destroyed the scene. We knew it was David—all of it—we *knew*. With today's technology, it would've been so easy to get him, but back then…knowing wasn't enough. The fire at the mansion was labeled accidental, the deaths of Felicia's parents remained unchanged, and the fire department faulted a wiring issue as the ignition source at her house."

He stroked Paresh's hair. "Try to remember that they were happy in the end. I know it's not easy. I'm sorry for hurting you like this."

"It's…not you," she said, wiping her hands on her skirt and leaning into him. "Please, keep going."

"Okay," he whispered, kissing the top of her head. "David skipped the funeral, but surfaced for the reading of the will, unaware of the Senator's changes. I could see it in his eyes—he'd fallen from the Flock, and that tempted the darkest corners of my soul. I could've ripped the life right out of his body and been done with it.

"He was blindsided by the conditions of the will, especially when he learned that Andrew intended to retain control of the majority. He knew he couldn't contest the will, so he threw a tantrum and I got to drag him off the property with the warning not to fall before my sight again if he valued any portion of his life.

"It was years before he reminded us that he was alive and not well, but in the meantime, Andrew repaired the mansion and abandoned it into the care of a skeleton crew, then prodded me to live my own life. He'd matured overnight into the responsible and proactive man who was your father, saying that Death was part of life, and it would come for him whether I was there or not. He didn't want me to waste my life watching over him. So, to make another long story short, I built my house and found a balance between the life he thought I should have and the life I'd settled into for over a century.

"He married Felicia during the nation's bicentennial, and they immediately tried to conceive, which led to their next period of trials. Years passed without any luck, and when they did conceive, they lost the babies early on. When Felicia made it past the first trimester with you, she allowed herself to hope. When she got to the third trimester, she was ecstatic. There weren't any complications until you were born, but you already know how that turned out.

"That week, the *Daily Sunset* ran an article about everything they'd endured and the hope they'd found in a miracle baby. It even credited you with shifting your birth date to June 23 by taking your first breath at midnight, and explained why your parents changed the spelling of your name to join 'perish' and 'parish' to celebrate life and faith.

"Days later, the church burnt to the cinders. David's nothing if not consistent, but he didn't even try to make it look accidental. The scene reeked of his blood, and it was ruled an arson, but, once again, we couldn't connect him. He was in Wisconsin and the authorities who interrogated him reported that he had an alibi. Walter was a lieutenant then and knew the truth about me, but my sense of smell was hardly admissible as evidence. The case was never officially solved, and David vanished—no one's seen him since.

"I thought the article had forced David to see his brother married to the only woman he'd ever loved, living the life with her that he'd desired. That it had reignited anger he couldn't let go of—but that was before I saw the address of the house you lived in. It's the same as her parents' house, where Felicia lived when they dated. His twisted obsession with her clearly runs deep—so much so that he stole away the only surviving piece of her."

He paused in preparation for the worst part. Regardless of his infatuation back then, David must've grown to hate Felicia as much as he'd loved her. Why else kill her alongside his brother?

Eric cleared his throat, but the words refused to come.

She knows enough, he told himself. The truth would only tear open a fresh wound and add in fear. *But she doesn't know that David wants you dead or how he plans to make that happen, you coward. He's on his way to kill her because of you.*

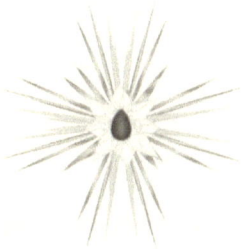

CHAPTER THIRTEEN: THE HUNTERS EMERGE

I

The sun had begun its descent—an orange sliver barely hovered over the canopy in a sky smeared with vibrant color. Clouds loomed on the opposite horizon, hiding the moon and threatening to blank out the stars.

They stood at the clearing threshold. It was quiet. Still. Eric's hand was on Paresh's arm, holding her back under the guise of forgetting something in the car. The serenity belied the menacing energy of an ever-present, watchful eye.

He grabbed a satchel from his trunk and curled an arm around her waist. Paresh melted against him, her head on his shoulder as they lazily strolled up the flagstone. She scanned the sky, focused more on her thoughts than the summer gloaming. Eric physically relaxed, but scrutinized the forest's dimming depths, one inner voice arguing that Jonathan's challenge was too deliberate to chase down, and another countering that his sudden shift from Paresh to him was too pronounced to ignore.

Eric felt like he was balancing on a precipice and the wind was about to shift. He sensed that Jonathan was giving him a final chance to avoid conflict—which put them at a stalemate. Jonathan would never reveal specifics, and without them, Eric would never give in.

When they entered the cottage, he nudged the door shut with his foot and pulled Paresh to him, capturing her lips for a lingering kiss. Parting with some reluctance, he stroked her hair and said, "You haven't eaten much. I know it's been a long day, but how about if you and Molly grab a bite? I'd like to go for a run in the woods."

Paresh distractedly orbited a button on his shirt with her finger. "I'll be fine while you're out." She sounded exhausted. "It's getting late and I'm not really that hungry."

"I didn't think you'd want to be alone, so I texted her earlier," he said, grimacing lightly as though he'd overstepped. "She's already on her way. I can call her back. I don't want you to feel like she's babysitting you."

Resting her palm over his heart, Paresh sighed. "I don't feel that way. I know you're worried about me. Besides, I'm used to having people around. It's fine, really. I like Molly."

She shuddered involuntarily as she glanced out the window. "To be honest, you're probably right. I would be jumpy here alone. Especially with Jonathan…and my uncle…out there."

Alarm prickled the hairs on Eric's nape, but she'd only meant that as a generalization. Forcing a smile, he smoothed his thumb over her cross. "Don't take this off and you'll be fine as far as Jonathan's concerned, and don't worry about the rest. Maybe getting out of here to a public place with Molly will help."

Nodding in agreement, she fingered the cross and turned out of his embrace. "It's cooled off a bit outside—I'm going to put on something warmer."

Resisting the urge to follow her, Eric took his satchel into the bathroom. He removed his contacts and quickly changed, then perched on the hearth to lace up his running shoes. He heard Molly's car pull up at the carriage house a moment before Paresh came from the hall wearing jeans and a lightweight, pale blue sweater. She swept over his simple black t-shirt and track pants with a soft, appreciative gaze.

Tenderly kneading her lip between her teeth, she approached and he stood, intensely focused on her movements—the hesitant reach for his abdomen, the delicate touch of her fingers tracing his muscles beneath the cotton, the occasional pink of her tongue flicking over her lower lip. She didn't see the fire behind his glasses burning hotter with each caress or know that the stronger her attraction grew, the more intoxicating her aura became.

Closing his eyes as his control frayed, he rubbed his hands firmly along her arms, breathing slowly and deliberately. The air between them didn't move. But her lips were suddenly against his, warm and eager, eroding his willpower, and making him forget why he needed to go on this run.

For once, he was silently grateful for Molly's timing. When she knocked, he cupped Paresh's cheek and hungrily responded to her kiss. Parting with a seductive smile, he whispered, "Perhaps later we can see where this leads us."

With blushing cheeks, Paresh opened the door for Molly. He gave his thanks for coming to his aid yet again and walked them to Molly's car, asking that she call his cell on their way back.

When her car disappeared beyond his sight, he contemplated the clearing. The sun had descended behind the trees, staining the deepening blue sky above the forest a shade of deep persimmon. Like boats sailing calm waters along the path of the sinking sun, the clouds, with fiery hot magenta peaks and rich indigo valleys, had crept to hang directly overhead. An embedded silhouette, Sunset Grove's shadowy core was darker than the deepest coal.

The familiar prickle strengthened as he faced south. He set off in a paced jog, rounding the cottage and crossing another few hundred yards to the tree line. The worn path cushioned his feet as he hit a comfortable rhythm, each step thudding into the ominous silence. He didn't feel the usual release that came with an evening run, especially knowing it would end with Jonathan.

The path ahead opened into the mammoth silver maple's empty clearing. The instant he crossed the threshold, air charged with hostility knocked him back into the woods. He struggled to stay afoot and erect a barrier with his aura.

The blow destroyed the final thread of his patience.

Fury-filled adrenaline surged throughout his veins, overloading his senses and plunging him into the raging bloodlust of his inhuman alter ego, the hunter with razor sharp, dagger-like nails, ferocious fangs, and vision that tinted everything the shade of blood. The sheer force of the pressure behind his teeth drove him to salivate like a starving beast. Clenching his fists so tightly that blood dripped between his knuckles, he issued a guttural growl into the clearing. An invisible miasma sheathed him with a violent intensity that was more than capable of defending against Jonathan's venomous essence while attacking on its own.

His engorged, dilated eyes snapped up. Jonathan emerged from the far side, similarly monstrous and bearing his fangs. Briefly noting that Jonathan's pins were absent, Eric kicked off his shoes and reentered the clearing with a weighted pit growing in his chest.

"This is what I've wanted to see," Jonathan smirked. He flinched when Eric's essence struck him. "Impressive."

With a snarling war cry, Eric lunged across the field, hands and fingers extended like the claws of an eagle diving for prey, but Jonathan had the same powerful talons and Eric, flying at him with deadly intent. They collided, their gnarled hands slicing through skin and muscle as they speared each other's shoulders.

Grimacing through searing pain, neither withdrew. They cut deeper, driven by anger and a natural urge to maim. Deadlocked, they growled like the preternatural animals they'd become, ejecting negative energy that fused with the air's molecules and created a potent mixture capable of driving a human insane with one breath.

Eric spun to the side and kicked his bare foot at Jonathan's knee. The joint bent the wrong way and forced Jonathan off balance. Staggering backward, Jonathan threw out a fist and struck Eric's jaw with enough force to shove him out of striking range. They circled each other warily, Eric flexing his jaw and Jonathan shaking out his leg, each waiting for the other to make the next move. Glistening with sticky moisture and the scent of fresh blood, their thirst and rage edged them dangerously close to the true beast's territory.

"What the hell do you want, Jonathan?" Eric barely recognized his unearthly voice.

"I've been ordered to bring you in," Jonathan spat grimly, visibly struggling for control, backing away from that pivotal point where he'd turn into the instinctual killing machine of days long past.

"That's not happening." Eric shot a challenging look over the rim of his glasses. The hunter's crimson view spurred an inhuman desire for bloodshed. It was reflected to him in his brother's eyes.

Jonathan suddenly sprang up with a funereal yell and slammed his fists into Eric, driving him into the tree. He impaled Eric's chest with his fingers and a surge of strength, narrowly missing his heart as his nails extended and pinned him against the aged bark. "I do *not* want to kill you," Jonathan seethed.

Fire ravaged his lungs as blood bubbled up Eric's throat and oozed a steady stream of scarlet from his mouth. He grabbed Jonathan's arms with a clasp so tight it would snap human bones, and slowly inched the flesh and bone weapons out of his body. "That's good, because you can't."

Jonathan scoffed. "Don't delude yourself with false securities. The conditions of the Treaty only apply to the hunter within us. That trinket around your neck can't protect you from my beast. Lucien has requested your presence at any cost. If you push me over that edge, I'll forfeit my soul and tear you into pieces for the VaSH to pick up and reassemble before him. *That* is a testament to the Vampiric Nation's loyalty."

"How can you talk about loyalty when you removed your pins to forsake your allegiance? Do you think that will save your race from the consequences of your actions?" Intentionally smug and provoking, Eric laughed. "How will Lucien feel when he beheads *you* for killing a member of the Flock? Will he feel anything? Even then?"

The darkness within him savored the agony visibly biting at Jonathan. Eric's lips curled into a sneer. "This is a death match that you cannot win, *Brother*. Either I kill you, or you kill me and Lucien kills you."

Eric laughed harder. The evil sound echoed off the trees and filled the tight space between them. He whispered, "That means *I* win."

Jonathan's face contorted first with fury and then with an underlying misery in his eyes. "Do you think he gives such an order lightly? Lucien has deemed you worthy of my life. Even if you defeat me, others will come. He'll send all of the VaSH squads after you—come with me, now!"

"What a reward for the fierce loyalty of his lifelong companion." Eric rolled his eyes.

"And you seriously expect me to fear the VaSH where their championed Second Born failed?" Eric asked in an icy voice. The wounds in his chest had closed and the bleeding had tapered to a trickle. "I know your pack is here, and you know I'll kill them easily. You picked the wrong day to do this—I'm not going anywhere with you. Or them. What about *her*?"

Jonathan pressed his full weight into his attack and his arms began to slide through Eric's grasp toward his chest again. Eric dragged

Jonathan's arms out to the sides and let go. Jonathan plunged furiously into the trunk as Eric kicked his legs out and slid down the tree barely wincing as bark splintered into his back. He hopped up into a crouch and shouldered Jonathan's abdomen, kicking off the tree with all his might.

The force of Eric's momentum knocked the wind from Jonathan when he bounced off the ground yards away. Clutching his chest, Jonathan tried to gulp air down a closed off airway. His face turned a deep shade of crimson.

Eric backed away. He didn't see any movement in the shadows. Jonathan was too proud to involve his pack when it came to anything involving him—although pride wasn't an accurate descriptor. It was more like conquest.

As air returned to his lungs, Jonathan gulped greedily and found his feet again. He snapped, "*She* is no longer the Elders' concern."

"Then why do I need to go now, when David is on his way to kill her?" Holding Jonathan's gaze, Eric shook his head. He clenched his teeth and demanded, "Why *now*?"

Jonathan charged again, brutally piercing through Eric's shoulders, the force lifting him off his feet as Jonathan screamed, "*Because those are my orders!*"

Eric's head cracked against the maple's rigid bark with a sickening sound. Jonathan clamped down on his throat, his teeth savagely tearing into Eric's skin. Even with the intent to kill, the bite's effect was euphoric. Eric exhaled involuntary pleasure, helpless as he battled within himself to stay afloat in a mental haze controlled entirely by Jonathan.

Distant ringing dunked in and out of his awareness. Lustful sparks scorched the sound away every time it started. His entire body was awash with tingling nerves yearning for touch, and pressure built within his core that was desperate for release. Then the ringing started again, and somehow, from somewhere deep within his psyche, his logical brain managed to scream over the endorphins Jonathan had forced onto him. *Cell phone!*

He stopped fighting Jonathan and forced every bit of focus on that internal voice. The ringing came through more clearly and he was able to latch onto a thought of Molly and Paresh. They were on their way home. Moaning despite himself, he wrenched Jonathan's head to the side and ripped him free of his neck with a spray of blood that splattered the side of Jonathan's face and left a gaping hole in Eric's throat. The trees and night sky spun around him as Eric frantically clawed at Jonathan's throat, slippery with blood, so weakened that he barely managed to hold off a second attack.

The ringing stopped again.

Jonathan's tongue slid along his garnet-stained lips as he peered at Eric with intense, arrogant eyes. "I have waited so long to taste you again," he whispered with a seductive sneer. "And her blood makes it even sweeter."

Eric's body suddenly felt engulfed in flame as he furiously charged forward with a head-butt that sent Jonathan reeling backward. He advanced in pursuit and felt the wound in his neck, glancing briefly at the blood dripping from his fingers after he pulled them away.

He grabbed Jonathan's throat with one hand and punched him with the other, his cheekbone absorbing enough energy to shatter steel. The mighty blow dented Jonathan's face and crushed Eric's knuckles. "I warned you that if you ever did that again, I'd break your teeth off! Do you think they'll grow back?" Eric growled in disgust, shoving Jonathan to the ground. "What the hell has gotten into you?"

It was taking everything he had just to stand. Jonathan had taken too much for Eric to fend off another attack. He backed away in case Jonathan lunged again. Pain radiated from his hand. He was healing at a vastly slower pace in this depleted state.

Jonathan's facial structure was regenerating, but he was largely unresponsive and oddly stunned—sluggish, like a drugged human—sprawled in the grass, trying to sit up. He eventually managed to get upright and rested an outstretched arm over his knee, shaking his head in a daze as though to get his bearing. Keeping a wary eye on him, Eric backed farther away and pulled out his phone.

Straining to level his voice when Molly answered, he said, "Turn away from Paresh so she can't see your face. I've hit a snag. Tell her I got farther away than I intended, but I'll be back soon. Stay inside with the doors and windows locked, but don't alarm her." He didn't wait for confirmation before pocketing the phone.

Huffing with exasperation, Eric pointed north, toward the

cottage. "*She* is your savior! Why are they throwing her away?"

Jonathan's eyes were vacant as he stared ahead and answered in a breathless voice, "Ours. She is *our* savior—you forget what you are. No one argues with Lucien, not even me. I will not question his decision. He wants you."

"I never forget what I am. You refuse to acknowledge that I'm not like you." Eric glared at Jonathan for several long moments. "I've done nothing to warrant Lucien's attention. Giving her life is no different from what you did when you altered me."

Jonathan shot him an annoyed look. "You don't think that was special? The fact that you exist warrants his attention. I created you. You have a soul. Feel love. Live a successful life in the Realm of Man, among *them*." He waved in the direction of town.

"Do you really think those humans don't know what you are? How many of them knew you when you raised Daniel? When you went to law school with Andrew? When you rallied them to search the forest and fields for her? Hell, some of them may even remember you from Joshua's days!

"They wonder. They suspect. They know. They accept you and say nothing. You are what the true bloods have desired to be for more than a thousand years. How is that not special? You're a vampire, but you're a member of the Flock—an outstanding achievement."

"It's not as great as you think. I hear their whispers, what they say. I have a steady stream of people marching into my office asking questions they have no right to ask. I may not care much about your laws, but I do care about exposure, and I know my days in the public eye at the firm are expiring. I'm only successful because Andrew wanted to keep a low profile.

"And you know I constantly battle my emotions. You talk about how great it is when all you've ever done is exploit it to destroy the part of me that won't conform to your ideals. The human I was before has never melded with the vampire you created, until *her*. I'm finally at peace and *she* made it happen. Cry heresy if you want, but Lucien is wrong."

At a loss for words, Jonathan merely shrugged. Pangs of compassion tugged at Eric's heart. Love might elude Jonathan, but not betrayal. Lucien's order must've struck his heart like a sword. Eric's patience began to return as he contemplated Jonathan.

Shaking his head, Eric sat across from him, legs outstretched, leaning back on his palms. Despite their stormy history, he and Jonathan shared an eternal bond by blood that Eric's human heart couldn't ignore.

"I don't understand this...*you*. Why would you throw your life away, fighting me, because of his orders? Surely, any threat I pose isn't worth that sacrifice. Why not send the hunters after me?"

"You see us as cold-hearted creatures that care only for ourselves, and perhaps that is mostly true, but you don't understand the nature of my existence. I will do anything Lucien asks of me." Jonathan exhaled loudly and stared up at the sky. For a time, he was quiet.

The negative energy around them diffused and Jonathan's impassive gaze fell upon Eric once they resembled humans more than bloodthirsty demons. Jonathan wiped his face with the back of his hand and eyed the smear Eric's blood left on his skin as though the substance was foreign to him. "I needed to know what you're capable of."

Eric shook his head once more and made a slight, perturbed noise as he looked down the trail. "Look, let me deal with David and make sure she's safe. Then I'll go willingly, I promise. If they can't wait for that, then send the damn VaSH hunters. Fighting will get us nowhere and I'll feel less guilty about killing them."

Eric stood, ripped off his shredded t-shirt, and tossed it at Jonathan. "Get rid of that. And don't you dare ever bite me again, because I swear to God—you will never bite anything else."

Jonathan caught the bloody fabric with an absent nod. He watched silently as Eric examined his bloodstained body.

Bark had splintered off into Eric's back, but the punctures in his chest and shoulders had closed. The gash in his throat was sticky and his swollen hand throbbed. Jonathan's attack had weakened him enough to impair his healing process.

He couldn't return to the cottage like this. It'd scare the hell out of Paresh. He called Molly. "Can you discreetly dampen a large towel and meet me at your car?" At her affirmative answer, he said, "I'll be there soon."

He threw a stern eye at Jonathan. "I trust we have a deal—or that I'll at least get the courtesy of a warning next time. If anyone comes for me before this thing with David is done, they're going to have a hell of a fight on their hands."

As he turned to go, Jonathan quietly said, "Beware of that woman. Lucifer lurks in her heart. She may be human, but she is cunning."

"What woman?" Eric picked up his shoes without looking back.

"Nicole."

"Speaking of—Paresh is dreaming about a man in a red cloak chasing her with a dagger. Do you have anything to do with that?"

"No."

"Very well, then." Eric jogged up the path and left Jonathan alone in the clearing.

II

Jonathan watched him go with a queasy, unfamiliar feeling settling in his gut. Sparring with such raw inhibition had tempted him beyond control—and that had been his critical mistake. Paresh's blood in Eric's veins was a subduing mechanism that had acted more efficiently than any attack or defense Eric could ever throw at him. It had hit hard and fast, a tranquilizer of crushing emotions that he'd never experienced before.

And that parting question further bothered him. Alongside the weapons he'd taken from the VaSH armory, he'd grabbed a bundle of Aegis Cloaks, whose red wool offered protection from vampiric aura attacks. He couldn't explain Paresh's ability to have a premonition at all, let alone one involving a cloak she'd never seen.

He gripped Eric's tattered shirt in a tightening fist and stood, plagued by doubt. The thought of Paresh dying upset him greatly. He agreed with Eric, because he could feel it—could feel *her*, inside him, trying to override thousands of years of loyalty.

He pulled a hard case from his pocket and gazed upon the pins within before attaching them to his bloodied shirt. Since the day Lucien had given him these symbols of their freedom from Lucifer, he'd worn them proudly. Not so much for allegiance to the Vampiric Nation, but as an affirmation of his devotion to the one man he obeyed without question. He rarely took them off.

Despite Lucien's outwardly apathetic nature, he and Jonathan shared a unique kinship for their kind, and the Arch Elder wouldn't approve of the risk Jonathan had taken. Eric was right—the Vampire

Shadow Hounds were more expendable, but he was wrong to believe that Lucien had given such an order to *him* in the first place. Even after all these years, Eric was too naïve, and too quick to fall for emotional manipulation. Giving clues and keeping Eric guessing was always part of the game, but this time, Jonathan had tried to give stronger fragments of honesty within his lies—because the game was over. Lucien was in control now.

"I needed to know what you're capable of."

Eric should have wondered why Jonathan suddenly needed to know that, particularly at the cost of his own life. No one truly knew how strong Eric was and Jonathan had never been ordered to determine it. It should have stuck out as a misnomer. He'd wanted Eric to catch on, to notice that this entire situation had changed. To ask more questions…enough so that one might warrant an indirect answer that didn't go against his orders.

But the fight hadn't gone as Jonathan expected. Eric's blood was the nectar of temptation that erased all logic. Being with him had always been a test of restraint, but this…Eric's anger had pumped so furiously hot, and the faster his blood swished, the sweeter its heady scent. Coupled with Paresh's influence, it'd been impossible to resist—

Jonathan had lost control and bungled his last chance to give Eric any kind of warning.

He rolled his eyes up at the moon and let its ghostly luster steal his thoughts until a twinge in his jaw brought Eric's punch to the forefront of his mind. The power behind that fist had been shocking. Eric had shattered Jonathan's cheekbone despite losing a massive amount of blood. Jonathan had long suspected that they were equal in strength, but now he doubted that.

Eric shouldn't have been able to stand, let alone lash out—which Jonathan knew from his own history with blood loss—and that was a concern. The VaSH had created the Ivor bow with the strongest true bloods in mind, but they'd never tested it on beings with the strength he and Lucien possessed. As Jonathan opened the hazy white portal to Animus Hollow, he hoped the maximum voltage would work. If not, then only Lucien himself could overpower Eric without lethal intent.

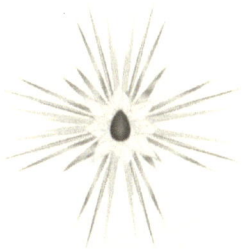

Chapter Fourteen: Checkmate

I

Subtle, tingling pleasure rippled over his every nerve, scratching with the compassion of sandpaper and scorching the tips with equally cruel heat. Jonathan's bloody sneer flashed behind his eyes. Eric jerked up in bed and threw his legs over the edge, clawing at his throat to choke the feeling out, but it was futile. He couldn't escape it any more than he could escape Jonathan.

Eric rose with a heavy, frustrated sigh, whisked his pants up from their crumpled spot beside the bed, and paced a narrow swath of the floorboards. Jonathan was there for every step, engraved as deeply in his memory as his name was on his tombstone. He paused at the window. Thick clouds governed a gloomy night—a perfect match to his mood. He stepped into his pants and sat on the bed, hanging his hand off his neck.

The damned tickle pulsed in his jugular. It was the same feeling that made Paresh blush when she stroked her throat, delighted and sighing at intimate memory of skin on skin. Of heated moans. Of panting and touching. Of his fangs and her blood. But that had never been Eric's experience. He'd only ever seen Jonathan.

And now Jonathan had given Molly a nightmarish memory of her own. Eric had been exhausted when he met Molly at her car, but not so self-absorbed to miss the shock she tried to hide or the glimpses that lingered over his oozing wounds as she pulled on nitrile gloves.

She'd never seen him bleed.

But, she had dealt with his anger and violent moods after the accident, and had chosen to approach this aspect of their relationship with quiet fortitude. Therefore, she said nothing to him, pursing her lips tightly white as if to sharpen her focus away from imagining what beast could inflict such damage to him.

She plucked wooden slivers from his back while he worked to loosen dried blood from his chest with the damp towel she'd brought. She discovered a chunk of bark lodged into his scalp and carefully removed it, her touch so delicate and skilled he might've forgotten they'd never done this before. As his wounds failed to heal and fresh blood dripped, Eric knew he was too weakened and too bloody to return to the cottage. He hated it—hated Jonathan, in particular, for it—but Paresh couldn't see him like this. Molly promised to stay with her while he went home.

When he finally returned to the cottage, Molly performed superbly, re-explaining that he'd pushed himself too hard on his run and gone home to clean up. Since he could've showered there, he added that he'd needed *sustenance*, staving off questions and omitting the reason why. Later, as he walked Molly to her car, he told her to stay away unless summoned. Shadows of anxiety had deepened the creases in her face, but—again—she hid her thoughts and bid him goodnight.

He'd leaned his head and bare arms against the carriage house awhile after she'd left, hoping the brick's sharp edges might rouse him from his funk or counteract Jonathan's bite. But, despite healing physically, the mental imagery haunted him then as it did now, and he'd trudged up the flagstone destitute, wondering if he could hide his angst from Paresh, and quickly realizing he was a fool. She'd opened the door wearing a robe and nothing else, and her intoxicating purity had lifted his spirits instantly. Perhaps an unknown future awaited him, but he'd known, at that moment, exactly what she wanted from him.

Unlike the raw urgency of the night before, their lovemaking was tender and sensual, as if both had known it was their final embrace. He'd drunk of her, reveling once more in blood that upended his world, scattering him into dreamlike teetering and spinning. Then the calm set in and everything slowed down. She was his everything, even strong enough to overcome Jonathan where he had always failed.

But now only a trace of her warmth remained, falling away from the weighted pit in his heart, Jonathan's nagging tickle, and his own doubts about his future. Eric buried his face in his hands, closed his eyes, and emptied his mind. At the slightest glimmer of a thought, he counted from his age backward. Too much had happened. He needed to refocus. He pressed against the throbbing in his throat. But he couldn't stop it.

He clenched his teeth and waited for it to subside. Jonathan had bitten him before, but never with such savagery. They'd both started to cross into the true beast's territory—the divide between vampiric logic and uncontrollable bloodlust—but Eric had felt restrained, like a wall had gone up between him and madness. Something had pulled Jonathan back, as well.

What pushed you that far, Brother? What did Lucien do?

If Jonathan was telling the truth, this mysterious new order finally gave Jonathan what he wanted, which made his anger that much more confusing. As Jonathan's seductive smile flashed across Eric's mind, he groaned and shoved away thoughts of his future at the Arc of True Blood. He'd never be the partner Jonathan truly wanted, and loathed that his fate depended on a cold-hearted creature's whims. But, no matter what the order actually *was*, Lucien had seized control. Eric might fight the rest of his life to get it back without winning.

The front door's hinges squeaked almost imperceptibly. "So it's happening tonight then," he muttered, listening to five pairs of feet move about the cottage: two tiptoeing toward the hall and three outside—all human. His eyes snapped open, blazing with fury and crimson light. The clock read three a.m.

The witching hour.

He crept to the bedroom door. Outside, two men were nearing the master suite's windows and another was by the guest room. Faint conversation to the south, likely in the Grandfather Wisdom clearing, indicated three distinct voices, one of which he knew disturbingly well and had not extended the courtesy of a warning.

The knob turned in his hand. He moved in a blur, throwing open the door and clamping onto throaty flesh, driving the male and female intruders down the hall while tugging the door to shut softly with his foot. He forced them to their knees in silence, squeezing until they fell limp and letting go before he killed them.

He bound them with the dining room's phone cord and checked on Paresh. She was out. Standing at the front door's threshold, he heard only the three others in the immediate area. He slipped out like a shadow and snuck behind the man by the guest room window.

Whispering in a commanding voice, Eric told the man to turn around and then bore into him with swollen eyes, searching through every dusty corner for his soul. Heat poured into Eric's palm as he made a circular motion in front of the man's chest and drained his energy until he slumped against the cottage.

Eric listened for the positions of the other two men near the master suite. He selected a stone from the flowerbed and threw it over the roof. It landed with a clatter on the far side, drawing one to investigate while the other waited. Eric ran up behind him and similarly drained him, and was lowering him to the grass when his partner returned.

The burly fellow hesitated as Eric straightened and then charged. Eric flicked his gaze up. When the man was almost within reach, Eric flaunted a devilish grin that exposed his fangs. He'd resisted the hunter's natural desire to kill thus far, but the darker side of his soul enjoyed the man's horrified expression.

Narrowing his eyes, Eric slid his tongue along his teeth and whispered, "You are not of the Flock."

The man froze and paled, eking out a timid yelp. He took off for the southern trail, screaming for help. Eric watched him go—he'd heard Paresh awaken. Getting her to safety came first.

An emerging form on the path realigned his priorities. A new surge of adrenalin coursed through him. Thirty-one years had passed since their last encounter, but he instantly recognized those piercing dark eyes and the Hawthorne genetics in that skinny physique.

David's emotionless gaze traced the burly runner's escape route to Eric before he retreated. Eric's pulse exploded. His lungs burned. His fury surged. The beast of madness roared.

That man had stolen so much from him.

He should have turned into an instinctual monster. Should've opened the beast's cage and set it loose. But, as before, a barrier blocked the way. Fresh within him, Paresh's palliative essence restrained the beast, but the hunter's desire for David's blood was just as strong.

A low, steady growl vibrated in his throat. Sharp teeth tore into his lower lip as he clenched his jaw, fighting against his instincts. Paresh's heartbeat galloped in his ears. She was scared and alone. She needed him.

But the urge to follow David was too powerful.

Fuzzy words crossed the distance. He only heard his name and "get the bow ready." The thought of getting vengeance at last released another course of adrenaline. If he'd killed David at the will reading, Andrew and Felicia wouldn't be dead. This was his chance to end an ordeal that had plagued a fifth of his life. If David vanished again, Paresh might never be safe.

He set off for the southern trail with grim determination. Paresh was fine. He'd locked the door, and he'd return before the intruders woke up—only three humans and Jonathan waited ahead—and his fury stood between her and them. Eric may have taken mercy on the intruders, but David Hawthorne had walked the Earth for far too long.

II

A shouting voice startled Paresh awake. Her heart was already hammering from the man in the crimson cloak chasing her dreams again. She swore she could feel him nearby—his presence raised the hairs on her nape—but her pulse pounded harder as her eyes adjusted to the moonless dark and she realized that Eric was gone.

She fisted the sheet, her mind reeling and lungs laboring as she strained to listen for Eric's voice. The yelling faded into the distance. The hall clock ticked out long seconds. Finally, she peeled off the sheet and looked out the window. A shirtless man in black jogging pants was running into the forest.

This isn't really happening. Wake up, a voice in her head commanded. But she knew she was awake. And that Eric was doing exactly what she'd seen in her nightmare. Fright licked her gently. Her legs trembled.

Call the police and stay inside. She threw on a silk night slip and grabbed her robe. She shuffled down the hallway, leaving the lights off. Only the dimmest glow of an overcast night outlined the windows of the living area.

She tripped over a lumpy mass and screamed as her hands slammed down into something that was both soft and hard. A hollowed croaking noise came from in her throat as her fingers dug into a nose, an eye, an ear, hair. Horrified, she dropped the robe and scrambled over the bodies, her chest heaving under full-blown panic, her mind certain that hands were going to pop up and trap her. She cried out and lurched to get clear, landing on her butt and scurrying backward along the floor, clutching her mouth.

She rammed into the sofa and the voice yelled, *Get to the phone!*

But fear held her paralyzed, legs folded beneath her, eyes frozen on the hidden fleshy pile. Somehow, she managed to scoot to the door and pull herself up using the sideboard. She swallowed hard and reached a shaky hand toward the phone.

Clinging to it as a lifeline, she hit the talk button. Silence. A small cry came from her mouth as she stared at the handset in disbelief. She was about to reach for the base when the scrape of metal on metal stopped her cold. She snatched her hand back.

Someone had slid a key into the lock.

Her heart thumped so hard it shook her whole body. Without thinking, she stepped to the side, feebly sheltered behind the door. She clutched the phone at her breast and held her breath. The handle turned and the door slowly opened. Her lungs were on fire, but she didn't dare breathe.

A large form passed through the doorway. She clamped down on her chattering teeth. The ringing in her ears muffled the man's expletive as his massive frame tripped over the hidden bodies. The cottage shuddered under his landing.

She was woozy and lightheaded but this was her one chance. She slipped around the door and silently dashed outside. Gulping for air, she sprinted down the path, her feet hitting the stones hard as tears blurred her vision. She glanced back at the cottage's black entrance. It was empty. Maybe she'd make it to the carriage house before he noticed she was gone.

Another hulking man stepped from the shadows ahead. Terror locked her legs so quickly that she almost tripped. She hugged the phone, quaking as he crept toward her. She recognized him. He was her uncle's friend—and he wore a glowing black ring on his middle finger. Visions from her nightmare flooded her mind, holding her captive as though the cloaked man had already seized his prey.

Time seemed to crawl as she watched him in a daze. Intensely focused on her face, he tried to coax her into taking his extended hand. She squeezed her eyes shut and gritted her teeth. She shook her head and whispered in a shaky voice, "No. *Run!*"

She threw the phone at his head and shot off to the left, arcing toward the southern trail as she ran.

He swatted the phone off and chased after her, angrily yelling, "She's outside! What're you doing in there? Let Simon worry about the damn vault!"

His partner—also wearing an obsidian ring—appeared at the door and jumped out to lead the pursuit. A body slumped on the cottage's west wall jarred free a memory of a man smiling at her— her uncle's neighbor.

All of them—every single one—were people from her childhood. For years, they'd given her support and treated her as a friend, but now they were breaking into her home and lurking in the darkness, and two were chasing her with the scowling faces of men with wicked hearts. None of them resembled the people she'd known. Had *anyone* actually cared for her? She still didn't know her uncle's true intentions, but she was swiftly getting the gist.

Goosebumps riddled her flesh as the cloaked man flashed into her mind. She studied the void of his face and peeled off the shadows. Her uncle stared back at her with eyes so cold they froze her heart. His presence loomed like a black storm cloud.

She shivered involuntarily and a heavy pit formed in her stomach. Knowing she'd lived with such a monster made her feel sick.

Labored breathing and thudding feet closed in behind her. She needed to clear her head and focus. If she let the past consume her in the present, it'd devour her future, too.

The tree line was close, but seemed so far away. In a meager silk slip, and out in the open, she felt naked and vulnerable. She pushed her muscles harder so she could disappear into the forest and finally reached the trail. Taking advantage of her smaller size and slight lead, she jumped off the main path into the dense undergrowth.

And instantly regretted her decision.

Tranquil to wander by day, Sunset Grove mocked her attempt by night. Trees snatched her hair and twisted it around their branches, breaking off or wrenching strands from her head. Low limbs whipped her arms and face, and thorny bushes lashed her belly and raked her legs, tearing at her nightdress and leaving burning welts and bleeding lesions all over her body. Sharp pangs shot up through her bare feet as each hard-hitting footfall landed on twigs and prickly plants. She focused on Eric. On his vow to protect her. On the safety she always felt with him—the safety that lay ahead.

A talon-laden hawthorn branch clawed the length of her cheekbone. Paresh whimpered and pressed her fingers against the gash. The jagged edges seamed back together and, within seconds, her skin was smooth under a slip of blood.

A sizeable black mass loomed ahead. She tried to vault over it—a fallen tree trunk—but its girth was too wide. She scraped off skin from her inner thighs, knee, and shin before crashing onto unforgiving ground.

Hot, stabbing pain shot up her heel through her leg. She yelped and bit down on her lip. Grimacing in eerie shadows and the smell of dank earth, she gripped her ankle and tried to catch her breath as quietly as possible.

She could hear them farther back on the path as she cowered against the damp, moss-covered bark. A scuffling noise to her left might've made her leap up if not for ruthless fear pinning her in place. Fresh tears spilled down her cheeks when a raccoon waddled over and pawed at her breast like a scared child. Its little heart was beating faster than hers. She hugged it close and used its fur to muffle her breathing. She couldn't stop the cry that escaped as the gravity of the situation hit all at once and tears gushed.

"You hear that?" a gruff voice.

Booted feet crunched the trail as the men thrashed the thicket on both sides. She panicked and searched for a useful distraction, but even if she found something, the brush was too thick. She looked at the squirming raccoon in her arms.

I'm sorry, my friend—please help me, she thought as she stroked its fur and set it down on her right, giving it a gentle, insistent nudge. It obediently scampered through the bushes. She flattened herself along the trunk, wedging her way partially beneath it, and held her breath. Making slight shuffling noises, the raccoon scurried across the dirt trail and disappeared into the shadows on the other side.

"There goes your noise," replied the gruff man's partner. "Damn animals. Keep moving. She could be at that tree by now."

They were right next to her. One swivel of the neck and they'd see her pale skin against the darkness. But they didn't. They dashed off to the south as her lungs reached their limits. She huffed out a quiet, shaky breath and sucked in shallow breaths until she couldn't hear them anymore. Then she sat up and gasped.

Her foot *hurt*. So much. She bit down on her lip and drew blood as she brought her foot up to her knee and gingerly felt around her heel. She blew out a bolstering breath and tried to prepare herself. She bit down harder and screamed mentally as she pulled out a pointed fragment of wood. It had stabbed into the bone on that last leap to get over the trunk. Now that it was out, sharp, throbbing pain consumed her entire leg. She thrust her head back against the trunk and grunted through clenched teeth, gripping the shard in a trembling hand.

Squeezing her eyes shut, she prayed for the pain to stop, too aware of how alone she was in the silent gloom. She yearned for Eric so badly that she almost started crying again. The pain's intensity gradually began to fade, her chest stopped heaving, and a semblance of calm replaced panic. She evaluated the wound and felt splinters surfacing as the puncture regenerated from the inside out. All welts and scratches had also healed, although, with her adrenaline fading and draining her energy, exhaustion and chills were creeping in. She hugged her knees to her chest and rubbed her arms for warmth.

She had to think. Needed to *do* something. If those men came back, they'd see her. If she returned to the cottage, she could get Eric's car keys and cell phone—but she'd be out in the open and the others might wake up. Plus…they'd mentioned something about the vault—

"Oh no, Simon, too?" she whispered, thinking back to Eric's argument with him the day before.

Eric had suspected him. It'd been part of his theory—the theory,

Paresh realized, that he hadn't told her. The reasons for Simon's involvement and why the man in the crimson cloak—her uncle—wanted to kill her were mysteries. She shook her head against a defeated urge to cry and forced herself to think it out.

She couldn't chance getting inside and out again without being seen, and then making it safely to the carriage house—assuming no one else was waiting there. And suddenly the thought of running o Eric made her shudder. She'd followed him to her death in her nightmare. The way reality was going, she couldn't assume safety was a guarantee.

Her choices dwindling, she decided to stay hidden by taking the long route through the forest to the main road. The police department was only a few miles from there and running across private properties would shorten the distance. The only real danger there was getting lost.

At over a half dozen square miles, Sunset Grove was a blanketing giant that made it easy to lose sense of direction by day. Even with clear markers, she could wander in a straight line for hours without getting out. Add in the shadows of night and that straight line would twist into an endless series of loops in any direction at any time.

She knew she was near the northern edge, so as long as she used the clearing as a guide, she could reach the break by the carriage house and walk parallel to the rocky drive the rest of the way. It wouldn't be easy. Without the push of adrenaline, her feet would suffer and she'd struggle with obstacles—holes and fallen trunks—but the longest route was ultimately the safest route. Pain would subside and injuries would heal. She needed help to survive.

She stood, leaning against the trunk to keep weight off the injured foot, and bent to whisk a clump of mud from her calf. She needed to get moving, but the throbbing spot in her throat kept turning her thoughts to Eric.

He hadn't come back yet.

Knowingly heading into danger would nullify his efforts to protect her, and if they'd defeated him, she definitely needed Walter Hodges. It was the best she could do with the knowledge she had. She looked to the left, the direction of escape. Nothing but darkness.

She gingerly tested her foot. It was healed and pain free. She took a few steps and stiffened when a twig snapped ahead. The force of the break signaled something heavier than the average woodland creature—and bears didn't live in Sunset Grove.

Her heart skipped as she held her breath and listened. Lifeless air snaked around her and squeezed until the weight of stillness reached an unbearable level. It was too quiet. She swallowed hard and took another tentative step.

Snap! Another twig. Closer than the first. Dread's icy fingers slipped up her spine and drew out an involuntary shiver.

Her heart was beating too fast. She couldn't hear over her thundering pulse and she was taking in too much oxygen. A bead of sweat formed along her forehead. The air was different, energized with unearthly tension. Beyond the instinct to survive, true terror held her in its grip. Whatever was waiting ahead had remained silent until it wanted to make its presence known.

Tingling pressure raced along her cheekbones. She felt like a mouse using its whiskers to sense air currents disturbed by an unseen predator. It came from two separate spots ahead.

They'd been there watching the whole time.

Adrenaline shattered her paralysis. Bright silvery-blue light blew away the shadows. She glanced around, bewildered and searching for a source because the moon was still blocked by cloud cover and the canopy. Then she realized that her eyes felt strange and could suddenly see...*everything*.

The wall of silence crumbled, too. Soft breathing came from the two spots she'd sensed. She wasn't interested in meeting her mysterious stalkers face-to-face. She fled in the opposite direction and crossed the path.

Over her shoulder, she saw two figures cloaked in black with hollow faces emerge from behind the trees. But they didn't advance. They didn't need to. Others were present. She felt them. Heard them. They surrounded her. One was directly ahead. Close.

She swung her head around too late and hit a brick-like mass. The force knocked her to the ground. She crashed onto her elbows, catching a glimpse of a forbidding, yet surprisingly slender and tall, masculine form blocking her way. The figure's face was fringed in thick darkness, impenetrable even by her newly enhanced eyesight.

Not that she had time to try. Noises behind him and to the north and east signaled that the others were moving in. The ominous man reached a gloved hand toward her, but she scurried back, scrambled to her feet, and ran. They'd only left one direction open: south.

Déjà vu nipped hard, but she shook it off. This wasn't the man in the crimson cloak. This was someone else.

The tall man alone chased her initially. Then his cloaked companions swarmed behind him like locusts and fell completely silent. Even the steady footfalls of her pursuer faded away until she heard only the sounds of her forceful breath, her furious feet, and her deafening pulse.

A shattering contrast to her wild flailing, he followed at a regal pace through the trees and cruel undergrowth that raked her body once more. He was unfazed by obstacles, as though Sunset Grove had graced him with a clear path to her, and a wide stride let him catch up with ease. And yet, he'd fall back to lag behind her, as though relishing the hunt.

She barely managed to jump over fallen trunks and limbs, and had to concentrate on the ground to avoid tripping over exposed tree roots. Trying to scream for help only resulted in choking and desperate gasping. The instinct to flee forced her burning legs to keep moving, but no matter how hard she pushed herself, she couldn't gain any ground or widen the gap—he had complete control over his proximity.

Suddenly, the very earth tugged on her ankle. She'd slipped into a rabbit den. Falling at an awkward angle, she threw an arm out but couldn't catch hold of anything. Her knee locked and over-extended, and a violent, head-splitting crack echoed through the trees just before she crashed onto her side. Stars shot through her vision as it tunneled to black and she felt her wrist snap beneath the weight of her body.

☽ ❋ ☾

She was face down in the dirt when she came to. Rapid-fire flashes filled her visual field like thousands of miniature black and white fireflies flickering in a summer eve. She tried to blink them away as an overwhelming urge to flee wormed up her spine. Her mind was fuzzy, but she knew she needed to get up and keep moving.

She gripped the closest tree. Something wet slipped beneath her thumb and she vaguely recalled hitting her head. Her temple on that side was sticky, too. She groaned and tried again, pulling herself up, sharp pain shooting through her limbs and her throbbing head. Her left wrist was disturbingly swollen, limp, and unresponsive, and her knee, bent at the wrong angle, screamed in breathtaking agony when it popped back into place. Uncontrollable sobs shook her whole body, and fat drops fell off her jaw and plopped loudly onto the leaves and dirt.

Somehow, she summoned the strength to rise.

Both legs were wobbly, but she was able to support herself on her good leg with the help of the blood-slicked trunk. The surrounding trees and shadows swirled into a dizzying blur that seemed to spin faster the harder she tried to lock onto a singular point. Her stomach lurched. She wrenched to the side and vomited.

She closed her eyes, but even then, the spinning sensation wouldn't stop. Feeling her stomach contract, she threw up again, and then heaved for breath, choking out acidic residue and streaming tainted snot.

"Why?" she croaked, wiping her mouth as she glimpsed the tall man in her gyrating peripheral. He was mere feet away.

Ghostly whispers floated on the stagnant air. They grew louder and surrounded her like a rioting crowd. "Run! Run! Run! Ru—"

The chanting ceased when the tall man lifted his head. The shadows clinging to his face fell away.

Paresh gasped at his beauty and smooth, blue toned skin that was light as alabaster and far more translucent and luminous than Eric's.

His eyes glittered like diamonds, but drilled into her with the darkness of polished hematite. Two curved, sharp fangs appeared when his petal pale lips parted and a deep, commanding voice escaped his mouth. "Run, Paresh."

Her eyes widened and her mind pitched into a whirl as unsteady as her vision. Eric had said the High Council thought she was their Servator, but the tall man was a vampire. *Vampires* were chasing her through the forest. Yet again forced to acknowledge a grim reality, her confidence in Eric's ability to protect her rapidly dissolved. He possessed strength unknown to men, but so did all vampires.

A giant lump formed in her throat. She choked out, "*What did you do to Eric?*"

She shook with panic and terror as she stared at the vampire through a burning liquid haze. Her mind yelled to run, but her body was rooted. Any of them could have killed her at any time—she refused to run for their thrill of the chase.

The tall vampire pulled off a glove and held his hand out to the side as though reaching for a sword. He splayed his fingers and Paresh watched his nails lengthen to resemble daggers. In an instant, he was in her face, peering deeply into her eyes. Mesmerized, she saw violence and blood from thousands of years pooling in his pupils.

Lowering his gaze to her neck, he ran the back of one daggered claw down her throat. It slid beneath her necklace and traced the delicate silver links, stopping before touching the cross.

"*He* would not want you to give up so quickly." His empty eyes narrowed. "You have been bitten. Obey me. *Run.*"

Her resolve fled with her body. Instinct drove her forward, not permitting her to think or fight back. The tall vampire walked in pursuit as she hobbled through the brush as fast as her wounded body would allow.

She climbed over a thick branch that had splintered under its own weight. None of these trees looked familiar. She was disoriented, but it shouldn't take this long to reach Grandfather Wisdom—especially if she'd been running due south. The tall vampire controlled the pace, but his companions dictated the direction.

They'd been herding her.

Bile rushed up her esophagus. She bent over another tree to spit it out and faltered off balance, collapsing into a blubbering heap. Wondering about the point of it all, she tried to prop herself up with her right hand, but her body suddenly felt heavier than concrete. Lacking the will and strength to hold herself up, she crumpled back down. In her weakened state, she had stopped healing.

The tall vampire, close, yet out of her sightline, reiterated his command, "Run, Paresh."

It sounded like a trace of concern underlined the words, as though her distress was a torment to him. But then he sinisterly added, "You *will* run or you *will* die, right here."

The whispers started again, sailing through the air like fine wisps of spider thread. "Eric." One soft voice after another echoed his name again and again, growing in tempo until it became a steady chant intermixed with, "Run, Paresh. Run."

"*Stop it!*" she screamed, crying into the dirt as she tried to push herself up again.

"Run, Paresh. Run! Run to Eric," the disharmonized voices chanted.

Half crawling, half dragging herself along the ground, she reached for a sapling and hauled herself to her feet. The forest wobbled and stars shot through her vision as she pressed a palm to her head and glanced at the tall vampire through hooded eyes. She swore she saw a line of concern in his apathetic expression, but anything she might've imagined was replaced with a sinister glare. He took a step toward her and she pushed off the tree into a slow, lopsided trot, moving like a live, leaden statue, but he no longer kept his distance. The hem of his cloak brushed her calves and his breath was hot on her nape.

"*Run* for me, Paresh," he whispered, his lips skimming her ear.

Her heart jumped into her throat and she darted ahead, too gripped by fright to register the jarring pain in her knee and ankle. She needed to get away from him, *now*. She hadn't noticed the blue light dimming from her sight, but it faded completely and plunged her into the forest's charcoal veil without warning. She tripped on a tree root and staggered to stay afoot, hopping ahead and barely staying upright on her good leg.

She saw orange flickering ahead. There was a break in the tree line and the area to her right seemed more open. She knew this place. That was the southern trail and the light was coming from the second clearing. Maybe a half mile directly behind her was the bulky trunk that she'd hidden against—the point where this pursuit had started. The vampires had chased her around the perimeter in a giant circle, running her ragged, like that was their sole intent.

She reached the edge of the forest and her fear of the tall vampire collided with her dread of setting a single foot into that clearing. Her legs cramped and refused to carry her any further, but her momentum was still moving forward. Throwing her eyes over her shoulder as she fell, she saw the tall vampire stop, and as she collapsed into the clearing, she lost sight of him, but knew he was there, lingering unseen, silent in the darkness.

The breeze in the clearing swept over her sweaty and bleeding skin, and the tension drained from her body into the grass. Her heart thundered. Her lungs burned for oxygen. Her body screamed for respite. Pressure pounded her head.

But even as heavy tears obscured her vision, she recognized the polished black leather shoes that appeared before her eyes. And the crimson hem that hung above the laces. Terror squeezed her heart as she choked out denials and hyperventilated at the sound of his voice.

"My dear, you look absolutely dreadful."

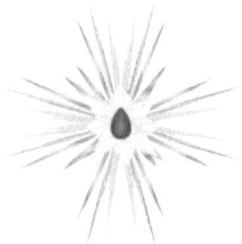

CHAPTER FIFTEEN: PROPHECY

I

Two roaring bonfires flung sinister shadows high into Grandfather Wisdom's waiting arms. Flames nipped at their heels and kept them afloat like demons trying to save their feet from the fires of Hell.

She closed her eyes to shut it all out. Her mind screamed not to give up, but every inch of her body ached and throbbed. She dropped her nose to the ground and futilely tried to push herself up. With one arm completely out of commission and the other refusing to obey her brain, she stared out over the grass. Defeated, she waited for her uncle to speak again.

She grew aware of a static-laden buzz and her heart lurched at the sounds of low, broken grunting. David's hem blocked her view of the source, but Nicole, flanked by the men from earlier—all wearing blood red cloaks—looked wickedly content, if not a bit impatient.

"Da...vid!"

The pained, unearthly growl stole what was left of Paresh's hope. Perhaps the vampire swarm had truly been the shadow of Death, escorting her to the end of her life.

"Eric," she whispered sadly.

"May I help you up?" David asked in a smooth voice. "We've been waiting so long for you to join us. You missed quite an exciting family reunion, I must say. I don't think our *friend* was too happy to see me again. But that feeling was mutual."

Unable and unwilling to accept his outstretched hand, she stared helplessly at his fingers, noting that he wasn't wearing the large obsidian ring from her nightmare. He crouched and drew her into his cloak, leaning her spent frame against his chest. Dirt and blood streaked his white shirt.

"Please just tell me why?" she whispered into his shoulder length hair. The strong scent of his aftershave turned her already queasy stomach. His quiet smile did nothing to soothe it.

The pounding in her head worsened with each step he took. She tried to look over his shoulder, but slid from his grasp and forced him to hoist her up over his shoulder. The movement was quick and effortless. David was stronger than he looked.

When he was almost at Grandfather Wisdom's base, his grip loosened and her angle shifted, finally letting her see the whole clearing. Two men lay on the ground: one motionless and contorted into an unnatural position as though hurled like a doll. The other was pinned to the ground by what appeared to be a pulsing, neon blue blanket of electricity.

"*Eric!*" Her weak and scratchy voice barely crossed her lips, but she knew he heard her. Seeing him in agony broke her heart. "Please...don't hurt him."

The mask of desperation and rage on Eric's face twisted his handsome features into something devilish. His darkened and engorged eyes softened as they landed on her, but then his lips curled over his teeth into a vicious snarl and he flicked his bloodthirsty glare to David.

"*Let...her...go!*" he seethed, his inhuman voice broken and raspy.

Invisible, icy veins snaked through the air to encircle Paresh and David. It made her skin crawl and prickled the hair on her nape. A vice tightened in her chest and she shivered from renewed terror as the air thickened and clawed at her exposed skin like it was peeling it off layer by layer. She moaned in pain.

David spun around to face Eric. The hatred in his voice lent the image of a cruel sneer to her mind.

"This superb material provided by your dear brother blocks your preternatural attacks, demon. You're only affecting one of us. Care to guess which one? Go ahead and make it that much easier on me. Her death is on you, anyway. Then again, aren't they all?"

The savage, cold air withdrew instantly.

"Please don't hurt him," she repeated sadly. The High Council must have rescinded their order restricting Jonathan's involvement and the only man capable of saving her had already been subdued. The presences of the vampires in the shadows made sense now. Even if Eric could escape that trap, they wouldn't let him intervene.

Nicole ran a hand through her fiery hair and snapped, "You two make sure he's secure! And take those damn rings off. You're not hiding from him now." She turned an unnaturally bright emerald gaze on David. "Let's get this over with and be done with it."

Paresh had seen through Nicole's attractive facade to the ugliness in her heart long ago, but not to the depths of the evil that had rooted there. Nicole's hatred was probably the driving force behind many of David's actions, not that he needed much of a push given his history.

The men grunted profanities and slurs at Eric, and horror took its turn to embrace Paresh as she heard the sound of metal sliding from a leather sheath. Facing death was scary enough, but fearing for someone else was far worse. She mentally screamed for Eric's life, but he was yelling for hers.

Confused, Paresh tried to find the blade. Before she could figure out what was happening, the desperation in Eric's voice and all other noise faded away. She felt Grandfather Wisdom's bark on her backside and a church choir's somber euphony rose within her, consuming her mind with "ahs" and "ohs" that carried high over sad violins and a woeful pipe organ as baritones dipped into underlying chanting.

Deafened by this...delusion, Paresh saw Nicole's devilish smile and realized the blade wasn't intended for Eric—at least not yet. Powerless to protect her and growing more frantic by the second, Eric was screaming at David and fighting against the electric current. The chorus sang over his voice as she glanced into the shadows and wondered if the vampires there would save him after she was dead.

The instruments and chorus sifted into the background and the male voices grew to prominence to dynamic a cappella chanting. David maneuvered her arms over wooden stakes driven into the trunk to support her weight, but she flopped loosely between them. He held her in place while Nicole barked orders at her goons, who came running with a wide leather restraint. The belt pressed tightly into her abdomen and ribs, the rigid material restricting her to short, shallow breaths. Additional belts were wrapped across her chest and legs, and two urns were placed beneath her arms.

The chanting quieted and the choir returned in prominence with its sorrowful refrain, and the organ and violins flourished. Paresh watched the fires' tiny reflections frolic inside her tears as they fell to the ground. David's back was to her, but as he turned and pulled the cloak's hood over his head, her stomach clenched at the silver dagger in his hand.

Without looking at her, he pressed the blade into the underside of her left forearm. The blade cut deep and sliced through skin and connective tissues down the full length. Blood gushed out and an electric shock sensation shot into her hand, stinging her palms and fingertips, followed by fiery pressure that intensified as though a ferocious animal had clamped down to tear her arm off.

Her fingers went numb and she lost the sensation of his hand holding hers. But when he yanked her arm straight and stabbed the dagger into her wrist, burying the hilt into her skin, the immense pain stole her breath. He thrust the dagger's tip into the tree, firmly securing it to let her blood stream into the urn below.

Nicole handed him a second dagger. He brought it against Paresh's right forearm, but didn't break the skin. The baritone chanting rose above the weak whimper she felt rattling in her throat. David paused, as if in thought, but swiftly repeated the motions, hesitating again only after running the blade through her wrist. His fingers lingered on the handle.

Short, rapid breaths labored to supply Paresh's constricted lungs as the chorus reached a feverish pitch. She waited for the final thrust. But David wasn't moving. He stared at her as if seeing her for the first time, his eyes tortured with despair.

The choir clipped their notes short and fell silent. The crackling of the fires seemed far away, Eric's shredded yelling was a distant echo, and David's voice sounded flat and dull.

"Why did you do it?" he asked quietly with a disturbing gentleness. "It didn't have to turn out this way."

He lifted her chin and smudged her tears with a gore-slicked knuckle, sighing as his eyes wandered over her face. Furrowing his brow, he carefully pulled twigs and leaves from her hair with bloodstained fingers, and smoothed her tangled strands. His hand slipped down to stroke the back of her neck. The slight smile on his lips turned her stomach.

"Your hair is such a mess, but you're still so beautiful to me. I've always thought so. You know, all those years ago, I meant it when I told you I loved you. I was such an angry young fool. I didn't really care that you didn't feel the same way. You would have, in time. I know it...except that *Andrew* stole you away." He spat his brother's name as his tender words twisted and became bitter. "But oh no! Everybody loved him—perfect as a peach *Andrew*. Our parents. Their friends. Their colleagues. Acquaintances. The staff. That *creature* over there. Even *you*."

He clenched his jaw and released her chin. Paresh's head dropped, and she struggled against heavy eyelids and blurry vision to watch him pace before her. Nicole's eyes darkened and narrowed, but he was oblivious to her.

"What was so damn special about Andrew? I should have killed him that night—none of this would have happened. I had my hands around his perfect little throat, but his protector, his 'guardian' was there—"

He glared at Eric. "Always there. Always watching over my perfect brother, *Andrew*. Well you failed, didn't you? Your time will come. You will see—karmic retribution for the sins against our family, for innocent blood spilled because of your selfishness. Andrew met his end, his punishment, and I'll gladly send you to join him. You liked him so damn much, it's only fitting."

"*David!*" Eric growled. "You won't...get what you want. Jonathan's...a *liar!* Let...*Paresh*...go!" An anguished grunt followed as he thrust his head against the ground in desperation.

But reality was gone to David. He whipped around, ogling Paresh with wild eyes. "Andrew wasn't happy enough being perfect and getting everything that he wanted. He found something that wasn't his and took it anyway. *He stole my love.* He ripped out my heart and tore you away from me. He—no! *They!* Destroyed. My *life!*" He shrieked the last word with a spray of spittle at Eric before turning a sinister, narrowed gaze upon Paresh.

"But you weren't so innocent," he seethed. "Oh no. You shattered my heart. Did you think that would go unpunished? I took away what you loved most. Oh, so sad—you didn't have any family left, did you? You should've stayed with me. I would've given you everything and more. You were all I ever wanted."

He sucked in a deep breath and rolled his head back, bobbing it dramatically with each statement. "Yet you stayed with *him*. You married *him*. Then you had a child with *him*. That was supposed to be my life. *Mine!*"

He faced away, muttering, "That child. That spawn of my brother's seed, a stain upon the Earth, evidence of the love my brother stole, the love that should have been mine."

He looked at her without seeing her. He shot his hands angrily into the air and shook his head. "Ha! I couldn't sit by and watch him enjoy you any longer! I saw what he was doing to you, how broken and weak you were—how sick you'd become. He did that to you. I never would have caused you such pain."

He tucked in close to stroke her cheek, pleading in a quiet voice, "I had to kill you. It was the only way to spare your misery and mine. But then, seeing you lying there, bloody and lifeless in that wreckage...you crushed my heart. How could you do that to me, again? Were you put here only to torment me?"

Moisture surged around his dilating pupils. "But then you came back to me. You haunted my existence, my dreams, only you were real. You were there—*really there*—and you were strong, like you used to be. I wanted to go to you. I wanted to be with you, but—"

Recognition briefly flickered as he glanced at Nicole. "Our time had passed. No...*no!* I don't believe that! I'd never give up on us! It's not too late. You came back! You knew you'd made a mistake."

He whispered, "I always loved you. I only wanted you back. You should have come to me. *I would have taken you back!*" He screamed in her face, sneering and glaring like a feral animal.

"Uncle David, please, don't do this," she whispered, barely conscious. She felt herself slipping away; she could just close her eyes and drift off.

"David!" he mocked in a high-pitched voice. He punched the trunk beside her head, huffing and gritting his teeth, staring at her with rampant frustration.

Then, something shifted in the way he was looking at her. His expression relaxed and softened. "It's not too late," he said in a quiet, affectionate voice. "I'll forgive you and we can be together, at last. I do love you. I never stopped."

He held her right hand against his chest and tugged the dagger free. As he reached for her left hand, he paused and lifted her chin instead. His eyes bore into hers and slowly closed as he leaned in. Bile burned her throat. His lips pressed against hers and his face contorted with pain. He gasped, falling limply and clutching at her body and breasts as he slid to the ground, crying, "I only wanted...your love...Felicia."

He collapsed into a pile of red fabric at her feet, the glint of a silver hilt in his back. Nicole stood over him with a look of disgust on her face. Anchoring her foot against his body, she yanked the dagger from his heart and kicked him so that he rolled face up. She recovered the other bloodied weapon from his hand.

"Sick bastard. I'll never understand why *He* insists on loving you people," she muttered with a scowl. She motioned for her goons to drag David's corpse to the edge of the circle, then faced Paresh with a wicked twinkle in her eyes and a mischievous smile on her lips. "As much as I love to watch y'all torment each other, I really must move this along. Time's awastin' and I can't have him undoing all our progress, now can I?"

Nicole roughly squeezed Paresh's jaw and peered into her eyes. Licking her lips, she taunted, "He'd lay awake at night fantasizing about you. Jonathan regretted his decision to have you live with us real quick. You have no idea how many times he had to convince David that you weren't *her*."

Nicole cracked Paresh's head against the tree as she inspected her throat and flashed an evil grin. "Of course, I knew better than to believe Jonathan's bullshit, but he had quite a hold on David. He believed every line that came from that rotten vampire's mouth. But me? Well, I have always wanted you dead. From the moment I learned of your existence."

Her face took on the look of soured stone as she raised a dagger high over her head. Inhuman hatred burned in her eyes as she curled her lips into a snarl and plunged the blade into Paresh's chest.

II

Veiled in the forest's inky swell, Jonathan wrestled with emotions he'd never before felt. A restless urgency nipped at his ribs to leap into the clearing to stop the very thing he'd spent decades orchestrating. He clenched his teeth and fought an internal battle unlike anything he'd ever faced.

It's only a game, he thought. *Another death like all the rest!*

In the clearing, David speared Paresh to the tree. The scent of her blood snaked up Jonathan's nostrils and awakened something hot in his gut.

If Eric wasn't so vexingly stubborn! If David wasn't so sniveling! If only you'd killed them all so long ago!

His thoughts raged uncontrollably. Pathetically. Surely, someone as powerful as him could conquer a voice that didn't exist.

And yet it prodded, relentless.

Why? Why? Why? He grabbed at his head, claws digging into his scalp as he let a silent howl fly into the canopy.

He knew the why. Of course he did. He'd succumbed to the thrill of the fight. And he'd released a monster into his blood.

But enjoying a good kill, any kill, is only natural!

Lucifer had given him the most savage bloodlust of his kind. And it was the truest, purest joy he'd known all his life.

Until the Treaty shut him down.

Then came Eric. And with him? Ecstasy. Human marionettes prefilled with hate and betrayal, as ready to maim and kill themselves as they were each other. He'd seen it in every single one, on every single day, since Lucifer delivered him to Earth.

Humans were primed for violence and so malleable that they deserved all that befell them. Finally, after a thousand years of peaceful drivel, he'd found a thrill rivaling the War's fields of blood.

Because this one came with a reward: Eric.

Oh how he'd thrived pulling the Hawthorne strings! Walking among them unseen. Whispering. Influencing. Careful to tiptoe that line protecting the Flock. Devouring Eric's misery. Watching his human spark dim with each precious death.

But this...

This was distressing.

And he didn't like it.

For thousands of years, he'd satisfied his every desire. Why did he suddenly feel so *bad*?

The anger he usually craved to see on Eric's face was a torment. And Paresh—

Pare...

He couldn't bear to look at her. A thousand daggers piercing his heart would hurt less.

The jagged holes in her slip. The bloody scrapes. The head to toe dirt and mud. Her sorrow. Her heartache...David's mad lust.

How could he have anticipated the effect of her essence? That he'd grow fond of her? That he'd want to protect her? That he'd hated the thought of sending her home?

And he'd been so exactingly cold with David, too. Building upon his paranoia. Goading him to exact his revenge. Dutiful in his assignment, all the while infuriated to be raising a human. Him. The Second Born. Stuck in the Realm of Man, rearing one of *them*—he knew nothing of such a thing.

And yet...it was undeniable. He and Paresh had bonded. The connection formed unbeknownst to him, over the barest fraction of his life, and while he couldn't say he felt any better for it, he finally understood Eric's attachments to these fleeting, fragile things.

He thought back to her departure in Kansas. The pit in his gut when the train arrived. The sick feeling that clung uncomfortably close as she stepped on board without him. The desire to tear out David's throat before he could follow her.

A side effect of spending too much time with humans? He'd immediately recognized it for what it was: the protective instinct of a father. That sickened him on a different level.

The Great Second Born...

He sighed deeply and instantly regretted it. The air was thick with her blood now. It covered him like a wet blanket, heavy and claustrophobic.

That is guilt, you idiot. You think yourself a father? You killed her entire family. And now you're killing her. You can't deny accountability—you're the one holding that dagger with David's hands.

He wanted to scream aloud. To lash his talons out and shred

David into unrecognizable pieces. To sate his wrath and emerge bathed in blood as he had so many days during the War.

That war had upended a simpler life alone with Lucien. They left a wake of crimson in their footsteps and basked in the freedom to do what they wanted, when they wanted. Nothing had ever been the same. The Treaty delivered a pacifist lifestyle that challenged Jonathan's all-consuming thirst, but Lucien had slid into his new role with ease, able to hide behind all the pomp.

The Lasting Peace had been anything but that for him, and yet he'd rather face that again than deal with this hell. These emotions were plagues upon plagues. That much he knew, though he knew little else—even about his infatuation with Eric.

Some unexplainable *thing* had drawn him to Eric. A thirst beyond the blood flowing in Eric's veins—although, to be sure, that sweet nectar had driven Jonathan mad numerous times. Yes, he wanted Eric. All of Eric. But he also wanted more. What he shared with Lucien—a companion—but on equal footing. Someone free to roam the world, who didn't wield power over him, with whom no formalities existed. Someone he could spar with, who understood his thirst—a vampire on his level: just like Eric.

A low groan scraped past his lips as he wiped his face and peered into the clearing. Desperation and rage contorted Eric's face as he fought to free himself. The Jonathan of Yesterday would've salivated at the sight and of the promise that lingered within. But the Jonathan of Today saw Eric differently. And he didn't like it. A switch had been flipped and turned infatuation off—but not by choice.

He scratched at the scowl on his own face. His skin was too tight. He felt constrained in his body, unable to relax. He flexed his fingers and huffed in another blood soaked sigh of frustration.

David had sliced through both of Paresh's wrists and her pulse was slowing. A crushing, panicked jolt gripped Jonathan's heart. He skewered a tree trunk and struggled to contain the growl rumbling louder in his throat. It had to be enough that her spirit would rise above her violent death and find peace. But it wasn't. It never could be—not without her essence there to brighten his world. And he had only himself to blame. Forced by Lucien's order to use David's ridiculous plan.

He'd rather give her a quick, painless death.

No—you'd rather not see her die at all, he thought bitterly, realizing that he had yet to wrangle with Eric's fury in the aftermath, and that a good share of that would be directed at him.

He ground his teeth in disgust. Like Eric, he disagreed with Lucien. Paresh's blood was inside him, enhancing the feelings he'd felt for her more than a hundredfold. That decade with her had only given him a taste. Real love was a violent, dominating force, and it wouldn't let him pretend he was as powerless as he felt. Or that it wasn't his place to question Lucien—that his duty to Lucien came above all else.

Lucifer's intent for his life had always been clear—Jonathan was made for Lucien, a creature who knew of no equal and only two beings to be above him: *Him* and Lucifer. Lucien knew well the power he commanded, having spent his solitary years on Earth as an apex predator. The Treaty had changed Jonathan's life, but it had not changed the nature of his creation. He was beneath Lucien in the hierarchy, and that was true even in their intimate moments—figuratively and literally.

But that was Lucifer's intent. Lucifer's will. Lucien had never given Jonathan any reason to question it—until now. Lucien had agreed with Lord Ceallach and the other naysayers. The sting of that betrayal made Jonathan wonder what *he* wanted to do with his life. Dared him to think of rebellion. To say, *'Everything Lucien does, he does for the Vampiric Nation,'* be damned!

They were wrong. He knew it. Felt it. Felt *her*. In his blood.

Narrowing his eyes on David and Nicole, his anger sparked anew. Suddenly it was so imperative that Paresh die. Why? Letting her live might prove that the time for prophecy had come. Surely, if *He* had sent her as the fabled Servator for their salvation, Lucien wouldn't risk the Nation like this. Would action or inaction avoid eternal damnation for them all?

If he was wrong and he rebelled, Jonathan would reunite a race that had been damned from the start with their creator and the souls of the wicked they'd killed. Perhaps Jonathan hadn't shared the true bloods' desire for the lives of men, but he wanted more from Fate than that.

Grinding his teeth, he speared another tree and huffed harder.

Oh, how he wanted—*needed*—to lunge into that clearing! Over the course of human history, others had fallen further from the Flock than David and Nicole, but they had gone quite far, surely deep into the ranks of those destined for the Lake of Fire, beyond salvation or forgiveness. The world would welcome their deaths.

Lucien ordered the death of a member of the Flock. Humans are merely a tool. Will that technicality truly matter to Gabriel in the end?

Where was this doubt coming from? Lucien's wisdom and guidance had given every vampire a chance to enjoy life while awaiting deliverance. With nary a complaint, Lucien had ruled despite never wanting to command an army of thousands in a war not his own.

But…

What if Lucien's thirst was stronger than Jonathan knew? What if this wasn't about the solitude that came with being Arch Elder? Did Lucien secretly prefer the raw freedom of destruction and wanton carnage? Maybe he didn't want salvation. Perhaps he'd merely bargained a furlough for the true bloods in the face of slaughter.

From the moment of inception, the Vampiric Nation had lived by a treaty with loopholes that allowed them to prey on the fallen and wicked. If Lucien planned to return to war, their current populace vastly outnumbered their original army. He may have set up a governing body, but Lucien always had the final say and no one questioned him. Lucien alone ruled the Vampiric Nation. The High Council was a farce.

As that realization sank in, he watched Nicole stab David in the back and kick him aside. A sudden chill fell over him and he shivered, dreading what would come next. As a heavy pit grew in his gut, he forced his gaze forward. He would not permit himself to look away. This was his doing. He would bear witness.

Nicole plunged a dagger into Paresh's chest with visceral hatred and Paresh's heart failed to complete its final beat. Blurring wetness surged into Jonathan's eyes. He balled his fists, driving his nails into his palms. He didn't know what else to do but let the emotional wave crest over him.

Lucien's desire had become reality.

Jonathan's jaw shook too badly for him to whistle to his pack to begin the cleanup process, and the weight of that anger, or guilt, or sorrow—whatever the hell it was—spread to his entire body. His chest rose and fell rapidly. He thirsted for Nicole's life, but couldn't move. And that's when he noticed the dislodged stakes holding the electrified netting in place over Eric, and saw what the humans didn't: the current flickering out.

He dared not interfere now. He was about to witness what he'd yearned for: Eric fully embracing his true nature.

"Sate your thirst for revenge, Brother," Jonathan whispered. "You're finally coming home."

III

A satisfied grin crept across Nicole's face. After years of Jonathan's interference, she'd finally killed the girl—and with Lucien's blessing, no less. There was one more, though. *His* blood had brought her back once before, she could not risk it happening again. She kicked over one urn of Paresh's blood. Before she could tip the other, guttural sounds turned her around.

"How?" she demanded upon seeing Eric freed of the electric webbing. He was wrestling with her two remaining men, and while she didn't care if he killed them, she needed him contained.

He cast one man off and viciously latched onto the other's throat. The man's cries died the instant Eric's teeth sank into his flesh. The other tried to attack, but Eric used the body as a shield while replenishing some of his massive energy expenditure. Savagery burned in the eyes Eric turned on the final man as he lifted his mouth from the dead man's neck. Twisting his lips into a bloody snarl, Eric tossed the body aside and took a menacing step.

"No!" Nicole marched over, and, at her signal, the surviving man leaped beyond Eric's grasp and grabbed a black crossbow from the grass. He moved to her side as she eyed the discarded carcass and shot Eric a sly smile. Firelight danced in her eyes and glinted off her glossy lips.

"If I didn't know better, I'd say the rumor I heard is true—that you do share the bloodline of the first two creations. And I cannot deny that your power is impressive." She cocked her head like an innocent child studying a new peculiar *thing*. "I want to know why, but not more than I want you dead."

She motioned for the man to raise the weapon, which he did with a quivering arm. Eric's engorged, watery stare shot beyond them to Paresh's bloody frame hanging limply from the leather restraints. Every muscle in his body quaked and rage shaded his face dark red.

Ensuring that she was out of the line of fire, Nicole stepped to the midpoint between Eric and the weapon. She lifted her chin and looked down her nose in mock sympathy, relishing his pain. "Her death was long overdue, and the sight of you makes me rethink many of the things I've done, but I must send you to join her. I simply cannot permit you to live."

Eric dropped to his hands and knees and howled in unearthly anguish. His chest heaved and saliva dripped from his fangs as he growled at the pair in a timbre below the range of human hearing. Nicole couldn't hear it as clearly as she'd like, but she caught enough. Without Paresh's calming aura, there was nothing left to hold him back from that vital precipice. The beast's insatiable bloodlust was in control.

As his growl rumbled to a higher frequency, Eric's animalistic gaze darted from Nicole to the weapon. The moment he bolted up, she snapped her fingers. The man's finger twitched on the trigger. Eric lunged.

Inhumanly swift and fluid, Nicole spun on her heel, kicking the weapon out of the man's hands, and settled into Eric's path. She accounted for his momentum and threw a punch. He blocked with his right arm and grabbed her throat with his left, but before he could squeeze her head off, she thrust up from below and pierced his chest with the last dagger.

His hands dropped limply to his sides. He couldn't even grab the hilt. Death had claimed his eternal soul the instant the blade impaled his heart. Nicole watched him collapse with a heavy, lifeless thud.

"I created you bastards. I can definitely kill you," Nicole spat.

"*No!*" came an unearthly growl from the forest.

Jonathan stepped from the tree line, grinding his jaw as he gawked at Eric's body in disbelief. His eyes narrowed and his lips formed a loathsome sneer. He flew at Nicole, running so fast he seemed to glide over the grass.

"Lucifer!" he seethed.

Nicole lifted her chin with confidence, but the man behind her fled in fear to the edge of the circle. Nicole met Jonathan's demonic countenance with a smug grin.

"Second Born." Her voice was seductively feminine with an unearthly edge. "Don't mind this body. Come give Daddy a kiss…if you think you'll survive it." She arched her neck and ran her fingers down her throat.

"Do you dare mock me? You may lurk in her heart, but you are confined to her human limitations. Your ability to kill him was a fluke. You won't be so lucky with me." His eyes mournfully shifted to Eric's corpse.

She shot Jonathan a fierce look. "He *does* belong to you, doesn't he? With that face…just how did *that* happen?"

Jonathan wrapped a hand around Nicole's throat. "Why did you kill him?"

"Oh, you are such a fool, Jonathan. Surely, I gave you more intelligence than that. He's a pawn. He could have brought her back to life. Do you really think I'd permit your Servator to save even one of you traitorous wretches? I gave you existence and the ability to take over *Heaven*, and you repaid me by switching sides—which is why I'm terribly curious to know why the First Born ordered her death. Our shared desire intrigues me. Tell me why that is. Do you know?"

She studied him, and for a brief moment, childlike wonderment filled her eyes—she truly expected Jonathan to give her an answer just like that. When he failed to respond, the illusion shattered.

"I see. You don't know a thing, do you?" She smirked. "A betrayal like that might bring one to question one's master, wouldn't you think? I mean, I—for one—am *thuh-rilled* that she's dead, but it makes you wonder whose side Lucien is really on, huh?" Her tone dripped with sickly sweet sarcasm. She beamed a fake smile, unfazed by his choking hold.

Jonathan glared at her and clenched his teeth. Grief and uncertainty were eating away at him. He didn't know what to say.

Nicole wrapped her hands around Jonathan's forearm, tightened her grip to force his muscles to relax, and slid free from his grasp. "I am not as powerless in this body as you think."

She glanced up at the sky and tapped her cheekbone a few times. "Hm, you know what?" She pointed at Jonathan and smiled again. "It may interest you to know that you were the one who alerted me to her presence in the first place. Your desire to kill has always made you easy to track—the scent of freshly spilled blood trails you. You make me so proud, I swear," she said, batting her eyelashes and marking an "X" over her heart with her finger.

Jonathan's jaw clamped down tighter. She continued on, inspecting her nails as she spoke.

"As a restless creation, you've never stayed in one place, yet for the last century and a half, you've lingered here with the lovely stench of innocent death hovering around you. I knew something had gotten your attention."

She dropped her hand and met his eyes, dramatically feigning dissatisfaction. "Really, Jonathan, I am terribly disappointed. Your lust for him makes you just like *them*." She shook her head and waved her finger at him. "Tsk, tsk."

Her finger stopped in midair and began drumming against it instead. She licked her lips and nodded in thought, saying, "But then again, imagine my surprise when I saw *Him* at work in the background. Sure enough, she showed up. It seems I'm not the only one watching you, so I've been careful, waiting for the right moment. And Lucien simply handed it to me."

Anger lit her eyes ablaze with an unholy flame as she sneered, "The thought of you joining the Flock sickens me even more than watching them revel in His undeserved love." Her palm smacked against her chest. "*We* were the creations of love incarnate, living in a perfect utopia free from pain or want, but He had to share His love—and with such imperfect things, too."

She made a frustrated sound in her throat and shook her head. "I'd much rather watch you suffer your own damnation on Earth with the rest of us than to fall into His good grace. You deserve that even less than them."

A wicked smile spread across her face when Jonathan continued to simmer in silence. "You were always my favorite, you know, even though Lucien's cold heart makes him the perfect creature. I hate to say it, but I should've left well enough alone and created the others like him. Oh well. C'est la vie. Enjoy your eternal unrest, Jonathan. You personally brought it onto your entire race."

Jonathan growled and snatched her by the throat again. Nicole seductively lowered her lashes and smiled. "Without her energy to supply her blood, that urn is useless. I'm sure it'll make a sweet snack for you though. 'Til we meet again. Rest assured that I'll reserve a nice, toasty place in Hell for you. Bye-bye, Jonathan. Have a nice life." Nicole gasped and the flame in her eyes was snuffed.

With Lucifer gone from Nicole's body, Jonathan took immediate control of her. "You sold your soul to the Devil and sealed your fate to burn for all eternity in the Lake of Fire," Jonathan growled at her. "Perhaps he promised that you'd stand at his side. Foolish human! He will not rule over Hell. He'll burn. Just like the rest of us."

He flicked his hand and a dozen cloaked figures emerged from the forest to attack her terror-struck manservant. A tremor appeared in Nicole's jaw as she listened to his screams and blood choked gurgles, but Jonathan did not permit her eyes to move from his.

He slid his hand up her throat and held her by the jaw, curling his lips back over his teeth. Utter terror contorted Nicole's façade as her focus shifted between Jonathan's eyes and his fangs.

"Lucifer thinks he has won, but he missed a crucial detail. His blood—" He roughly twisted her jaw to force her to look upon Eric's corpse without allowing her to see the commotion behind her. "Flows in my veins, too."

He tilted her head to the side and observed the pulse in her throat. "You are beyond redemption. I should throw you to my pack to be devoured. But you don't deserve that honor. You threw away your life—your death will be equally meaningless."

Returning his hand to her throat, he squeezed without mercy and turned away to kneel at Eric's side. She lurched down with him and convulsed on the ground, digging her nails into his fingers, desperate to break free. He didn't spare her another glance.

With his free hand, he pulled the dagger from Eric's chest and wiped the blade on his slacks before tossing it aside. A despondent sigh fled his lips. Anger and sorrow had filled his last moments, but, in death, Eric looked serene and peaceful. New feelings of grief and guilt crashed into Jonathan like a brick wall. If he hadn't hesitated...

Eric's death had been avoidable. He could have stopped Nicole. He should have.

Jonathan affectionately stroked Eric's cheek until the woman stopped clawing the flesh off his arm. Only when her heart stopped completely did he loosen his grip. It was unfathomable to think of a human so easily slaying Eric, possessed or not. He'd underestimated Lucifer's ability to control human reflexes.

"Eric…" The feeble voice of a young woman sailed past Jonathan on a lone current of air. Movement on Eric's chest drew his attention—the wound there was healing. Jonathan caught his breath.

"Eric…" The voice circled back and lured his gaze to Paresh. His brow dipped as he studied her and stood. It was her voice.

He tossed Nicole's body like a rag and flicked his hand, a signal to the others to remove her. "She is still warm, do what you will."

Only the Commander of his pack approached. Darkness veiled his face as he nodded a silent acknowledgment.

Gazing at Paresh, Jonathan told him, "Gather the bodies. The survivors are not of the Flock—do not suffer them to live or allow them to join our ranks. David killed Simon earlier this evening and dumped his body in a ravine west of here. Retrieve it, as well, and return to the cottage to await my next directive. I need a moment."

"As you command." The vampire's voice was masculine and gentle. He collected Nicole and motioned for others to remove the corpses of David and the two men that Eric had killed.

When they left, Jonathan swept his hand over Eric's eyes and took a few minutes to mourn his brother. But then the whisper floated past again and he acknowledged what he needed to do.

He left Eric for Paresh. Blood trickled from her arm into the crimson pool of the remaining urn while it dripped from her other arm onto the tipped pot and dribbled down the side. She hung there with no breath to feed her life and no soul to fill her body, but she had always existed outside of nature's typical boundaries. Eric's blood within him would revive her.

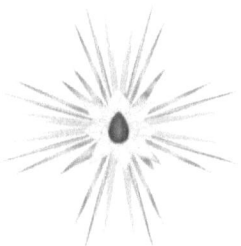

Chapter Sixteen: Serendipity

I

A voice in his head screamed that he was a heretic and traitor—words he knew in the deepest part of his core to be true. All his life, he had blindly followed Lucien and—until now—had obeyed him without question. But that was before the Elders' fear had killed their only path to salvation.

He removed his suit jacket and rolled up his shirtsleeves, well aware that his actions would jeopardize his future. But facing Lucifer for the first time in millennia confirmed what he'd already felt. Even if it meant facing Lucien's wrath, Jonathan would risk his life to restore hers, and would spend the rest of his days defending her. He pulled the daggers from her chest and wrist and tossed them aside.

Seeing Paresh like this made him feel like *he* had a dagger in his heart. Her ragged appearance was a testament to the agony she'd suffered before her death, broken both mentally and physically by unlikely allies: the humans created by *Him* to exist in the Realm of Man and the creatures designed by Lucifer to eradicate them.

And it's my fault.

The fires reflected off the diamonds embedded in the cross around her neck. He didn't feel the usual compulsion to shy away from it. Curious, he inched a finger along her collarbone and traced the necklace down to the tip of the holy trinket. He sucked in a nervous breath and slid his hand beneath the cross.

He gasped. He was holding it. In his hand. *Him*. The Second Born. Palming a cross without searing burns or the slightest discomfort. He couldn't believe it.

Looking from the cross to the sky as though searching for a sign, he drew in another nervous breath. No—he didn't need a sign. There'd been purpose to his fight with Eric after all. She'd already saved *him*.

Lady Rainne's voice of reason streamed through his mind: *A true blood can be a soldier of Destiny, but not the bringer of our salvation.*

Wanting to be that soldier, he bit a chunk of flesh from his wrist. He tipped Paresh's chin with his free hand and let his blood flow into her mouth. It pooled and overflowed, and stained her skin as it spilled down her chin onto her body. He flattened his index finger to hold her tongue down to help it slide down her throat.

It'll drain into her lungs, he thought, pulling his arm back and watching for any indication that this was going to work.

His eyes widened as the blood that had spilled over collated and formed into an unnatural flow that ran the length of her body, snaking and branching off to fill her open wounds. Each tender area soaked up his blood like a sponge and slowly began to regenerate. Even the stab wound in her chest began to heal, just as Eric's had.

Jonathan glanced over at Eric's body and realized that Paresh's blood had been on the dagger that Nicole used. Tentative hope began to bloom beneath his ribs.

He grabbed her right hand and turned her wrist up so that he could stream his blood into the deep gash. The fibers and cells absorbed every drop and began reconnecting. He repeated the action with her left hand, and then waited and listened closely.

Seconds passed. Then minutes. He clenched his jaw. It was foolish to think he had enough of Eric's blood in his body to bring her back. What had he done by allowing her to die? He doubted there was hope for any of them—

Thump...

...thump.

It was so faint he almost missed it.

He pressed his ear over her heart and held his breath.

Thump...

...thump.

It happened again and again, getting louder and stronger and faster with each passing second. Disbelief hung suspended in his chest as he straightened and listened to the slow progression of reanimation. Bit by bit, he could hear the blood moving farther and farther away from her heart, swishing through her fingertips and down through her toes. Before long, her pulse was throbbing visibly in her throat and a subtle glow illuminated her skin.

A gurgling noise came from deep in her throat and her heart began pumping erratically. She was choking on the blood in her lungs. Jonathan ripped through the restraint belts with his bare hands and lowered her to the ground, setting her on her side and rolling her slightly forward. He gently patted her back and knelt in the grass as she regained consciousness and coughed up bloody spatter in between violent, rasping breaths.

"Come on, Pare. You can do it," he whispered. "Please, Pare. Come back to me."

Second by second, the coughing fits grew further apart and eventually ceased. She wheezed hoarsely with every breath, but that, too, began to even out, transitioning into a slight whistle that also faded. Soon, she lay quietly in the grass—just breathing. *Alive.* He rubbed her back and watched the miracle of her lungs rising and falling, his mind vacant.

She suddenly pushed herself into a sitting position and tried to stand, but couldn't quite rise on her own. He helped her up and let her use his arms and chest to get her balance, gaping in disbelief the whole time. Her restorative ability was incredible, easily surpassing both his and Lucien's—after all, this was the second time she'd defeated death, not a feat either of them could claim even once.

Before he could think of what to say, or how to begin to apologize, her hands floated down to her sides and she stood before him completely on her own, poised with sudden strength and confidence. Her eyes glimmered with a brilliant blue flame and her expression was soft and peaceful as she reached a delicate hand to his face and cupped his jaw, stroking his cheek with her thumb.

Total serenity enveloped him the instant she made skin contact. Her eyes were mesmerizing. He felt detached from his body, as though she had freed his soul to fly away, holding it in place with her touch alone.

"Gabriel has a message for you, Jonathan," she told him in a voice that was both melodic and commanding, and wholly unnatural. "A human who looked like a vampire—the Second Born no less, the 'Gift from God'—entered the world over a century and a half ago. Where this man is concerned, there are no coincidences. He was designed to garner your attention.

"Eric's path was determined before his conception. But after you altered him, you mistook your interest for attraction and your lust clouded your judgment. You interfered with his destiny and the pool of innocent blood surrounding you drew Gabriel's attention. He's been watching you for a long time. You are guilty of more than Eric knows, and you must repent. Reveal your sins to Lucien and seek his guidance to save your soul."

She softly continued in her own voice, "I don't know what you've done, but for what it's worth, you were always good to me and I forgive you for your involvement here. As far as the High Council is concerned, you followed your orders."

The flame in her eyes faded. She threw a slight smile over his shoulder. "That's why he's here."

Jonathan followed her sightline. The tall vampire who'd led her pursuit stepped into the clearing, resembling the Grim Reaper in a full-length ebony cloak. He removed his remaining glove and lowered his hood with long bony fingers to reveal silver hair, luminous blue skin, and silver-flecked, crystalline eyes.

"Lucien?" Jonathan whispered, dumbfounded that his master was outside the Arc of True Blood for the first time since the High Council's inception.

The Arch Elder's impassive countenance resembled that of a young elven man, but his eyes conveyed the wisdom of thousands of years. He stood upright and unmoving at the tree line. Nodding respectfully to Paresh, Lucien shifted his gaze to Jonathan and tipped his head slightly—a beckoning gesture.

Jonathan glanced at Paresh uncertainly.

"He's your master," Paresh said. "I'm not permitted to say more."

"I don't know what that means, Pare." Jonathan was reluctant to leave her, but when she remained silent, he went to Lucien, bowing his head and kneeling as tradition dictated. Lucien's eyes narrowed as he lifted Jonathan's chin and studied his face.

"Her blood is in you." Lucien's gaze darkened.

Guilt nipped at Jonathan again and he almost dropped a shameful stare into the grass. "Earlier in the evening, I tried to persuade Eric one last time...and I drank from *him*."

The darkness eased, but the narrowed slits remained. "You've changed."

Jonathan didn't know how to interpret that nondescript comment. Lucien held his gaze for excruciatingly long seconds—time had never felt so apparent as he waited for his master to elaborate.

"Tell me—" Lucien slid his hand up and brushed Jonathan's cheek tenderly. "Do you love me?"

If not for the skip in his heart and the surge of warmth at Lucien's touch, Jonathan might not have known how to answer that either, but, as he closed his eyes and leaned into Lucien's caress, he softly moaned, "Yes."

"Do you love her, as well?"

Jonathan hesitated only because the warmth flared in his heart so much that it hurt. Thinking of Paresh brought him a type of joy he'd never before known. "Yes, I do."

Lucien's thumb stopped mid-stroke. "I know what I must do, then." He looked past Jonathan to Paresh, who was kneeling over Eric's body with her head on his shoulder. Lucien stepped toward her. Jonathan grabbed his cloak. Lucien stopped.

"Does your love mean that you no longer trust me?" Lucien asked in an empty voice. "Does your desire for her overshadow the greater good? Would you sacrifice yourself to save her, even if it meant you must defeat me in order to do so?"

"I do not *desire* her, Lucien," Jonathan said. "I—"

"Do you desire him, then?" Lucien interrupted.

"I did, but—"

Lucien took another step. Jonathan stubbornly tightened his grasp. Again, the Elder stopped. "Why are you obstructing me?"

"I do care about the greater good." Jonathan stood to face Lucien eye-to-eye. "And...yes. I would sacrifice myself to save her. Even from you."

A trace of amusement glimmered across Lucien's face, but Jonathan couldn't tell if it was sinister or humored. He'd never seen that expression and Lucien's voice was as emotionless as usual. "After three thousand years, a woman comes between us? Lucifer has gotten into your head."

Jonathan brazenly stepped in front of Lucien to block his path. Lucien's eyes darkened again. "Perhaps you know something that I do not? Do not be disillusioned. Time does not stop for us. Decide right now if you trust me or not, and do not allow your emotions to influence your decision. Remember what you are. I do not love you and you cannot defeat me without *him*."

"*She* is the Servator."

"If you truly want what is best for our race, move aside." Lucien stepped closer and looked down into Jonathan's eyes.

Jonathan stared back defiantly, initially confident, but his uncertainties resurfaced and ate away at his resolve. He lowered his head and begrudgingly let Lucien pass. The Arch Elder hesitated a few feet away.

"This is not how this was supposed to happen," he said in a quiet voice.

Jonathan turned and watched Lucien's back as he approached Paresh. His graceful movements barely disturbed the cloth of his cloak—it scarcely swayed, even near the hem above his feet. Paresh was lying across Eric's chest. The elder vampire stooped and took her hand in his.

She lifted her head sadly. "He's so cold."

Lucien nodded and pulled her up with him. Locking their eyes, Lucien gently tilted her chin and swept her hair from her throat. Paresh glanced at Eric and drew in a shaky breath as Lucien lowered his mouth to her jugular.

"You will see him again soon enough," he whispered before his teeth sank into her skin. She whimpered in pain and went limp in his arms.

Not only was Jonathan watching her die again, but he'd let it happen. Again. No human had ever survived Lucien's bite.

Despair and anger collided violently within him, ravaging both his body and mind, and yet he felt too defeated to fight. How had he so easily resigned himself to follow his master into the grim future he desired? And what made him think he'd survive the punishment for his disobedience? His future had never been this uncertain. Only one truth played on loop in his mind: Lucien's cold heart did not permit forgiveness or mercy. That one, undeniable fact hung like a noose around his neck as Lucien beckoned and he sullenly advanced.

Withdrawing from Paresh's throat, Lucien said, "Take her, I don't have much time."

Lucien carefully placed her into Jonathan's arms. She'd lost consciousness, but she was breathing. Jonathan shot a curious look at Lucien who was removing his cloak, scattering the scents of vanilla and incense that invoked intimate memories, and using it to cover Paresh's tattered body.

Dressed formally in a black kimono with Japanese pleated trousers, Lucien resembled a swordless modern day samurai warrior. A brief glint of silver beneath his haori revealed the Vampiric Star pinned near his heart. The jacket contained an embroidered crest of the star on both sides of his chest and at three traditional points along his back: on each sleeve and near the collar, hidden beneath his hair.

Lucien stepped over Eric and met Jonathan's eyes with emotion devoid in his. "You still do not trust me. Perhaps that should hurt?"

Kneeling, Lucien propped Eric against his chest and tilted his head to rest under his chin. "From the moment of my creation, my private desire—all I have ever wanted in my life—" Lucien confessed quietly, "has been to feel something, anything at all, in my heart other than empty coldness. I cannot see that become a reality as long as he is dead. Without him, she is powerless."

Jonathan's expression softened as he joined Lucien and knelt in the grass with Paresh cradled in his arms. Lucien he sliced through his wrist with a sharp talon and streamed his blood into Eric's mouth. "You had the right idea…"

Lucien focused intently on Eric as he continued, "Eric's blood in your veins sparked the return of her life, but it was your blood that gave her exhausted body the energy it needed to regenerate itself. Similarly, her blood in me will lure life back into his body, but her essence is too weak to sustain it. My blood should supplement hers to kick-start his heart and get him healing. Right now, they are dependent on each other to survive—if one dies, they both die. I believe she is mortal without his aura to supply her vampiric cells, and not only does that mean that my bite will kill her—and soon— but also that without him, she cannot save us."

Lucien glanced at Jonathan through hooded eyes. "You surprised me. She was calling you to save him, but you saved her instead."

Uncomfortably averting his gaze, Jonathan asked, "Why did you order her death in the first place?"

Lucien lowered his arm. "Humans cannot visit the spiritual realms in their physical form and she needed to meet with His emissary, the Archangel Gabriel."

Pointing up, he added, "Often they can hear His voice but don't know He is speaking to them. He can lead the way and hope they follow, but sometimes He must be persuasive, as seems to be the case with you three. It appears that Gabriel saw to this personally."

Jonathan returned his gaze to Lucien. He'd kept his promise. He hadn't betrayed him after all. A strong feeling overwhelmed him—like a hybrid of joy and despair. He felt compelled to reach out and touch Lucien. But he resisted. He'd doubted Lucien. Challenged his orders. What right did he have to witness this historic moment with him?

In a low voice, Jonathan confessed, "I've done horrible things in my efforts to persuade Eric over the years and they culminate in Lucifer's arrival here. If not for me, he wouldn't have noticed her."

Lucien nodded. "It's true that Destiny had to work harder to reach this end, but she gets her way, eventually. Lucifer would have found her one way or another, and his involvement created more problems than yours did. Listen…" He cocked his head and tapped his ear.

A faint, prolonged beat came from Eric's chest. Another beat followed, and then another as his heart fought to pump coagulating blood through constricted veins and arteries. It was slow and erratic, and the minutes plodded by as Eric's pulse gained momentum.

As his swishing blood hit a regular rhythm, the man who'd been stabbed through the heart by the Devil moaned his first new breath. His eyes struggled to open. They landed on Jonathan without focusing. After a long pause, he flicked his gaze up to Lucien and blinked repeatedly. He didn't show a single sign of weakness as fury ignited his face and he grabbed Lucien by the throat.

"What the hell is happening? *Where the hell is that woman?*" he demanded through his teeth, returning his glare to Jonathan.

"How apt," Lucien said, regarding Eric apathetically as Jonathan replied, "Eric, meet Lucien. He brought you back to life. And that woman is dead."

Eric froze and stared at Lucien hard before hesitantly looking back at Jonathan. His already pale face blanched when he realized Paresh was beneath the black wool in Jonathan's arms. Eric's voice caught in his throat as he choked out, "Is she…she was…oh no…"

Lucien spoke before Jonathan could think of what to say. "Now that you are alive, she'll recover—give her time. Jonathan saved her, Paresh the Pure, so that she could save you, Eric the Anointed. We don't have one Servator. We have two. You balance each other."

Concern etched lines into Eric's face as he released Lucien and stroked Paresh's cheek. Jonathan quietly observed the tenderness of his touch before transferring her into Eric's arms. Eric tucked her closely to his chest.

When their eyes met, Jonathan looked away. "Eric, I'm sor—"

Lucien cut him off with a stern look. "Paresh needed to pass to the spiritual realm to learn of her destiny. You were supposed to revive her, but Lucifer interfered. That exception aside, everything happened with reason and there is nothing to be sorry for right now."

As his strength visibly returned, Eric cracked his neck and rotated his shoulders. He sighed as his body adjusted to moving again. "If this place isn't holy, then what ties her to it? Two days ago, that tree gave her a premonition that came true tonight."

"As a private gift given to her through the bond you both share, her connection to Him bypasses physical structure and land. As long as you are with her, she will feel it anywhere, but it will always be strongest here, at its point of origin, since the spiritual realm opened here at the moment of her birth," Lucien replied. From his waist, he removed a case, about the size of a small journal, and held it in his lap.

"When Jonathan met with me yesterday, the effect she had on him was evident. He sounded fond of her and I needed no more proof than that." He opened the case. "I understand her favorite color is blue? These seemed more fitting than ours."

Peeling back a layer of rich blue velvet, he revealed a pair of pins. The Vampiric Star held a sapphire in place of the ruby, and the silver, black, and blue silk ribbon bar had two stars tacked into it.

"I understand that you don't care much for our ranks, but I hope you will accept these on her behalf." Lucien offered the case with a respectful nod.

"Thank you." Eric accepted and snapped the case closed. "What happens now?"

"She must tell us, when she awakens," Lucien said. "You should take her to your house. I will follow soon—if I am invited."

Eric's eyes narrowed as he stood. "You may enter my home," he said and carried Paresh toward the trail without another word. When he disappeared into the shadows, Lucien caught Jonathan's eye and tipped his chin to the north.

"Call your pack and have them clean up," he said. "Secure the urns and send them to my quarters."

Jonathan loosed a low whistle. Moments later, his VaSH hunters appeared to erase all signs of what had transpired. "Account for the inventory: two Hilja Rings, one Ivor Bow, and five Aegis cloaks. Secure the urns—to Arch Elder Lucien's sole attention. Take the bodies to storage and clear the premises," he commanded. As they scattered, he looked at Lucien. "Shall I go with them or you?"

With others present, Lucien sat in a meditative pose and impassively stared at Jonathan, saying only, "Wait."

Once Jonathan's pack departed, either en route to the Arc of True Blood or the Arc of Mourning Eidolons, Lucien lifted his gaze from Jonathan to the overcast night. The hunters had put out the fires, leaving behind only the scents of smoke and smoldering ash to linger over that of spilled blood. Without the haunting flicker of orange, the darkness was soothing and peaceful.

Lucien breathed deeply in through his nose. "It's been so long since I've gotten out into the world. Even with the pollution, the air seems fresher than the recycled atmosphere of the arc." He tilted his head back and closed his eyes, clearly enjoying each even expansion of his lungs.

Caught in the moment and ensnared by Lucien's beauty, Jonathan could only watch him. He could stare at Lucien forever like this. After a few minutes of silence, Lucien cracked an eye to look at him but said nothing.

Jonathan's brain eventually jarred loose the fact that they were outside the arc. "Why did you come yourself? It's dangerous for you to be here."

"I'm not the only Elder who has left the sanctity of the arc lately."

Lucien met Jonathan's eyes with a dark streak in one iris. "We have a traitor in our midst and I will rely heavily on you to deal with it as our race adjusts to the Second New Age." He closed his eyes again and took in another deep breath.

"Do you know who?" Jonathan asked in a solemn voice.

"I do."

"Who?"

"I don't want to get into it now." Lucien swatted the concern away. "The High Council can't continue ruling from one arc. We need leaders free to move among the ranks anywhere in the world, guiding and helping them cope with their new emotions. You've learned firsthand what they will do to us."

He gave Jonathan a pointed look.

"I didn't understand, Lucien. I should have trusted you, but I knew what I was feeling. This was the prophecy, our future—you should have told me," Jonathan returned the look. The casual exchange felt natural, like a return to their days before the Hosts fell to Earth.

"Perhaps, this time. But you had your orders."

"And I did as you asked despite my doubts."

"Someone is leaking information to Lucifer," Lucien revealed.

"How do you know?"

"No one outside our circle knew about Eric's origin and you never told the humans, but Lucifer knew—had heard a rumor—whether he believed it or not. I didn't expect him to take matters into his own hands tonight, or for you to underestimate his abilities, but things do not always go as they should."

Fear briefly knotted Jonathan's countenance as he wondered about any hidden meaning to the accusation. Lucien responded with a small smile. "Don't look at me like that. I know you aren't a traitor. The instant Lucifer saw Eric he knew there'd been *other* involvement."

Jonathan sighed. "So what do you intend to do?"

"For now, give her blood to the Elders and the VaSH Commanders, and let them adjust before distributing it to the masses. I'll assign the True Blood Elders to specific domes and allow them to set up sub-councils with guidance from the High Elders. Coping and evolving is not going to be easy. You and I need to convince Eric to assist us."

"Eric knows nothing of our ways and has no desire to govern our race," Jonathan said sourly.

"He understands these emotions better than any of us. He'll accept his destiny in time," Lucien replied lightly. His voice softened as he confided, "Jonathan, I want you by my side at the Arc of True Blood. You are the only one I can trust completely." Lucien met Jonathan's eyes with a look that made his heart skip.

"Lucien, I—" he whispered, guiltily staring at the narrow spot of grass between them. He clenched his jaw, not knowing what to say.

"Forget about that, and ask me—" Lucien said in a gentle voice as he tipped Jonathan's chin up. "What I feel in my heart, right now."

"What…do you feel in your heart…right now?" Jonathan asked quietly. His pulse was racing. Lucien seemed so unlike the distant man he had long known, but then, he felt strange himself. A sensation swelled inside him that was different from anything he had ever experienced. He felt light and dizzy, like a gossamer feather caught in a vortex swirling ever upward even though he'd never left the ground.

"I feel warmth. It's not cold anymore." Lucien stroked Jonathan's jaw and slid back to grasp Jonathan's nape. His fingers dipped into Jonathan's hair. "I don't want you beneath me. I want you next to me. Always."

"Lucien, I—" A lump formed in Jonathan's throat. He glanced down at the grass again and nodded.

Tipping Jonathan's chin up, Lucien leaned in and gently pulled him forward. He caressed Jonathan's cheek and his eyes softened with a tenderness that had never before existed. Jonathan's heart erupted and a nervous sigh escaped his mouth. His eyelids slowly closed. He moved in closer until he felt the heat of Lucien's breath on his skin. A surreal moment of tingling anticipation raced over his nerves, and then their lips met and they shared their first truly passionate kiss in over three thousand years. The Vampiric Nation's salvation had finally come.

II

Relieved to be home and safe in the darkness of his room, in the comfort of his bed, Eric lay on his side anxiously watching Paresh's chest rise and fall. What they'd endured…what *she'd* endured…if only he'd stayed behind instead of chasing David—

…*everything happened with reason…*

Even if that was true, Eric couldn't help feeling guilty. He'd gently washed and rinsed, and then re-washed and re-rinsed, the mud and blood from her body, alarmed at the color of the water with each pass and wondering what had happened in that forest. To take care of her hair, he'd sat behind her in the tub, shampooing until the suds were clean and white, and later cursed owning only a fine-toothed comb as he worked to detangle the mess on her head. But he wouldn't have made it far in life without patience, so he persisted and later dressed her in one of his t-shirts and tucked her into his bed before hurriedly tending to himself with a drink and shower.

He swallowed over the lump in his throat, trying yet again to make it disappear, and traced the features of her face. Even in the bath, she'd shown no physical injury, but she'd been hot to the touch, and was still feverish as her immune system fought Lucien's lethal protein. Otherwise, she looked peacefully asleep, like an angel. He kissed her crown and lightly rested his forehead on hers, offering a silent, thankful prayer that she'd survived.

Her aura awoke and drifted lazily about him. The soothing essence relaxed his muscles and dissolved the lump. The guilt driving his thoughts finally calmed and seeded the wake for inner peace to blossom. The moment felt so natural—as though he'd lain beside her every night of his life—that he couldn't believe she'd only come to his office three days ago.

He sighed into her hair and kissed her again. "You can do this. Please wake up," he murmured. Inky darkness cocooned him in her scent, and in the sounds of her breath and heart, a soothing balm for his aching soul.

His mouth turned up at the corners in a contemplative smile. "It's customary to knock before you enter someone's home, whether invited or not," he said. "Jonathan has that same bad habit."

"It's been awhile since I've been out in civilization and I don't tend to make house calls," Lucien said in a deadpan tone. His movements were as fluid as water as he approached the foot of the bed.

"Where is he?" Eric propped himself up on his elbow, his gaze on

Paresh, and coiled a curly lock around his finger.

"Waiting outside until he is invited in."

Eric nodded without extending the offer. "Did you know what was going to happen tonight?"

"To an extent. I didn't know when, nor whom, only vague details about the prophecy that I kept to myself. I suspected you initially, but you never passed to the spiritual realm. Until tonight, I hadn't considered you both together."

Lucien seemed more relaxed and informal than before, as though comfortable in his skin for the first time. After a thoughtful pause, the Elder said, "It is the rare fool who turns his back to me. For someone who fought so hard to avoid meeting me, I seem to have your implicit trust. Why?"

"She let you bite her to save me."

"She also trusted Jonathan with her life and he plotted to kill her on my order."

"Jonathan has saved her more times than I ever knew she was in danger." Eric sat up to face the Arch Elder.

Lucien half-smiled. "I see why he likes you so much. It feels rather ordinary to be here with you, although I can't say that anyone has ever talked to me in such a way. I thought you would be like him, but you are quite mild mannered. Humbled, if you will."

"I have my moments…as do we all. You're quite different from what I expected, as well. Then again, I suppose I'm privileged to see this side of you."

Lucien nodded. "And yet, somehow I don't think you see the honor in that. Eric, you have strong leadership qualities. I'd appreciate your assistance in the time to come. Consider my request knowing that you'll never need to leave her. I will come to you."

Eric started to answer, but Lucien held up his hand. "Think it over. You, Jonathan, and I are the strongest of our kind. The survival of our race will depend on our support. The Second New Age brings with it the need for a new style of government. The time for Lucifer's ranks has gone. As far as I am concerned, the three of us are equals above the High Elders."

"What about her?" Eric threaded his fingers through her hair.

"She is beyond us. Special, a being unlike any other on this planet, and she will be treated as a queen. I would bow to her, if He meant for that; however, He did not intend for her to guide us. 'Find salvation in the purity of the vessel and leadership from its anointed strength.' Gabriel transcribed those words from God's order. Though you both possess great power, she is the vessel and you are the strength."

Lucien circled the bed and knelt beside her. "The prophecy has begun, but that doesn't mean Lucifer or others will not try to kill her again. Never leave her side. As long as one of you lives, the other will always defeat death."

Eric's eyes flashed at the warning. "You know something."

"An elder plotting with Lucifer—the extent to which I do not know, but it will be dealt with. I do not wish to go to war again and I am certain, as a former soldier yourself, that you wish to avoid that as well."

"What makes you think I would fight in your war?" Eric asked suspiciously, pausing mid-stroke.

"You wouldn't have a choice. They'd come for you. Do you think there is anywhere in this world that you can hide?"

Paresh suddenly moaned. "Mm...Eric?"

Eric shifted down to lie beside her, saying softly, "I'm here."

"Eric!" Her eyes snapped open. She reached for him, faltering as though afraid he wasn't real.

"I'm here," he whispered again, pressing her hand against his cheek. He leaned over to kiss her and savored the feel of her lips on his. "Oh, honey...you're safe now."

"You were dead."

"So were you."

"You're warm." She kissed him again and cupped his face. "You were so cold...I was so afraid..."

"I know," he whispered, stroking her hair. "But we're okay now. Both of us."

"What about Uncle David?" She sat up with Eric's help and pressed her ear to his chest. She closed her eyes and sighed in relief.

"You don't need to worry about him. Any of them. Everything has been taken care of, my love, I promise." Eric shared a look of confirmation with Lucien before kissing her forehead. "Lucien is here. Jonathan is outside."

"Can you believe that I…I met an angel?" she asked with a dreamy quality to her voice. "Gabriel. He was so beautiful— swathed in the palest blue with wings like the air, and his skin gleamed like a star. Beyond description. Lucien?"

"I'm beside you, here. Perhaps you'd like some light?"

"No, it's all right. My eyes are adjusting. I can see you. I just needed to hear your voice…to make sure," she replied. "Everything's a bit blurry. I'm not used to this—it's not the same as it was earlier. It doesn't feel real yet."

"Please forgive my behavior in the woods. I did not relish the task of weakening your body," Lucien said with an element of disdain. "David hadn't planned to stab your heart—which would have killed you outright—and altering his plan would've been considered direct involvement in killing a member of the Flock. The Celestials behind the curtain are unforgiving when it comes to the rules."

"I understand—I got a taste of that myself. And there's nothing to forgive." She smiled warmly at him. "Destiny, a Dominion from the Fourth Angelic Choir, designed my death before I was born, and honestly, I think they partially pulled me out once I touched the tree—it was like I could hear them singing."

"I am still sorry for the suffering we caused you." Lucien bowed his head. "I imagine Gabriel wasn't happy about that, either."

"He didn't say. But I got the impression that he's like your guardian angel. He was charged with watching over the Vampiric Nation after the Treaty was signed, and he even had Destiny try to deliver the prophecy once before."

Lucien looked up sharply. "With Eric?"

Paresh glanced up at Eric and nodded.

"But I never crossed over." Eric shot a brief look at Lucien. "You said—"

"That's true, but Lucien's right. It did start with you, Eric," Paresh said. "God designed you to gain Jonathan's attention and survive. You and your son were supposed to fulfill the role of the Servator—a human soul for Darien never existed. But to combat the thirst you share with Jonathan, God had to leave much of your humanity intact. It was the only way you could fight the beast—and because of that, your grief overwhelmed you and…you—"

She stroked Eric's cheek. "I'm sorry—you couldn't hear His

voice."

Eric nuzzled her hand and closed his eyes. "I'm so sorry," she whispered again.

"No..." he said with a sigh. He threaded their fingers and kissed the back of her hand. "Lucinda and Darien are at rest together. It's best that way. I'm at peace with that, but you...I was just...so scared of losing you. Terrified. I couldn't do anything—"

He huffed and shook his head.

"Me, too...with you. I hated seeing you suffering." Paresh bit her lip, her eyes misting.

Eric held her hand against his mouth, squeezing his eyes shut tight against the filthy, bloody water he'd washed down his drain. He hadn't thought anything about himself—the fight, the electric bolts, his death—or how any of that had impacted her, had made her suffer even more. "Oh honey—"

"It's okay, my love," Paresh whispered. "It doesn't change the pain, but it was all supposed to happen. Destiny foresaw the hurdles in my life and used them. She withheld my soul at birth, similarly to Darien, but this time you heard The Voice. You did what you were supposed to, when you needed to do it, so don't blame yourself. For anything. Please."

Eric pulled in a calming breath and nodded. She snuggled closer and dotted his cheek with a kiss. He might've forgotten they weren't alone if she hadn't faced Lucien and cleared her throat.

"And that meant they had to tweak the prophecy for a human body and soul. Eric's essence supplies my vampiric cells and sustains my immortality, and my blood gives him strength and calms the beast in his heart. Together we are the Servator, but without him, I will age and die. Without me, he will constantly fight for control."

Eric shook his head again. "I just..." Eric's voice broke. "Why did you have to die to have a *conversation?*"

"It wasn't about that. I had to die a human death." She bit her lip again and sniffled. Tears dripped onto her cheeks. "And I can't say I'm okay with that, but hopefully I will be in time. I can accept that this is my destiny and that I'm fulfilling it, as I should. I'm proud of that, no matter what."

Eric buried a sorrowful sigh in her hair and even Lucien must have felt something, because he touched her arm in an awkward gesture seemingly meant to be reassuring.

Paresh patted his hand. "Gabriel said it's about balance. That life becomes death out of necessity. The physical world is the axis on which the spiritual realms pivot. I had to be reborn to be like Darien since I'm bonded to the soul destined to open the path for the Second New Age."

Eric kissed her and tucked her head under his chin, wrapping both arms firmly around her. She pressed her palm against the beat of his heart and smiled. He felt at peace with the moment, enveloped in her warmth and her love.

"You're whole now," she said. "You'll always be whole with me."

Paresh smiled to herself. "I am grateful to you both, and to Jonathan, too. They didn't anticipate that he'd become so vital. They initially only used him to keep my vampiric cells alive with his DNA."

"They?" Lucien asked.

"Um, yeah…" Paresh paused in thought. "Destiny worked with Serendipity, a Virtue from the Fifth Angelic Choir. They planned my life and accounted for obstacles. They saw Jonathan's presence as an opportunity because he and Eric are so similar. But, they didn't know he'd be vulnerable to my essence, and that gave Destiny access to you, Lucien, that she wouldn't have had any other way. You alone possessed the power to accept or deny salvation, and you saw the change in Jonathan for what it was."

Paresh glanced away from Lucien and gave Eric a knowing look. "You and I came together as intended, and that let Serendipity create a backup in Jonathan. I know he attacked you and that's why you had Molly there with me. Jonathan became a bridge between us, capable of saving us both because of our bonds in blood. If Lucien had tried to resurrect me, it wouldn't have worked."

"Without Jonathan, Destiny's plan would have failed?" Lucien asked quietly.

Paresh nodded. "And the order to kill me violated the Treaty, so this was her final chance. They left very little to chance, but Serendipity can't function without it."

"The rules," Lucien said grimly.

A tear slid down her cheek. "And I wasn't permitted to intervene—as much as it broke my heart, I couldn't tell either of you how to…to——" More tears fell.

Eric smudged her cheeks dry with his thumb. "Oh, my love."

She shook her head and sucked in a shaky breath. "I'm just so thankful that Lucien knew what to do when he saw salvation slipping away," she whispered. "I can't imagine what it would've been like to live without you."

"We're together now," Eric whispered. He swallowed hard and kissed her crown. "I'm not going anywhere."

Lucien moved to the foot of the bed, withdrawn as though in disbelief at how perilously close they had come to losing everything. He sat and turned to face her. "What happens now?"

Paresh took a moment to compose herself and sucked in a deep breath. "Eric withstanding, one drop of my blood seals the beast and unlocks your hearts. Your souls are free and open to the grace of God and love, and initial judgment is no longer suspended. Since it's the natural order to live and die, your immortality is no longer a given. It's a gift. The wicked will age and perish, but can still repent before they die, and those who pass initial judgment will wait alongside humans for Final Judgment. He's not holding you to a higher standard. We're all imperfect, so there's room for error, forgiveness, and…mercy."

She lowered her eyes and quietly said, "Gabriel said that Jonathan has been granted another chance at redemption, but Jonathan must choose penitence—truthfully, from his heart. Quickly."

Though Lucien's expression didn't change, Eric felt like he'd been gut punched. He clenched his jaw and stared at a spot on the bed.

Lucien's eyes swept over Eric as he asked Paresh, "What did the Archangel tell you about the End of Days?"

"Not much. Just that the righteous among you will stand alongside the Heavenly Host to protect the Flock from Lucifer's wrath. The triumph over evil is preordained in the Book of Revelation. In you, His army has found additional strength."

"We came into the world fighting and we will exit the same way. Lucifer accused Jonathan of switching sides. I don't suppose he meant that literally." Lucien again eyed Eric, seemingly struck by his reaction, though he said nothing about it. "Did He amend the conditions of the Treaty?"

"He lifted them," she said. "You control your own fate. With the beast sealed away, you can't lose control to its rage. That leaves only choice. To sin or not to sin. To kill or not to kill. Same as humans. Your existence is no longer a test. The Flock is still protected, but they may choose to join you without forsaking God."

She smiled pensively. "Gabriel told me that you are an honorable leader, and that he has faith in your guidance. You should adapt the guidelines given to humans—although, he did say that the commandment to honor your father is counterproductive."

Lucien briefly returned her smile. "It may be in our best interest to continue living by the Treaty for a time. Such freedom may prove too tempting to some."

He stood and bowed. "I'd be honored if you'd visit the Arc of True Blood for Winter Solitude, though, of course, you are welcome anytime." He met Eric's eyes and then walked toward the door. "I'll be in touch."

"Lucien, thank you for saving Eric's life," Paresh said quietly. "Please thank Jonathan for saving mine."

The Arch Elder nodded as he stepped into the hall. Eric glanced down at her. "I'm going to see him out. Will you be all right here?"

"I'm not going anywhere," she replied, caressing his face. "I love you, Eric. With all my soul. I-I thought I'd never be able to tell you—"

He tipped her chin up. "I love you, too. Forever." He gave her a tender, loving kiss and held her gaze a moment longer before following Lucien outside.

The sun tried to pierce the dawn's half-light, but clouds shrouded the waking horizon in dim grayness. Slumped against his car, Jonathan was soiled from head to toe with dirt and dried blood. Once a pristine white, his shirt was unbuttoned to the center of his chest and his sleeves were loosely rolled up to his elbows. He held his jacket haphazardly folded over one arm and his hair fluttered loosely around his shoulders. He looked haggard and worn out, as if the night's activities had taken their toll on him physically and mentally. He seemed almost…human.

As they approached, Jonathan straightened and gazed at Eric with guilt and sadness deep in his eyes. Looking at Lucien, he asked, "Well?"

"If we live by His word until Judgment Day, we will perform a new Heavenly duty. If we fall from His Grace, we will face an eternity in Hell. Destiny has been fulfilled. We now control our individual fates."

"That's not what I meant. I heard...*everything*." Jonathan's forehead creased as he stared between them, unable to bring himself to look at Eric. "How is she?"

"Fine," Eric said. "I can't say that I'd trust you with my life, but I trust you with hers. Thank you for saving her and watching out for her over the years. I didn't know how deeply disturbed David was."

"Yes, well, I told you he was a sick man. And, for what it's worth, you weren't wrong about Simon. He confronted David and it cost him his life."

Eric lowered his gaze for a moment. Then, he looked up at Jonathan and extended his hand. Jonathan backed away and headed for the driver's door. He and Lucien had driven alone.

"Know that I cared for her like a daughter and always will," Jonathan said. "But that's a small penance for everything I've done to you and her family."

Eric nodded and let his hand fall back to his side. As Jonathan got into the car and started the engine, Eric opened the passenger door for Lucien. He caught the Arch Elder's arm before he sat.

"I'm here whenever you need me," Eric said in a solemn voice. Lucien's lips turned up slightly, but he said nothing as Eric closed the door.

Watching the car pull away, Eric's eyes darkened. One disgruntled vampire, let alone an Elder, held the power to organize a coup, several could wage a battle, and a dozen could resume fighting the Great Holy War with dire consequences. That truth had spanned the ages, but with love and their souls caged in their hearts, the vampiric race had forged a nearly collective conscience—only a few stragglers had threatened to shatter it in the past and the VaSH had handled them. The remainder had desired the peaceful lives of men and patiently awaited the arrival of their Servator.

Now Death's hand threatened to eviscerate their eternal souls from their bodies as they withered away like humans. Although only a few would face such an immediate fate, even an aging vampire with a vile heart posed a great threat to the rest as each member of the Nation faced a powerful new emotion capable of overshadowing the logic of thousands of years. How it ruled them determined the fate of their souls, just like those in the Realm of Man.

Eric had experienced the positive side of love and witnessed the negative side's ability to rip families apart. Most vampires had not. And the sudden ability to care for others above themselves paved the way to guilt and self-loathing. Eric had seen that in Jonathan.

How they reacted to the Second New Age remained to be seen, but the collective would falter, forcing their society to evolve. Some would stand strong. Others would fall. Individuality loosened the High Council's iron grasp and opened the door to anarchy. Only time would tell if that meant disaster or peace for Paresh, himself, the Vampiric Nation, and the world.

He strolled up the walkway comforted by the melancholy coo of a mourning dove, the first bird ever to perch upon his roof. Paresh opened the door, watching him with loving eyes. He crossed the threshold and pulled her close.

He'd begun a new chapter in his life, freed from all vows of servitude and Jonathan's manipulation alike. Free to live with the woman to whom his heart belonged for all eternity. No longer alone. Finally whole. As they shared a kiss filled with the raw passion of star-crossed lovers, he held fast to his faith that as long as they were together, they'd conquer all that was yet to come.

☽ ✷ ☾

Jonathan clenched the steering wheel in white-knuckled fists as Eric's house grew smaller in the distance. Lucien was a stoic statue beside him, contented to remain silent, but Jonathan's mind was not so quiet. Or as kind.

A young boy appeared on the shores of memory, hair black as midnight and blue eyes clear as crystal. The bustling brick and mortar downtown of the newly incorporated village populated around the boy, followed by the sounds and odors of the mid-1800s.

It'd been his eyes.

Those eyes had changed everything. Had changed *him*.

His golden-brown orbs reflected in the rearview mirror. He flicked his gaze away in disgust. His sins—his confessions—what he'd done to Eric... He didn't deserve forgiveness.

BONUS CONTENT

DELETED SCENE

This deleted scene was cut during initial edits and is referenced when Eric reintroduces Paresh to Walter at the end of Chapter Three: Reunion. It takes place during Paresh's homecoming once she's inside the cottage.

She was back in the place where animals followed her everywhere and had played with her as one of their own throughout her childhood—a feat that had amazed the town's veterinarian, Doctor Grimley. He came by the cottage on a near-weekly basis. There was always a wing or leg to bandage. Permanently etched crinkles around his eyes had been a testament to his warm and gentle nature, and his lips could morph into grins wider than his narrow face should've allowed.

Doctor Grimley's hands had nurtured countless creatures, but none had been more important to her than a coyote named Greywolf. She hadn't simply met Greywolf—the coyote had searched for her. He'd appeared one night in the clearing, limping up the flagstone, and pausing to lick his paw after each step. Another animal had bitten him and the resulting infection threatened his life. An immediate call had gone to the doctor, who, used to handling animals like rabbits and squirrels, and the occasional deer, raccoon, or even skunk, was frightened at the thought of treating a dangerous animal with a grievous injury. His fear quickly waned, however, once he saw the predator as little more than a whimpering dog at her side.

Greywolf stayed with her for several years after that—outside, of course, since her mother wouldn't let her bring her friends inside. But then hunters trespassing in the woods shot him. Local people treated their land as a sanctuary, so it hadn't taken her father long to find the culprits: two men new to the area who claimed they hadn't seen the "no hunting" signs posted around the forest's perimeter.

Whether genuine or false, their ignorance couldn't protect them from her father's wrath and threats of legal retaliation. They left town, but that offered little consolation to a young girl with a devastated heart. Greywolf's passing took a long time to grieve…although, ultimately, the pain she'd felt then was trivial in comparison with what she would face only a short while later.

A DAY DREAM

This new, short scene is based on a note shared by the author in the reading group on Facebook. It correlates to a brief detail in *Last Born Daughter*, Chapter Seven.

Sometimes I daydream for my characters. Today a young Paresh dreamed of buying a nice tie for Master Jon since he's always impeccably dressed, but she doesn't have any money. Timeout—his suits are custom made, so does that mean there are vampire tailors? (Shrugs) Not that it really matters, because he can't take her to one of *them*, anyway. He'd have to see a human tailor. Ug. Can you hear his feet dragging? But doing it for Paresh? Without even realizing it?

Hm, if only there was another option...

Upon learning of Paresh's simple wish, Jonathan arranged a special excursion. He drove her to an outlet mall and parked in front of a shop whose window, covered with disintegrating brown paper just the day before, gleamed as the mid-morning sun spotlighted headless mannequins stretching back to admire their colorless fingers instead of their fashionable suits. The gloomy, abandoned atmosphere inside and dusty bare shelves were all gone, aired out and revitalized, popping with color from wood cabinetry brimming with enough fabrics, trinkets, and accessories to make her heart soar.

Not that he was doing this for her. He needed a new suit and, ruse or not, he would get one.

She knew to stay near him even if she didn't know the real reason why. In public, he used his aura and Hilja ring to keep them unseen and unheard. When it was necessary, Jonathan might be seen and heard, but never her. Today, onlookers saw a door that appeared to open by itself, which wasn't at all interesting in these automated days.

A silver bell jingled when he pushed the door open and let her pass. She stopped almost as soon as she entered, gasping at the organized array of suits on wooden hangers, shiny leather shoes, and glass counters that glittered with bejeweled cufflinks, pins, and watches galore.

"All this for a tie," said a soft, masculine voice that only Jonathan would hear. The leader of his pack, Alexander, swept out of the back room in a crimson pinstriped vest over a black shirt that matched his creased pants. He reached up as though to ruffle his usually spiked blond hair, but remembered at the last second that he'd combed it neatly to the side and smoothed his hand over it instead.

"Are you the tailor?" Paresh asked, slowly moving inward, her jaw gaping in awe.

His smile was warm. "No, I'm—"

"Not important," Jonathan interrupted. "Pare, he's a *friend* filling in for today. I thought we could do something extra special—I need a new suit, and want you to pick out the colors."

Her eyes blew wide open and reflected the overhead lights. "More than the tie?"

Oh, her exuberance was infectious. He beamed a genuine smile back at her. "Definitely more than a tie, Pare."

Dutifully rooting himself near the tailor dummy at the full length mirror, Alexander's eyes followed every move Paresh made. No one else had ever seen her and he was the only VaSH Commander who knew about Lucien's suspicions.

"Explore to your heart's content," Jonathan told her, able to relax for once in a controlled environment. "What color do you like?"

She gnawed her lip and circled the room, seriously thinking over each option. Jonathan caught Alexander smirking and shot him a look of warning. But he couldn't help thinking the same thing and it confused the hell out of him: she was adorable.

Not surprisingly, she lingered longest at the section for her favorite color and lightly petted a royal blue sleeve. "This would look prettiest with your hair, Master Jon."

Alexander pulled a thick catalog from the drawer behind him and crouched, waving her over and whispering like a conspirator, "What options do you want to pick out? Pockets, pleats, the vest—there's so much more to choose!"

Jonathan glared at Alexander and was deliberately ignored. She was only supposed to select the colors and even those he'd controlled to avoid winding up with something garish in pink or yellow. His tailor knew what he liked. What was he going to end up with now?

"Hm." She studied the illustrations and pictures that Alexander showed her and listened to his explanations. She flipped through a few pages and pointed at various selections.

Alexander snapped the catalog shut and finally looked up at Jonathan, triumphant. "We're going with royal blue Italian wool, slim fit, vented, no pleats, and a double-breasted vest patterned in royal blue and burgundy."

"And a light gray shirt," Paresh added with a firm nod.

"Burgundy?" he asked Alexander lowly, maintaining his smile for Paresh.

"Lady's choice," Alexander replied with an impish grin.

Jonathan clapped his hands together and threw them out to the side. "I didn't hear anything about a tie? We're missing the main attraction here."

"Oh…" Her brow dipped as she looked at the closed book in Alexander's hands. "Can I—?"

"Not to worry!" Alexander tossed the catalog aside and pulled out another drawer behind him before racing around the room, whipping out drawers in each section. Rows of colors and patterns were rolled up within. He spun a few wracks of cheap ties, too, before leaping back to Paresh and the dummy like a king's idiot. "Pick whatever you like."

"But—" Jonathan cut himself off. With the *burgundy* exception, Alexander had guided her well, so far.

Clasping her hands behind her back, Paresh deliberated over each option—of which they'd provided too many, Jonathan decided, given the time it was taking—before narrowing them down and wavering between a few survivors. She plucked up a silver tie in a diamond pattern and its matching pocket square.

He briefly touched his fingers to his forehead. The colors and patterns on the tie and vest broke the rules for a gent's three-piece suit.

Alexander appeared beside him. "She's so happy."

Jonathan sighed. Once his tailor put it all together, he'd wear this odd combination just for her. The slight swell of emotion in his chest told him that wasn't all bad.

She was stooped over the glass counters now. "She'll pick out the cufflinks and pins with sapphires," Jonathan quietly predicted. "And you'll guide her to brown leather for the accessories, understood?"

Alexander winked. "Of course."

A short while later, Paresh confirmed Jonathan's prediction, Alexander talked her into brown leather for the wing tips and belt, and she'd even selected a complimenting banded and feathered fedora. And, while she didn't understand why they'd spent so much time in the store only to leave with nothing, her glittering smile was brighter than a star and sparked a warm bloom in Jonathan's chest.

He'd made a heartbroken little girl's day. And his own, too.

...And so, thanks to Alex, I brought in a new option for Paresh and Jonathan's special bonding moment. Jonathan's not such a bad guy...all the time—but he can be a really bad guy. Can you imagine it, though? Her happiness alone would give him a high to ride out the whole day. Maybe she'd try to get him to wear a blue ribbon? It wouldn't work. Lucien gave him that crimson ribbon and he wouldn't change it out for a blue one. Not even for her. I guess dapper chaps come in good and bad, or both.

NOTATIONS

Author's Note & Acknowledgments

In addition to the abbreviated acknowledgments from *The Arrival* below, I'd like to thank authors Megan Deppner, Ruth Miranda, Serene Conneeley, Julie Embleton, & Andrew Franks, to my friends Brenna & Beth, & to Magpie Press. As my debut novel, the original acknowledgments were long, but informative. I am still grateful to those listed!

When I was 13 or 14 years old, I had a nightmare: a cloaked man with a dagger chasing me through the woods. It inspired a tale of witchcraft that I saved to discs that actually flopped and printed on a dot matrix printer. Decades later, Paresh's life evolved with experience, research, and education. I named her Paresh at the beginning to join death, *Perish*, with the house of God, *Parish*; however, Eric didn't exist until a few years later and David was the love interest—and not as her uncle.

Much gratitude and thanks to early supporters, my English/Literature teachers: Miss Wilson and Mrs. Rinkel, my best friend at the time, Rachel, and my mom, who read anything I wrote.

Thanks to all of my friends and family who have supported me: Jennifer, Liz, Betsy, Debbie, Amy, Ed, Jacque, Linda, Linda, Wilma, and my mom, Carol, and my daughter, Meredith. Thank you also to Ethan for his professional editing services.

A huge THANK YOU to the Civil War re-enactors from the 8th Regiment of Illinois Volunteer Cavalry out of Chicago for inviting me to "play" with them in Marion, Illinois, in October 2007. Amid white canvas tents and crackling fires, these guys answered questions, and then decked me out in a uniform with a Carbine Sharps rifle and black powder to use while marching and battling. Playing in battle is immeasurably different from watching—extremely chaotic and confusing—but I survived our skirmish with the Confederates.

I got to shoot an old revolver and even got onto a horse for the second and final time in my life—with *much* help. It was great fun and truly difficult. They call it "playing," but they're serious about drills and marches, and some re-enactors authentically live only on hardtack and burnt coffee.

All of it was worth being very…very…sore the next few days. I cannot thank them enough for the experience and everything they taught me. To learn more about them, visit: www.8thillinoiscavalry.org/home.

Thank you to Pastor Ron for discussing Christianity and Lucifer—*at length*. He helped me understand the way Lucifer might see the world in 2006. "Do you think, if Lucifer truly wanted it, God would forgive him?" I asked, surely not a question clergy get often, and Ron said that if Lucifer was truly penitent, then yes, God would forgive him. The point here is genuine remorse when seeking forgiveness.

Thank you to friends and authors Jaleigh Johnson and Serene Conneeley for insights that lit a fire under my butt to get this story out!

A special thank you goes to Robin, my dear friend who passed away suddenly in January 2017. I love you and hope you are proud of me. Thank you to her husband and son, John and Connor, who shared their wonderful woman and opened their lives to me. I love you all.

The biggest thank you goes to my husband, Tim, for his tireless patience. He is my soul mate and I love him with all my heart.

The strangest thank you goes to my cats, forced to share my attention with a bright screen and clacky keys. The David in my dedication was my best friend in a fur coat. Always there as a skilled lap ninja, he even helped Tim propose to me. He suddenly passed away Christmas 2007. There is no link between him and the David in the story.

The obvious thank you goes to YOU! I hope to see you again in *CONFESSIONS OF THE SECOND BORN* and beyond!

I'd love to connect with you! Learn more on my website: www.kastiepavlik.wixsite.com/author. I have a neglected blog at *kastiepavlik.blogspot.com* and a neglected Twitter account. I am most active on Instagram as @kastiepavlikauthor, and have author pages on Facebook, Amazon, and GoodReads.

Reviews are lifeblood to authors! Please let other readers know what you think of this book by reviewing on Amazon and/or GoodReads! It's as easy as telling a friend!
Thank you so much for your support!

Historical & Content Notes

Poison Spring, Arkansas, April 18, 1864 & the 10th Illinois Cavalry

The battle at Poison Spring was a particularly brutal chapter in the US Civil War. At the time of the original writing (2007), information was sparse; however, there are now (2021) many resources to learn more. The battleground is an Arkansas State Park.

The historical 10th Illinois Cavalry, Company I (Champaign County), was in Camden, Arkansas when 200 wagons and soldiers from other units left in search of food and supplies, and was not present at the ambush/battle at Poison Spring. Artistic license puts Eric there.

After initial deployment, the 10th Illinois Cavalry, Company I, did not return home for 3 years. Soldiers who re-enlisted received a 30-day furlough prior to disembarking from Camp Butler, Illinois, now a cemetery in Springfield, the state capitol, to return to war.

This unit was heavily involved in the Western theatre of the war.

Colonel Thaddeus Hawthorne & the Army of the Potomac

The fictional Colonel Hawthorne rode out with the historical 8th Illinois Cavalry, out of Chicago, Illinois. This unit fought with the Army of the Potomac in the Eastern Theatre of the war.

Lucifer Translation Note

Most biblical scholars agree that the name "Lucifer" is a mistranslation that references the astronomical Morning Star—generally Venus, also known as the Evening Star—and that it is not among any of the names used biblically for the Devil. Some even believe that "Lucifer," as the Light- or Dawn-bringer, is an influential title in Heaven now held by Jesus Christ.

Angelic Choirs, Dominions, Virtues

This is a reference to the heavenly tiers described in The Book of Enoch. Enoch was the great-grandfather of Noah and much of the alternative religion in this fictional series is influenced by this ancient text. Its canonical role in the world's religions varies.

Family Tree

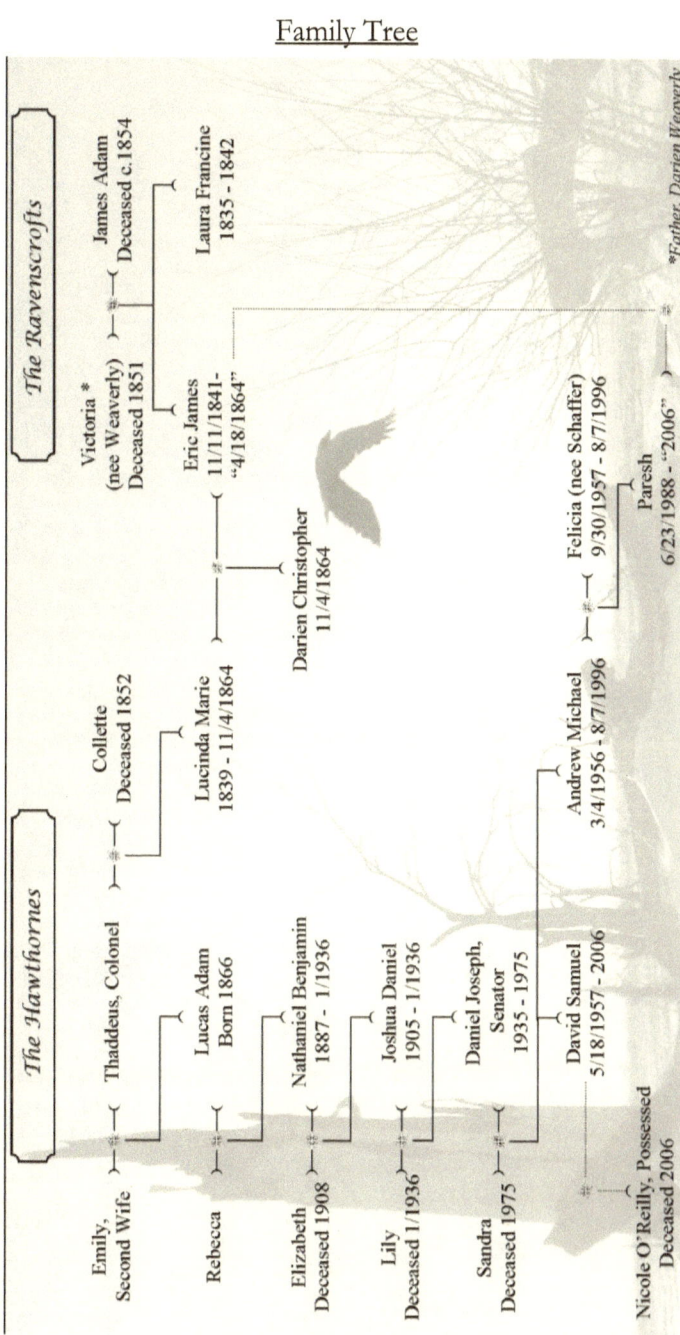

The Ravenscrofts

James Adam
Deceased c.1854

Laura Francine
1835 - 1842

Victoria *
(nee Weaverly)
Deceased 1851

Eric James
11/11/1841-
"4/18/1864"

Darien Christopher
11/4/1864

Collette
Deceased 1852

Lucinda Marie
1839 - 11/4/1864

Felicia (nee Schaffer)
9/30/1957 - 8/7/1996

Paresh
6/23/1988 - "2006"

Andrew Michael
3/4/1956 - 8/7/1996

*Father, Darien Weaverly

The Hawthornes

Emily,
Second Wife

Thaddeus, Colonel

Lucas Adam
Born 1866

Rebecca

Nathaniel Benjamin
1887 - 1/1936

Elizabeth
Deceased 1908

Joshua Daniel
1905 - 1/1936

Lily
Deceased 1/1936

Daniel Joseph,
Senator
1935 - 1975

Sandra
Deceased 1975

David Samuel
5/18/1957 - 2006

Nicole O'Reilly, Possessed
Deceased 2006

271

The story continues in…

CONFESSIONS OF THE SECOND BORN

CHILDREN OF THE MORNING STAR BOOK 2

**As salvation sinks into darkness and blood,
Sin preys upon the Sinner.**

Tethered to Lucien at the top of the world, Jonathan divulges the horrors of his past and questions his chance for redemption. Beyond the Arctic silence, Death stalks those closest to Eric and edges the Vampiric Nation toward the brink of civil war.

Paresh's blood is out—and with it, the volatility of raw emotion that threatens to shatter an already splintered High Council. And, as a murderous rogue prowls the streets of Sunset Grove, the bloody crusts on the victim's throat turn narrowed eyes and poisoned tongues on Eric.

The Vampire Shadow Hounds descend and the body count rises. With trust wearing thin and the hunt closing in, Jonathan is tempted to join the fight—but the cost means forfeiting the very soul he's struggling to save.

Then a traitor targets Paresh both in the Realm of Man and within the Arc of True Blood's supposedly safe borders, and Jonathan realizes no sanctuary remains. He can only protect her if he finds a penitent heart.

Have his doubts cost him everything? Is he already too late?

This revised edition features new bonus material:
Interviews with an Unwilling Vampire!

Author Sketches

Sketch (pencil) by Kastie Pavlik, Spring 2007. Eric, Paresh, and Jonathan.

Lucien, circa 2013, by Kastie Pavlik

Above: Grayscale (pencil and charcoal originally; digitally retouched face 2018)

Right: Digital sketch

Digital sketch of Vampiric Star by Kastie Pavlik, 2007.

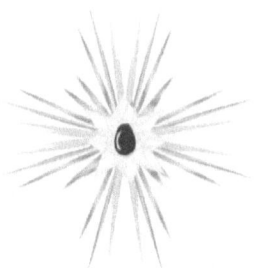

About the Author

KASTIE PAVLIK is a gamer, artist, techie, and hopeless bibliophile who grew up loving all things macabre and creepy crawly, with an affinity for mythology, vampires, the paranormal, and psychology. Diagnosed with Multiple Sclerosis in 2008, she has subsequently beaten breast cancer, and manages a rare genetic disorder, Ehlers-Danlos Syndrome. She spends her days entertaining (annoying?) her feline overlords while adapting to her endlessly changing needs. Surrounded by the starry cornfields of Illinois, she enjoys a quiet life with her husband and their cats. She is the author of the *Children of the Morning Star* vampire series and the horror novelette *How to Make Lemonade*. Her writing influences include *Edgar Allan Poe, Anne Rice, James Herbert, Alfred Hitchcock,* and *Hideyuki Kikuchi*. She is a member of The Alliance of Independent Authors.

www.ingramcontent.com/pod-product-compliance
Lightning Source LLC
Chambersburg PA
CBHW050319200626
46808CB00023BA/1572